STILL MINE

NADIA LEE

To all the members of the Monday Suzugamine class. Thank you for your friendship and love. Miss you so much already.

1

BOBBI

EVERY TIME I tell someone that my dream is to (a) own a bakery, (b) get married and (c) have as many babies as possible, people look at me like I'm sprouting broccoli from my forehead. Apparently, those things simply can't be what a girl like me wants.

There's nothing soft on me. My breasts will never look bigger than a B, no matter how much I spend on pushup bras "guaranteed to create cleavage that would make Dolly Parton jealous." And I'm never going to have the gorgeous flaring hips that so many of my celebrity clients had.

Six feet of mostly sinew and muscle means physicality and strength. I'm those things—I was also a nationally ranked judoka in high school, and worked for a while as a bodyguard for some of Hollywood's more famous faces.

Still, that doesn't mean I can't dream of the softer things in life. And work to get them. "Live your life to the fullest" were my mother's final words to me, and I'm going to honor her wish, even if we didn't have the best relationship.

Now one goal is about to become a reality—Bobbi's Sweet Things. Up to now I've only done relatively small items like birthday and wedding cakes without an actual physical store to sell them from. But tomorrow, the very first location is going to open in downtown L.A., complete with a ceremony and after-party to celebrate.

The timer dings over the sound of my favorite Latin playlist. "Oh, yeah..." I go to pull golden croissants out of the oven. A heavenly smell fills my kitchen, and I close my eyes to appreciate it fully. Then I visualize what everything is going to be like tomorrow:

A bakery full of delicious fresh bread and pastries and cakes. Cupcakes with colorful frosting, each one with unique and interesting decorations. I don't just want my creations to be tasty; I want the kind of creations that my customers will loathe to eat because they're just that pretty—the ultimate sensory experience.

Excitement fizzes through me like soda from a freshly popped can.

"You never change."

I open my eyes. That damn velvety voice. Never thought I'd hear it in my kitchen again.

I turn around. Noah is standing there, butt propped against the sink. Dark eyebrows slanted at the most perfect angle; eyes brilliant in the bright light of my kitchen. They seem to change color depending on what he's wearing, the weather and maybe other random factors—right now, they're polished silver. A gray shirt made of some silken material fits his wide shoulders and flows over his perfect torso. I've felt that body more than a few times, up close and very personal, and always marveled at how powerful and tireless it was. Hard to believe he's a wildlife photographer. I joked once that he got his stamina from running away from hungry lions, and he laughed, then kissed me like he couldn't stop himself from showering me with affection.

His gaze softens, and he smiles, his beautiful mouth curving into the slanted grin that never fails to make my heart hop and spin.

"How did you get in?" I ask in my coolest voice, not wanting him to know how his presence affects me.

"You gave me a key, remember?"

He sounds playful, which is both painful and a relief. He forgot about coming to pick me up when I was discharged from the hospital after getting shot in the belly. Same story with having drinks together after I'd had a particularly nasty incident involving a client's ex—one who'd decided to run both me and the client over. Both times he had to be out of the country to film cheetahs. But at least Noah hasn't lost the key I gave him. So that means he must care about what we had...at least a little bit, right?

"The cheetahs couldn't keep you in...wherever...?" I wave my hand vaguely, hiding all the old doubts and disappointments behind a light tone.

"Cheetahs wait for no one, but..." His boyish smile is charming enough to sell sand in the Sahara.

I do my best to fix a matching smile to my face. "And me?" I don't mean to sound needy and desperate, like I've been emotionally clinging to him, but the chiding question rolls out of my mouth anyway.

A hint of guilt cracks the light, winsome mask on his gorgeous face, revealing raw affection underneath. It gives me hope that I haven't imagined this connection between us. Some men are forgetful, but that doesn't mean they don't care.

"Bobbi," he whispers, then "Adiós Amor" plays from the speakers. I go still as sweet memories of when we first met in Mexico flow through me. I was trying to sort myself out after my father's death, and having a hard time since I didn't know how to feel about the loss of a man who was more stranger than family. How Noah made me laugh, made me feel special. Somebody had a party on the beach, and this song played, and we danced to it—our first—under a night sky brilliant with stars and beside an ocean whose waves were limned with the light of a thousand tiny sea creatures.

Noah reaches out, takes me tenderly in his arms like he did on that wet, silky sand, and we sway to the music. He feels so good, all warmth and strength, even though I can't rely on any of it. But that doesn't mean being wrapped up in him won't soothe the searing, jagged edges of my heart, so gingerly I place my arms around him, too. With a shuddering sigh, he drops his head, resting his face in the crook of my neck. I'm tall, but he's taller, even when I'm in heels. I've always loved that about him. There aren't many men who can physically overwhelm me, but he qualifies.

"My light," he whispers. Whenever he calls me that, my insides turn to mush. He has an inexplicable power to make me believe I'm as important to him as light itself. His breath feathers over my neck, and my whole body goes tingly. His lips brush my jaw, then my cheek and finally my mouth. I sigh softly with longing—realizing how much I miss him and this connection we have, even though part of me grieves that I'm the only one feeling and yearning for it. His tongue glides into my mouth, and I taste him, shivers spreading over me. Our mouths fuse as if we've never been apart, and he holds me like I'm the most precious treasure in his life. I can almost believe it as we sway to the music and share our breath and heat and presence.

Then his arms tighten around me, and his erection rubs against my belly, over the scar from my bullet wound. A small groan tears from his throat, and I want to cling to him.

Come on, girl. He's just here for your body, the cold logical voice in my head points out, with a disapproving *tut-tut.*

The possibility hits me like a bucket of ice water, and the dreamy mental cocoon shatters. I pull away. "I'm not sleeping with you."

He blinks a few times, a picture of innocent confusion. But I'm not buying it. Not after so many broken promises.

Thankfully "Adiós Amor" ends, and another, more upbeat, song comes on. Something like awareness and surprise fleets over his gorgeous face, and he shakes his head with a rueful laugh. "You think I'm here for sex?"

"Part of you sure seems to be."

"She says, stiffly," he responds. He shakes his head. "I was dancing with you in my arms. Of course I got hard. That doesn't mean I'm *here* for sex, especially if you don't want it." He adds the last part like it pains him. But I'm probably imagining that—I've been wanting a genuine emotion from him for a long time. And sure enough, he smiles. "I love you, you know."

It hits me like a rabbit punch, even though he's said it many times before. Always lightly and brightly, without any weight. But when I heard it the first time, I didn't know any better than to believe it, to dream of a beautiful future together—him and me creating a family with children at some point.

It didn't take too long before I realized his idea of "love" was nothing like mine. If he really loved me, he wouldn't have let me down over and over again.

"You need to go." My tone is brisk to hide the achiness in my heart. "I have to get some sleep. Early start tomorrow."

"Yeah, I heard about your bakery opening. I'm really proud of you for making your dream a reality."

"You know about that?" I've done some advertising, but why would he notice? And it isn't like he's been around for me to tell him. Noah can be surprisingly perceptive, but also totally oblivious at times. During our first few months, I thought he was the former, but as time went on I began to realize with an increasingly excruciating sting to my heart that the latter was more common...

At least with me. I was an open book with him—kind of embarrassing, but my fault for letting my guard down.

He plucks a croissant from the pan and takes a bite. "Jesus. This is like crack. I've missed your baking so much. I'd sell my soul for this stuff."

My insides flutter, and my mind wants to interpret his comment to mean he missed *me* so much, too. It's irritating as hell because I should know better.

"If the stuff at your bakery is half as good as this, you're gonna make a killing," he says with a grin.

"Thanks," I say gruffly. Do not let his compliment warm your foolish heart.

"I'll be there to congratulate you."

"Wait... You're coming?"

"Of course! I want to be the first person to congratulate you. *And* bring you your favorite flowers."

"My favorites, huh? Do you know what they are?" I cock an eyebrow.

"White calla lilies," he says promptly with an I-know-everything-about-you smile. His eyes darken with profound affection as he looks at me, and the wall inside me weakens. This man knows how to lay siege to my emotions.

Still, hope swells. We've never talked about what flowers I like, so for him to know that means he must've been observing and thinking about me.

Maybe this time will be different, and he will be there.

THE NEXT MORNING, colorful flowers are everywhere inside my new store. But none of them are white calla lilies.

My friend Yuna comes with her husband, Declan. She's a Korean *chaebol* heiress, and one of the biggest champions of my dream. As usual, she's dressed to the nines in a gorgeous designer ensemble that fits her slim body beautifully, a cute wide-brimmed hat completing the outfit. A pair of stylish heels encase her small feet—but then I've never seen her in flats. She hugs me with a small excited squeal. "This is incredible! I'm so happy for you!"

Declan nods and smiles, lifting a half-eaten éclair and looking like some kind of advertisement for the pastry. But then he used to be an underwear model before he turned to acting. "This is amazing. The best I've ever had."

"Thank you." I smile brightly, even though it's hard to focus on what's going on.

Where is Noah?

When Yuna and her husband chat with some other guests, I check my phone to see if Noah texted to let me know he'd be late. *Nothing.*

My belly pinches. It's been two hours since the party started. If he was going to come, he'd be here by now, so that he could be one of the people who congratulated me, if not the first like he said.

The door chimes as it opens, and my eyes dart to it, my heart trembling with uncertain hope again, only to deflate fast. It's Ivy—another good friend—coming back in after taking a call outside.

He's not coming.

The buoyant sensation I had earlier this morning has ebbed away. Every time the door opens and it isn't him, bitter disappointment slices another sliver off my heart.

When the party ends, my friends and guests begin to leave, giving me hugs, wishing me well. I say goodbye with a smile so professionally frozen it actually hurts my cheeks. If anybody notices, they don't say anything. They probably just figure I'm nervous.

Customers come in all day. As soon as they take a bite of the samples, their eyes widen, then they grab whatever is calling their name the loudest. When the last person finally leaves, I lock the front door and stand in the empty store, my legs sore from being on my feet for hours without a break. I'm going to have to get busy tomorrow to restock. Everything sold out, even the crusty multi-wheat bread, which was a pleasant surprise. But instead of feeling like a million bucks, I tighten my jaw and tap my fingers on the cool countertop for I don't know how long as thoughts churn through my head.

He didn't come. No text. No flowers.

The special mini-cake I baked for the two of us—to share later, in private—mocks me from its silver tray. The dancing modeling chocolate couple seems like a monument to my ludicrous hope that *this time would be different.* But how was I supposed to know? He said he'd come yesterday. He knew my favorite flower. And he was so sincere.

But then when was he ever not sincere?

Sudden rage erupts, incinerating what feelings I still have. I dump the cake in the trashcan. It breaks into ugly pieces, the couple upside down with chocolate frosting splattering the girl's face, like she's been made the butt of a joke.

Who am I kidding? Nobody made me the butt of a joke. I *let* myself be one.

I let out a shuddering breath as I struggle to swallow my tears. One of the most important moments in my life, and it basically meant nothing to him. Waiting is hard, but waiting for someone who never comes is just wretched. I gave a man who doesn't care the power to ruin what should've been an amazing celebration.

Never again.

Impatiently, I wipe the tears streaming down my face. It's well past time I cut Noah loose. Forever.

2

NOAH

—A YEAR later

"EVERY WOMAN LOVES *the guy who rescues her,*" *says the senior coordinator.*

Spoken like a man who's probably still a virgin. I resist the urge to face-palm myself again over the lack of creativity and medieval sensibility of the people I have to work with. I don't need their help picking up a woman. I certainly don't need them to come up with a moronic scheme to have three would-be thugs "attack" her while she's on vacation in Mexico, so I can "rescue" her.

I tell them it's unnecessary, but they look at me like I just told them to kill her. The fake thugs are already on their way, and if I don't do my part, horrible things could happen to her.

"Make sure to get punched in the face or get knifed on the side because then there'll be a logical reason for her to stick around."

You'd have to have the brain of a single fat cell to come up with this. I've never had to do more than flash a twinkle-eyed smile to get laid. There's no need to get punched or knifed.

I keep track of the target in the crowded club. Bobbi Bright, the only child of Otto Bright. I need to retrieve his dossiers, which nobody has been able to recover so far despite a fine-toothed combing through all his known associates. His daughter's the only one left to check.

She might have them...or she might not. She didn't seem that close to her father. After finishing college, she started working as a bodyguard for Hollywood celebs and influencers while Otto continued with his career at the State Department. But you can't trust a traitor—or even a potential traitor, and not even if they come in a package as beautiful as Bobbi.

All that soft golden hair tumbling down her back, the smooth lean muscles of her long arms and legs flexing as she dances. Her breasts aren't big, but they only need to be big enough to feel good in my palms with sensitive nipples. The lithe torso dips into a tight waist and somewhat narrow hips, her body wrapped in a tight black top and flaring skirt. She's not voluptuous, but she keeps in shape. And that's sexy.

As she tilts her chin at the climax of the music, a smile curves her soft lips. Her long lashes cast crescent shadows around her wide eyes, and the dim lights from the ceiling creates shadows that showcase the perfection of her cheekbones.

Unlike the many women who contour to bring out their facial structures, Bobbi is one hundred percent natural. She buys a cocktail, smiling at a bartender who grins at her like he's in love, then fans herself.

She finishes her drink and steps outside. The air in the club is cold and stale with sweat and alcohol. I follow her out.

Her hands on her hips, she inhales and exhales slowly. The parking lot isn't too well-lit, and drunken tourists and laughter from the locals shatter what little silence the night would've brought.

I stay out of view and do my best to avoid becoming impatient. The "thugs" should pop out of the shadows any time now. I would, if I were as boring and unimaginative as the people who orchestrated this farce.

On cue, three scruffy looking types strut forward. All big beefy guys with thick muscles underneath stretchy shirts and jeans. Three gold rings flash on the sausage-like fingers of the guy in the middle. Impressive. Maybe even scary if you didn't know they're fake gangbangers.

They approach Bobbi, then say something in fluent Spanish, getting a little too close. They're the kind of folks the State Department website warns you about, and the Mexican authorities want to eliminate to allay the fears of the gringo tourists.

The one in center steps into her personal space, then grabs her wrist.

Guess that's my cue. I take a step forward—

There's a sudden movement; Bobbi twists his arm, bringing the guy's head down a bit and then kicks him hard on the point of his chin, her leg shooting up at an impressively vertical angle. He drops like a rock.

I blink. That was quick. So much for me playing the hero.

The other two pull knives, the blades glinting. She's going to back away now, which will give me my chance. I start forward—

Nope. She traps the arm of the first guy who comes at her, grabs him by his shoulder, twisting violently, and tosses him in a spectacular judo throw. Holy shit. Her foot connects with his belly, and he curls into a ball with a pained groan. The third one lashes out with his blade, and I am finally in position to help out. I grab his wrist, spin him around and punch his jaw in one motion. He collapses, feigning unconsciousness—I didn't hit him that hard.

She huffs out a breath, then looks at me. "You okay?"

I feel like an actor who just realized he's been studying the wrong script, but I nod. Didn't anybody study this woman's background before setting this up?

Her critical gaze rakes me top to bottom. "Thank you." She speaks in a calm, gentle voice. "But you didn't have to do that."

"Apparently not. You can obviously handle yourself in a fight. But it was one against three. Not really fair."

She smiles. Feeling the full impact, I realize why the bartender grinned like he was in love. A woman who can take care of herself with ease, then smiles at you like an angel is positively nuclear. My heart thunders hard and fast.

Suddenly, the smile vanishes, and a frown pinches her eyebrows. "You got cut."

She reaches out, fingertips brushing my bare arm gingerly. A delicious prickling sensation spreads through me.

"Probably should put a Band-Aid on that." She looks up at me. "I have some at my place."

"That'd be great—"

A jolt that travels from tailbone to skull wakes me up. *Dammit.* I blink at the bright light of the Airbus cabin as I remember I'm on a commercial flight. What was the pilot thinking? The older passengers probably had their backs thrown out.

There's a roar of deceleration and creaks from the fuselage as the plane tries to slow down on the tarmac. Rain drops splatter the window, streaking and blurring the view.

I wish I were on my private plane. My personal pilot would've done a better job of landing, for one thing. But this is work, and incognito is the name of the game. To the point that I'm traveling under a fake name and ID.

The cabin attendant smiles as I deplane. "Have a great evening. We'd love to see you again soon, Mr. Everson."

I give her my flirtiest grin and start walking up the ramp. See? I can easily charm any woman, no faux heroism necessary. If my idiot handlers hadn't set up the moronic plan behind my back, I wouldn't have fallen for Bobbi so hard and so fast.

And I wouldn't be here, in the dreary, rainy Pacific Northwest.

TWO HOURS LATER, I'm standing in front of a fancy intercom at my mom's mansion. "I'd rather fornicate with Mozart," I say loudly into the mic. Otherwise, Mom will claim she couldn't hear me over the howl of the storm and keep me outside until she's satisfied.

Two beats...and nothing happens. *Goddamn it.* She's kept the old passcode. I sigh and say, "There's no one I'd rather fuck than my mom." I grit my teeth to avoid gagging. It'd only amuse her, and I'm not in the mood to entertain her perverse sense of humor.

Finally, the lock clicks open. I walk inside the huge château, topped with soaring witch-hat turrets, overlooking the Pacific from a cliff. Mom doesn't like the sun—or people—so she loves this place. It's remote, very defensible and made with marble and stone in various hues. Fifty Shades of Grey, the Real Estate Edition.

I stride past the solid double doors at least fourteen feet in height. The ceiling is even higher. The place holds very little warmth by design. The moist chill of the rain lingers in the air.

It'll be easy to locate Mom in the vast home—she'll be in the kitchen, her favorite place. Not because she's that into cooking or eating, but because there are a lot of sharp objects close at hand.

"Careful you don't track mud onto the floor," she calls out.

"You think mud is what's on my mind?"

"I have no clue what's on your mind, and don't particularly care. *My* concern is you dirtying my floor."

"What's on my mind," I say as I walk into the kitchen, "is why you didn't change the passcode like we talked about."

"Because *I* never agreed to the change. You can't just use some common phrase—then it wouldn't be a passcode."

"But fucking your *mother*?"

"I was accommodating your objection to fucking a cow," she says carelessly.

"Yeah, well, I don't play with my food." *My brothers were smart to not work with their mothers.* I should've followed their lead. Nora Blane is an exceptional agent, but she's a terrible boss and handler. "What's wrong with 'I'd rather fornicate with Mozart' anyway? It's not like anybody says *that*."

"Bo-ring." She puts down the glass of chardonnay she's been sipping, and cuts into a loaf of crusty bread, creating a slice that without measuring will be precisely half an inch thick. A sleeveless black turtleneck and black leotards stretch over her tall, lithe frame. She's wearing a pair of stylish boots, but if she ever kicks you, you'll know the pointy tips aren't for fashion. Short black hair frames her pixie-like face. Some say I got my coloring from her, but it isn't true—my six half-brothers all have the same dark hair, and we're related on our father's side. The smoothness of her skin is more befitting a teenager than a woman with a grown-up son.

Mom tosses the breadknife in the air, catching it smoothly while her green eyes are still on me. Those eyes, which hold whatever emotion she wants them to, are currently impassive.

"Show-off," I mutter.

"We all have our fortes. Mine happens to be blades." She gestures with the knife. "Want some?"

She knows how much I love carbs. "Thank you." I take the rest of the loaf from the cutting board.

She shakes her head. "Bread was probably what went through your mind when that plane was going down."

I pull out jars of honey and raspberry jam from the pantry. *Not bread, but the birthday cake Bobbi made for me.* It was the last time we spent any meaningful time together.

Mom hands me a glass of the chardonnay, which I realize is chilled once I take it. We sit at the counter with a couple of knives and our respective glasses. I smear a generous dollop of honey on the bread and bite into it. It's excellent, with a good subtle flavor of grain. Maybe the bakery this came from is another reason Mom doesn't want to leave this godforsaken area.

"We flushed out the mole. So next time there won't be another plane crash." This is about as emotional as she's going to get about what happened to me.

She can fake situationally appropriate sentiments, convince you she feels them from the bottom of her heart, but in reality, she feels nothing. Sometimes I'm tempted to poke her with a needle and see if she bleeds something like oil or hydraulic fluid.

"Nicely wrapped up?" I ask.

"With a pretty bow." She smiles like a divine messenger. The mole probably wishes he was dead. If he isn't already.

"Then there won't be a problem with me taking some time off." My tone is casual, like a billionaire carelessly expressing desire to purchase a private island.

She frowns. "Some time off?"

"Uh-huh."

"How much time, exactly?"

"Not sure, actually."

Understanding dawns in her penetrating eyes. "You want an indefinite leave."

"Unpaid," I add, like that has to be the most pressing thing on her mind.

All warmth leaches from her face. "That isn't the point. Making it unpaid won't make you return any faster."

True enough. I invested my money with two of my brothers, Emmett and Grant, who founded a venture capital firm together. They made me filthy rich. If I didn't have my job, I wouldn't know what to do with myself all day. Hell, I might spend the time making babies, which would make my father so happy. I spread my arms. "Some people just have clever brothers, and they're smart enough to know who to listen to."

Mom lost a huge chunk of her retirement savings when her financial advisor bet against the companies Grant said would be good to buy. Dunno why she ignored Grant. He made at least a million a year trading stocks in college. Beating the market is his forte, just like delicately fileting a man is hers.

Mom looks like she'd love nothing more than strangling me. Not that she will, because she hates working with her bare hands.

"Besides, some quality time at home will ensure my brothers won't suspect anything. A billionaire wildlife photographer is bound to say no to projects here and there and spend time slothing around on a beach."

"*Sloth* is not a verb."

"And yet you understood my meaning."

Her eyes narrow. "I doubt 'slothing' will be necessary. Your brothers are about as perceptive as deaf, one-eyed donkeys."

"Or I'm just that good."

Her snort says I'm still an amateur compared to her. "Is this about Bobbi Bright?"

I consider denying it for a second. I'm good at lying, having inherited the ability from my mother. Polygraphs and barbiturates are powerless against her—or me. Torture is basically futile since we both have incredibly high pain thresholds. Not only that, when our bodies have had enough, they start to register pain as some kind of weird high. Mom says it's convenient, but I think it's unnatural. Still, it's preferable to screaming and writhing like most people.

But if she suspects I'm lying, she's going to poke her nose into my business until she's satisfied, a.k.a. until she's proven correct.

"When the plane was going down and I was facing possible death, I didn't really feel anything. I vaguely thought I'd miss my brothers—but I was confident you'd come up with a good reason for why I wasn't around anymore. You always have a good cover story."

She sips her chardonnay, her unblinking eyes on mine.

"My mind emptied, and I couldn't decide if I should care whether I lived or died. Then I thought about a birthday cake Bobbi made for me." I give Mom a small, empty smile. The cake wasn't the only thing on my mind. I also remembered Bobbi's sweet smile. As I gazed at her beautiful face, for the first time in my life I was glad to have been born, and I told her so. The rose that spread across her cheeks was mesmerizing, and my heart thudded as though it yearned to leave the confines of my chest and run to its true master.

And my heart pumping hard on that plane with black smoke billowing out of its engines was just like that time, but it was more of a mourning that she wasn't going to smile at me like that anymore. She might not even miss me. Hell, she might go out dancing when she heard I was dead.

The possibility was soul-crushing, even though I definitely gave her just cause.

I was exasperated with myself as the plane dipped lower. If I missed her so much that she was the only one on my mind when my plane was nosediving, why was I staying away?

If I survived this, I'd go see her, I vowed. I didn't know what I'd do next, but I'd go say hello. If she felt nothing for me...

Well, I'd deserve that. But one step at a time, and first things first.

I survived the spectacular crash that wasn't covered in the media. And returned to the States in one piece.

"I just wanted to have her cake again." A lie, but one with enough truth to sound plausible. Plus, Mom is aware of my carb addiction.

"You're eating bread from her bakery. I special ordered it from Bobbi's Sweet Things."

I pause for a moment, wondering if Mom has some ulterior motive. But her face betrays nothing. I take another bite, savor it. It's amazing bread, with thick crust and perfectly soft inside. It tastes even better knowing it's Bobbi's. "Thank you. But bread isn't cake," I say between bites.

"You didn't want it before."

"I was on a diet."

She narrows her eyes. "Mike Swain and his fiancée had nothing to do with it?"

My gut does that tight and uncomfortable twist it did when I first heard of their deaths. Fear runs its fingers up my spine. It's all I can do to not shudder. I bite into the bread to buy some time.

I meant it when I told Bobbi I'd come by for the bakery opening, but then Mom called at the last minute to have me dispatch some terrorist trying to get his hands on a dirty nuke. I told her to have another asset handle it, but she said that wasn't possible. Something ugly had happened to Mike Swain, the one who was supposed to do the job. His face was removed, and his fiancée raped and shot—collateral damage. Their deaths hit close to home.

The fiancée had tried to flee. She was just a civilian, but the assholes didn't care. An image of Bobbi's honey-gold hair spread around in a pool of blood with her dark eyes staring blankly haunted me as I read the report.

I felt secretly relieved and ironically unwanted that Bobbi didn't text or call to ream me out for breaking my word. It's like my absence didn't bother her. But I didn't dare contact her because I had no clue what to tell her.

Hey, sorry, someone got killed along with his fiancée, and it sort of messed me up. Oh, how'd that happened? It was a hit. But you know... Things like that happen all the time, they don't even report it on the news, ha ha ha...

Yeah, try to explain why a carefree billionaire wildlife photographer thinks the possibility of getting gunned down with his significant other is a thing. Not even I can come up with a good story for that. The only sensible solution was to stay away—or so I thought.

But my biggest regret when that plane was plunging was breaking so many promises to Bobbi. And I would've given anything to be able to see her again.

"Things have changed. I think of cake, I have to have it. You'll understand, if you're about to die and your favorite food pops into your head. We give prisoners whatever they want before they're executed."

"So? You weren't being executed, and Bobbi is a civilian."

Guess she didn't buy my bullshit about wanting cake.

"You'll get restless," she adds. "You always do."

"Then I'll be back. But until then, let me have my cake."

3

BOBBI

"Do you think we should make more croissants? Everyone who comes by seems to want them," my apprentice Victor says.

Only four remain under the clear cover, even though we started baking more just a couple of weeks ago.

"They do seem to be flying off the shelves. So yeah, I guess so." I smile.

He's the only employee I have. He says he's lucky to have met me, but I'm the fortunate one. He's one of the hardest working and most honest people I know. I wouldn't have been able to grow the business this much without him by my side.

His head is shaved smooth—says it's cheaper to do it himself with a razor than see a barber—but given his thick black eyebrows, he'd probably have stunning hair if he let it grow out. And he has beautiful wide-set brown eyes that look at the world with earnestness and quiet pride.

Although the weather is warm, he's in a long-sleeve shirt and slacks. I told him he could wear short-sleeve shirts, but he politely declined. He was sporting a black eye and busted lip and crouching under the awning of the bakery at five in the morning when I met him a year ago. I figured him for homeless or a runaway teen, and felt bad for him, especially since he was nothing but skin and bones. So I gave him a couple of Danishes from the day before that I'd saved for breakfast.

Instead of accepting them and disappearing, he asked me what he could do for payment because he wasn't taking something he didn't earn. So I told him he could take out the trash.

After that he kept coming by and I kept giving him the stuff from the day before for helping out with little chores. Two weeks later I just hired him outright and started to pay him enough money for a modest studio apartment and decent food to put some flesh on his bones. I had to when I inadvertently saw the cigarette burn scars on his forearms and realized he had nowhere safe to go. Everyone deserves a sanctuary.

The kid has his pride, so I've never let him know I noticed. We all have scars we'd rather hide from the world.

I check the time. It's four, an hour before closing. I hand him a carefully packed box of cupcakes that I made while he was busy manning the cash register earlier this morning. I used pearlescent blue and white frosting—his favorite colors—and decorated them with modeling chocolate that I molded into a house, people and dogs. It's my wish for him to one day find happiness and love with people who have his back. "Here."

"What's this for?"

"Happy nineteenth. Sorry, didn't have the time to make a birthday cake for you, but there was that emergency custom engagement cake in the morning."

His eyes widen, like he can't believe anybody would bother. "How did you know?"

"You filled out the job application, remember?" It's terrible that he has nobody to wish him a happy birthday. But then I didn't either until I met TJ and his family. Mom always pretended birthdays didn't matter, although she remembered Dad's, and Dad was too busy doing important jobs for the government to remember anyone's.

Noah wished you a happy birthday.

Yeah, and then bailed on me. Broke too many promises. I'm not going to include him among the special group of people I can count on.

Victor shakes his head. "Well...wow. Thanks."

"I would've done the whole candle and song bit, but I didn't want to force you into therapy. Good employees are hard to find."

He grins. "This is fine."

"You can take off an hour early. And here." I shove a hundred-dollar bill into his hand. "Birthday bonus."

"Oh, man." He runs his free hand over his shaven head. "You already gave me a Thanksgiving bonus. Christmas one, too."

"Those were for holidays, this is for your birthday. Just say thanks and enjoy the day."

His eyes film over. It kills me how easily a little bit of kindness can overwhelm him. His parents have to be absolute shits. I wish them a fitting punishment of eternal diarrhea.

Tears will only embarrass him. Time to lighten the mood.

"You still have to come in on time on Monday, so don't party too hard over the weekend." The bakery is closed over the weekend because most of our business is from commuters in the area. And I do special orders on weekends—weddings and so on.

"Of course." He laughs. "I'll be here on time."

I give him a hug. "Happy birthday. Hope all your wishes come true."

He hugs me back hard. "They did when I met you. Thank you, Bobbi. You're the best thing that's ever happened to me."

"Aww. Now you're going to make your big mean boss cry."

I wave at him as he disappears into the employee area to get out of his Bobbi's Sweet Things apron and take off. He's beginning to smile more, like a kid his age should.

I run my hands lovingly along the counter. When I opened this place, I just dreamed of creating amazing baked goods and making people happy. But now it's enabled me to make a difference in someone's life. And I know it's going to bring me even more joy and fulfillment.

I hear the little bell on the door tinkle. I lift my head with a smile... then freeze at the sight of Reggie Hopkins, Ms. Pain in the Ass herself, walking in. A third cousin once removed on my mom's side of the family, she grew up in the same neighborhood as TJ. We went to high school together when my father left Mom and me in SoCal. The place the State Department sent him into was too unstable and dangerous to take us along.

Reggie did everything in her power to be my best friend in high school, mainly because she's had a crush on TJ since forever, and he and I were tight from holiday dinners and a few vacations Mom had with her family. To him, I'd led a fascinating life in parts of the world he'd seen only on YouTube, and I found comfort in his steady nature. She meant to use me to get close to him, and I became friendly with her without understanding what she really wanted. When she realized that he would never like her, she accused me of poisoning him against her. She won't accept that the real reason TJ dislikes her is because she's an insufferable know-it-all who called his dog stupid and regarded every other woman around him as a competition for his affection.

TJ and I have moved on from our high school years—along with most of the other students—but not Reggie. She didn't bother to come to my mom's funeral and stopped by during the first week of my bakery opening to complain about how horrible my croissants were, then posted crappy reviews everywhere. Given that she's a minor celebrity, it almost ruined my bakery before it could get started. Thankfully, Yuna's husband Declan, who is a far bigger star, mentioned how much he loves our croissants and cupcakes, which dwarfed Reggie's negative posts and bitching.

Now she's apparently bleached her hair platinum and gotten lip injections that blew them up to four times their normal size. Her eyes are an unnaturally bright green with extra-large pupils, probably from cosmetic lenses. She might've done something with her chest as well— her cleavage is now Mariana Trench class. She's in a hot pink maxi dress with a plunging neckline—of course—and the rest of the outfit is straining to keep her properly covered.

Her belly protrudes rather overtly. I hope this ugly dress isn't maternity wear, but with Reggie, anything's possible.

"No hello for your customer?" The grating nasal voice, unfortunately, hasn't changed.

"Are you actually a customer?"

"I'm here to order a cake for my engagement party. So, *yeah*, I think I am." She extends her left hand, chin held high like a queen expecting a lowly peasant to drop and kiss her ring. Sure enough, a huge rock blinks under the bakery lights. She puts her other hand over her belly. "My fiancé and I are expecting a baby, so we want to have a lavish engagement and wedding as soon as possible."

A corner of her mouth lifts as she shares her plan. She knows I've always wanted a family.

"Congrats," I say dryly, more for the pregnancy than the engagement. It isn't the baby's fault that his mom is a horrible human being. But this fiancé? Obviously a terrible judge of character.

"You're invited to both, you know."

"I am?"

"Of course. It's important to experience these kinds of social events, if only vicariously."

"Ah, I see. Yeah, no thanks."

"Don't worry, I won't ask for anything too expensive," she says, completely oblivious. Or maybe she just can't believe I'd say no. "You know how to decorate an engagement cake, don't you? Even though you aren't engaged or anything?" She shakes her head. "What's making your guy take so long, anyway? What's his name again? Noam? Nolan?"

The girl can't quit talking. She probably thinks she's doing a fantastic job of throwing verbal jabs. I paste on my blandest smile. "Noah."

He and she met when he took me to Jean-Georges for brunch. She was at the restaurant with her sugar daddy, a man literally old enough to be her grandfather. Her jaw slack, she ran her eyes over Noah, her face growing red as she catalogued his lean body, expensive clothes and stunning face.

"Is this a new client?" she asked, eyeing him like she'd like to strip off her clothes and jump him.

"No, I'm the boyfriend you've been hearing so many great things about," Noah said with a grin before I could respond.

Her mouth parted, and she sucked in air. The vein on her forehead pulsed hard—but unfortunately didn't pop.

"Right." Reggie snaps her fingers. "Noah."

"Can't believe you forgot already. But I read somewhere that

21

memory and recall require at least two brain cells. So, not your strong point."

Her eyes narrow. "Maybe, but getting engaged *is*. Unlike some women, I'm not just fucked but *kept*." She declares it with pride and triumph.

The attack slides into my heart like a well-honed knife. I fantasize briefly about shoving her smug face into a vat of butter cream I've got in the back, but no. That butter cream deserves better.

"Anyway, about the cake—"

"Talk to your baker."

She stops, then lets out a grating laugh. "Uh, isn't this a bakery? Aren't you the baker?"

"I am the baker. Just not *your* baker."

"What? I'm a customer! With good money!"

"Who left shitty reviews of my bakery everywhere." For the baby's sake, I hope her fiancé is smarter than Reggie.

"I'm giving you a chance to redeem yourself. You bake me the cake, and I won't even charge you for the opportunity." She positions her hand so I can't miss the ring.

"Okay, are you seriously asking me to make you a cake—for *free*—so you can then decide if it's good enough?"

She brightens. "Yes!"

"Reggie," I say sweetly, "go fuck yourself."

She lets out a loud gasp. "You bitch!"

"And then go fuck yourself again."

The bell on the door tinkles.

"Oh, look. Here comes a *real* customer." I turn away from her, then realize it's just my landlord swaggering in.

The second Floyd crosses the threshold, he pulls out a stained hanky and places it over his pug nose. His white muscle tee stretches painfully around his short torso. Hair that should be on his head sprouts in black wiry tufts from his chest and back, and he has on his usual cowboy boots with the elevator heels. He claims they're fashion items made with "genuine cowhide that costs thousands of dollars" from Texas.

If anything on him cost more than twenty bucks, I'll give up my ovaries.

"Baby!" Reggie exclaims with the dramatic flair of a telenovela actress.

Baby?

She rushes to him, looping her arms around his. "Can you believe how rude my cousin is? She won't make us an engagement cake!"

"That's terrible, but at least she can't poison me with gluten." He sounds nasal through the handkerchief. I don't know what that green-yellow patch on the wrinkled fabric is, but I hope it's full of cooties.

"*This* is your fiancé? Floyd Baggett?"

Reggie turns to me. "Yes. And he's valiantly fighting his allergy to win my heart." She gives me a cloying smile. "That's how much he wants me."

Floyd takes her hand and kisses the back of it. "Anything for you, my love."

Gag me with a dirty plunger. But at the same time, they do kind of suit each other. Like a praying mantis and a cockroach.

"This explains the fifty percent rent increase Angie wanted," I mutter, recalling the unpleasant, awkward meeting with the property manager over the lease renewal. I should've just signed the five-year contract the property management wanted, but fear of failure stopped me from making the commitment. I straighten my spine, ready for a battle.

His dark eyes narrow in his round face. He loathes that I'm as tall as he is, even though I'm in flats and he's in those boots. "Gluten tax, Bobbi. The existence of this bakery destroys the quality of life in the city. Not to mention the health of the people."

"Has anybody tried to tax you for damaging their *mental* health?" My tone is drier than the bags of flour in my kitchen.

He blinks for a moment, then turns bright red. "How dare you!"

"Why you gotta be so mean? All we want is to be happy for our engagement," Reggie whines.

Right, because newly engaged couples always go see people they've insulted to share their happiness. Happens all the time.

"Relax. Can't you take a joke?" I give him a fake laugh, and he backs down a little. He told me more than once that if his mother hadn't forced him to go into engineering, he could've been a taller, more handsome and funnier version of Danny DeVito. His mother was one of the nicest people I've ever met, and contempt stirs at his delusion and ingratitude to the woman. If it weren't for her, he'd be unemployable and homeless. He certainly wouldn't be in a position to come into my bakery and harass me. "Maybe you should lobby the city council if you want to ban bakeries." *Good luck.* Probably a quarter of the council buys Danishes from my bakery every morning.

"Oh, I intend to. But meanwhile, I do what I can. You see the reaction I'm having because of gluten? I have to take so many precautions to even be near this place." He indicates his belly. "Look at this! I used to have a six pack until you opened your bakery." Reggie makes a sympathetic noise.

"You weren't even here when I started Bobbi's Sweet Things. You were in Denver, working at an engineering firm." His mother was so proud of him finally becoming gainfully employed, rather than hopping from one get-rich-quick scheme to another, that she asked me to bake a set of special cookies for him. She was such a lovely woman, it's astounding she ended up with a man-child like Floyd. The family lottery can be pretty shitty for some people.

Of course, the same can be said for the landlord lottery. If I'd known he'd be the one to inherit the building Bobbi's Sweet Things is in, I would've thought twice before signing the lease, regardless of its fantastic location or his mother offering me the flexibility of committing for only one year rather than five.

"It's the gluten in the air," he insists. "It's hurting me even now." He waves a hand, then closes his eyes as though torn between unbearable pain and intolerable bliss.

He's probably dying inside that he can't eat anything in the bakery because of his "gluten allergy." Who does he think he's fooling? I saw him scarf down two burritos from a food truck just last month. Afterwards, I asked the guy manning the truck if they had gluten-free tortillas, and he looked at me like I was crazy.

It's extremely tempting to put Floyd in a headlock and shove a cookie down his throat just to show him I know he's a filthy lying roach. Except my cookies are rewards, not punishment.

He props an arm on the counter and leans closer. "But regardless of my struggle, my fiancée would love a vanilla chiffon cake with strawberries and white nama-cream frosting from your bakery. So you're going to make it for her."

"And if I don't...?"

He stiffens like the possibility of rejection never entered his mind. "You will."

I lean closer as well. "*No, I won't.* I don't have to do business with people who come here to insult me."

"Oh, I get it. You're jealous of Reggie, now that she and I are engaged." A leer creeps over his face, and I resist the urge to shove it away. He thinks he's this generation's Casanova, despite all the evidence mirrors must provide. "The prototypical woman scorned. Devastated because I am now taken."

"I'm really not that invested in your personal life." Somehow, he's gotten into his head that I harbor an unrequited love for him because I baked the custom cookies his mother ordered to celebrate his employment.

"But if you don't make that cake, I won't just raise the rent by fifty percent, I'll kick you out as well."

"If you kick me out, you won't get *any* rent."

"You could put in a comedy club, Floyd. It would be classier than this," Reggie sneers, and I really want to smack her a few times. It takes talent to make me want to hit a pregnant woman.

"We need a cake big enough for a hundred guests. Something impressive and pretty," Floyd says. "I expect it to be ready whenever we set the date!"

"So you're expecting in two ways now. Hopefully a baby will satisfy you."

"Ow, my back." Reggie puts a hand at the small of her back with a small smirk at me. "Man, it isn't easy carrying this child."

"I told you you didn't have to take care of the cake. Let's get you home and comfortable," Floyd says, running a soothing hand along her back. He turns to me with a snarl. "Make the damn cake or else, Bobbi!"

He escorts her out. Although he's nobody's idea of a great catch, part of me does feel sad and lonely. He's a jerk, but even he knows how to treat a woman he's having a relationship with.

Noah, on the other hand? He has a prettier package and an amazing ability to make me feel like the most special person in his life, but he doesn't treat me like I mean anything.

I shake my head. Time to think about something more urgent and relevant to my life than an ex I haven't seen or heard from in a year.

I really need to look for a new location with a saner landlord. But that feels like surrendering, and why should I have to relocate just because Floyd is an asinine pig? Besides, I'm not sure if I'm going to be able to find a spot as good as this. Relocation will also mean unexpected expenses.

I make a mental note to consult a lawyer. There's no way what Floyd is doing is legal. Tenants must have some rights.

Breathe out. Relax. The nastiest part of the day is over. Friday can't get any worse than a visit from those two. Besides, I have a date to look forward to later this evening. This guy I found on a dating app sounds promising. If even half of what he said is true, we'll hit it off great. Reggie and Floyd are just a blip on the radar.

The door chimes. I paste on my friendliest smile, which instantly cracks.

Noah!

He saunters in, like all the broken promises aren't still lying between us. What's worse is that he's even better looking now. Sadly, nobody has found him annoying enough to break his nose since last time I saw him—its bridge is still narrow and straight. His cheekbones are more prominent, probably from a bit of weight loss—*and why do I have to notice that?*—although his wide shoulders and thick chest fill out his pale gray T-shirt beautifully, and well-worn jeans hug his thighs perfectly, hinting at his lower body strength.

It's infuriating that he's wearing the same smile full of empty charm, and even more so because I'm noticing how gorgeous it is. I despise that he's tall enough to tower over me, and his entire body somehow looks both large *and* lean at the same time. He should be a dork with a pencil neck and skinny arms. A wildlife photographer doesn't need that height or that much muscle.

"Hi." His tone is friendly. Charming even.

I can't respond. I might crack under the weight of my fury and what he meant to me. He can't possibly expect me to say anything friendly, and I'm not going to hint how much his last disappearing act gutted me.

Noah can stand in front of me all he wants. But in my heart, where it counts the most? He's in my past. Forever.

4

NOAH

I STAND outside Bobbi's bakery. She said she was building her dream...but what she's really built is a catnip factory.

Bobbi's Sweet Things. A bakery filled with amazing treats that only she can create. It's been difficult to resist stopping by since the place opened.

I could always go to a different bakery. It isn't like Los Angeles is lacking options. But none of them is Bobbi's dream. And none of them makes me wish I'd reacted differently back then. Now all I've got is regret for what I've done—and grief for the loss of all we could've been, but weren't because I was terrified of the darkness my secret life could bring.

Bobbi's Sweet Things is psychological warfare at its finest, and nothing I've gone through in life has prepared me for it. If I didn't know better, I might think Bobbi was working for the enemy.

Even the location is diabolical—right near GrantEm Capital, my brothers' VC firm, which still has a lot of my money. I've thought of different ways to approach her, but the only option that feels right is to act like nothing's wrong. Shameless, but it's better than lying about why I missed the opening party.

I simply cannot tell her the truth. So it's best I don't bring it up at all, shove our past under the rug and try to smooth things over. I screwed up badly, but Bobbi has feelings for me. Despite her tough exterior, she's too soft inside to ignore my efforts.

Yeah, but when a woman as sweet as Bobbi decides to cut you out of her life—

I short-circuit the thought, then kick it out of my mind. Don't need that kind of negativity before a critical mission. Although it's just recon for the moment—gotta figure out how deep of a hole I'm in before I can build a ladder tall enough to get myself out.

Pasting a shit-eating grin on my face, I walk in. I made sure to look my best because I'm aware of the impact my appearance can have. Women always check me out, and I've caught Bobbi staring more than once. On top of that, I know exactly which of my assets she likes the most. I'm in a shirt that emphasizes the width of my shoulders. My jeans are fashionably worn and fit to show off the musculature of my long legs. My hair is neatly cropped and styled to look careless without appearing sloppy.

The place smells of sweets and home. She's always had a magical ability to make me feel like I can take an easy breath and let my guard down.

You'll be lucky if she doesn't spit in your face, you bastard.

I'm okay with that. Anger is better than apathy, although given her deafening silence over the last twelve months, her reaction to seeing me again might involve more than just some spit. I haven't forgotten that kick she delivered in Mexico.

Bobbi turns her beautiful face, and our eyes meet...

Boom-boom-boom, my heart thunders. I realize that until now it's been barely functioning on life support without her. She looks even more amazing—and happy.

Although that happiness is rapidly vanishing from her face faster than water on a sun-roasted rock in Death Valley.

"Hi." I smile.

"What the hell are you doing here?" Her words shake with barely suppressed fury.

Hallelujah. I can still make her feel something. "Hey, babe," I say with all the joy I feel at being in her presence again.

Her burnt-caramel eyes narrow dangerously. "Don't you *hey babe* me."

Is it fucked up that I want to hug her? Even knowing she's probably fantasizing about throttling me, I want to tell her how much I love her because it's the most honest thing I can say. "Sorry, my light, that wasn't appropriate. You're a goddess, not some mere babe."

Her hands curl into fists. If there were a rolling pin nearby, she'd grab it and try to brain me. Actually, forget rolling pins. If I were closer, she'd just swing and break my beak.

Not that I can allow that. My pretty face is one of the reasons she likes me. But she can punch the other parts...well, some of them, anyway.

"I was in the neighborhood and had a craving for croissants. I've heard great things about your bakery. And listen, congratulations! Really. You've done an amazing job here." I mean it sincerely. I'm so proud of her for doing what she set out to do. Plus, I'm happy she's no longer somebody's bullet catcher. Mom told me I needed to toe the line, but I really should've done more than sic the IRS on that Instagram model client of hers. That idiot bitch staged a fake stalking and kidnapping for likes and shares, except she was too brainless to use blanks. Bobbi took one in her belly while protecting her client like the top-notch pro bodyguard that she was. Since Mom vetoed shooting the moron, I should've poisoned her. There are so many substances that can give you heart failure.

"*Thank* you," Bobbi says with a smile, although her eyes scream, *Fuck you and your fashionably distressed jeans!* "Unfortunately, we're all out of croissants."

"You are?" I point at a tray, which has four left.

Her smile remains frozen as she pulls out a paper bag with the Bobbi's Sweet Things logo and places all the croissants in it.

"How did you know I wanted four?" I tease with a wink, hoping to coax a genuine reaction out of her. It doesn't have to be anything big, but even a crack would be enough to start thawing her out.

A sharp glint flashes in her eyes. "I didn't. See, these are croissants reserved for somebody else."

"Who? I'll buy them from them."

"A regular. You wouldn't know him, of course, since you've never been by."

Okay, I deserved that. I should've at least sent flowers, but when I saw those photos of Mike and his fiancée, I thought it might be best to just cut ties. If I could turn back time...

"Are you still upset about the calla lilies?" I say, trying to communicate that I haven't forgotten anything about her. That she means so much to me.

The faux serenity slips from her face. "No, Noah. I was, but not anymore. I've decided to quit you."

"Ah, come on. We both know you're not a quitter." I give her my most winning smile, which never fails.

"I am when we're talking about a cigarette." Her gaze sweeps over me meaningfully, lingering on my crotch.

I let out a reluctant laugh. All right, she wants to take a cheap shot about my dick. Understandable, given the situation. I can be the bigger man, no pun intended. She can do a lot more if she'll just forgive me. "I'm at least a cigar, based on girth and length. And, you know, class."

Her eyes are like stones. "You're a cancer-causing agent, and I'm not going to tolerate your toxic BS."

For a moment, I'm speechless.

"Get out, or I'm calling the cops for trespassing."

5

NOAH

As a last-minute customer walks in to grab whatever's left, I walk out of the bakery like Bobbi wants. No matter how happy I am to see her or how much I want to make my case that I'm back for good, she obviously needs a bit of time.

I head to her place. She lives in the house she inherited from her traitor father. The SoCal sun warms me inside and out, driving the chill from the Pacific Northwest—and Bobbi's cold shoulder—out of my system. I'm clutching the bag of Bobbi's bread I got from Mom's pantry like a security blanket. I know Bobbi will come around. I've never failed to charm her, and soothing her is the easiest thing in the world because all I have to do is spoil her the way I want to.

The two-story house hasn't changed. Squat. Unassuming. Dark brown roof and pale green paint on the exterior. A two-car garage and well-maintained yard with a couple of orange trees. I know there's a basement as well. The property blends in with the middle-class neighborhood, and nobody would look twice while driving past.

Wonder if Bobbi got to redo the kitchen floor. When she inherited the house, it had the ugliest tiled floor imaginable: bright lime green and reddish-brown tiles with cracked, yellowing grout. Whoever picked those shades was at least color-blind. Her father never bothered to redo it, probably too busy being a traitor, and Bobbi swore she would replace it as soon as she got a chance.

I slow down, then stop. I have to blink...but yes, there is in fact a pair of human legs sticking out of one of the windows. Shitty old jeans and ratty white tennis shoes. Not Bobbi's style. Not her ass, either.

I park my Bugatti on the road and climb out. Munching on the bread, I approach the person—a skinny Caucasian guy in his twenties, with mousy brown hair that could use a comb. His white T-shirt doesn't look that old, but it's still dingy. Mom would say that's what happens when you don't separate your laundry correctly.

He's wriggling his bony ass, legs kicking, like he's trying to air-swim. Given that the upper half of his body is inside, it's obvious he's trying to enter Bobbi's home and failing. Not sure why he's using the window when there's a door. He can't possibly be a burglar because he'd starve. Even crime requires some level of competence to earn you a living.

"You stuck, buddy?" I say conversationally, like it's normal to see a person wiggling in a window.

He twists a little and something cracks. "Ow."

"You okay?"

"Think I pulled something. Shit."

Definitely a starving criminal. What an opportunity to practice the enhanced interrogation technique I've always wanted to test. I'm trained to do it, but unfortunately never get a chance. The top brass assigns me targets they want dead, not singing.

"Just trying to get back inside, man," the guy says with a faint Nova Scotian accent. "Got locked out."

"Didn't leave a spare key under the welcome mat?" The fucker broke one of the glass panes to unlock her window. What an asshole. I thought Canadians were supposed to be nice.

I pull his wallet out of his back pocket, which he doesn't seem to notice. A California driver's license, issued last year. Lorcan Duncan, with an Orange County address. My God, what was his mother thinking? She should've at least given him a dignified middle name he could've used. Lorcan Duncan sounds like a particularly stupid tropical bird.

"Nah. Bobbi doesn't do that," Lorcan says. "Says it's begging to be robbed."

I smile. Smart girl. Although...trying to rob her would be a mistake. She owns at least four guns and isn't afraid to use them. On top of that, her license and permit are up-to-date. I know because I checked. If they weren't, I was going to take care of it. I can't have my girl getting into trouble over some bureaucratic bullshit.

"So why are you going this way instead of asking her to let you in?"

I flick his license to the ground—just because it seems like a fitting punishment for trying to break into Bobbi's house—and look through his wallet. Two Visas. A Master Card. Four AmExs. All of them well used. A few small bills that look more worn out than a hooker after a busy night, and I remove them as a penalty for damaging her window. Four Powerball tickets. *Hoping to turn your life around?* The latest jackpot is one-point-two billion. A life-altering amount of money if you can beat the odds of two or three hundred million other lottery players in the country.

Oh wait, those tickets are for previous drawings. Guess he wasn't so lucky after all.

"Okay, so get this." Lorcan groans. "Wait, can you lift the window up? I can't stay like this anymore. It's killing my back."

I lift the window, and he slides out, landing inelegantly in the dirt. Wincing, he pushes himself up and smooths his wrinkled shirt to make himself more presentable. Not that it really works. He needs a shower.

"Thanks, man." Lorcan straightens his back, placing his hands on his hips for support, and winces. He doesn't seem to notice the wallet in my hand. "I'm, like, totally ready to ask her to marry me, you know?"

"You are?" I let go of his wallet and shove more bread into my mouth. That's better than murdering this irritating Canadian guy. Unsanctioned kills are frowned upon.

"Hey, did you drop something?"

"No. You were saying?"

"What? Oh, yeah. About the proposal. I know she's gonna say yes."

What the hell? When did she start dating this guy? And when did her standards drop so low?

I might—*possibly*—acknowledge with great bitterness and

reluctance that she found another man. After all, I've been gone for a while. But that's only if the guy she replaced me with was God's gift to humanity. Like, the perfect man.

Lorcan doesn't qualify. I can spot ten things wrong with the guy just at a glance. If I spend more than a few minutes with him, I know I will be tempted to terminate him for the betterment of humanity. If nothing else, it would make me feel good about saving Bobbi from this loser.

"Did she say she loved you?" I ask, the bread suddenly tasting like dust in my mouth.

He looks at me. "Not really relevant, dude."

What?

"I mean, I'm not sure if I'm really going to marry her. I just need a fiancée, you know?"

"You need a fiancée who might not love you? A fake fiancée?" It sounds like one of Nicholas's romance novels. Except Lorcan doesn't strike me as the type to read anything other than Instagram captions. If that.

"Yeah, exactly! I knew you'd get it!" His eyes go bright. "See, I need my parents to understand I'm leading a stable life here, but not so stable that they'll want to come visit, you know?"

"Not really." I should probably go ahead and do some enhanced interrogation to get straight answers out of this guy.

"Well, it's pretty simple. My parents are worried that I'm in another country by myself. But if I'm settled here, with a fiancée, they won't be 'cuz I wouldn't be alone."

"Why wouldn't you want them to worry about you?"

"Look." He gives me a don't-be-so-naïve smile. "I don't really want to go back home. This area has all the good shit, you know? Plentiful and cheap."

"Good shit?"

"You know." He tries to elbow me, but I move out of the way. He sniffles. "Mostly club stuff. You can't find anything good at a reasonable price in Halifax."

It finally dawns on me. A druggie.

"Bobbi doesn't have much going for her, you know?"

"Is that so?"

"Nobody wants to date a girl that tall. And she's, like, *hard*. Her body." He lets out a just-between-us-boys laugh. "I like a soft woman. With some heavy artillery up front." He mimes holding a pair of cantaloupes.

"You touched her?" I ask with a smile, placing my hand over the blade I carry in my pocket. It isn't big, but plenty sharp enough to emasculate him. Knives aren't my thing, not like Mom, but they'll do in a pinch.

"Nah." He scoffs. "She couldn't get me up."

Spoken like a true loser, blaming his problem on a woman. It isn't Bobbi's fault his dick is softer than soggy rigatoni. Mine works better than fine around her.

He continues, "She isn't my type. Probably isn't anybody's type. Maybe one of those bodybuilder freaks. But the girl can bake. Gotta give her that."

He's lucky he never touched her because he would've lost his balls—and tongue—otherwise. I make a noncommittal noise, then look at the window. "Want some help getting inside?"

He immediately perks up, but his eyes hold as much intelligence as a lobotomized turkey. He doesn't suspect I want to filet him—we both have dicks and so I must agree with everything coming out of his mouth.

"Yeah, sure! You're the best, man."

I clap him on the shoulder, bro to bro. "I aim to please."

6

BOBBI

I WANT to be the first person to congratulate you on achieving your dream. And bring you your favorite flowers.

I have to consciously relax my hand on the steering wheel as I drive through the pre-rush hour traffic. Noah's broken promise—the one I've tried so hard to forget—is back, buzzing around in my head like the world's most annoying gnat. He never apologized or explained himself.

The *gall* he had to walk into my bakery and want to buy my croissants! Like I'd serve him. Ha! I really wanted him to stay and be a nuisance so I could call 911. It would've been hilarious to have him hauled away. That would've proven I'm not letting him ruin my life with his toxicity and mind games. Not anymore.

So why am I still thinking about him?

Ugh. I need to find a way to permanently evict him from my mind. The fact that a year apart hasn't made me immune pisses me off to no end. He lives in Malibu. He could've come by any time and apologized, but didn't. That says so much about where I rank in his priorities.

I don't want to beg for crumbs of affection from people who don't care. That only brings pain.

Just look at my dad. I park my Tacoma in front of the house he left me. He died in some third-world country, doing God knows what for the

State Department. He never told me anything about his work—everything was supposedly classified and above my pay grade—and he never, ever had time for me. I'm sure the only reason the house became mine is that I'm his only surviving family member. He certainly didn't bother with a will. The life insurance money I got is what the federal government provides to its employees. He just never found it urgent to opt out, probably because the premium was so low. At least his neglect worked in my favor that one time—the payout became my seed money for the bakery.

Still, I would've preferred it if he'd shown he cared about me, rather than leaving me that life insurance and the house. Spending a few years in L.A. with TJ's family when I was in high school showed me what a family could be. They were always laughing and cheering each other on. And hugs. So many hugs. I was hugged more in a month with them than my whole life with my parents. TJ's family was always so secure in their belief that they weren't alone—that the family had their back. I was never certain. Mom was inconsistent in her love, showering me with it one day then unable to bear the sight of me the next. Dad always had something more important to attend to.

If the house wasn't located so conveniently in a nice neighborhood, I'd sell it and move in a heartbeat.

I kill the engine and climb out of the truck with the bag of the last four croissants. As I unlock and enter the house, Señor Mittens, so named because the hair around his paws is dark orange, comes over with a soft meow. He's a stray I took in after discovering him crying in a park, his left forepaw bleeding. The vet told me he'd lost a toe, and the little cat tugged at my heart. He was so scrawny, I could almost see the ribs through his dingy white fur, and I couldn't let a toeless kitty out on the streets. The world might not want him, but I did.

Now, he's plump, his pelt shiny. And he walks around like the missing toe doesn't bother him at all.

I should be able to function like that, too. Like cutting Noah out of my life doesn't bother me at all. He should mean as little as Señor Mittens's missing toe.

Actually less. Toes don't lie to you—

The sound of the dryer tumbling comes from the laundry room. I scan the kitchen island. The dirty glass I left on the counter this morning is now in the sink.

Okay. Señor Mittens is a great cat, but he doesn't do domestic chores.

Quietly, I put the bag of croissants on the island, open the left drawer and pull out the Glock. I creep toward the laundry room—which is empty except for the dryer with something that looks like a bedsheet tumbling inside.

Weird. I don't have a housekeeper. And a burglar wouldn't be doing my laundry.

Is TJ messing with me?

Nah. If it were my cousin, he would've made his presence known. He knows I have guns.

Then I hear a muffled noise, like somebody trying to scream against a pillow, coming from my bedroom. Señor Mittens dashes past my legs and in through the partially open door.

Shit.

I kick the door fully open, aiming the Glock. What I see overloads my brain. It's like the world is ending and I only have two bullets, but there are five zombies after me.

Some guy is hogtied with a rope, a big piece of duct tape over his mouth. That explains the muzzled screams. Meanwhile, Noah is sitting on the floor with his long, muscled legs stretched out, ankles crossed, scarfing down half an apple pie on a blue Disney Cinderella plate, which means he grabbed it from my kitchen.

And that pie must be the one I made last night and was saving for the weekend.

Noah smiles. "Hi, Bobbi." His gray eyes crinkle, like he couldn't be happier to see me.

I hate it that he's still heartbreakingly beautiful. And I loathe it that my hormones are perking up, and something inside me wants me to preen.

Hell, no. Have some self-respect!

Señor Mittens hisses at Noah. Even my cat has more dignity than me. Of course, he doesn't like any of my friends, either.

I lower the gun. "If this were Texas, I'd've shot you."

"Thank God we're in civilized California." Noah's smile widens, annoyingly charming.

Maybe I should just shoot him and claim self-defense—*he tried to attack me with his fork, officer!*

"This is a *great* pie. You're an even better cook now."

His compliment only pours gasoline on my temper. "You think you're so fucking clever, don't you?" I say, shoving the gun into my waistband.

"Don't just think it. I know it." He gazes at me softly. "I love you, my light."

I inhale sharply at the easy way he says "I love you." The fact that I want him to mean it makes me feel pathetic and even more furious. How is it that he can still manipulate my emotions? He has a unique ability to make me feel so good and so bad at the same time.

"I even nabbed this guy for you. He says he knows you, but he was trying to break in through a window."

"And you helped him inside?"

"Well...yeah. But afterward I tied him up. As a peace offering. You might know him. Lorcan Duncan?" Noah's tone is sweet and understanding. *I knew you were slumming while I was away. I get it. I'm here to save you from your own poor judgment.*

I glare at the piece of shit on the floor. He's trying to get free of the ropes, but not having much success. I should've known it was a bad idea to try to date some random dude named Lorcan Duncan of all things, even if the dating app did swear that it could match me up with the other half of my soul.

Unfortunately, the app didn't promise the guy would have a brain. I'm convinced Lorcan doesn't because I've never met a dumber guy.

But God gave him plenty of perseverance. Not only does he not understand the meaning of "no," he apparently doesn't give up. Noah witnessing my date-shame only makes me want to scream. I'd bet my bakery he's been with some hot chicks in the last twelve months. Women are always eye-fucking him. My arms around him didn't stop them before, and without that, forget it. They would've been rubbing themselves all over him like cats in heat.

"Leave. Now. And take out the trash when you go."

Noah doesn't point out that Lorcan is *my* trash. "Okay."

His tone is agreeable. But I know the truth. He's just playing with me. When he's done, he always leaves without a backward glance, then after a while, he checks up on me, like a child remembering a toy he discarded in a corner of his room. I didn't realize that when we first met because I was in a weird headspace after my dad's death. Then Noah came back only after I got shot, thanks to an idiot client who was trying to stage an attack against herself for social media cred.

And now he's back again, when Lorcan was trying to break into my house. Un-*fucking*-believable!

"You're bad news. Don't ever come back," I say. "And stop eating my pie!"

"Come on. Don't be so hard on me." He stands up.

I glare at him. "Not even my cat likes you."

"So if he likes me, will you give me a chance?"

"Ha! He'd eat raw broccoli first."

"You didn't answer the question," he says, all sweet and charming.

I'm not falling for you, buster. "Yes," I snap, knowing he's more likely to get struck by lightning. Señor Mittens will never love Noah, or anyone other than me. He doesn't even love my friend Yuna, who fed him premium cream. There's nothing Noah can do.

"Deal." He smiles.

My foolish heart does a funny thing that feels like a little pirouette of joy. It better not start dictating to me because I'm not listening. When it comes to Noah, I'm only relying on my head. And my head says it's unfair that I don't have the superpower to make him spontaneously regurgitate the apple pie he already ate.

He hefts the hogtied Lorcan with one hand and carries him out like an oversized toolbox, banging him a couple of times against the doorjamb and a corner of the hallway. More muffled screams. I remain in the bedroom with the cat. I don't want to do anything stupid to let Noah know he can still affect me, especially not when my heart is still doing that ecstatic spin.

The front door shuts. I wait a few minutes, then go to the kitchen and put away my Glock.

Señor Mittens hops onto the island.

"Hey, get off there. You know better than that."

He meows, pawing the smooth marble surface.

"I'm going to feed you, don't worry." I rub the spot behind his ears which should settle him down.

He smacks the counter harder. If he could talk, he'd call me an idiot.

"What's the deal?" I look at my annoyed cat, unsure what to do to soothe his temper, then realize what's wrong.

That son of a bitch stole my bag of croissants.

7

BOBBI

MY FIRST INSTINCT is to run outside and snatch the croissants from Noah, assuming I can catch up to him. But I don't have the time to get ready for my date and deal with him.

The date matters more, my mind says. It could be your future. Noah's your past.

Right. I inhale, then go back to my bedroom. My hands shake with rage as I try to curl my hair and reapply my mascara and lipstick. It's all Noah's fault. Closing my eyes, I breathe, trying to settle my temper. But it isn't easy. I'm imagining wrapping my hands around his neck and squeezing. *Hard.*

Except he'd just laugh. He got a minor scratch in Mexico when the trio of thugs attacked me, but he's no pushover.

Before rage can consume me further, I look at my vision board. The photos of a hot guy and four kids—I'd be okay with two, but four seems ideal—a house complete with a yard and white picket fence, beautiful baked goods, and Señor Mittens. I'd love a big, loving family that has dinner together every night and laughs, cheers when things are good and hugs and cries when things are bad because I never had that growing up. And firm roots. No moving all over the place. We constantly relocated all over the world due to my father's job, and Mom was always busy trying to adjust to a new place, a new language and culture.

The photos make a perfect vision for my future. And hopefully I'll be closer to it after tonight's date.

Señor Mittens comes over and meows in that secretive I-know-something-you-don't kind of way. I scratch his head. "Don't worry. My future includes you."

He shakes his head, then sits in front of my vision board. His tail swishes in front of the picture of the guy—the one representing my future husband. I smile. "That's the one I'm going to get tonight. Hopefully."

Señor Mittens stares at me disdainfully, his tail swishing faster.

"What? I'm sure he's not allergic to cats. You're on my board, too." I step forward and put my finger on the board. "This is you... Hey, wait a minute..."

I look closer and realize that *Noah has pasted a photo of his own face and taped it over the hot model.* He did it so slickly that the colors and shadows blend together almost perfectly, which probably contributed to me not realizing earlier.

"Son of a *bitch!*" I snatch the picture from the board. Noah's head is smiling, his eyes crinkled. That bastard. He must've done this before he decided to raid my fridge for the apple pie!

Okay, *that's it.* I'm going to murder him. I *so* fucking will!

Señor Mittens's eyes turn to slits as he yawns and stretches. Obviously, he's annoyed at the lack of proper appreciation for pointing out the problem with my vision board.

"Thank you, buddy. You're the only one I can count on."

He purrs. Even though he can't speak, I know what it means: "Pay me with tuna."

"Okay, fine. One can of your favorite tuna for pointing out the problem." The stuff is pricey, which is why I don't buy it for him all the time. But this definitely warrants laying out a little cash. What kind of future am I going to manifest with Noah's smiling head on my vision board?

I toss the crushed photo into the trash and resume getting ready. No way is Noah going to derail me tonight.

Resolutely, I finish applying makeup, then I change into a sleeveless cream scoop-neck top along with my favorite red and black plaid pleated skirt over fishnet thigh-highs and medium heels. The man's profile says he's six-three, so the shoes will make us about even in height.

You could've worn high heels if it were Noah.

I shove aside the irritating thought. This isn't about him. It's about *my* life, which does *not* include him.

Determined to forge ahead into a Noah-less future, I drive to Gion Shiyaki. The restaurant is much fancier than the places I normally frequent. It opened not too long ago, so I've never been inside, not even guarding one of my high-profile clients. Assuming they could get a table. It's apparently always booked, and not even celebrities can get a table on short notice. My date must've pulled some serious strings to grab a table on a busy Friday night. And that earns him lots of bonus points. A man who can make magic happen to make a girl feel special? Sold!

The entrance is the definition of understated elegance with a Japanese stone garden set with a small water feature. A quiet melody consisting of some Asian string instruments comes from speakers, the plucked notes lilting and pretty. A slim Asian woman in a deep purple kimono comes out with a smile.

I give her my date's name.

"Oh yes, he's here already. Right this way."

"Great." See? Normal men show up when they say they will.

Stop comparing every one of your dates to Noah.

Right. That wouldn't be fair to my date, potentially my future husband. He should be judged on his own merits.

The lady leads me through corridors with hardwood floors and off-white walls. Little nooks and crannies hold wood carvings and Asian potteries in earth tones.

Excitement starts to build as I focus on what's to come. Most people fudge a little on their dating profiles, but we'll probably hit it off even if he's exaggerated his charms a bit. Not only is he stunning, but he's looking for someone who knows what she wants, is seeking commitment and shared dreams and values. He loves movies, dancing on the beach and singing. He enjoys musicals and loves to travel to tropical places with turquoise water. A lover of animals and an expert surfer, too. When I messaged him that I'd love to learn, he said it'd be his pleasure to take me out on the water. He added, "I'll plan everything. All you have to do is show up."

That let me know he might actually be the one. Noah has never offered to plan anything—but then he can't even remember to come to stuff *I* planned.

Time to stop thinking about him. Even though it's been a year since I resolved to evict him from my life, he's managed to occupy a small corner of my mind, popping back up now and then like he can't bear to let me forget him. My cousin Josie, who's a shrink, would have a field day with this—which is why I haven't said a word to her. I don't need to get my head examined. My problem is that my heart is stubbornly fixated on Noah for some reason, and I'm making slow progress freeing myself. Once I find a man who cherishes me and I can stake my future on, Noah will be history. A discarded and never-to-be-revisited chapter in my life.

The lady pushes a sliding door open. I start to smile, then my face freezes.

There's no way this...person can be my date. The photo doesn't match the guy in front of me. The profile pic showed a stunning man with beautifully tousled auburn hair and smiling green eyes, full lips stretched into a boyish smile. The jawline was tight, the cheekbones high and sharp enough to cut wood. But the guy sitting in front of me has flaming orange hair slicked back with gel, showcasing a massive forehead. The angle of his cheekbones is nothing special, and the tip of his jaw is round enough that it can't even be called a "tip." Owlish green eyes stare at me, and his thin lips are colorless.

The photo was an eight or a nine. This guy is maybe a four.

He doesn't stand up. "You're finally here! Great. You look just like your profile."

And you don't. I can't decide how to say it without sounding rude.

"Have a seat." He gestures with a small, smug smile.

I sit, more or less on auto-pilot. *What am I supposed to do now?* I should've known the day could, in fact, continue to get worse after running into Reggie, Floyd and Noah. "Was your profile name your real name?"

"Nope. Joey Martin, at your service." He pauses expectantly.

"Am I...supposed to know you?"

He spreads his hands, giving me incredulity. "I work for Ted Lasker."

"Oh, okay. The movie producer, right?" The man's a legend.

"Correct." Joey beams proudly.

"And...?" I prompt, unsure why he's bringing up his boss.

"I'm his right hand. And left hand."

Color me skeptical. This guy is maybe his left foot.

"I'm glad we were able to meet in person." He gives me a once-over like he's assessing merchandise at a yard sale. "You'll look pretty enough with a bit more makeup."

Is he serious? At least I posted a regular selfie pic, not something that had twenty filters on it! "Thanks. So will you," I say with a fake smile, then gesture at our server for some warm sake. I can't do this without alcohol.

"The magic of make-up, darling." He sighs with satisfaction. "It can make anybody beautiful."

"Whoever did yours must've been amazing."

The sarcasm flies right over his head. "She does make-up for Ryder Reed," he says.

Ryder Reed. When the actor announced his marriage, my client at the time wept because she was convinced he would've married her if she could've engineered a meet-cute grandiose enough for her rep. She didn't seem to understand that it's meet-*cute*, not meet-crazy.

"His looks aren't from the makeup," I point out coolly.

Ryder is a very good friend of Ivy's husband Tony Blackwood, and I've met the man in person. Doesn't matter what he's wearing or how sweaty he's become. Still ridiculously hot. Joey, on the other hand...? Not exactly.

"Meh. He still has a whole team dedicated to that, unlike me. I don't need to bother." Joey waves a hand dismissively, and I raise an eyebrow. Does he honestly think he's better looking than *Ryder Reed*? "My accomplishments alone..." Joey spreads his hands again with a meaningful look.

Except...I don't know what his accomplishments are, other than that he works for a movie producer. He doesn't elaborate. He probably doesn't have anything else.

The dating app must be cursed. Lorcan frickin' Duncan. A few go-nowhere dates. And now *this*.

The server places a small bottle of hot sake in front of me, thank God, and I start drinking. The food follows, coming out on delightful little plates and bowls, tiny portions of fresh fish, tofu, meat and seasonal items broiled or simmered in various sauces. I lift my head and look at Joey, then back at the food. I don't have much appetite. As a matter of fact, I'm beginning to have a headache. But given the amount of care the chef put into creating this meal, I should try to enjoy it and endure this moment. I have to eat dinner anyway.

I've just taken a small bite of the horse mackerel when Joey says, "I'd love for you to have a grandbaby for Ted."

"What?" This is maybe the weirdest thing I've ever heard, and I've been around some *very* weird people. "Are you Ted's son?"

"No." He frowns in confusion. "What does that have to do with him wanting a grandchild?"

"You said you wanted children in your profile...?"

"Oh." He laughs, then pops a small chunk of chilled tofu topped with spring onions into his mouth. "I put that so I could find a woman who's open to the idea."

My chopsticks go still in the air. "I'm not sleeping with you."

"Not now, obviously—"

"Not ever."

"—since we're trying to get Ted an accessible grandchild first," Joey continues, completely oblivious to my rejection. He's probably one of those guys who only hears what he wants.

"An *accessible* grandchild?"

"Well, yeah. There's no point in having a grandchild he can't take to parties. Grandchildren are meant to be displayed, not hidden." He takes a healthy bite of beef simmered in savory sauce.

"I'm pretty sure taking a young child to a Hollywood party wouldn't be considered good parenting." I put my chopsticks down and pour more sake into my thimble-sized cup.

"He wouldn't *be* the parent. He'd be the *grand*parent. A jovial man of great accomplishments. Someone everyone loves. All you have to do is produce a beautiful baby that coos like a dove and sings like an angel."

Maybe I snorted something without meaning to—Noah might've left it; after all, he's the kind of bastard who defaces vision boards—and now I'm hallucinating. "I think I'd need a loving husband first."

"Ted will make sure you're taken care of. And your kid."

Joey's making no sense. Maybe he's the one who snorted something. "I thought he wanted a grandchild?" I lift the sake cup to my mouth.

"Yes. You're going to sleep with one of his sons."

The sake goes up my nose. Oh *shit*, that burns!

He hands me a tissue with a small frown. "I hope you present yourself better than this. But anyway, one of the available sons is a great catch. Women fawn all over him. He's basically perfect."

"Mmm, so perfect he can't find a woman to marry."

"It's called outsourcing, honey." Joey informs me in a slightly pitying tone, like I'm some cavewoman who hasn't discovered the wonders of delegation.

"Yeah, sure. What does this perfect and available son do?" Maybe he's an actor. Not the hot kind, but the weird kind.

"Nothing. He's rich."

I make a face. A spoiled overgrown man-child. How sexy. No wonder he needs to have Joey find him a woman.

"He's working on some novel, but I don't think he plans to finish it any time soon. Which is fantastic because it leaves him with a lot of free time. So all you have to do is sleep with him and have his baby."

"So simple!" I snap my fingers. "Where's the proposal and wedding?"

"Don't be plebian. Who does that in real life anyway? It's just for shows and movies."

I just can't.

"Besides, you should be honored. I've hired escorts—and I mean *hot* ones—models and actresses, but he didn't find any of them good enough. Which is why I've expanded the pool to include, you know, regular women. If you looked the slightest bit less hot, I would've walked out the door a long time ago."

That's it. I have no appetite and I'm not putting myself through the torture of nonsense coming from Joey. I start to rise.

"Bathroom's down the hall, to your right," he says.

He must've been here a lot with his important boss to know where the bathroom is! Except that isn't where I'm going.

I open my mouth to tell him, but then a waitress enters, placing a fresh bottle of sake on the table. Don't remember ordering it, but I certainly deserve it.

The server holds the sleeve of her kimono just so and pours me an elegant thimble-full, but I grab the bottle and take a direct swig. I turn to thank her, but then shock knocks me back on my ass.

Noah. What the hell?

He's in a freakin' suit, which of course fits him perfectly. It also adds that extra edge of power and authority which makes him look even hotter than he did earlier. The fact that I notice at all burns my gall.

"Good sake, isn't it?" he says.

He's smiling, just like on the vision board. But I ripped that picture off, so why isn't he disappearing?

He sits next to me, takes the bottle and places it on the table. "Feeling better?" he asks. "You really should be more selective about your dates. Joey isn't much better than Lorcan Duncan." His chiding tone says I should've been out with him.

How does he know my date's name? Just what the hell is going on?

"How did you find me?" I manage finally. My voice is hoarse, and I clear my throat. "Are you stalking me?" I wouldn't put it past him. He showed up at my bakery without warning, then broke into my home. He could've bugged my house. Or maybe planted a tracker on my truck on his way out. Those things are dirt cheap and small enough that the victim would never notice.

"No. I just keep my eyes and ears open when it comes to you," Noah says softly.

"Probably social media," Joey says. "People post pictures when they see someone important." His tone says he's the important someone.

After struggling to process the moment, I give up. The sake bottle is sitting there on the table, taunting me. I grab it and take another swallow.

"So, you two know each other?" Joey asks. The excitement in his voice slithers over my back like a snake. Cold goosebumps cover my body despite the alcohol.

"No," I say, at the same time Noah says, "Yes."

"Perfect." Joey grins. "Please. Meet Noah Lasker. He's the one I told you about. You know, the guy who doesn't do anything but be rich."

Displeasure twists Noah's handsome face as he turns to Joey.

"I believe you. He doesn't even stick around." I spit the words out between clenched teeth.

"Right?" Joey says with a broad grin. Noah shoots him a murderous look. If gazes were tangible, Joey's brain would be splattered all over the unfinished meal. "But don't worry. Ted will take care of everything, as I said. With my assistance, of course."

"You don't want this leper colony reject near us," Noah says.

"Hey," Joey protests.

"Come on, Bobbi. Let's go." Noah puts a hand on my arm, the feel of his skin on mine sending warm shivers through me. "You and I will have a better time alone with each other. We can catch up and talk about our future."

"There is no *our* future. There's only *my* future and *your* future."

"Joey upset you. I have a reservation at La Mer," Noah says, mentioning a high-end seafood restaurant that also has a long waiting list.

"No!" I stand up and shake his hand off my arm. "I'm not having dinner with you whenever you decide it's convenient *for you*. We don't have that kind of relationship. In fact, we don't have any kind of relationship. We might as well be strangers."

Noah looks like I just slapped him. And the hint of vulnerability shakes me more than the charming façade he wore this afternoon. But I can't afford to let myself weaken. Give him an inch, he'll take five or six miles. I'm not putting myself through such cruel and unusual punishment out of some misguided hope that he'll be different this time. "It was an *interesting* evening. I hope I never run into either of you again."

"Bobbi," Noah says. "Look—"

"Wait, we have to hammer out the details!" Joey sounds slightly desperate.

"Better not to. Bring a hammer anywhere near me, and I'll be forced to kill you with it to save my sanity."

8

BOBBI

I TOSS AND TURN, then punch the pillow next to me hard. Breathing out roughly, I turn on the lamp on the nightstand. The pillow stays dented, like it's sulking about the unfair treatment it's received.

"Shit." *I'm personifying inanimate objects,* and I only do that when I'm stressed or frazzled. I glare at the clock-radio. 11:23. Way past bedtime. I make it a habit to go to bed at the same time because I have to get up so early to open my bakery.

But sleep eludes me. It's all Noah's fault for showing up again after so long and acting like there isn't anything wrong between us.

I love you, my light.

The easily said confession rips a long, ragged scar into my heart. Do I look so starved for affection that he thinks a carelessly tossed out L-word will make me fall to my knees? Especially when he's proven—repeatedly—that he has no problem abandoning me and breaking his promises? Just how pathetic does he think I am?

And ruining my vision board? Joey happened because of Noah. I know it. The universe totally got the wrong message when he put his face on the photo I'd so carefully curated.

I feel wounded and frustrated, and my pride bristles. It demands I stop wasting my time trying to get some sleep and just get even.

Except I can't think of a way.

I trudge to the kitchen to grab some ice water. First step is to cool my temper—fast. Señor Mittens stops in the middle of grooming himself and watches me open the fridge.

"Just getting something to drink," I say to my cat.

He stares at me, unblinking. He knows I go to bed early.

"It's Noah. That rat bastard. He comes back into my life, and now I'm so off balance I can't even sleep."

Señor Mittens's eyes narrow into slits.

"So you think he's a piece of crap, too, right?"

He meows. I don't speak Cat, but it sounds like a *yes*.

"I need some revenge, but I can't think of anything good." I drum my fingers on the countertop. "He said, 'I love you' to mess with me, and I don't know what I can say back to shut him up. He wouldn't care if I said, 'I love you, too,' since..." I rub my forehead. "He never cares about anything I do anyway, except when he's just bored." The last part comes out in a pitiful resigned sigh. "And why did he put his face on my vision board anyway? It's like...he wants to be a permanent part of my future, but we both know that isn't true. There can't be any *our* future when it only lasts until he needs to go photograph some cheetahs in Zambia or wherever."

I hate Noah for stirring the tiny, romantic part of me that had stupidly fantasized that he could be the one to marry and have children with. It took so much effort and heartbreak to quash the illusion a year ago. He doesn't get to simply pop back into my life whenever he wants and disrupt my emotional harmony *just because*. I can't give that much control over my life to someone who constantly lies.

Señor Mittens gives me a judgmental look. Bet he doesn't let anything shake him. He's a simple cat, clear on his likes and dislikes.

Suddenly, he starts retching. I jump with alarm, but before I can panic, a glob of hair lands on the counter.

"Eww! That's *super* gross, Señor Mittens! I told you no puking hairballs on the kitchen counter."

He hacks a couple more times and then looks away disdainfully.

"What is *up* with everyone today?" I mutter. Reggie, Floyd, Lorcan, Noah, Joey and now Señor Mittens...

I grab a paper towel to clean up the hairball, and my cat makes a sound somewhere between purr and growl. Then it strikes me. Except for that first time, he's never thrown a hairball up on the kitchen counter. Ever since I told him not to, he takes care to cough them up in the bathroom.

I study my cat closely. He's a feline of habit. Is he sick?

His bright eyes stare back at me. Smugly. If he could speak, he'd say, "You may thank me."

My gaze drops to the hairball. "You want me to throw it at Noah the next time he shows his face?"

Señor Mittens smacks the counter with his paw, the way he did when he was trying to tell me Noah filched my croissants. Then he stretches, extending his claws, and moves his head from side to side.

Okay, so apparently that would be a *no*. But he's trying to tell me *something...*

An idea pops into my head. Depending on what Noah's done with my croissants it may not work, but what do I have to lose? It's better than tossing and turning all night, fuming about what happened.

I change into a black sleeveless turtleneck and my darkest blue jeans, grab some supplies—and the hairball, carefully wadded up in a paper towel—and drive to Noah's Malibu mansion. Thankfully, traffic's light at this hour. I guess even L.A. has to sleep sometime.

His place is a beachfront property, highly prized, so I doubt he's sold it in the last fourteen months. And he obviously doesn't need money. Besides, unless I'm mistaken, his brothers are loaded. He can always borrow money from them if he needs to buy another Bugatti.

I stop my red Tacoma in front of the security pad. It's the same as before. It sits there, silently mocking me.

The last time I was here, it was to celebrate him selling an entire set of cheetah photos he took to a private collector at an art auction. I even baked him a special cake. It was super cute, with chocolate cheetahs and a swirly "Congrats to My Special Guy" in the center.

Just thinking about it makes me want to writhe in shame. This is why we can't do nice things.

I glare at the pad and punch in 0729. It's the date we met. Noah told me he chose it for his security code because that's when he found *the one.* I fell for that line so bad, it was like an elephant through a plate glass skylight.

The gates open, and I stare in shock. *The code still works.*

Well, July twenty-ninth must also be the day his doctor cured his gout. Or erectile dysfunction.

Spotlights dot the driveway. I do my best not to notice how nothing has changed in the garden with its vines and little shrubs. The landscape might have stayed the same, but that's not true for me and Noah.

I park my truck a few yards away from the main structure and get out with my supplies. The door to the mansion is shut tight, and I inhale. There's another security pad inside by the entrance. That one is —or was—0412. My birthday.

"The day you came into the world," Noah said, then gave me a smile that made my belly flip.

I'd never experienced that until I met him.

Smooth talking asshole. I input the code. The light turns green, and inside my heart blossoms a tiny bit of hope—which I immediately shoot dead with a bazooka.

He's just been too lazy to change the code. If I really meant that much, he wouldn't have left the way he did or broken so many promises.

There's enough moonlight coming through the floor-to-ceiling windows facing the ocean for me to move around with ease. The soft soles of my tennis shoes make no sound on the marble floor. I pad toward the kitchen and flick on the light. The first floor is the same—the wide open space with the foosball table and the giant picture of Marilyn Monroe on the wall. It's weird that for a wildlife photographer obsessed with cheetahs, he doesn't have pictures of them plastered everywhere. But then he's a guy, so maybe he likes to look at a woman more than furry animals. And of course not just *any* woman but a sex symbol, the kind with a soft, voluptuous body and full breasts—the exact opposite of me.

A desk with an old-fashioned typewriter on it stands in one corner of the living room in front of a massive window that looks out onto the beach. Noah did say he was working on a novel, which according to Joey hasn't been finished yet.

Okay, enough dilly-dallying. On the kitchen counter is—*bingo!* The Bobbi's Sweet Things bag. I open it and find the motherlode—all four croissants. Guess Noah is saving them for breakfast. Or maybe he doesn't intend to eat them and just took the bag to piss me off.

Nothing would surprise me. But I sincerely hope he's planning on having them later.

I lay out my supplies on the counter. A tub of buttercream I made a couple of days ago. A piping bag. A small bread knife. And a whisk.

Perfect.

Jesus, what if you get caught? What if he calls 911?

He could, but I'm past caring. If he can break into my house, I can break into his. Besides, this house is basically soundproof. You can't hear anything from the kitchen or living room in the bedrooms upstairs. My heart pounds with an illicit thrill. I'm not turning back now.

I make decent-sized incisions into the croissants, then pull out a bowl from Noah's pantry and whip the buttercream and hairball together until they're well-mixed. Señor Mittens has short, white fur, and it's not so easy to tell that there's anything in the buttercream. I shove my gooey vengeance into the piping bag, then squeeze the glop into the incisions.

Then I put a thin, decorative plastic sheet over the cream so it doesn't make a mess and put the croissants back in the bag. Noah will never suspect, unless he checked them out earlier. But he probably didn't look that closely in the bakery. And even if he does notice, he'll probably assume I did this before leaving work. After all, who hates buttercream?

I quietly wash the mixing bowl, dry it and put it away. Then I deposit all my supplies back into my bag, making sure not to leave anything behind. Being a bodyguard isn't the same as being a cat burglar, but there is some overlap in the skill set. It helps to notice things that are out of place.

I look around. *Perfect.* My only regret is that I'm not technical enough to install a camera to film him biting into my newly reborn Frankencroissants.

Ah well. Can't have everything. But that doesn't mean my revenge won't be sweet. I flip the bird in the general direction of Noah's bedroom and sneak out, re-arming the alarm.

Once I get back home, I sleep like a baby. And dream of hairballs and a particularly annoying but hot as hell wildlife photographer.

9

NOAH

My scope finds *four targets in green camouflage, laughing around a campfire on the African savannah. Probably reminiscing and joking about all the innocents they've killed.*

It's been almost a year, but we found those responsible for Swain and his fiancée's deaths. And Mom sent me to mete out justice because she knows I'll make it good.

Most importantly, I won't miss.

They erupt in laughter again. One of them gets up and mimes holding something in front of his crotch while he thrusts.

Rape is all fun and games to you, isn't it?

The image of Swain's fiancée's body flashes in my head as I exhale and pull the trigger, blowing the asshole's pelvis into a bloody mist. The next bullets hit two of his companions; their skulls explode like watermelons dropped from a skyscraper. The fourth one rolls away, pulling out his gun, and starts shooting wildly.

Bang, bang, bang!

The sound stops abruptly as the lead slams into his head. The reports of the shots fade off, and the savannah is quiet again.

The first one I shot is writhing on the ground, leaving blood everywhere.

Could leave him to die like that. Shitty way to go, but then what they did to Swain and his girl was worse.

But then the paranoid voice in my head—the one that makes me so good at my job—warns that he might get lucky and survive.

Which wouldn't do.

I get up and walk into their camp, unholstering my Sig Sauer P365, and stand over the man. He looks up at me and tries to say something as I put a round into him. Red blooms over his heart; he twitches a couple of times, then stops moving.

I tilt my neck left and right. The tension in my shoulders refuses to ease. So what if the couple got justice? They're still dead. If vengeance could bring them back, I might've gone to Bobbi's bakery opening. But the finality of death is absolute.

It's best that I stay away from Bobbi. No matter how much I love her, we simply can't be together. Can't let her become a target for animals like this, I think, looking dispassionately at the bodies strewn on the ground. The hyenas will probably devour them before sunrise. A fitting ending.

I go back to my hide site and pack up my beautiful cheetahs—the moniker I gave my guns. Fast, precise and deadly, they're very similar to the gorgeous cats I love so much. My Jeep bounces over the uneven ground until I reach a small landing strip. It's just long enough to accommodate a prop plane, and sure enough, one is idling there, waiting.

A darkly tanned pilot squints at me. "Finally. You good?" he says, then spits in the dirt.

The bloodshot eyes, a grimy used-to-be-white wifebeater, dirty pants rolled up to two inches below the knees together with the hint of alcohol on his breath don't inspire confidence. But the team wouldn't have hired him if he wasn't good.

I nod, then climb into the plane.

"All right." He situates himself in the pilot's seat. "If anything happens, there's a parachute under each seat." He laughs. "If any of 'em work."

I pray the plane's better maintained than the man's clothes, but the craft rattles horribly as it gains speed on the short runway. The cockpit door has been ripped out and never replaced, so... I bounce in my seat, and almost hit my head against the low ceiling despite the seatbelt. Jesus, I know I'm supposed to play the unserious adventurer, but this is ridiculous. Should I be grateful the seatbelt is working?

But the plane takes off, climbing up and up without sputtering. Apparently, the engines are solid underneath the garbage exterior.

—Me: All taken care of. Toilets unclogged.

—Mom: Great.

I thumb through photos that have just arrived on my phone. Lots of fantastic shots of cheetahs in the wild. If anyone ever gets nosy enough to want to see my work, I'll have something to show them.

We turn on to our heading and level off and everything's fine for about ten minutes. Then the plane starts to roll.

For fuck's sake. I know the pilot was drinking before, but is he so drunk that he can't fly straight?

"Yo, keep the plane straight!" I yell.

Nothing, and the plane tilts further.

What the hell? I unbuckle and go to the cockpit to give the pilot a piece of my mind. I'm not flying like this all the way to Nairobi.

"Hey, what's—"

The pilot is slumped to the side. I pull his head back and see white foam mixed with blood around his mouth. His eyes are blank. I don't need to check his pulse to know he's dead.

There are sudden explosions on each side of the plane—shit. I head back and look out the dirt-crusted windows. Black smoke billows from the engines and we start to nosedive.

Panic, terror, fury—something should hit me, but instead, the only thing filling my head is a blasé "Guess this is how I'm going to go."

In a fraction of a second, the meaning of my life flashes by—and the fallout from my death. At least it'll be a clean, quick one. Painless. I deserve that much for all the horrible actors I've killed over the years. My brothers might wonder—but Mom will feed them a good story. Hopefully she doesn't tell them I'm dead. No need to dump grief on them. They have their wives and families. They should be busy enjoying what they have.

On the other hand, maybe they'll be fine even if they learn about my demise. They might even console themselves, thinking I died doing what I loved the most.

Shooting cheetahs.

They would've been right two years ago. Now...

Bobbi.

Longing wraps a fist around my heart. I miss her so much. My eyes land on the yellow bag by the pilot. It's the same color as the beautiful birthday cake she baked for me in Mexico. I'd never felt so loved and cherished in that moment, when she woke me up from a nightmare after bringing the cake and all I could see was her looking down at me with concern in her eyes. Even as guilt poked at me for lying to her, I basked in her warmth.

Dying means never seeing her again. Never putting her in danger. She'll never end up like Swain's fiancée.

My heart sputters, then beats hard at the notion that I'm never going to see her smile again. She won't miss me. She might even be glad when she hears I'm gone.

After all, what have I given her in the end except deception and heartache?

The knot in my chest grows unbearably tight, enough to make me wince and put a hand over it.

If you're going to miss her that much, why did you stay away? *a voice in my head asks.*

Can't go like this. I won't let Bobbi think she meant nothing to me. If I survive this, I'm going to go back to her. Show her what she means. I'll prove it to her...

Adrenaline pumps. I reach for the bottom of the pilot's seat. He won't be needing his parachute. And bingo. It's so dusty and stiff... Is it still in working order?

Only one way to find out.

I put it on quickly and look outside. Still some distance to the ground, although not much. Time to see how much Lady Luck loves me.

Grabbing my cheetahs, I jump. Then land on my side so hard, my whole body jars with the impact. Ow.

I wince, then blink at the feel of smooth hardwood floor against my cheek and torso. What the hell?

Slowly, my senses take in my whereabouts. Cool airconditioned air without any dust. A faint scent of pine my housekeepers used to clean the mansion. *Damn it*. I push myself up. Sheets are tangled on the mattress, like a coil of twisting snakes.

I huff, then flop back on the bed. I slept like crap, which is unusual. I make it a rule to sleep well because to be healthy and happy a man needs three things—sleep, food and sex—and I strive to ensure I'm at least generally healthy if not always happy.

Perhaps I'm not sleeping well because I haven't had sex in a while. Not since that last time with Bobbi. Which might explain my strong reaction to Lorcan now that I think about it. And my strong desire to modify and enhance her vision board because she doesn't need some random dweeb she found in a magazine when she can have me.

She's even more beautiful than I remembered. The height and the strong frame and lean muscle. The long golden hair that cascades down her shoulders and back. The confident tilt of her head, those slightly slanted, dark caramel eyes and those lips I could kiss for an eternity. Her breasts aren't huge, but I don't need anything larger than my palm. What's important is sensitivity, and in that respect Bobbi's are the gold standard. I've made her come just by sucking on her tits.

And she had no idea the kind of filthy thoughts that went through my head when she burst through the bedroom door. I wanted to gobble her up the way I did her apple pie. I might've tried to kiss her if I was one hundred percent certain she wouldn't shoot me with that nice Glock of hers. Bobbi has a temper—gloriously fiery. And I love her even more for it.

Last night, though... The disappointment was crushing because I was waiting for her call. I was sure she wouldn't be able to put me out of her mind like she did a year ago. I expected her to ream me out. Call me names for stealing her food, altering her vision board or crashing her ridiculous date with Joey. If I wasn't worth a call, I figured she'd at least text. I'm open to any name—asshole, dickhead, thief, jerkface.

But no. I haven't even merited a text. *What a letdown.*

Still, she was beautiful in that skirt, which Joey The Sycophant doesn't deserve to see her in. I wondered who the date was when I saw her note under the vision board—and didn't plan to let her see some loser, but it was worse than anything I could've imagined. Why is she scraping the bottom of the barrel? She could do so much better than the Lorcan Duncans and Joeys of the world.

Like *me*. I'm back. I'm available and more than willing.

I stare at the ceiling, wishing I didn't have to get up. But the catering people are coming soon to set up Saturday brunch with my brothers. I volunteered to host since Griffin wasn't in any condition. His triplets have been keeping him and his wife up round the clock for six days in a row. They might grow up to be the best interrogators this nation has ever seen. Enough sleep-deprivation and people will say and do anything you want them to.

At least it's just us seven guys, so the food can be kept simple—lots of eggs, ham, sausages and bacon and a mountain of bread and pastries. The wives don't join in—they call our monthly brunches and dinners "the boys' time." Instead, they get together and do their own thing, mostly spas or tennis or reading while gobbling up chocolate fondue.

Look at the bright side, I tell myself as I drag my ass out of bed. A bag of Bobbi's croissants is waiting in the kitchen. She was always a fabulous baker, and she's even better now. I was never that picky about bread or desserts until I met her.

Starchy carbs aren't the only things I've become selective about after Bobbi. My life is divided into pre-Bobbi and post-Bobbi. And I've become *very* particular about women. Nobody else measures up. They aren't as beautiful, or capable or sexy. Not that I'd say that out loud any time soon because I don't want my married brothers to give me shit. Love has blinded each one of them into thinking their particular wife is the best.

After a quick shower, I change into a blue T-shirt and black shorts and make my way downstairs. The catering people text that they're at the gates, and I let them in as I head to the kitchen.

The Bobbi's Sweet Things bag is sitting on the counter just as I left it. The logo is pastel blue and purple, just as lovely as the woman herself. Anticipation curling in my belly, I take a pastry out and note the buttercream. Hmm. Does she sell buttercream-filled croissants? I don't remember seeing any in the store. But who cares? Maybe she stuffed them specifically for herself. Crème de la Bobbi, mmm-hmm. If they taste fantastic—I'm sure they will—I'll ask the catering team to add buttercream croissants to the menu.

I start to bite into it as the catering team comes in and starts setting up. A thought pops into my head. *Bobbi could've lost her phone in the last twelve months—and thus my number.* So even if she wanted to call or text and call me an asshole, she couldn't.

I have her number memorized, of course, but she probably doesn't have mine. After all, not everyone has a photographic memory. I partied all night and got straight As in school. My brothers wanted to know what magical ass-kissing I did but I've always hidden that particular talent.

I chew on the croissant. *Delicious.* All that perfect flaky goodness. The buttercream is light and sweet, but not overly so. The texture is great. No wonder Bobbi's bakery has become such a success—

Wait. What was that?

I run my tongue over my teeth to get the weird thing out. But it isn't enough. I spit into the sink, but that doesn't work either.

Sonya, one of the catering people, looks over from setting up the brunch spread. "You okay?"

Shaking my head, I grab a glass of water and rinse my mouth. Little bits of hair remain in the sink. *What the fuck?*

Sonya walks up, stares at the hair, then at me. Her eyes are wide with alarm, probably wondering if the hair came from the food her team has brought.

"It's not you," I say before grabbing another croissant. Again, buttercream filled. But is it untampered with?

This time, I scoop up a generous glob using a finger and rub it with my thumb. Sure enough, there's hair hidden in the cream.

No need to check the other two. Bobbi wouldn't have done this if she'd planned to have them herself. And she didn't know Lorcan would show up to be her fake fiancé. So that means she did this afterward, specifically for me.

I start to laugh, ignoring the rich-people-are-so-weird look on Sonya's face, then go check the security feed from last night on my phone. Bobbi stopped by at 11:54. She is scorching hot as she glares at the security pad out by the gates and punches in a number. Given that there was no alert, she remembered the date.

And again, she input the right combination for the door. Did she also recall what I told her when I gave her the code? Did that remind her of what she means to me?

I watch her mix something in a bowl, then sabotage the croissants. Jesus, she's sexy as hell. And the intense look on her beautiful face? I want to blow it up, print it out and frame it so I can hang it in my bedroom.

Maybe I should do it and text Bobbi a snapshot. Sure, it's immature, but I need some validation—no matter how inconsequential—that I matter enough for her to react. It's possible I never grew out of the tug-the-girl's-hair-for-attention phase of boyhood, although I never felt the urge until I met Bobbi.

I laugh again as she flips the ceiling off. *Yes!* It might not be love, but I don't care! As long as she isn't indifferent to me. Disgust, dislike, even hate... I can work with that.

But first. Her excellent effort shouldn't go unrecognized.

—Me: You didn't have to be so cruel, my love. Wasting perfectly good croissants... Think of the starving children somewhere in the world.

I pour a cup of coffee from one of the pots Sonya's team has laid out and count. Three... Two... One...

—TLOML: Señor Mittens sends his regurgitated regards.

That must be the cat. He disapproved of me, but absolutely hated Lorcan. What a good, sensible little kitty.

—Me: I love you too, light of my life.

—TLOML: I hope you choke on a gaggle of dicks. Heavy on the gag.

—Me: Not my thing, but I could do an MMF if you really want. Just as long as nobody gets to touch you but me.

Three dots appear then disappear. Although I wait a good minute, nothing happens. Probably too overcome to respond.

My phone vibrates with a new text. I raise my hand eagerly, then glare at a photo my dad sent.

—Dad: What do you think? Erika is five-eight. D cup. Nice ass. Holds a brilliant conversation.

The photo is a woman, naked from the waist up. She has hair so bleached it looks like straw and plastic tits with nipples the size of dinner plates. Her face is spray-tanned to the point of looking more tangerine than human.

The only correct thing is likely her name and her cup size. But that's only because I know it's Joey doing the menial job of texting me. And unlike my dad, who still can't remember his daughters-in-laws' names, Joey keeps track of such details.

Besides, is he blind enough to think I'm going to downgrade to Erika after Bobbi?

—Me: My walls can probably hold a better conversation.

—Dad: But can they give you a baby? Josh Singer just got another grandchild. She sings like an angel.

—Me: Newborns don't sing like angels. They scream and cry like demons burning in eternal hellfire, day in and day out.

Except for my nephews and nieces, but then they're the most precious, precocious babies. And since my brothers are smart, they keep our father and Joey away from their offspring. Nothing good comes from being around those two.

—Dad: His does. And I want you to create a child who can outdo her!

By that, he means outdo Josh Singer. Dad has some kind of weird psychotic rivalry with the man. Who the hell knows why. Not even Joey can explain it. I'd bet my left nut that Josh Singer doesn't know, either. And I'm not having a baby just to hand it over to my dad so he can parade it around as a prop to boost his already overinflated ego. Children deserve to be loved, not used.

—Me: If I ever have a baby, it'll outshine everyone just by existing. Now go away, Joey, before I decide to get myself snipped.

I open one of the eight social media apps on my phone. Everyone thinks I'm addicted to these brain-rotting sites, but actually they're search engines and intel for government assets. I scroll the feed—a lot of general gossip about celebs and stuff—so that if anybody happens to see my screen they won't notice anything unusual. Then I stop at a post of an apartment building. In front is a tree heavy with red pomegranates.

I can't believe moving means saving 50% on rent! But then my landlord is a jerk.

It's one of the profiles we use for communication, and I asked Keelan to keep an eye on Bobbi and my brothers. A picture with red fruit means it's about Bobbi. I skim the comments.

So much greed, man!

This is why everything costs so much! Price gouging! I had to pay almost $10 for a loaf of specialty bread today. I used to pay only like $5!

I go to the search section on the app and look up the landlord for Bobbi's bakery. Floyd Baggett. I hit the profile, then tap on the gear icon at the top and enter my passcode.

The screen fills with details about him. God must've been in a hurry when He created Floyd. The man's been mediocre—or worse—all his life. Hasn't been able to hold a job or a relationship for more than a few months.

He inherited the building Bobbi's bakery is in when his mother passed away six months ago. Floyd quit his job in Denver the same day, ostensibly to deal with his grief and work on mental health and self-care. Apparently, such care involved strippers and hookers.

His financial situation was shit, but the money left by his mother took care of his debt. But now he's buried in IOUs again. He even owes money to Uncle Sam and the state of California. He's got some balls to take on both the federal and state governments. They won't break your knees to get paid, but they do have a lot of excruciating methods to extract money out of you. Since a nine-to-five would interfere with his degenerate lifestyle, he's trying to jack up the rent on Bobbi's Sweet Things.

Which won't do. Bobbi isn't laboring away to fund this disgusting man's existence. I tap the corner of my phone. How should I deal with him? Arrange for a seemingly innocent incident that puts him out of commission for a while, since his property manager seems saner? Bury him in so much debt he has no choice but to sell the building?

As I ponder my options, my brothers start to arrive. We're all busy, but we make sure to keep in touch and have regular brunches and dinners. It's just the seven of us against the world. Unfortunately, our dad is an oblivious, self-centered piece of shit who didn't really want to have kids. But he sure got stuck with some when the seven of us were born within four months of each other after his vasectomy failed. And our mothers... Well, they have their lists of priorities. And we aren't always on them.

People in L.A. view our parentage with envy. After all, our father, the vaunted Ted Lasker, is one of the most successful movie producers of all time—having had nothing but mega-hits during his prolific career. And our mothers are generally successful in their fields as well. Any one of us could be a star any time we wanted, with throngs of women screaming our names and paparazzi taking pictures of our every private moment. What a glorious life!

Ugh.

"Good morning," Emmett says with a wide grin. He's happy because a new business he funded made more money than he expected. GrantEm has been raking money in like crazy. The firm has made all of us ridiculously wealthy as well. A lot of people incorrectly assume we got our fortunes from our father. To be fair, his idea of parenting *is* throwing money at his children, but he doesn't throw billions.

Griffin just grunts. There are dark circles on his face larger than Texas, but he's still a handsome bastard, inheriting his chiseled features from his fashion model mom. He can be grouchy as hell and people still love him. Well, except for his econometrics students because he hands out Cs and Ds like candy on Halloween. They're probably deserved, too —Griffin is anything but unfair.

Currently his T-shirt has a mysterious yellow stain that didn't come out in the wash. His attention to fashion has degraded significantly since his wife had triplets.

Grant, Nicholas, Huxley and Sebastian walk through the door. The latter looks like there's a chunk of lemon in his mouth.

"What's the problem?" I say as we start to grab food and coffee.

"Preston being a dick?" Grant asks.

"Yes. My piece-of-shit half-brother got arrested for dealing drugs."

"Well, you wanted him to work—" Emmett begins.

"Stop sounding like my mother," Sebastian says.

"—and that was probably the only thing he could find." Preston is the type of guy who's dumb enough to stick his finger into a pile of dogshit to see if it's chocolate.

We go to the table and sit down. I grab two extra croissants because I need some carbs if I'm going to stay alert and fuel my brain.

"Will Jeremiah take the case?" I stuff my mouth with half a hair-free croissant. Jeremiah is Huxley's mom. A scary Harvard-trained lawyer who believes the only acceptable outcome isn't just victory, but complete evisceration of the other party. She can make anything go away—if you can afford her and *if* she feels like taking you on.

Sebastian shakes his head. "She refused."

Huxley raises his hands, palms out. "I'm not getting involved. She said she'd only do it if I joined the firm."

He'd rather jump into a pit of fire carrying a case of Chinese fireworks than become a lawyer. He went to Harvard Law for the sole purpose of showing his family that he wasn't cut out to be an attorney, except he graduated summa cum laude. That just made his family want him more. The obvious solution would have been to flunk out, but his ego is too big to feign stupidity, even if it's for a good cause.

Eye on the prize, man. Eye on the prize, I think. But what I say is, "Ah, she shouldn't have to waste her time defending that dumbass." I'm brimming with good humor because that's the mask I wear and that's what I want my brothers to see. It's safer for them. "I would've dealt better drugs and also not gotten caught."

"Not something to be proud of." Griffin sounds like a teacher imparting the wisdom of life: *Just say no.*

"I'm proud of *all* my abilities." I wink, then chomp down on a piece of bacon and try to resist telling Huxley about a possible betrayal brewing in his family. His grandmother has been meeting with Andreas Webber, one of the name partners at Huxley & Webber. I'm certain they're plotting against him behind his back since they have no reason to meet and they aren't having a clandestine affair. They show photos of their grandchildren to each other every time they meet, and nobody coos over pictures of grown-ass adult grandkids or tries to pair them up like they're playing some kind of fantasy wedding match up. But what am I going to say if anybody asks how I know? Huxley's grandmother doesn't do social media, and Andreas only posts about golf. I'm not admitting that I keep an eye on my brothers to make sure nothing dangerous is headed toward them. They might take it the wrong way.

Suddenly, Grant says, "Hey, you bought stuff from Bobbi's Sweet Things and aren't sharing?" He gestures at the mountain of carbs, then at the bag from Bobbi's bakery I left out. "This doesn't taste like her stuff."

"There's nothing to share." I'm happy she made the effort to come over, but it would've been better if she hadn't ruined the croissants with cat hair. She could've just spat on them instead, so I could've eaten them in innocent ignorance. If she tried to taunt me later, it wouldn't have mattered. We've already exchanged saliva—many times—during other activities. "I saw the bag and took it."

Sebastian looks at me like I left my brain back in Africa. "You *stole bread*? What's wrong with you?"

"It's like something out of *Les Mis*," Emmett says.

"Jean Valjean." Griffin sounds typically professorial, although he teaches econometrics, not French literature.

Hux shakes his head. "You're on your own, man. Mom doesn't defend petty criminals. It's beneath her."

"I also broke into Bobbi's house," I say. "Does that elevate my criminal status?"

Huxley laughs. He thinks I'm joking. But then all my brothers do.

"You probably shouldn't say things like that because you're making us witnesses to your confession. If her house was burglarized for real, you'd be a prime suspect even if you hadn't done anything," Nicholas says. He's always so calm and sensible.

"Oh ye of little faith. If I broke in, nobody would notice." None of my brothers take me seriously. I've done my job well over the years.

"Are you even allowed inside her bakery?" Emmett asks.

I give him a smug smile. "Of course I'm allowed in."

"And you stole from her. Way to go." Griffin shakes his head.

"Hey, she wouldn't sell any to me," I grumble.

"Should've taken some money," Grant says with a laugh. "At least a credit card."

"Join the modern world, bro. Nobody takes credit cards when they have a phone." I shrug. "Anyway, she wouldn't sell me anything. Told me she was out of croissants when there were four sitting right in front of me. *Taunting* me. Who does that?"

"Somebody who doesn't want you as a customer. What have you done to her?"

Grant's assumption that I'm the bad guy is mean, but not entirely unfair. Still, I put on my best I-didn't-do-nuthin' expression. "Not a thing. I'm completely innocent."

"That's why you will never get croissants from her bakery. When a woman's mad at you, you just say, 'I'm sorry. I won't do it again.'" Sebastian's tone is half-smug and half-chiding. Dickhead. He turns to Grant. "By the way, did you make up with Aspen?"

I swivel around. "Uh-oh. What's going on?"

"Grant's in the doghouse," Nicholas says.

"He's being a bad boy," Huxley agrees. "Tell us what you did wrong."

Grant shakes his head. "Wrong? Nothing."

Seb points to him and mouths, *See? Wrong thing to say*, to me.

"I'm sure Grant is innocent as well," I say.

Seb throws his hands up in the air, rolling his eyes.

"Depends on your viewpoint. Aspen wants to invest in a bar that her friend is starting, and Grant here is a little annoyed." Emmett's eyes twinkle with evil brother humor.

"Not just a *friend*. *Zack*, who's been panting after her like a fucking dog since college!" Grant's outrage reminds me a little of Bobbi's cat.

"But you're going to smooth things out," Griffin says gravely.

"Obviously. My problem is with the asshole, not Aspen."

"How?" I ask. My brothers have healthy relationships with their wives. I want to know what they do when they anger their women for real.

"I'll simply explain to her why I'm upset. Calmly, of course," Grant says.

"Better bring flowers," Emmett says.

"And jewelry. Jewelry always works," Sebastian says. I wonder how many pieces he's given his wife so far?

"So you just tell her why you're upset...and then she's cool?" I ask.

Huxley tilts his head, his eyes narrowed. "Why are you so curious? Did you piss a girl off? Perhaps a certain baker in the greater Los Angeles area...?"

"Me? Are you kidding? Ladies can't resist my charms."

"Right. Which is why you're forced to steal from a poor, hard-working baker lady." Sebastian snickers.

I point my fork. "Shut your pie hole."

The snicker turns into a full-blown laugh. "At least *this* hole gets to eat pies from Bobbi's Sweet Things."

10

BOBBI

MY MORNING STARTS LAZILY—BECAUSE I've decided to sleep in. Triumph deserves some celebratory sleep. The day would've gone even better if Noah hadn't texted me though. *Starving children my ass.*

Señor Mittens hops onto the bed and slowly pads his way to my chest. He gazes at my phone with distain. He hates it when I don't start the day by scratching behind his ears.

So I start doing exactly that with one hand and text with the other.

—Me: Señor Mittens sends his regurgitated regards.

—Noah: I love you too, light of my life.

Still throwing out "I love you"s like they're going to make a difference. If I didn't know him so well now, it might work. Even though he doesn't mean anything by "I love you," my heart picks up speed, which makes me irritated. Does he honestly expect me to swoon? And *light of his life*? I'll fall for that when the sun starts revolving around the moon!

I send him a text telling him to choke on a bag of dicks.

He responds, saying he might be okay with a threesome if certain proprietary rules are in place.

I grind my teeth, trying not to throw the phone against the wall. My

74

emotions are a source of entertainment for him? I simply can*not* take a man like this seriously.

I start to type as much, then stop. *Why am I even trying?* He won't understand, and will just crack another lame joke. I'm not wasting my morning like this.

Okay. Phone, on the night stand. Me, out of bed and into the shower before TJ shows up with the power tools I asked to borrow. Unlike some men—who I am definitely *not* thinking about at the moment—TJ is both reliable and punctual...although he kind of sucks at remembering anniversaries and birthdays.

Just as I'm done drying my hair and have put on a black tank top and yoga tights, TJ walks in, carrying his precious toolbox. He's a human Rocky Mountain, huge and solid with arms and legs designed to deliver maximum damage. Enormous muscles all over his body strain against a gray T-shirt and shorts, and he can't even buy shoes off the rack because his feet are too large. He used to shave his head bald, but now he lets it grow like an eighth of an inch because his daycare teacher girlfriend wants to feel his hair. His eyes are two shades darker than mine, and when he shows up, kids get quiet because he has a definite I-eat-children-for-snacks look. Unfair—he's a softie inside and loves children, but his psychopath expression works well professionally. He's in charge of security for a billionaire, Anthony Blackwood, and his family and companies.

His existence kept the boys away from me all through high school. Nobody was brave enough to face him to ask me out. To be honest, most grown men aren't either, which left my dating life rather sad until Noah. I'm not giving him any credit, though. He's never met TJ. If he had, he might've fled.

Maybe I should introduce them.

"Thanks," I say as TJ sets his toolbox down by the couch in the living room.

"No prob." He looks around my kitchen. "You sure you don't need any help?"

I scoff with affection. "No need for arms bigger than my thighs. It's just some tile." I haven't had time to do anything about the foul kitchen floor until now, what with Bobbi's Sweet Things opening and all.

"I promised your mom I'd watch over you."

"I don't think she meant for you to do my kitchen." An odd conflicted feeling rises up. My mom acted like she couldn't bear the sight of me, then hugged me like I was the only bit of sanity in her chaotic world. I might've thought she was bipolar, but she never behaved that way toward anyone else.

Well, whatever. I decide her final wish for me is how she truly felt. "I'll let you know when I need your muscles. But thanks for the offer. And since you're being so nice, I'll serve up your favorite breakfast."

"You made an apple pie?" He perks up like a puppy about to be walked. He's addicted to my baking, and for an apple pie, he'll do pretty much anything.

"Yup." I pull out the half—that damn Noah ate the other half yesterday—and cut it into two pieces. I put the bigger one on a Disney Frozen plate with Elsa and microwave it because he likes his pie hot. Once it's reheated, I put a huge scoop of vanilla ice cream and set it on the dining table. I have my own piece cold on an Olaf plate.

He takes a seat, then lets out a sigh of appreciation as the smell hits him. "You're the best cousin a man could have."

"Don't I know it." I laugh as he digs in. "Want something to drink?" I say when his lips form an O and he fans himself. He always burns the roof of his mouth, but never seems to learn.

He nods.

I pour him the last of the OJ, then reach for a bottle of vodka and fill my glass half-way. I top it with cranberry juice and sit down with my portion of the pie.

TJ's thick brows jump three inches on his forehead. "A little early for that, don't you think?"

"It's a Christmas gift from Yuna, and it's like midnight where she's from."

He gives me a look. "She lives in Beverly Hills."

"But her Korean roots are strong." I take a big bite of the pie. So delicious. I *am* the best.

He frowns, all concerned now. "Did something happen? The bakery struggling? If so, don't stress about it. I can always get you a job."

By that, he probably means a position in Tony Blackwood's vast empire. But I don't want to manage security for his clubs. Or go back to guarding his wife, Ivy. Not because she was a difficult client, but bodyguarding just isn't my dream. I got disenchanted real fast.

"The bakery's going great," I say before TJ starts making calls. I don't bring up Floyd because TJ might do something. Like permanently rearrange his face, which wouldn't accomplish anything. Besides, since my dad's death, TJ's overprotectiveness has gone into overdrive. He means well, but I'm an adult. He doesn't need to treat me like some uncoordinated toddler left by a pool.

"Then why are you drinking before noon?" His tone says *you ain't foolin' nobody, especially me.*

"It's Noah." Don't want to say it, but if I don't fess up, TJ will drive me insane with questions.

"That shithead?" My cousin's eyebrows pull together. He's never met Noah, but knows how he's ghosted me over and over again. TJ's meaty hand gets tighter around his fork. "Did he at least apologize for hurting you?"

"Ha. No. He would never. He has no clue that he did anything wrong."

"Then keep him out of your life. Simple." To TJ, everything is black and white. Gray is a weasel category for doing things you know you shouldn't but refusing to admit it. I wish my mind was that uncomplicated.

"Not so easy. He's back in town." I take a big swallow of my cocktail.

My cousin looks confused. "Doesn't he live in Malibu? So he's always been in SoCal?"

"Yes. But he was *here*. In this kitchen." I point my fork at his plate. "The reason you're only getting a quarter of a pie is because he ate half."

TJ's face slowly turns red. He probably feels personally violated. "What the fuck? Why did you let him in and feed him pie?"

I bristle at the unfair accusation and at the humiliating realization that maybe I look that clingy and desperate when it comes to Noah. "He broke into my home!"

"And you didn't kill him?" His gaze slides to the drawer where I keep the Glock.

"I might've, if I'd thought I could get away with it. But he isn't worth going to jail for." Plus his very rich, very famous movie producer daddy wants him to make babies. Offing him before that happens would bring a lot of heat.

TJ seems somewhat mollified. "So why was he here? I mean, your apple pie is great and all, but..."

I sigh, then tell TJ what happened, including the incident involving Lorcan.

He starts to turn red again. "Son of a bitch! I told you meeting the men you found on those apps was a terrible idea!"

"TJ, everybody does it. It's really hard to meet a good guy these days."

"Because you keep using those apps."

"It's not the apps, it's Lorcan. What kind of weirdo thinks there's something between us after exactly one disastrous date?"

"The kind who uses apps!" TJ says, absolutely refusing to give in on this point. "Let me set you up. I know just the guy—he'll treat you like a princess and make you happy. Why should you go through more disappointment and heartbreak? You deserve better."

"No, thank you." My cousin means well. But he's going to pick the kind of guy who'll ask for permission before holding my hand. Consent is important, but I honestly don't want a guy who's too scared of TJ to overwhelm me with hot sex. I didn't put a picture of a couple having passionate sex on the vision board, but that doesn't mean it isn't part of the deal with the loving husband I'm yearning for.

"Fine. If you're going to insist on allowing crazy losers into your life and not use your Glock on them, you should at least upgrade your security. Also, get yourself a mean-ass dog. No offense to Señor Mittens, but he's no attack kitty."

My cat scornfully swishes his tail. It almost looks like he's sneering.

"He coughed up a hair ball to avenge me," I say, defending poor Señor Mittens. TJ is a hardcore dog person, and he can't fathom why I don't get a "real pet."

"Oooh..." TJ gives me a mock shudder. "Yeah, I hear that home invaders are terrified of hairballs."

"Don't be dense. I put it into some buttercream." I lay out what I did to the croissants Noah stole.

TJ looks at me like I've broken out of an asylum. "Wait, so you broke into *his* house?"

"Of course. He did it first."

"Yeah, but don't you think he's going to think it's an invitation to escalate?"

"What? No."

"Cuz, the best way to deal with a guy like that is to ignore him completely."

"Uh-uh. That's silently endorsing what he's doing."

"Don't believe me? Talk to Josie."

"Josie? Why?" TJ's sister is his exact opposite—petite and delicate with an inviting, friendly face. It works well for her career as a psychiatrist. People tend to pour out their entire life story, which she absolutely loves, and is great for her. But if I had her job, I'd be jailed for murder.

"Because she's going to side with me and say you still have feelings for this motherfucker."

The remark hits too close to home. It's all I can do not to grind my teeth. "I don't need my head examined. I'm fine!"

"Sure, you're fine. *And* dandy. That's why you have guys like Lorcan and Noah around," he says. "I always thought your dad was crazy, but he wasn't totally wrong when he said nothing keeps unwanted people out better than landmines."

"Oh my God." I close my eyes briefly. *Landmines.*

"I'm just saying you're putting me in a bind. How am I supposed to keep my promise to your mom that I'd take care of you if you keep finding crazies who stalk you and break into your house?"

"TJ..." I debate how much to say, but eventually just settle for, "I can take care of myself."

"Physically, maybe. But you're letting that asshole weasel his way back into your life. And he's gonna screw with you and break your heart all over again. Why should I have to sit around and watch it unfold?" His concern is touching, but there's something else there, too. Something evil glinting in his eyes.

"TJ, if you're plotting something—something I'm not going to like —that'll be the last apple pie you'll ever get from me."

"Jesus, all I'm trying to do is be nice to you. No need to get all cruel about it." He looks as betrayed as Caesar when he realized it was Brutus who stabbed him.

I lock eyes with him and start to reach for his plate.

He leans forward and physically covers the pie with his torso. "Okay, *fine!* Have it your way. But if that shithead isn't gone by the end of the month, I'm getting you a Doberman!"

11

BOBBI

AFTER TJ's GONE, I stow the tools and head to Ivy and Tony's mansion. Thankfully my cousin's off today, so I won't run into him and have to suffer another *you're dating wrong* lecture. Ivy and her best friend Yuna became my good friends, and their daughters Katherine and Lilian treat me as an honorary auntie. The two have been begging me to show them how to bake cookies. Apparently, nobody else will do. "You have the best bakery in the world! Oh please, oh please, oh please!"

When the two little angels put their hands together and looked up at me with all the earnestness in the world, I promised to stop by today. They're just too adorable, and I love children.

The mansion Tony built for his wife is in a quiet area with tight security. It's enormous, but—unusually for Los Angeles—doesn't have a pool. The reason being that Ivy almost drowned twice. Although she can swim now, the experiences are still too triggering for him. There is, however, a very shallow water garden covered with lotus blossoms.

I park my Tacoma, which looks out of place among sleek European cars that cost more than most houses, then head to the door. The housekeeper, Felice, lets me in.

Once I'm inside the foyer with a cathedral ceiling and brilliant crystal chandeliers, I can hear the faint sound of the pianos. Ivy has two

—a white Steinway baby grand and a Bösendorfer Imperial concert grand that Tony specially commissioned for their first wedding anniversary. It was handcrafted in Austria with a tiger lily—her favorite flower—and entwined T&I embossed on the side.

"Yuna and Lilian are here," Felice says as she gestures me toward the music room.

"Thanks." I flash her a quick smile and head down the familiar corridor. One side is made entirely of windows that face the garden, and I look at the stunning flowers and lawns that seem to spread out endlessly. Tony spares no expense to please his wife, and a pang pierces my heart.

I'm not envious of Ivy's wealth, but I would die for the kind of connection she has with her husband. And their beautiful children. Tony fell in love with her at first sight, and he's been crazy about her ever since. For him to make a promise to his wife and break it would be unthinkable. Nothing short of death could keep him away from her.

I, on the other hand, sort of have...Noah. Who puts no weight on his promises to me. Or his professions of love. Then there's Lorcan...who is obviously unhinged because just what kind of weirdo breaks into the house of a woman he only met once through a dating app? And Joey, who only met with me so I'd sleep with his boss's son and have a baby. What a creep.

When I walk into the room, a tiny strawberry blonde and an even smaller dark-eyed brunette squeal. "Bobbi!"

Their gazes are bright as they rush me in their pink tutus. Tiny tiaras sit on their heads, and they wrap their arms around my legs, hugging me. I crouch down and embrace them, one in each arm. They smell like baby powder and innocence.

"Hey, girls!"

"Hi!" Ivy stands up from behind the Bösendorfer, her gray eyes warm. She's pulled her reddish golden hair into a top knot, which exposes the delicate line of her neck and the smooth slope of her shoulders. She looks casual and at home in a loose gray V-neck shirt and cropped teal pants.

Next to her, Yuna waggles her long fingers. Unlike Ivy, her auburn hair is unbound, and she's in a stunning crimson dress that matches her take-charge personality. I've never seen Yuna in anything but beautiful clothes and the most fashionable shoes. Today's no exception.

"Bobbi, how do I look?" Katherine spins, her hair flying everywhere.

"Look what I can do!" Lilian leaps around, her arms up in the air.

"Amazing, both of you." I make sure to keep my tone and expression serious and admiring, even though I'm dying with laughter at their antics. Over by the pianos, Ivy and Yuna smile and shake their heads.

"I'm going to be a Sugar Plum Fairy!" Lilian declares.

"Me too!"

"I thought you wanted to be Cookie Fairies?" I say.

"We can be both!" Katherine says.

"Our grandmama said so!" Lilian adds.

I laugh. Yuna's mother, a formidable woman, took it upon herself to sort of adopt Ivy as her own child and considers Ivy's twins her own grandkids. Which was nice because Ivy's mother passed away a long time ago and Tony's mother is a sociopath. If Margo Blackwood ever came near the girls, I'd have to drag her away by the hair—she's just that insane and dangerous.

"Girls, ready to bake some cookies?" Ivy says.

"Yes!" They dash out of the music room, squealing.

"Thank you for coming over. They're exceptionally energetic today." Yuna sticks her tongue out with her eyes rolled heavenward, then laughs.

"You know they're going to get high on sugar, right? I can't imagine them not gorging on the cookies after we're done baking."

"Oh, I know. But by then, Declan and Tony should be here." Yuna gives me a wink.

"Are the boys out with their fathers?" I say.

"Yes. Thank God." Ivy sounds sincere. "While the girls want to be Sugar Plum Fairies, the boys want to be Jedis."

Yuna rubs her forehead. "It didn't help that Mom had her assistant buy them light sabers. She doesn't know what it's like because she's in Korea most of the time."

"They broke Yuna's favorite tea set," Ivy whispers to me.

"Oh." Although Yuna loves her coffee, she occasionally likes to sit down and enjoy tea with a slice of cake. And she takes out one of her numerous fancy tea sets, even if she's drinking alone.

"They don't make them anymore." Yuna's shoulders sag. "I checked everywhere."

If she can't get it, then it really isn't available. There's nothing her fabulously wealthy conglomerate father wouldn't get for her.

The girls are already in the kitchen. Felice must've laid out everything we need when I arrived because the counter is littered with baking sheets, a bag of flour and so on.

I show the girls how to mix everything together—and teach them the most important lesson: follow directions and don't improvise until you have the basics down. Knowing Katherine and Lilian, they'd dump two bags of sugar into the bowl because, hey, we're making sugar cookies.

We get the gobs of dough onto the sheets and turn on the oven. When it's been preheated I carefully help each girl load her sheet into the oven and soon the kitchen starts to smell like cookies—all warm and sweet. When the timer dings, I pull out the sheets and let the cookies cool while the girls vibrate with anticipation, their eyes glued to the freshly baked goodies.

"You're a goddess," Yuna says, propping an elbow on the marble counter and resting her chin in her hand.

"It's just cookies." I start making the royal icing myself. I was planning to teach the girls, but they're too distracted. They'll be more than happy to help decorate the cookies later.

"Yeah, but I can't do them. Mom tried to send me to a cooking class, but I totally said no."

"Why? I thought you always wanted to cook better." Ivy reaches into the wine cooler and pulls out a bottle of Riesling. "Want some?"

I nod, and Yuna makes a gimme gesture. Laughing, Ivy pours three glasses. One of Yuna's nannies pours milk for the girls in clear plastic cups because of course they're going to want something now that we're drinking.

We toast. "To friendship," I say.

"And surviving another weekend," Yuna says, making big eyes at the girls.

We clink glasses. Lilian and Katherine bump cups and laugh. I take a sip of the wine—crisp without being too dry. Tony doesn't keep bad wine.

"Anyway, tell me why you didn't take the cooking class," I say. Yuna always has a good reason for what she does, but I can't think of anything in this case.

"Oh, she was trying to pad my bridal résumé." Yuna rolls her eyes. It's no secret her parents were trying to set her up with a man of their choosing. She ran rather than submit to their selection, which is how she ended up marrying a former underwear model.

"Don't you regret it now, though?" Ivy teases. "I mean, poor Declan. Deprived of awesome Korean food."

"Nope. Mom sent someone."

"Another of her 'spies'?" I ask.

"No, the chef from my parents' house. That's how I know they love me." Yuna grins. "But enough about my past as a marriageable item. How's your lease thing going? Did you finally get to renew it at a fair price?"

"Ugh. No." I take a swig of the wine. "Floyd came to the bakery on Friday to tell me he wants fifty percent more and..."

Ivy frowns. "And...what?"

"And I have to make him and his fiancée an engagement cake," I spit the words out. "He's going to marry Reggie."

Ivy's face turns bright red. "*What?*"

"Who the f..."—Yuna's eyes slide to the girls—"who does he think he is?" she asks in a low hiss. "Why should you make anything for that horrible human being?"

"My landlord and God's gift to women? I don't know. He's convinced the reason I'm refusing to bake them anything is because I'm jealous."

Ivy looks completely lost. "Jealous...?"

"Yeah. That he's marrying *Reggie*," I say.

"Eww. He's so gross!" Ivy scrunches her face.

Yuna makes a gagging sound. "He makes Jabba the Hut look like a catch!"

There's nothing like the support of good friends. "Then he accused me of creating some kind of health crisis. He's claiming he's gluten intolerant." I roll my eyes.

"He's such a piece of work." Yuna purses her lips. "And I can't believe he's threatening to raise your rent by so much."

"He thinks he can intimidate me, which is ridiculous." I cock my hips as I consider how short and pathetic he is. "But I do hate the idea of having to move to another location. I'm in the best place I could be right now."

"Then don't. I'll cover the increase," Yuna says.

The offer, given so quickly, is kind of stunning. But at the same time I should've expected her to want to help. Yuna can never sit by when one of her friends is in trouble. Still... "Thank you. But no, I can't let you do that."

She shrugs. "It really isn't that much money."

"Yuna's right." Ivy pats my forearm gently. "You shouldn't have to move just because your landlord is a creep."

"Yeah, but it's the principle of the thing. I don't want him profiting unjustly." I'd rather give the money to TJ to fortify my home as he sees fit.

"But you shouldn't have to move *unjustly*, either." Ivy's tone is soothing—and slightly coaxing. "Don't cut off your nose to spite your face."

Yuna drums on the countertop. "Wish I could find a way to force him to sell the building to me. Then you could have a lifetime of free rent and I could have a lifetime of free cake. Seems like a fair trade."

I laugh. It's so great to have people on my side. I never had close friends as a child because we had to move constantly for Dad's jobs.

"Actually, Tony tried. But Floyd won't sell. He doesn't have anything else left."

Yuna shakes her fist. "I want to kick him where it hurts. Then he *really* won't have anything left!"

"Target's too small, so the chances of you missing are high," I say. "I'd hate for you to kick into thin air and pull something."

"What's too small? We can have TJ take care of it if somebody's bothering you," Tony says as he walks into the kitchen. He puts a hand on Ivy's shoulder and kisses her.

"Welcome home," Ivy says at the same time Katherine runs over, her arms stretched upward. "Daddy!"

Laughing, he picks her up as though she weighs nothing. Lilian dashes over as well, and he swings her up, making her giggle.

You wouldn't think a billionaire could be unhappy. But when I first met Tony, that's what he was: the most miserable looking rich guy on the planet. But now his eyes are full of laughter, shining with adoration for his wife and children. And Yuna's kids too, who he treats as his own niece and nephew. He doesn't care that the kids are touching his four-figure shirt and pants with sticky fingers. Or that Katherine just grabbed his hair.

Wistfulness swells. If I'd touched my dad's tie with sticky hands, he would've pulled away with a disapproving frown. He hated any possibility of not looking his best. Although I'm an adult now, there's a little girl inside who wishes I'd had a better father, one who put *me* first, not his hair or clothes.

"Where are Declan and the boys?" Yuna asks.

"Getting ice cream," Tony says, his eyes stretching comically upward as Katherine tugs on his hair.

"What about *us*?" Lilian whines.

"That's why I'm here! To take you out for ice cream," Tony says.

"Yay! Uncle Tony, you're the best!"

"Daddy, I love you!"

He smiles like he's just inherited the world. "Let's go get changed real fast first, okay? Have fun, ladies!" he calls out as he carries the girls away.

"Thanks, love!"

The vibrancy sizzling in the air vanishes, leaving nothing but peace and silence. "Wow," I say.

"Yeah. Whirlwind of energy. I love them, but I also enjoy my adult-only time." Yuna sips her wine.

But I already miss the boundless vigor of the children. I sigh with longing.

Ivy peers at me. "You okay?"

"Just sad at being alone," I blurt out, then bite my lip. I sound too envious, which isn't right. Ivy and Yuna fought for and earned their happy marriages. In my case... Well, I never got a chance, but it makes me feel small and petty to feel this sharp pang over the fact that they have loving families like I've always wanted.

"You are *not* alone," Yuna says. "You have us. And wasn't there something about a date yesterday?"

Ivy leans forward. "Wasn't that guy supposed to be the perfect hottie? The one who would make you forget all about that shitty ex of yours?"

"Yes. But I should've known he was too good to be true." I take a big swallow. "Talk about embellishment."

Yuna frowns. "Everyone embellishes a little. Even my parents spruced up my bridal résumé."

"I find that hard to believe. You're perfect," I say.

She scoffs. "They said I was 'biddable.'"

Ivy and I chortle at the idea. "So what did he lie about?" Ivy says, turning to me.

"Everything! His profile was, like, at *least* an eight. He was barely a two!"

Yuna cringes. "That awful?"

"He apparently had pro-level movie makeup applied and used professional lighting and stuff to make himself look about a billion times better. And I thought he was maybe a four when I first saw him. But the real problem was he kept opening his mouth. It cut that four in half. And get this: he didn't even want to date me! He was trying to find someone to sleep with one of his boss's sons and get pregnant. And to top it all off, the boss turned out to be Ted Lasker and the son turned out to be Noah!"

Ivy and Yuna's jaws drop in unison. It's almost comical.

"Why am I having such terrible luck? I didn't think it could get any worse after Lorcan Duncan."

Yuna's eyes widen as she covers her mouth. "Oh my God. *Lorcan Duncan?*"

I just swig more wine.

"I'm sorry. It was my fault." Ivy shakes her head ruefully as she turns to Yuna. "This happened while you were in Korea visiting your family last month. I told Bobbi to be open-minded when she wasn't sure about seeing him."

"Still. *Lorcan Duncan*? I mean, just the name..." Yuna cringes.

Ivy shrugs helplessly. "I thought it'd be unfair to judge him when it was probably his mother who had bad taste."

"Yeah, and Bobbi would've been stuck with a mother-in-law with shitty taste. Friends don't let friends marry into families with shitty taste." Yuna shudders.

I sigh. "I just feel *stuck*. And frustrated. Why is it so hard? All I want is a loving husband and family. I'm not asking for the Nobel Prize!"

"Maybe dating apps aren't the way to go." Ivy purses her lips. "Isn't Lorcan, like, the third guy you've tried?"

"Fourth," I mutter.

"I'm so sorry." Yuna pats my hand. "Nature abhors a vacuum. You need to manifest your dream husband so you quit attracting trash to fill the slot."

"Believe me, I'm game. But how?"

"A vision board full of hot men?" Ivy says.

"I have one of those already."

"Which is obviously defective," Yuna says firmly. "If it weren't, you would have had at least a couple of acceptable dates." Her eyes narrow in thought.

I watch her and wait. She always has either the most outrageous or the most amazing ideas. I'm praying for the latter.

"I know!" she says snapping her fingers. "You need a vision *object*."

"Uh... Okay. What is that?"

"Another way to manifest your desires. I've read about them. They're for people who live in tiny homes and have no space for vision boards. You have the space, but your vision board is worthless. So I say a vision object will work better. Since you want to get married, you should get something that symbolizes matrimony."

Ivy purses her lips. "Like a wedding dress?"

Yuna nods. "Or a ring."

"Isn't that kind of extreme?" I ask, wary.

"No, because you're trying to have a physical representation of your future." Yuna taps the rim of her glass. "The more I think about it, the more it makes sense. Let's say you see a ring so beautiful and perfect, it calls to you and makes you go, 'Oh my God, this is it.' Imagine how much that feeling of excitement will stay with you when you wear it on your finger as a constant reminder of the future you deserve."

I cock an eyebrow. "So all the single guys will assume I'm married."

"Annnd any guy who approaches you will probably be a cheating jerk. Or someone trying to break up your 'marriage.'" Ivy shrugs helplessly. "Kind of counter-productive."

Yuna blinks, seemingly nonplussed for once. "All right, fine. Get a super pretty chain and put the ring around your neck. Then you can look at it as often as needed, but most importantly, you'll constantly feel it against your bare skin. Every time it happens, you manifest the qualities you want in your perfect husband. And the universe will give you the man of your dreams and he'll propose to you with a ring just like your vision ring—or better."

"I don't know." Yuna's idea is pretty wild as manifesting goes. And insanely expensive. "A ring is way more than a simple vision board."

Yuna scoffs. "Don't settle because you're afraid you can't afford it. Remember, you are going to spend the rest of your life with this man. You deserve the best."

The words sink in, and I let my mind process. Maybe I wasn't getting the best men because I was afraid and uncertain after the pain of Noah's callous treatment. He's never apologized for not showing up for the bakery opening, and it's possible that subconsciously I haven't been able to bring myself to be brave and embrace all the possibilities like when I started Bobbi's Sweet Things.

"If I didn't have to go see Jin," Yuna says, referring to her brother, "I'd totally take you to Peery Diamonds right now." She reaches into her purse and pulls out a black AmEx. "Here. Take this and go get yourself the perfect husband. My treat."

12

NOAH

AFTER MY BROTHERS LEAVE, I shove another Danish into my mouth. It isn't as good as the ones Bobbi makes, but it'll do.

I chew contemplatively and look at Marilyn smiling at me from the wall. She's hot in the picture, but not as hot as Bobbi. I pull up the security feed again and watch her. The heated, resolute expression on Bobbi's face as she flips me the bird...

As I gaze at her, the world seems brighter and more colorful. My heart beats with more vigor. Guys have a name for this: *one-itis*. And probably a lot of them would say that sex with another woman would fix it, but they'd be wrong. If that's what was needed, it would've already happened. But the plain fact is, I'm not really interested in other women anymore, and Bobbi already feels like a necessary fixture in my life.

I don't want to experience that weird apathy again—the odd ennui that made me not care whether I lived or died on that plane. It wasn't until Bobbi flashed through my mind that there really seemed to be a reason to keep on living.

Since coming clean is out of the question, I'll need to use flowers and jewelry. Grant and Sebastian are correct about that. After all, their wives haven't left them yet.

Okay, decision made. I hop in the car and take a leisurely drive down to the Peery Diamonds flagship store in Los Angeles. Headed by my sister-in-law Lucie, it's full of exceptional items. But most importantly, whatever I do here won't end up in Sebastian's ear. If I purchase anything at Sebastian Jewelry, my brother will not only hear about it, he'll start a fraternal group-text just to give me shit.

My brothers can group-text to admire me later—after I smooth things out with Bobbi.

I cross Peery's pale champagne floor. Crown-shaped chandeliers glow over my head, and the speakers emit gently flowing notes from Debussy's Arabesque Number One. My eyes sweep across spotless glass cases, sparkling gemstones laid out on dark navy velvet like stars spilled across moonless night sky.

There are lots of nice pieces, but nothing really captures my attention. A crisply dressed clerk comes over. "Hello, my name is Albert. May I assist you, sir?"

"I need something for an exceptional woman." I tilt my chin at the displays. "I'm not seeing anything that really grabs me."

His smile grows broader as he slowly blinks. Guess every guy who comes here says, "I'm looking for something for an exceptional woman."

Now that I think about it, they probably all do. *When did I become such a cliché?* I think with disgust. I can do better.

"Perhaps some direction, sir, as to the character of the lady in question?"

"Right. Okay, she works with her hands a lot, so maybe a necklace. Not anything delicate." Bobbi's a woman of strength and resolute will. *And sassy*, I think with a grin at the memory of her on the security camera. "Fiery. Strong. But she's also a dreamer. And she doesn't just dream, she turns things into reality."

Albert nods with a smile as polished as the diamond in front of me. "Would you like to look at our catalogue, then?"

"Sure. Show me."

He leads me to a quiet room and brings out a glossy catalogue as an associate serves a glass of champagne. "Here you are, sir."

I flip through the pages casually while sipping the excellent Dom. Everything's pretty, but nothing screams, *I am what Bobbi deserves.*

Is Sebastian Jewelry really going to be my best option? I could wear a fake moustache...

Or maybe something custom made would be better. Masako Hayashi does great work, although she's probably booked until next year. But she owes Dad a favor, and I could probably cash that in. He'll say yes if there's a possibility of getting a grandbaby out of the deal...

And then, suddenly, *there it is.* Brilliant blood-red rubies, each stone surrounded by clear diamonds, the whole thing set in platinum. The red stone in the center is round like the burning sun, marquis-cut diamonds surrounding it. The necklace is big enough to make a bold, feminine statement, but not so big that it's vulgar. I can see it around Bobbi's neck, how it will glitter and enhance her already incredible beauty.

"This. This is the one."

"Ah. An exceptional choice." Albert looks at the picture. "It's currently in our store in Tokyo, but it can be overnighted for you."

"Do it." I hand him my black AmEx.

"Very good, sir." He gives me his most reassuring smile.

I sign off on the purchase agreement for the necklace and the credit card slip, then hear a familiar voice.

"Wow."

Bobbi?! My heart does a little samba, her voice music to my soul.

"It's so pretty."

She must be here to buy something sparkly to cheer herself up. What perfect timing. I can feel a grin start to spread over my face. I should go see whatever it is that she's looking at and spoil her.

"Just the piece for a romantic proposal," says a conspiratorial female voice.

A *what?* I get up, convinced the sales clerk must've misspoken. Through the doorway to the adjoining private room, I can see Bobbi standing over a display. The lighting in the store is designed to showcase the precious stones, but it's Bobbi who shines the brightest, her silken hair spilling over her shoulders and her beautiful eyes on some bauble in front of her. She isn't wearing any makeup, but her cheeks are rosy and her lips soft, so she doesn't need to. Her small smile widens, and the impact hits me like a wrecking ball.

My pulse flutters. Something warm and sweet and infinitely soft starts to fill my heart. Bobbi doesn't seem to notice me, her focus on the gleaming stone in front of her.

"Yup," she says to the salesperson, tucking a stand of hair behind an ear. "Super romantic."

13

BOBBI

As I DRIVE HOME from Ivy's place, my mind keeps going over what Yuna said. Although I wasn't sure about this whole manifest-via-the-perfect-engagement-ring idea at first, the more I think about it, the more sense it makes. I haven't had much success so far with the romantic aspect of my future, and I don't want to live without a vision. No way I'm waking up one day to realize I've been living a life I never wanted for myself.

Bobbi's Sweet Things became a reality when I visualized it, meditated on it constantly and then finally manifested it. Of course, there was a lot of hard work as well, but I was thinking about different recipes all the time, baking whenever I had the chance. I haven't put nearly as much effort into the family part of my dream, so of course I'm attracting all the wrong men.

So when Peery Diamonds comes into view, I park my Tacoma and go inside the glitzy jewelry retailers. Talk about manifestation—I never thought I'd have the chance to walk into this store, but suddenly here I am.

Every square inch of the store exudes affluence and luxury. Even the music is beautiful, some classical thing Yuna and Ivy would instantly recognize—and probably be able to play without any preparation.

A pretty brunette glides over to me. "Welcome to Peery Diamonds."

Her voice is professionally friendly. "My name is Jessica. Can I be of assistance today?" She peers up at me. Even in pumps, she's a lot shorter.

"Yeah. I'm looking for a ring."

"Any particular occasion?"

"It's for a proposal."

Her amber eyes glitter with good will. "Oh, how romantic! I'm so happy for you."

"Yeah." I will be, too, as soon as I manifest the right husband material and get married and have a family. "Thanks. Me, too."

"We have an incredible bridal selection." She leads me to a display. "These are some of our best pieces."

The rows of solitaire diamond rings under the glass take my breath away. I never thought diamonds were particularly pretty. Maybe that's why I haven't attracted a suitable husband candidate. I didn't appreciate this aspect of the whole engagement and marriage thing.

There is a gorgeous blue stone among the clear diamonds that catches my eye. It isn't traditional, but maybe sapphires are a thing? I mean, my ideal ring doesn't *have* to be a diamond. Tony proposed to Ivy with a stunning pearl ring.

Jessica notices. "That's our blue diamond. It's not overly large—"

"Wait, that's a *diamond?*"

"Yes, actually. It's not overly large at one carat, but it's exceptional in saturation and cut." She reaches inside with gloved hands, plucks it off the velvet and holds it out so I can see it more closely. "Look how it sparkles under the light. This is the best Asscher cut I've seen."

"It's *perfect*," I whisper, unable to look away. "Wow." Then, remembering my true purpose here, I close my eyes for a moment. Imagine a romantic scene with top-tier champagne bubbling in clear flutes edged with gold...something pretty and delicious on the table— maybe my favorite cherry pie, topped with a generous mound of whipped cream—and soft classical piano music floating in the air like fragments of a dream finally coming together. A man drops to one knee, holding out a beautiful blue diamond ring. Then he says, "Will you marry me?" in a sweet baritone voice, quavering slightly with love and devotion.

Giddiness rises like the champagne bubbles in my fantasy. I can't clearly see the man I'm going to marry, but I already know the qualities he has. Honest. Hard-working. Supportive. Puts me first. Ready to take a bullet for me—although that won't happen in real life because I don't want that kind of high drama. I left my bodyguarding career for a reason.

My mind still isn't revealing the man—it's just a fuzzy man-shaped haze where he should be. But the rest of my vision will take shape as I continue to work on my manifestation.

"It's so pretty," I say, opening my eyes.

Jessica nods in approval. "Just the piece for a romantic proposal."

I look down at it again, then at my finger. My smile widens. "Yup. Super romantic." I picture the life I could have with a loving husband, our wonderful children and Señor Mittens in a beautiful house—*our* house, not necessarily the one my dad left me—and building a fulfilling and loving—

Noah's voice shatters the reverie. "You're going to propose?"

What the fuck?! I whip my head around and there he stands, wearing a slightly stunned expression.

He looks unfairly handsome in a loose T-shirt and shorts, his hair tousled and stubble covering his square jaw. I used to love running my fingers over his chin, feeling the roughness there against my fingertips and marveling at how different we were, yet how compatible.

The incredulity on Noah's face is replaced by narrowed eyes and a furrowed brow, like he's upset. *Good.* Why should I be the only one suffering over his whim to butt back into my life?

"Since when did you start playing for the other team?" he asks, apparently taking my silence as a yes.

I mime checking a watch. "Since about, ah, half-past never. If you must know, I'm looking for a suitable ring for me and my future husband."

"Your future husband?" Noah repeats like he can't compute. "*Lorcan?*"

"Oh, God no." I shudder.

"Then who?"

"The specific *who* isn't the point right at the moment. I'm not waiting for somebody to give me my dream. I'm *manifesting* him."

He pauses, unblinking, for a full three beats. "You're manifesting a husband."

It's like I just told him I plan to hike barefoot to Mars. His reaction only makes me more annoyed, hurt and determined. "Yes. A good, *reliable* man. Someone I can *depend on*. Do you think I'm incapable of attracting a man like that?"

He looks like he just got punched in the solar plexus. "I—"

"Actually, don't answer. I don't need your bad mojo ruining this moment." I don't need a reply to know. His shitty treatment of me is response enough. I was somebody he fucked, nothing more. All I got out of our "relationship" were lies and disappointment.

"Bobbi, a husband is a serious matter. You—"

"Yes. Even more serious than a committed boyfriend-girlfriend relationship."

"You can't just go and propose to some random guy," Noah continues doggedly, sounding betrayed and...with a hint of worry? Maybe even anxiety?

I put on a smile as sweet as my buttercream. "Oh, it won't be to just any guy. But don't worry. That guy will never be you." I turn to Jessica. "Can we discuss payment options?"

Yuna offered to pay for the ring, but I can't let her. It's my dream, so I need to finance it.

Noah shoves a black AmEx at Jessica. "Here. My fiancée isn't going to pay for her own ring."

I freeze, unable to process what I just heard. There's no way he just called me his fiancée.

Then bitterness starts to swell in my heart. If he'd said this maybe even a year ago, I might've been ecstatic. But now? Now there's only pain and resentment. He must consider me a complete idiot to think I'll keep playing this game with him. Especially when the only prizes are my torment and a broken heart.

Jessica glances at me, her eyes uncertain, then back at Noah and starts to reach for the credit card.

I snatch it out of Noah's hand and slap it against his chest, putting some real force into it. "Who the *hell* are you calling your fiancée?"

He takes a staggering step back. "You."

"Since when? I haven't heard a proposal."

"You want me to do it right? No problem." He instantly drops to one knee, like he's been dying for a chance.

Once again, a year ago I would've been teary with joy. But now I know he isn't serious. He's only doing this because he can't bear the idea of losing one of the toys he occasionally pulls out and plays with. "No. I don't want you to do anything at all, because I'm not your fiancée. And you aren't going to be my husband."

He looks like I just backhanded him. "What's wrong with me?"

"Are you kidding? How long am I going to be your fiancée? Until you get a call that some cheetahs are about to fuck and they need you to take photos? *Hey Noah, Cheetah Only Fans needs more content.* Until you get another rush of inspiration for your novel and spend three days locked away not answering your phone? Remember that one? Or until you find basically *anything better to do* than keep a promise to me?"

Guilt and remorse twist his handsome face, and I steel myself. I can't let this display affect me when I know he doesn't care enough not to hurt me again.

"No. You'll be my fiancée forever. I mean, until we get married," he says.

"You know what I was doing before you walked up? I closed my eyes and envisioned a proposal. And guess what? *You weren't in it.*" I step forward and push him again, making him put a hand down to keep his balance. Once he realizes I won't be easy pickings, he'll move on.

"Bobbi—"

"Go marry some girl you really love. One you moan about in your sleep."

"That's *you.*" The confusion on his face is so sincere, its claws leave a vicious gash in my heart.

I smile to hide the pain. "Nope. Sorry. You chose your precious cheetah porn over me. I never meant anything to you, so stop."

He regards me for a long moment. That's right. You got nothing to say.

He slowly stands up and looks me in the eye. "You're wrong. You mean everything to me, and I'm going to manifest another chance to prove it to you."

14

BOBBI

THE FIRST THING I do after getting home from Peery Diamonds is place my vision ring on a chain and loop it around my neck so the piece rests snugly against my bare chest. Then I go about changing the locks so Noah can't invade my home using the key I foolishly gave him back when I thought we meant something to each other.

He's also probably changed his passcodes by now. If he hasn't...

My fiancée. The memory flashes through my mind—*so* irritating that he has the gall to believe there can still be anything between us. I expel the air from my lungs, imagining it's the toxicity of my past. *His delusion, his problem.* Not mine.

On Monday, Noah sends me a giant bouquet of white calla lilies. I drag the trash can out from behind the counter and drop the flowers into the gray plastic bin right in front of the delivery guy.

"You're, um..." The kid looks like he's about eighteen, and clearly isn't prepared for this.

"Supposed to sign for them before I chuck 'em out like old lettuce?"

"Uh, yeah," the kid says, shoving a small phone at me.

"Fine." It isn't his fault he's being forced to do Satan's work this morning. I slash my finger across the screen to make a straight line, pretty much the same motion my arm would make if I were to backhand the source of my annoyance.

My fiancée isn't going to pay for her own ring. Horseshit. Jessica the store clerk looked at me and Noah with a shaky I-don't-want-to-be-part-of-this smile, but ended up putting it on my account. His jaw dropped as though she'd backstabbed him. If she'd stabbed him for real, I'd have given her a nice tip.

"Uh... Okay. Now I have to take a picture," the kid says, scratching his cheek, mottled with acne scars, then lifts his phone.

"Why?"

"Proof of delivery."

"I just signed your thing."

"You put a line on it." He snaps a photo before I can stop him. "Thanks, though."

Noah probably offered to pay him extra if he texted him this little trophy. "Tell your client I'm allergic..."

He looks at the flowers with a *that's-too-bad* expression. "Okay. I'll do that."

"...to anything delivered from an *asshole*."

The kid either doesn't communicate well or Noah's defective brain decides I'm happy with his flowers because he sends white calla lilies every day for the rest of the week. If he thinks it's going to make up for him missing the opening of Bobbi's Sweet Things...

Hope isn't the only thing that springs eternal. Delusion's up there, too.

By Friday, no Mr. Perfect has gone down on one knee, but on the other hand Floyd and the other creeps haven't dropped by, so things are moving in a positive direction. My only worry is Señor Mittens, who has abruptly decided that he disdains the food I've been feeding him, but is gaining weight anyway. I google the symptoms wondering if he's sick, and it says he is likely suffering from heart, lung or liver malfunction and advises me to take him to the vet. But my cat seems alert and displays his usual contempt for humanity. I make a mental note to observe him for a couple more days. He could be stealing food from other felines that he considers lesser than him—which would be all of them—as a flex on his superiority and territory. He's done it before.

On Saturday, I head to the steakhouse where I'm meeting Yuna's older brother. He's visiting from Korea, and Yuna and her husband are planning to join us for a four-way dinner.

As I stop at a red light, I get a call from Yuna. "Hey, I hate to do this, but Declan and I can't make it. Lilian and Liam have both come down with some kind of stomach bug, so they have to stay home."

"Oh, no. Are they okay?"

"I think so. Just feverish, fussy and pukey." She sighs.

The light changes. "Thank goodness. We can always reschedule, no problem." I check my mirror and change lanes.

"No, no. You should go ahead and enjoy the meal. Jin said he'd love to treat you for being so good to the kids."

I raise an eyebrow. Jin, or Eugene to most people who aren't familiar enough to use his Korean nickname, has never given me an impression he has a favorable opinion of me. The man isn't easy to read, being overly serious and tragically divorced. Can't imagine the anguish of learning that the son he thought was his was actually another man's. I hope his ex falls into a ditch and breaks all her nails and her scheming, cheating vagina.

Yuna adds, "He's already on his way to the restaurant."

"Okay. Give the little angels hugs from me. Sending them good vibes."

Half an hour later, I'm at the steakhouse. Some jazzy sax tune swirls around along with the amazing aroma of perfectly grilled beef and freshly baked bread. This is exactly the kind of place my former clients loved to frequent when they wanted to splurge, especially since selfies taken here look fantastic with the moneyed backdrop. It's exactly the kind of place Yuna likes to visit when she's in the mood—lots of dark wood, class and gloss...and, of course, excellent food.

"Too bad about Yuna and Declan," I say to Eugene as our server leaves with our order.

"They'll be fine," Eugene says in great English, his voice a low baritone. "Part of raising little kids."

Since I was to dine with Yuna and Eugene, I dressed more formally than usual in a red dress with a side slit and my favorite stilettos. Declan wears whatever—but then he is a model and looks like a god in even rags—but Yuna always wears beautiful designer dresses, and I've never seen Eugene in anything but bespoke three-piece suits. Even when he's playing with his nephew and niece, he's in a suit that must have cost tens of thousands of dollars.

And this evening is no different. His black hair is perfectly coiffed, his suit dark-navy and formal with a burgundy tie that manages to add a splash of color without being flashy. A platinum diamond tie-pin blinks on his chest, expensive and classy. His outfit adds to his serious vibe. And the fact that his dark eyes and full lips rarely betray his emotions adds to the solemn air he carries. Whatever emotion he shows to the world, it's only what he wants to reveal.

"You're like the auntie they don't have. I'm grateful that you're so kind to them. I wish I were closer and could spend more time with them."

The server appears with our wine and food. He lays out the steaks and the sides of mashed potatoes, sauteed mushrooms and grilled veggies. Eugene tastes the Bordeaux and approves it with a nod, then raises his glass. "To friends and family."

I clink and sip the wine. It's drier than I'd prefer but the oak and berries at the end make it very drinkable. The grass-fed beef steak is perfectly grilled, and the bread is exceptional. As I cut into the meat, the table near us erupts with a cheer.

"Happy birthday, Adam!"

Eugene's eyes flick to the family celebrating a birthday. Some emotion lurks in them.

"Are those folks too loud?" When he's in Korea, he probably eats in quiet restaurants where people don't shout.

"No." He turns to me with a polite smile. "Just remembered... It's Minho's birthday."

Minho?

His dark eyebrows pull together briefly before he smooths his expression into a cool mask. "The child I raised," he says, apparently noticing the question on my face.

"Oh." I squirm a little as I realize Eugene is referring to the kid his cheating ex-wife passed off as his.

Yuna told me about it after one too many drinks: "It wasn't a love match, but it was a good arranged marriage. The right families. Good education on both sides. The right upbringing. But she's just an immoral adulteress whore. This is what happens when you stop treating adultery as a jailable offense. If Korea still put people in prison for adultery, that bitch and her manwhore would be *gone*."

I still can't fathom anybody cheating on Eugene. The man breathes success, and he's also quite handsome. Unless he constantly farts and belches at home, he's a great catch. "I'm sorry," I say after a moment.

A casual shrug. "It happens. Everyone knows about it, so it saves me the trouble of explaining."

I bet a divorce by someone like him would make the national news in Korea. "It sucks that you don't get the privacy you deserve."

"Comes with the job."

His tone is light, but his ex's betrayal must've hurt. Still might, if he's thinking of the boy even now. And the child... He did nothing wrong, but got separated from the only father he knew because his mom couldn't do the right thing. Children always suffer when the parents are self-centered shits, very much like my father.

I wash away the bitter taste in my mouth with the wine. "People suck."

Eugene laughs, but it's more polite than amused. "Should a newly engaged woman say something like that?"

"What?"

He tilts his chin at my hand. The chain for the ring doesn't match my dress, so I put my new ring on my finger for the evening, figuring I won't run into my dream husband tonight anyway.

"It's a vision ring. To help me manifest my future."

A corner of his mouth quirks upward. "Yuna's idea?"

"How did you know?"

"It's exactly the kind of thing she'd tell a friend to try. So what's it supposed to manifest for you?"

I pull the ring off and turn it around, studying the fracturing light off the beautifully faceted surface. "It's supposed to bring me a wonderful family. She said she read about vision items."

"And embellished them with her own twist. She always does. Like her soul sister idea."

I have to smile. She calls Ivy her soul sister. "'If you can have a soul mate, why can't you have a soul sister, too?'" I say, quoting Yuna.

He laughs. "Yeah. The way her mind leaps and makes connections. She'd make a great executive if she wanted. But she doesn't have the right temperament." He extends a hand. "May I?"

"Sure." I give him the ring.

He scrutinizes it. "Exceptional. I suppose my sister told you not to cheap out on your future."

"You know her very well. I went to Peery Diamonds for it."

A soft chuckle. "That's so like her, and Peery is where I would've gone too. The ring represents the first step in your future with a family—proposal."

"Right. I'm supposed to look at it and close my eyes and imagine what that's going to be like, what kind of man he is... You know."

"Maybe I can help you visualize." He extends a hand, palm up, holding the ring between his thumb and index finger.

"Oh, okay." I place my left hand on his. His skin and warm and dry. He smoothly slides the ring back onto my finger. Watching the masculine hand pushing the band up along my slim feminine finger makes my heart squeeze with longing for the future I've always dreamed of.

"Did you visualize your future?"

I nod, then smile. "Kind of."

"How does it feel?"

"Incredible." I laugh a little, then look up when I sense somebody approaching, thinking it must be our waiter checking up on us.

Instead, there's a quick peck on my cheek that causes me to start.

"You look lovely, my light."

Noah? Again? What the hell is he doing here? Stalking me?

He's looking down at me with a charming smile, but—stalker or not—his eyes are screaming, *What the fuck?* It gives me quite a bit of perverse satisfaction, even though he's completely misunderstood the situation.

That's right, buster, eat your heart out. I've moved on.

Eugene glances at Noah, then turns to me. "Do you know this man?"

"No," I say, at the same time Noah declares loudly enough for everyone in the restaurant to hear, "I'm her fiancé!"

15

NOAH

"Not that I have anything against spending a Saturday evening with you, but why are we here?" Huxley sips his merlot, his cool, wary eyes scanning the high-end restaurant that smells of well-grilled beef and freshly baked crack—I mean, bread.

"I just feel like having steak with my favorite brother." Actually, I brought him here so he can *just happen* to see his grandmother dining with Andreas Webber. I couldn't come up with a smooth way to let him know his family is trying to fuck him over. I don't want to tip him off that I'm keeping an eye on him and our other brothers, but I can't in good conscience let him get ambushed. Especially by a bunch of conniving lawyers.

Plus, I might be able to pick his brain a little. Hux could convince an Arab to pay for sand. He must know a few good ways to lay siege—successfully—to a woman's heart. Or, in this case, at least convince her I'm not the shithead she thinks I am.

Bobbi apparently hates white calla lilies now. I sent a bouquet every day of the week and she tossed each one into the trash, as witnessed by the delivery guy. Delivery confirmation with a note the last day: *I think she has a pollen allergy. Her face turns red so fast.*

What she has is a Noah allergy, which I plan to take care of before she proposes to some loser in a misguided attempt to "manifest a husband." Thankfully, she doesn't have anybody she can pop the question to at the moment. The only decent person with a penis in her life right now is her employee Victor, but he doesn't fit the bill—too young and not her type.

And now that I've wrapped up an intelligence report Mom said she needed last year—I rolled my eyes so hard I almost saw my brain—I have plenty of free time to devote to Bobbi.

"I mean, why are we *here*?" Huxley gestures around.

"Here? At this restaurant?" Damn it. If he won't let me get away with a bullshit excuse, I might have to abort my plan to alert him to his family's incipient betrayal. "Because it has the best bread...?"

"It does, but I feel like we're being disloyal to Grant and Aspen."

I hear you, brother. "Well, they don't need to know," I grumble, then try to ignore the weird prickling sensation I've had since we entered the steakhouse. It's probably guilt telling me I'm going to go to hell for giving money to this establishment.

My brothers and I used to come here regularly for our dinners because it has fabulous steaks and excellent bread—not as good as Bobbi's, of course, but still amazing. But then the hostess disrespected Aspen and her grandfather one time and we quit coming. There are plenty of great steakhouses in the city. We don't have to give our business to an establishment that mistreated one of the Lasker wives.

But Catalina Huxley and Andreas Webber don't know about the incident, and even if they did, they wouldn't care. So they're meeting here and I had no choice but to bring Hux.

But I'm not drinking anything other than the free water and have selected the cheapest cut of steak, no sides. I'll just devour the complimentary bread instead, even though Huxley is drinking merlot and ordered surf-and-turf with his favorite lobster mac and cheese and grilled asparagus. He doesn't believe in denying himself.

"Are we talking *here* because Bobbi's cut you off?" He slices into his steak while eyeing my plate. He knows something's up just from how little I've ordered.

"No, no, no. I wouldn't backstab Grant and Aspen over mere carbs." I stuff my mouth with a big chunk of bread laden with butter, which is fantastic—creamy with extra salt.

Huxley cocks an eyebrow. "Something more serious?" He frowns. "Are you having issues with women showing up everywhere and throwing themselves at you?"

"What? No," I say with a small shudder. "Wait... Is Joey still sending you hookers?"

"*Yes.*"

"Seriously? I thought he gave up after that first try and Griffin almost murdered him." Then again, Huxley isn't the one Joey really fears. When Griffin kicks you, you wish you were dead. But Hux? It's going to hurt, but you'll live.

From the way Huxley's face scrunches, the thought has occurred to him as well. "Motherfucker, I'm going to show him who he's messing with." His knuckles whiten.

"Actually, I don't think he's doing it out of disrespect. He isn't scared of me, either." Nobody's scared of me. That's the persona I picked for myself.

"Yeah, but you aren't having hooker issues. Are you?" Huxley's intense gaze says I better be honest. Man, he'd make a fantastic litigator. No wonder his family won't leave him alone.

"Nope. Maybe Joey doesn't think my DNA is worthy." I grin smugly. He acted all happy at Gion Shiyaki, but he only introduced me to Bobbi because I was right there. He would've done the same if Huxley had crashed the "date." A shitty thing for Joey to do, of course, but at least I stepped up and got her away from the human tangerine.

Huxley snorts. "Don't be ridiculous. If I'm getting them, you're getting them."

"But I'm not. Scout's honor. So..." A light shrug. "Pretty sure dad doesn't really want a grandkid from me. He needs a baby he can shove into Josh Singer's face." And I've done a great job of pretending to be not too bright, not too focused and not very talented in anything in particular except wildlife photography. Thankfully, Dad isn't interested in having a grandchild who's a photography prodigy. He wants a baby capable of singing like an angel or dancing like a prima ballerina—ideally both.

Huxley drinks more wine, then sniffs. Based on his expression, he's plotting some sort of gruesome murder. Joey better watch it because Huxley knows all the legal angles. If anyone can get away with homicide... "If you say so. Anyway, if this dinner isn't about the crazy women, what *is* it about?"

"I'm thinking about a career change." Not true, but I need a plausible reason for this meeting other than trying to save Hux's ass.

"Cheetahs no longer excite you?" He reacts like I just told him I get off on sticking my dick into a live socket. Understandable since I've spent most of my adult life acting like wildlife photography is one of the greatest joys of my life, up there with carbs.

If only he knew that "cheetahs" is actually what I call my rifles and guns. They're as sleek, fast and fatal as the gorgeous cats. The moniker fits.

"No, they're still good. But I'm getting a little...restless." I take a bite of the beef and sigh. Would've been better with some creamed spinach, but loyalty comes first.

"I thought you'd die shooting your precious beasts."

The comment reminds me of what Bobbi said. *Marry the one you love the most. The one you probably moan about in your sleep. Your precious cheetahs.* Totally unfair, of course. "Don't be ridiculous. I was never that weird about my love of cheetahs."

He snorts. "Ridiculous?" His eyes defocus a bit as he looks up at the ceiling. "'Cheetahs don't have retractable claws. Unlike other big cats, cheetahs can't roar. Cheetahs have those black tear-stripes on their faces to help prevent sun glare.' You know how I know all that? *You.*"

"Well, yeah, okay. But—"

"Weird, fetishistic cheetah-love."

"I don't really—"

He waves a dismissive hand in my face. "Stow it. My only advice is, if you want to be successful in your next career, don't be a novelist."

"Hey. You can't rush art."

"You can if art puts food on your table. Did you know Bach composed a mass a week?"

"Should've invested his money in venture capital or private equity."

"He lived three hundred years ago." Huxley points it out in that half-condescending, half-superior way he has. He always prides himself on being intelligent and well-versed in culture and history. Unfortunately, he's oblivious to the giant stick protruding from his ass.

"Well, I live in today's world and am well invested, as you know. So food will be on my table whether my book gets written or not." I pull out my phone and tap the screen to check up on Catalina and Andreas. *Ten minutes away.* "Actually, I'm thinking about going into advertising."

Huxley's fork stops in the air, butter dripping from the lobster tail. "What?"

"It's a stable career. I'll be great at it."

"No. You'll be *terrible* at it. You'll never make any money."

"I'm not asking you to pay me. Just show me the ropes. I can begin as an unpaid intern."

He blanches. "Hell no. Get an unpaid internship with Emmett or Grant."

"Why are you so against me working in advertising? It's a great place to learn how to appeal to different people's tastes and desires. Plus, I'm a great photographer."

He puts his fork down and looks me in the eye. "Noah. You're too independent. You can't follow directions and you do whatever you want. If I told you we were launching an engagement ring campaign, you'd bring me a photo of Marilyn Monroe with a blown-up diamond ring on her head like a crown."

I consider for a moment. "Nah. I'd hang it around her neck on a kind of choker, making sure the rock rested between her boobs."

"You're making my point for me. Look, if you're finally tired of cheetahs, why don't you just get married and give Dad the baby he wants? Or just bang one of Joey's bimbos and get her pregnant? That way Dad'll quit bugging the rest of us. It's too late for this year's birthday party, but next year..."

"Ugh. What did my not-yet-created baby do to deserve that fate?"

Hux shrugs, then downs his wine, hiding his face with the glass.

There's a good reason Emmett and Griffin refuse to let our dad near their children. Dad thinks the giant dick cannon we gave him was still the best birthday gift ever, not realizing it was a gag gift. He made replicas with some modifications so that they'd actually shoot out goopy white liquid, then had them at parties with kids around. "Bro. I thought you loved me."

"I do, but you're obviously bored and restless. Making a baby will be new and interesting. And you'll probably be pretty good at it, too."

"I'm not a virgin, you asshole."

"Of course. But have you done it without a rubber?" He raises both eyebrows.

"No." If you want something done right, you do it yourself. No condom, no sex, and I provide the contraception.

"So you're a 'raw' virgin." Huxley starts to reach for more wine, then looks across the restaurant. "Huh."

"What?" I say in a bored tone. Don't want to seem over-eager to know what he's looking at when it's probably Catalina and Andreas arriving a little early.

"Isn't that Bobbi?"

"What?" I swivel around immediately. "Where?"

"Over there." Hux points to my five o'clock and looks impressed. "She's hot in that dress. If she wore something like that at her bakery she'd make a mint off her male customers."

I spot her among the diners, and Hux is right. She's in a bright red calf-length dress with a slit that goes all the way up one creamy leg and stops at mid-thigh. Her golden hair is unbound and pretty. I realize my tingling sensation wasn't guilt at betraying Grant and Aspen, but an unconscious awareness of Bobbi since I stepped inside the restaurant.

An Asian guy is sitting opposite her. Something about him feels familiar, but I can't place it. I look him up and down, doing my best to find some fault. But his dark navy three-piece suit looks like bespoke Italian. It fits his lean frame perfectly, his shoulders straight and broad. His hair isn't flaming orange, and he doesn't look like a Canadian druggie searching for better and cheaper highs. *He's actually decent looking*, I admit grudgingly. His eyes are surprisingly intense, his lips full —the kind of face many women would find attractive, including Bobbi. His burgundy tie is impeccably knotted, the pin on it—probably a real diamond, if I'm reading the rest of him correctly—discreet and expensive.

The man exemplifies good taste and casual affluence. Likely born to money and comfortable with it. I watch him eat, hoping he'll slurp his wine or chew with his mouth open. But nope. Even my mother would approve of his manners.

He's the exact opposite of Lorcan Duncan—a true threat and a dangerous rival.

Something flashes in his hand. A blue stone.

Bobbi bought a blue diamond ring. The band was too small for his hand, but she could've resized it.

Is this guy the perfect husband she manifested?

Hell no. No fucking way.

But he fits the bill. He's the right age. Looks good enough if you like uptight corporate drones. Probably wants kids because Asians are big on family.

The idea of him and Bobbi in bed together kills my appetite faster than a roach puking in my food.

Mr. Perfect Asian Guy slides the ring onto her finger. What the hell? He can't even buy his own fucking ring to propose?

I slap my napkin down next to my plate and get up. Hux frowns as he follows my movement, but I don't have time to satisfy his curiosity.

I walk toward their table. Then, pasting on my most charming smile, I place a kiss on Bobbi's cheek, quickly enough that she can't move away or punch me in the face. Her fists hurt. "You look lovely, my light."

Bobbi gives me a poisonous glare while her date assesses this new development. Finally, he turns to her. "Do you know this man?"

"No," she says.

"I'm her fiancé."

"Ah." His gaze drops to the blue diamond on her finger, the one he placed there just moments ago. The gesture is a challenge and a fuck-you. "You seem to be a bit late."

For once, I hate my easygoing persona. Should have listened to Mom when she recommended an ax murderer vibe, then this asshole would be showing me more respect.

"This is what you managed to manifest?" I say. "A guy who can't even buy his own ring?"

She gives me a pat smile. "But one who can keep his promises."

"What promise?"

"He's here. For dinner."

"Which I'm paying for," the guy adds with a bland smile.

"*I* bought you dinner before!" I say, in case she's forgotten all the things I bought her, or if this is about her needing to be sure I can treat her better than this guy. I thank my lucky stars for my perfect memory. Every single thing we've done together is seared into my mind. "Mexico, July twenty-ninth, when we first met, and then for the rest of the vacation, lunch and dinner. After we came back to the States, a brunch at Jean-Georges on August fifteenth. Then—"

All this doesn't seem to advance my case. Her cheeks redden and she jumps to her feet, covering my mouth with her hand. The feel of her bare skin on my lips sends an electric jolt through me. She's close enough that I can smell the heady scent of her shampoo and soap, which haven't changed since I've known her. I kiss her palm, then lick it, holding her furious eyes with mine, silently communicating she's the only woman I want. That's the one true thing in my world, and I don't want her to resist it anymore.

Her face turns redder. Her beautiful eyes flash with incredulity, shock and *oh-no-you-don't*. "Excuse me," she says to the other guy. Then she snatches her hand away, grabs my wrist and drags me off toward the bathrooms. I follow, willing to go literally anywhere as long as she's with me.

We walk past the diners, some of whom turn to watch, then to the less brightly lit corridor outside the bathrooms. She starts to pull me into the ladies' room, which I instinctively resist.

"Hey, I can't go in there—"

"Get in here *right now!*" She grabs me with both hands and practically lifts me off my feet. I end up inside the ladies' room, which—thankfully—is empty. Bobbi seems worked up enough to toss any woman who might be in here out.

All the stalls have floor-to-ceiling faux-wood doors that have been left ajar. Spotless mirrors cover the walls in the vanity area. She reaches around behind me and locks the door.

"Okay," she says, hands on hips. "What kind of game are you playing?"

"No game."

"Are you trying to embarrass me in front of Eugene?"

Of all the things to be upset about. "Me telling you what we have between us is embarrassing?" I thought she was unhappy that she forgot some of our history, while I haven't.

"You were listing the meals you paid for!"

"I was listing all the times we had together, except for, you know, the dates and the sex stuff because I figured that might be upsetting for you. I haven't forgotten even a second of our history."

A hint of uncertainty fleets in her eyes before she stiffens. "Bullshit."

"What's bullshit is you letting that asshole put that ring on your finger. He didn't even pay for it." I glare at her, bristling with outrage that she's settling just to avoid me. "He doesn't know you the way I do. He doesn't understand you the way I do. He will never cherish you the way I do—"

Her eyes flutter as the walls around her start to crack. She covers her ears, squeezing her eyes closed, like that will keep me out of her mind and erase our history. "Shut up, shut up, *shut up!*"

I'm not going to shut up, not like this. But if she doesn't want to hear the words...

I take her wrists and pull her hands away from her ears. "Make me."

16

NOAH

BOBBI'S EYES SNAP OPEN, anger erupting in their depths. "Don't make me hurt you, Noah."

"I can think of a *much* better way to make me shut up."

I cradle her face and kiss her hard. I thrust my tongue in, claiming her, tasting her. Every nerve in my body tingles, my blood turning thick and hot and my heart racing hard. Just having her mouth on me makes me feel alive. She wraps her hands around my wrists and exerts enough force to bruise, trying to push me away.

I deepen the kiss, stroking her tongue and nipping gently at her delicate, soft lips. She tastes of wine and Bobbi and all the dreams that seem so impossible and beautiful when I lie hidden in the dark with my scope trained on a target. Of the gorgeous, shining vision that made me care about living on that smoking plane.

She doesn't kiss me back at first, so I kiss her enough for both of us. Drop a hand from her cheek and run it along the smooth slope of her shoulder, then the lean line of her biceps, then cup her pretty breast in my palm.

A low groan pulls from her chest, vibrating through the soft mound in my hand. She lets go of my other wrist and her fingers curl into my hair harder than is comfortable. The minor pain grounds me in the moment, reminding me I'm alive and with the only woman I'll ever love.

Her mouth is aggressive now, her teeth biting into me like she wants to vent her frustration and anger through the kiss. Laughing softly, I let her unleash it all on me. I want to own everything about her. Her laughter, her tears, her love, her hatred—all mine.

I move her until she's perched on the edge of the vanity. The mirror behind Bobbi reflects the one behind me, showing an endless row of images vanishing into the distance. Her glazed eyes, her swollen lips, her cheeks now rosy with lust as well as anger. Hot blood pools in my dick, and it begins to ache so much, even the top of my head tingles. She pulls my head down for another stark kiss; I kiss her back, plundering her mouth, while letting her take all she wants. I run my hands along her body, exploring and relearning the lean strength and feminine lines that never fail to incite my lust.

My palm glides along the smooth, warm curve of thigh exposed by the side slit, then slips under the dress. She's hot, and my blood boils. I want to drive into her over and over again until she's branded as mine.

I push away the thin strip of her thong, her heated slickness coating my fingers. She whimpers against my mouth, her fingers flexing in my hair like she can't decide if she should want the pleasure I'm offering.

Oh my light, you shouldn't just want it, you should crave it, demand it, take it.

I run my fingers along the crease between her thigh and wetness, giving her a moment to decide because it's ultimately her choice. She pinches her eyebrows as though in pain. Slowly the quivering tension in her legs eases a little, giving me better access.

Good girl.

Her eyes flutter open, glazed and beautiful. Maybe I said it out loud because she flushes. I push two fingers into her hot depths the way she likes, while my thumb toys with her amazingly sensitive clit. She tilts her head back, stifling a moan.

I bury my face in the crook of her neck, sucking and kissing the delicate skin there, as I pump my fingers. My dick is impossibly hard now, my pants unbearably tight, but I ignore it. This is for her. For my Bobbi—my light.

Her pussy tightens, a soft whimper escaping through her closed lips. Little shudders run through her, a sign that she's climbing higher—she's close.

I increase the tempo. Watch the pleasure building on her expressive face, her rosy mouth soft, her breathing going shallow and sweat misting over her soft skin. She lets go of my hair and clings to my shoulders, getting ready to ride out the climax breaking over her. No matter how many times I feel her come, every occasion is special. And it's no different now.

My fingers rub the inner spot that always drives her crazy. She doesn't hold back her moans anymore as every muscle in her body tightens.

"Noah." The call is half-plea, and I almost come in my pants. "Noah," she says again. But this time, it's tinged with uncertainty and fear, as though she's afraid I might disappear, just another ghosting act to add to many before.

My love, you know I've never disappointed you in bed.

"Bobbi, come for me, baby." I thrust harder, faster, ruthlessly pushing her higher. Her breathing grows hitched, uneven, a thin sound coming from her throat.

Then her orgasm hits. She wraps her arms and legs around me as she shudders. I hold her tight with one arm, guiding her climax, then pushing another one on her.

She groans against my neck, her scent enveloping me, and I shake with unanswered need. I stroke her back, then kiss her temple, taste her salt and sweetness.

A quiet moment settles over us, like peace after a storm. I hold her, cherishing it and glad I didn't give up when the plane dropped.

An impatient rattling shatters our delicate intimacy. "Why is this *locked*?" a young girlish voice complains from the other side of the door.

Bobbi stiffens, then pushes me away. Her eyes are no longer soft, but hard with self-recrimination and regret.

"Hey. Don't be sorry about what happened," I say.

"It wasn't the smartest thing."

"Feels like one of the smartest things *I've* ever done."

Refusing to look at me, Bobbi straightens, squirming to realign her thong and running her hands down her dress to smooth it. She can fuss with her clothes all she wants, but she can't hide the post-orgasm flush or the marks I left on her neck. "You think you're being clever, Noah, but this...encounter doesn't change anything between us. I'm not getting married for free dinners and a ring. I'm marrying for commitment, which you can never give me."

That hurts...and I can't even argue because she's right. I wasn't always around because I thought I could keep my distance every time my work might put her in danger. To make sure I couldn't go back to her, I broke my word on purpose...except I couldn't stay away.

Up to now, she forgave me because she liked me, and I shamefully took advantage of that, relieved that she still cared about me. The idea that she might actively push me away never seemed to be a possibility when I decided to see her after the crash. I had finally accepted that I couldn't live without her, and would just have to be extra vigilant to keep her safe—or even quit the business altogether. My work is important, but nothing's as important as Bobbi. "I'm here now."

Bang, bang, bang! There are more impatient knocks on the door.

"There's another bathroom right next to this one!" I shout in case she's the type to pee when she sneezes.

"Noah! Don't do this!" the woman yells from outside.

What the hell?

"Uh, '*Noah, don't do this*'?" Bobbi shoots me an *are-you-serious?* look.

"Bobbi, trust me, I don't even know her." I've never heard that voice before. It's so nasal the woman seems like an elephant with a cold.

"Yeah sure." Bobbi's lips twist into a humorless smile. "Let's just assume she's talking about some *other* Noah." She shakes her head. "But let's see if you can answer this question: How long are you going to stick around this time?"

"Forever. The answer is forever. I'll make up for everything."

She lets out a laugh. "How? By sending more flowers?" she says. "The bakery opening might've been some silly little event to you, compared to your amazing adventures and photography, but it was a milestone for me. A *big* one. And I need someone who recognizes what's important and can share those moments."

"And I will—"

"Until a year ago, when I thought about my future, you were in it. But now..." She shrugs. "You aren't part of the picture anymore."

She unlocks the door and stands to the side. A brunette in a skin-tight black dress is right in front of the door, arms crossed over a medically pumped-up chest. She pushes off the wall she was leaning against, uncrosses her arms and props her hands on her hips. Sharp eyes rake over Bobbi, noting the flush and the soft glow.

She turns to me with an almost unholy triumph. "Noah!" Before I can process her weird reaction, she launches herself forward, grabs my shirt and pulls me down as she stretches upward. I press my lips together hard just as her open mouth lands on mine. Her kiss is clammy, and smells of an eye-watering mint mouthwash. She tries to shove her slug-like tongue into my mouth, and I go cold.

I grip her arms firmly—but not so hard that they'll end up bruised —and push her away. Her overinflated lips are pursed in a perfect circle. It reminds me of a suction cup on an octopus tentacle and sends nasty shivers down my spine.

The whole thing happens fast, and my heart is thumping—for all the wrong reasons. Bobbi snorts in disgust. This has to look like a total shitshow to her.

"Noah, honey, I've been looking all *over* for you! I'm ready to have your baby now."

What?

"I just knew we were destined to be the moment our gazes collided." She sounds like a third-rate actress reading a fourth-rate script. "Don't you feel it? The galactic tidal pull?"

"Who are you?"

"Rammi." She winks. "Get it? Ram-Me?" She bats her eyelashes while trying to give me a direct *fuck me* look. It doesn't work.

Then it hits me: Joey apparently *has*n't forgotten about me after all, not after our run-in at Gion Shiyaki. His women just haven't had a chance to get to me because I've been holed up, working on the report Mom wanted. *Oh, shit.*

Bobbi looks half-humiliated and half-revolted. "Wow."

"This isn't what it looks like," I say, while Rammi is doing her best to squish her overflowing breasts against my chest. I don't know what's been done to her tits, but her nipples seem to be permanently erect.

Bobbi's eyes rake us up and down, taking in the whole tableau. "Nah." Her tone says, *How stupid do you think I am?* "It's fine. Have your fun with Rim-Me."

She starts to walk back to the dining area. I shove Rammi into the bathroom. "It's all yours!" I close the door and rush after Bobbi. Her long strides have already taken her halfway to her table where the Asian guy is faithfully waiting.

The door to the bathroom crashes open behind me and a rapid clattering of heels against the hard floor follows. There's no way I can have a productive conversation with Bobbi with Rammi in the picture. Because if the roles were reversed and some asshole tried to rub his dick against Bobbi...

I rush past Huxley. "Get the bill, Hux, thanks!" I say as I hurry to exit the restaurant before Rammi does anything to dig an even deeper hole for me.

Huxley gawks at me, at the woman in hot pursuit and then jumps up and stabs his finger at us. "Ah-*ha*! I *knew* it!"

17

NOAH

To KILL or not to kill, that is the question.

Of course, I'm not feeling anywhere close to poetic or philosophical as I seethe. It's been three hours since the encounter with Rammi, but my fury hasn't died a bit. I spent a few minutes running my hands along the cool barrels of my cheetahs. The cold hard smoothness of the rifles generally calms me down, but not today. I debated which one would be better to use, imagining Joey in the crosshairs and slowly pulling the trigger.

It would be so satisfying, and the fucker deserves it. I had a perfect chance to get closer to Bobbi and convince her I could be the one she's looking for. But then he had to send that crazy "I'm ready to have your baby immediately" floozy, and now I'm just fucked.

I should turn Joey's knees into mush. That way he won't be able to go around sending me hookers. Actually, I should destroy his elbows so he can't use his phone.

I sit in the dark amid the unfamiliar furniture and breathe slowly, trying to control my rage. But the scent of Joey's cologne is gasoline over an open flame.

If my dad's assistant didn't live in an apartment complex, I'd be tempted to set the place on fire.

I close my eyes to rein in all sorts of highly illegal impulses. Dear God, I know you love Nicholas the most because he's the nicest of us all and rewarded him by pushing Joey from the stairs, but you know... I've also done a lot of good deeds like sniping terrorists and running sting ops on arms dealers. So maybe do me one solid? Not asking for much. Just a divine drone strike. A literal deus ex machina.

But maybe it'd be better if Joey got struck by lightning. Sadly, there's no crackling in the air.

Guess I haven't killed enough terrorists to satisfy the Lord.

The door rattles; the lock turns with a soft click and I open my eyes. There's the click of a switch being flipped, but nothing happens.

"What the fuck?" comes Joey's voice. "I just changed the bulbs!"

Finally. The object of my ire is finally home.

His loafers slap the hardwood floor as he mutters with impatient irritation. "Nobody can do anything right! What the hell is wrong with the world? They have *one* fucking job!" The rapid complaints continue as he makes his way to the master bedroom, where I've been waiting for over an hour.

He flips the switch. Again, nothing. "Goddammit..." He glances out the window where the City of Angels glitters and sighs. I have excellent night vision, and can make out his scowl in the dark.

I stand silently. "Hello, you little fucker."

Joey starts violently. "Who's that?" His voice trembles with a tinge of fear.

I start to move toward him. "What's the matter? You fuck too many people over to recognize who I am?"

"Noah...?" He turns toward me. "What are you doing here? How did you get in?"

"Locksmith." Not telling him about my expertise with locks.

"What? That's illegal!"

"Illegal, but not as low as you sending me that porn star."

"Who?"

My little remaining patience vanishes. "Rammi, you moron!"

"Oh, her? What's wrong with her? She's fabulous. Headlights on high, all the time. Pretty face. Nice lips. No filler, by the way. Totally real, feel great, too. If you ever have them wrapped around your cock, you'll know exactly what I mean. I went above and beyond just for you."

The memory of that octopus tentacle-sucker mouth fleets through my head. Nausea rises at the thought of her anywhere near me. "Are you shitting me?"

"What? She's hot." Joey sounds genuinely confused.

"She's a freak!"

"Freakishly hot. The best of the bunch. Huxley got the *leftovers*, Noah! You should thank me."

Every blood vessel in my head feels like it's about to burst. "*Thank you?* I'm going to murder you!"

Joey raises his hands defensively. "Okay, fine, no need to get so mad. I tried to get a broad range of women, but the normal ones simply aren't interested in you that way. You saw how Bobbi was when she realized I was trying to set her up with you! So I'm telling you, buddy, it's you, not me."

"Wait—are you blaming *me*?"

"It's pretty obvious, man. Look, a little advice. Okay? No offense, but if I were you, I wouldn't be screwing around. I'd be busy making a baby with Rammi. She's fabulous mother material." He shrugs. "Don't like her lips? No problem. Just concentrate on her nipples."

My brain refuses to process the nuclear garbage out of his mouth.

"But until you give Ted the grandbaby he wants, I'm gonna do what I have to do." Joey lifts his chin, defiant and proud that nothing's going to stop him from pleasing my father.

The hot rage dies abruptly, leaving me surprisingly cold and focused, like I always become when I have a target in the crosshairs. I can't have Joey sending more Rammis when I'm on a mission to prove to Bobbi I love her and convince her to give me another chance.

I step forward, spin Joey around so he's facing the wall and shove him hard enough against it to rattle his picture frames. He grunts at the impact.

"What are you doing? This is assault!"

"Sue me." I press the tip of the blade I always carry against his fleshy side.

He flinches. "What's that?"

"Give you a hint. It's not Rammi's nipple."

He lets out a sound somewhere between whine and whimper. I slowly drag the tip all the way up until it's resting against the pulsing vein on his neck. His breathing grows rougher and shallower.

"You can't kill me." His whisper lacks conviction. "You're just a...photographer."

"Don't be so sure, Joey," I say into his ear. "You know what I had to do to get some of my best shots? To survive on the veldt for days at a time? To clear out animals that were in the spot I needed to be? Last time it was a Cape cobra. You know what that is?"

"A snake?" he whispers, trying not to move against the knife.

"That's right. A snake. An *orange* one. Highly poisonous. Reminded me of you, actually. Skinning it was fun." Joey's Adam's apple moves up and down. I add a bit more pressure on the knife, not enough to cut the vein—it's not the best way to kill someone; too messy and the spraying blood is a bitch to get out of your clothes—but enough to nick the skin.

"Oh God! Please don't!" There's the sound of something wet dripping on the floor.

"Did you just piss your pants?" I demand in disgust, hoping none of it splattered on my shoes.

"Please. Please don't hurt me. I won't tell anybody you were here."

Does he honestly think he has anything to bargain with? He can tell everyone what happened. I was very careful to avoid getting caught on security cameras. And my home security system is going to show I'm currently in the living room watching a BBC documentary on marine life while nursing a whiskey.

I spin Joey around and put the point of the blade under his chin. "Don't send any more women if you want to live. Ever. Got it?"

"But Ted—"

"You gonna risk losing an appendage for my dad? *No more women.*"

He inhales sharply.

"Joey, I'm serious. Don't fuck with me. You know what happens with nice guys when they decide to let go."

He bites his lip. Jesus. He's a weasel, but I have to give him credit for blind loyalty to my dad. I increase the pressure a little, causing him to go up on his toes. "What's it gonna be?"

His eyes are the size of dollar coins. Whatever he sees on my face must be pretty convincing because he tries to nod. With the knife under his chin, it comes out as a sort of vertical twitching. "Okay."

"Okay *what?*"

"No more women."

I let him go and step back. He crosses his arms over his torso, hands gripping shoulders.

"I'm glad we could come to an agreement." I fold the blade away with an audible *snik*. "I'd hate to have to cut something off you."

"Jesus, Noah..." Joey says shakily, desperately trying to cling to the idea that I'm the same old harmless Noah he's always known. But it won't work anymore.

"You get one chance. *One.* Understand? No more women."

"Okay, okay, I get it."

"Good. Because if there's another incident, I'll be back." I smile. "And next time, I'll wear an old shirt. One I won't mind ruining with your blood."

18

NOAH

My phone's been pinging nonstop with texts from my brothers since the Saturday dinner. Hux didn't mention that we ate at the blacklisted steakhouse, but he told them everything he witnessed between me and Bobbi.

Of course there's no way my brothers are letting such a great opportunity to rag me pass, so they're still giving me shit, even though it's Sunday morning now.

—Emmett: I thought there might be something between you and Bobbi, but an engagement?

—Grant: So when's the wedding?

—Griffin: The real question is, IS there a wedding?

—Sebastian: There are engagements and there are engagements. He didn't even give her a ring.

—Nicholas: What were you thinking?

—Huxley: I figured out who the guy she was with was. Eugene Hae. He's rich, and comes from an even richer family. We did some campaigns for his company.

—Me: Thank you, Hux. I would've never figured that out on my own.

I already hacked the security feed at the restaurant and looked the guy up. There's more information than I could read in a day on him.

–Huxley: You're welcome.

–Sebastian: Oh, he's from the Hae Min Group. A Sebastian Peery Collaboration partner in Korea. You've got some stiff competition. He's young, single and rich.

–Me: Thank you, Seb. But Hux already told me he was rich, and I saw him with my own eyes. I'm just as young, single and rich as him.

–Sebastian: Also handsome, in case you didn't notice that particular aspect.

–Me: And here I thought you had good taste.

My sarcasm doesn't stop Huxley, though.

–Huxley: Oh, Noah noticed. You should've seen his reaction when he saw Bobbi with the guy.

Asshole. I don't know if he saw his grandmother and Andreas at the restaurant, but it isn't my problem if he was too amused by my misfortune to notice. My priority is finding a way to dig myself out of the hole Joey put me in. I let my brothers give me shit while my mind whirls.

Bobbi probably won't marry Eugene Hae. He lives in Korea, and she isn't going to give up Bobbi's Sweet Things to go to Seoul to play the tycoon's wife. If that's the life she wanted, she would've said yes when I tried to drop to my knee at the Peery Diamonds store. I have plenty of money and I can set her up as a rich man's wife with unlimited access to my funds and properties.

On the other hand... She could just open a Bobbi's Sweet Things in Seoul. Koreans love good pastries.

Damn it.

After making sure Bobbi's not home—my job comes with unusual benefits—I stop by a supermarket and pick up a couple of things before heading to Bobbi's place. She's changed her locks, probably pissed off that she gave me a key after we came back from Mexico. But no lock can keep me out when I want to get in.

The inside of the house is the same—except for the new couch and the bed in the master bedroom. I helped her throw out the old sofa and bed, and my team promptly took them and ripped them apart, just in case. Mom stared at the mess for so long—without speaking—that I knew she was both disappointed and pissed. The dossiers are a splinter under her nail she can't get rid of, and they'll bother her until the day she dies even if she has accepted intellectually that they are no longer around. She's only satisfied if she has clear confirmation that the mission objective has been achieved.

Señor Mittens meows at me, nose held high in disapproval and disdain. If he could speak, he'd say, *You're late.*

At least the hair on his back isn't bristling. When I first showed up with Lorcan, he acted like I was a serial cat killer and scratched the back of my hand deeply enough to draw blood. The wound has healed, and now the lines are gone.

"My God, you are grumpy for such a well-fed cat. Traffic sucked, okay? It's L.A." I set my stuff on the kitchen counter.

He gives me a wide-mouthed yawn. *Yeah yeah yeah, excuses, excuses.*

"You could be a little more gracious. I never avenged myself for that hairball."

He stalks toward me, eyes slitted and paws padding over the ugly green and brown tiles. He makes an impatient growling noise.

"Just hold your horses, Señor Kitty."

I pull out a plate from one of the cupboards and put it on the counter. Then I reach into the paper bag I've been carrying and slap a fresh, sashimi-grade ahi tuna steak on the plate. Just by itself it's more than enough to tempt any feline, but I'm not done. I'm running out of time and need to make sure this cat is on my side as soon as possible. Soon a thick layer of caviar tops the tuna.

"Ta-da! A meal worthy of the emperor of cats. You should give me bonus points. I don't even feed my *brothers* caviar."

The cat licks his chops. I grin with triumph. "Oh yeah, baby. Come to papa!"

He jumps up to the stool, then onto the kitchen counter, his eyes on the feast I've created.

"Who's the best human?" I ask.

Señor Greedy doesn't deign to acknowledge me. Instead he starts scarfing down the tuna and caviar like he hasn't eaten in ages. Which is ridiculous—I've been feeding him fresh tuna for days now.

"Hope she appreciates what I'm going through to win you over."

He ignores me. Or simply doesn't hear in his feeding frenzy.

The fine hair on the back of my neck starts to stand up. It's the same physical reaction I experienced before the plane went down, and apprehension brushes its icy fingers down my spine. My fingers itch for the gun hidden under my shirt, but I restrain myself. There shouldn't be anything in this neighborhood that will require me to fire a shot.

Still, the unsettling sensation intensifies. Just to be sure, I check the house, then head outside, hand on my Sig Sauer, and look around.

This neighborhood has mostly middle-class families, and most of them are out working, their kids in school. A guy with terrible burn scars on his cheek is limping down the street. He doesn't look homeless —his cap seems new, and his white T-shirt and jeans are clean. His eyes are glued to his phone. He's walking straight, so not intoxicated or high. A few houses down, another guy is mowing his lawn.

A short blonde climbs out of her black Camry across the street and starts to unload groceries. Darcy, a nosy neighbor who keeps an eye on everything and loves to gossip. She's harmless, but has a scary memory for details. The only reason Mom isn't interested in her is that she can't distinguish what's important from what's mundane. The man pushes his cap down low on his head, probably to hide his scars from her and avoid any uncomfortable gawking.

Nothing's out of place. The man turns the corner; Darcy shuts her trunk and goes inside her house. Mister Lawn Mower does a one-eighty and starts down another swath of grass. The chilly sensation dissipates.

That was weird. No unusual cars or people sitting in their automobiles, thumbing through their phones. So what was that about?

Your instincts are fucked up, a voice in my head says. You didn't know your plane was sabotaged until it was too late, which you gotta admit is weird because if it were a few years ago, you would've noticed.

They aren't fucked up, I argued with myself. I scan the area again, then return to the kitchen where Señor Mittens is now cleaning himself. Or maybe he's trying to impart the tuna smell all over his body.

"Did you like that?" I scratch his head. Instead of acting like I'm a plague carrier, which he did before, he actually leans into it a bit. "You're an expensive cat."

He purrs, probably saying, *I'm not cheap or easy.*

I brush his hair, then give him a catnip toy out of a tightly sealed bag. "Make sure Bobbi doesn't see this. It's a secret between you and me —cat to man," I tell him as he pounces on the mouse-shaped toy, tail raised high.

While he's busy dominating his new toy, showing it who's the boss, I wash the plate, dry it and put it away. Bobbi doesn't need to know I've been feeding her cat behind her back or that I'm slowly winning him over. I'd bet my Bugatti that if she found out what I'm up to, she'd poison that innocent kitty mind against me.

My work completed, I head downtown to Manny's Tacos, arriving exactly at noon. The air inside one of the most popular Mexican restaurants in SoCal sizzles with grilled meat and veggies. Heated spices let off a pungent aroma, and everywhere I look cheese is melting.

The place is hopping with the lunch crowd, but I head straight to the private party room I've reserved. I had to bribe Lucie and Aspen with all the margaritas they could drink to get them to see me on such short notice, but this is an emergency.

Although Eugene Hae is an unlikely option, I'll be damned if I'm going to let Bobbi "manifest" some guy—*any* guy—and marry him.

Because when she spoke of marrying another guy and spending the rest of her life with him, my mind spun a montage movie of her life. Bobbi in a stunning wedding gown and veil. Her smile. The music. The vows she takes to accept another man into her life more intimately than before, while he pledges himself to her. And the fucker touching her...

That's about as far as my imagination went before it crashed and burned. I can't let her be with somebody else. I know that now. Mom was wrong when she told me to get Bobbi out of my system because she's bad for me. My mental state has suffered due to the fact that I don't have the woman I want most in my life. Most of my brothers have gone through the same thing when they had their crises with their ladies. It's just that they don't work in the same field I do.

Still, my situation with Bobbi isn't something I can discuss with my brothers. What do they know about how women's minds work? If they did, they would've never had any issues with their ladies. And they'd just take it as an opportunity to rag on me even more because that's just how we troll.

And I don't need that right now. I need a plan of action. And that means getting some female perspective—and not from my mother because there's some doubt as to whether she's actually human. But Lucie and Aspen...? They'll give me the straight scoop. And point out what about Sebastian and Grant's appeal made them give my brothers another chance after they'd dug themselves giant craters.

I head to the private room and open the door to a much bigger crowd than expected. Amy, Sierra and Molly are at the table along with Aspen and Lucie. I look at them blankly.

"Hey, my favorite brother!" Amy says with a cheery greeting. For a split-second I wonder if she has the day off, but she's in a business casual outfit—a cream-colored blouse and pale azure slacks. GrantEm never rests. Might be Sunday in SoCal, but a financial market somewhere in another time zone is humming.

"I invited them when you said you needed female help," Aspen says, pushing her bangs out of her face. Even seated, her amazing dancer's posture shows through.

"Cause in case you haven't noticed, we're all female." Sierra says, then takes a healthy swallow of her margarita. She's pretty with bright eyes that never fail to sparkle with good humor. You'd never know she's the CEO of a highly successful adult toy company from the cute baby-chick-yellow sundress she's wearing. "Have a seat."

"Um...thanks." I sit down and pour myself a margarita. Probably going to be necessary.

"Now what's this help you need?" Molly asks, all earnest. She's a gentle person, always eager to help. I should look into running her former boss down with an elephant. That would be hilarious and karmic.

"Okay. First off, it's a secret. So you can't tell anybody," I say.

"Not even Seb?" Lucie asks, blue eyes owlishly wide.

"Most especially not Seb. *Or any of my brothers*," I say, looking around the table. "Nobody, really. It's about my book, and you know how writers get about keeping their plots all secret." It's mostly true, so I'm not too upset about lying to my innocent sisters-in-law. The book is about my secret life with Bobbi. It's just that I keep getting stuck after the first scene. For some bizarre reason, my Muse makes Bobbi run into me while I'm about to snipe a target, and that is the wrong kind of future. She should never be where terrorists are.

"Why?" Amy asks.

"So nobody steals their good ideas."

"Seb said you still haven't finished your book."

"Of course he did." That asshole. And my brothers laughed at me over the now-deleted scene about riding zebras. It'd be fun to do, though. Bobbi would love to travel to Africa and see the wildlife and... stuff. "I'm getting there."

Our server interrupts, and I order the special without bothering to look at the menu. My sisters-in-law get platters to share.

Then we're private again. I munch on a salsa-laden chip for a little time to gather my thoughts. "Okay. So...my story is about a guy and a girl. And he sort of..." I start bringing them up to speed on what happened between me and Bobbi, changing several specific details.

Our server returns with more pitchers of margarita and food. Fast service is one of the reasons Manny's is so popular, but it's interfering with my story. Eventually, though, I get through it.

Sierra squints at me. "So... Not only did he forget to pick her up after the hospital stay—*and* see her after somebody tried to run her over—but he totally forgot to show up for her company opening, too?"

"He didn't exactly *forget*." I knew exactly when it was. And where. "But he had something else to do that was more pressing."

"Did his mother have a heart attack?" Lucie asks with a small frown.

"No." Mom doesn't have a heart. "His mother is healthier than most people in their twenties."

Amy looks up in the middle of dumping more guacamole over her shredded chicken and cheese. "So it wasn't life or death...?"

"Not for him." It was for the guy in the scope. But that isn't a detail they need. "More like a work-related obligation."

Molly shakes her head. "Please tell me this guy is *not* the main male character."

"What do you mean?"

"Your female lead deserves better."

Ugh. Molly is totally missing the point. "You're supposed to put yourself in the perspective of the man. And help him figure out a way to make it up to her so she'll forgive him."

"Oh." She smiles awkwardly then glances at Lucie, who is frowning. Aspen and Amy look like they're too shocked to speak. Sierra is still squinting.

Finally, Aspen clears her throat. "Why don't you just say it's about you?"

Uh-oh. "Because it isn't...?"

Lucie scoffs. "Noah, you're slick, but not that slick. You think you're the only one who's ever 'asked for a friend'?"

"Well, pssht, yeah, of course. Totally cliché." I laugh a little, glancing around the table. "But I'm asking for my *book*."

The women don't seem to be convinced. Looks are exchanged and some sort of silent consensus is reached.

"Grovel," Lucie says. "On your knees. Crawling in an expensive bespoke suit does the trick."

Amy asks, "Is that what Seb did to win you back?"

Lucie merely smiles.

"I don't know if that's going to work." Bobbi looked really upset when I dropped to one knee to propose. On the other hand, maybe it's the crawling that does the trick. Plus, I wasn't in a suit...

"Buying her a yacht is an option. Of course, you'll have to pay the taxes and other stuff, but..." Amy shrugs.

"Emmett bought you a *yacht*?" I haven't heard anything about that.

"No. But Gavin Lloyd did for his wife a while back. He also bought her a private jet, which was sort of wasted since she doesn't fly much."

"Money is nice, but you have to do more," Aspen says. "If the only thing she cared about was money, she would've gotten herself a sugar daddy a long time ago."

Molly nods. "Show her how much you appreciate her. Make sure she knows she's your Number One." She bites into a taco.

"Which means no missing big dates and anniversaries," Sierra says solemnly. "There are apps that keep track of things like that for you."

"Or you could get an assistant," Lucie suggests.

"Like Joey." Amy makes a face. "He *never* forgets a birthday. He sent

Monique a tennis racket with a gold-and-diamond edge trim. She can barely pick it up."

"I'm not getting myself a Joey. He'd repel her faster than crotch lice."

My sisters-in-law choke, then start laughing. Aspen's face is so red, it matches her hair perfectly.

Finally, they get over their laughing fit. Molly wipes tears from her eyes. "Just be yourself." She gives me an encouraging smile. "Share your secrets and let her really see the person deep inside. Once she does that, she'll fall in love with you."

I try to chew my burrito without choking. But there's no way I can follow Molly's well-meaning advice.

If Bobbi ever finds out I assassinated her father, any chance of her giving me a fair shot will be DOA.

19

BOBBI

SINCE DECIDING to be more serious about my manifestation, I've been getting up twenty minutes earlier than usual, while the sky's still dark. I close my eyes and sit crossed-legged on the floor of my bedroom, a pillow under my butt.

"Breathe in... Breathe out... Imagine yourself as the tide on a moonlit night..." The new meditation app has a soothing, hypnotic voice. I follow instructions, trying to settle my mind. Gotta shake off what happened on Saturday. Monday marks a brand-new week, which means a brand-new start.

You can do this. Visualize your future...

"Breathe in..."

I inhale slowly, trying for *tidal*, recalling how Noah sounded with his face buried in my neck. *His* breathing was labored. Desperate almost, as he worked his fingers inside me. And my breathing matched his, growing shallow, rough and strained.

Hot goosebumps break out over my back. I bite my lip.

"Breathe out..."

I try to expel the filthy imagery from my mind along with the air from my lungs. It doesn't work.

Noah's hot breath fanned my bare skin as he groaned at my climax, like he was the one coming.

Although I acted like what happened in that fancy bathroom didn't mean anything, I was shaken to my core by how easily my body succumbed to his touch. He's always known exactly where to caress, how to seduce me. I've been helpless against him, and he's used it to his fullest advantage.

I'm still not sure why he didn't finish the job. There was a moment before that weird woman showed up, dying to have his baby. In that mindless state I would've welcomed his cock. And he had to know that.

Liquid heat pools between my legs as I remember what he can do with his dick. I squirm. I'm not letting what could've been from Saturday derail my meditation. *I'm going to create the future I deserve.*

I curl my fingers around the ring hanging from my neck. There. That should help me center myself.

"Breathe in..."

Breathe in becomes begone. *Begone, Noah!* I focus on the words like they have an exorcistic power. My new mantra.

But no. As air fills my lungs, I get the craziest urge to huff it all out with a sexual shudder. My pussy clenches, like it's looking for the fingers that aren't there anymore.

Damn it, I'm too fucking wet for this! I scream soundlessly, frustrated beyond belief that I'm too turned on to meditate. I open my eyes, stop the app and clench my fists *hard*. Why? *Why?* All I'm trying to do is meditate, get rid of the toxicity in my mind and focus on the future I want.

So what if he can make me come? Why am I letting him affect me like this?

"So what"? It was the best damn orgasm you've had in the last year. And he was only using his fingers.

Argh! It's Noah's fault my peaceful existence has been disrupted. The day he reappeared, Lorcan decided to break into my house. And then because Noah put his face over my perfect vision board husband, I somehow ended up with Mr. Sweet Potato Hair, a.k.a. Joey the Fake Profile Photo because the universe and I got our wires crossed. Now Noah's a mind-worm I can't get rid of.

It's Monday morning for God's sake. I don't need to be horny! Especially over a guy who has a woman panting after him for babies. He acted like he had no idea who she was and was repulsed. But I'm too jaded now to buy that act. For all I know, if I threw myself at him like that he might shove me away, too. He just wants the thrill of the chase. And then, if he actually gets me, he'll ghost me. Again. That's his MO.

Plus, that woman was everything I'm not. She's shorter, with the kind of archetypical feminine curves around her huge breasts and flaring pelvis I'm never going to have. She has a small pixie-like face with a slightly pointy chin, and an overly lush mouth. She could be more his type, as long as she doesn't turn clingy. Bet he was too busy with her to come to the bakery opening. The thought is both infuriating and painful. I wasted my love on a man who doesn't deserve it, and even knowing the kind of person he is, I let him finger me.

I head to the bathroom to grab a quick shower. Meditation obviously isn't happening today. I resist the urge to touch myself because if I do, I'll be thinking of what happened on Saturday, and I'll be damned if I masturbate to that finger-fuck with Noah.

No! I'm going to shower like a good girl, dress like a boss, and get through the day like a goddess entrepreneur. Because that's who I've decided to be.

I put on a black sleeveless top and black jeans, and make sure to place Band-Aids over the hickeys Noah left on my neck. Just pulling my hair forward won't keep them hidden. I was so embarrassed when I saw them after I came home because Eugene must've noticed. But he didn't mention it, like the gentleman that he is. He carried on with our conversation like Noah's interruption never happened.

You know what? I'm going to manifest a guy who's better in bed than Noah. Who can make me come by just sucking on my breasts—

Of course... Noah has done that a few times...

Okay, STOP! Oh my God. I'm never going to manifest a proper sex-machine husband if I keep thinking about Noah!

I head to Bobbi's Sweet Things. Despite the less-than-ideal start to my Monday, everything comes out of the oven a delicious golden brown, and the bakery is soon replete with the comforting, mouth-watering scent of freshly baked goodies.

Mmm. Perfect.

Victor arrives, and we have a quick breakfast. The regulars begin to show up, and they snap up the still-warm croissants and Danishes along with the basic complimentary coffee we give out in the morning to any paying customer.

After the morning rush is over, I relax a little. Maybe the day isn't totally lost after all. "That went pretty well," I say.

"Yeah." Victor smiles. "I can't believe Amy bought two boxes of croissants for the office."

I grin. "Seven thirty sharp, just like always." She works in VC, but a lot of others from her firm come over to grab stuff around lunch time. "Those finance people... They love their carbs."

A young blonde in a UCLA T-shirt walks in, smiling shyly. She comes here for Victor, so I let him help her. It'll be cool if he finds love with somebody sweet who's his age.

Then the door chimes again and TJ walks in, clad in a black suit that barely fits him. I swear, if he has to take a swing at someone those shoulder seams are going to rip right out. He needs to quit buying suits off the rack, but he's a cheapskate when it comes to clothes.

"Hey you," I say.

He gives me a good squeeze, that lets me know he's got my back. "Looking good. Smells like sugar in here."

"Well, this *is* a bakery."

"That must be it." He pulls back, then frowns. "What happened to your neck?"

"Oh, that? Just...a couple of mosquito bites." Not telling TJ what happened with Noah on Saturday. Way too embarrassing and nothing good would come of it. Those meaty paws of his are murder weapons.

"Well, that sucks."

"Uh-huh. Literally."

"Gotta be careful. Those fuckers carry all sorts of diseases."

"I know," I say quickly before he lists all the horrible medical conditions I could develop. TJ is slightly hypochondriac, and he often looks up diseases on Google, supposedly for "reference." He hasn't realized yet that according to Google, even a sneeze can be fatal. I gesture at the gorgeous cupcakes, Danishes and croissants. "Want something?"

"Don't guess there's any apple pie...?"

"You know I don't make those here." I used to, but they weren't that profitable. My customers prefer cupcakes and muffins.

He heaves a sigh, but the twinkle in his eyes betrays him. "Fine. I'll take blueberry and chocolate cupcakes, four each. And five croissants."

I put the cupcakes in a box so the butter cream frosting remains intact, but place the croissants in a big paper bag.

"You sure you don't need help with those tiles?" TJ says.

"Maybe I already finished the job."

"Nah. You've been too busy. Ivy told me you stopped by their house, then went ring shopping and had dinner with Eugene. When would you have the time to rip out your kitchen floor?"

"You just want free apple pie."

"Obviously," he says shamelessly.

I smile. "Even if I needed your help, you'd have to wait. The tiles I ordered are taking forever."

"What's up with that?"

"Who knows? The store said the supplier is late with their shipment, so..." I shrug.

"Want me to look into it for you?"

"So you can use Tony's connections and take all the credit?"

"Hey, I'll get you those tiles. You just bake that pie."

"Ha! I might if you promise to make buffalo wings with your secret sauce this weekend." I'm heading to his place to hang out with him, his girlfriend Cassie and Josie.

"I can do even better. I'll have that raspberry beer you like so much, too. That deserves..." He pretends to add something up in the air. "At least two pies." He gives me a hopeful look.

I slap his shoulder, laughing. "Fine, fine. I'll bring plenty of everything because otherwise us ladies won't get any. And Buster can have some, too." TJ's golden retriever has never met someone he couldn't fall in love with, except when TJ orders him to attack. I don't know how my cousin managed to turn him into an attack golden retriever, but apparently he has his own methods.

"You're gonna make him too fat and lazy to bite bad guys in the ass."

"Don't be jealous just because he loves me more than you." In my peripheral vision, I notice a customer leave and a new one come in.

"Can I help you?" Victor says.

"I'm here for my fiancée."

Annoyance tugs my eyebrows together as I turn. I didn't want to deal with Noah right now, and most especially not in front of TJ. My cousin has never met Noah before, and I'd prefer to have kept it that way. An overprotective TJ is an overbearing TJ.

My cousin's jaw drops. "You've got engaged *and didn't tell me?*"

"No, of course not. He doesn't speak English natively, so he confuses fiancée with..." I try to think of some plausible word since "enemy" will only start a scene with TJ.

"The love of his life?" Noah says, unhelpful as usual. "His future wife?"

TJ looks even more confused.

"Baker," I say with a fake smile, then turn to Noah. "What are you doing here? Where's your Rim-Me blow-up doll?"

My cousin makes a choking sound.

Noah's expression remains sweet, his eyes shining as he looks at me. He must've taken some acting lessons in the last several months. "Bobbi, Rammi was an unfortunate misunderstanding. Really."

"Is that what you call the future mother of your children?" My voice is sweeter and smoother than the butter cream on TJ's cupcakes. Thankfully my cousin doesn't try to stick himself between me and Noah. He tends to stay out of the way if he doesn't understand the situation, unless there's an imminent threat of violence.

"She most definitely isn't pregnant," Noah says. "At least, not by me. Anyway, I was in the neighborhood and wanted to check up on *my fiancée* and get a croissant. Which you have." He gestures at the single one left.

I turn to TJ with a smile, this time genuine. "Since you've been such a great customer, I'm throwing this croissant in. Enjoy."

His dark eyes slide between me, Noah, then back. He shrugs his massive shoulders. "Yeah, sure. Thanks."

Noah languidly watches me put the last croissant into TJ's bag. He isn't upset about it. What's going through that mind of his? "I'll pay you a grand for that croissant," he says to TJ.

"Uh..."

"I'll trade you five apple pies for it," I say.

TJ shoves his meaty hand into the bag and gives me the croissant back.

As I take the flaky pastry, I let my fingers go limp. The poor thing falls with a plop on the floor. "Oops."

"You still owe me five pies," TJ says quickly, clear on what's important.

At the same, Noah says, "Three-second rule!"

"Of course," I say to TJ as I take a step forward and stomp on the croissant. Then I slide my foot around, smearing the croissant over about five square feet of floor. "Oh, darn. I slipped."

Noah looks at me like I stomped on his heart. "Cruel. Very cruel. You didn't have to do that, Bobbi."

"Actually, I did." It's all I can do not to throw Rammi in Noah's face. The only reason I don't is that I don't want him to know I still have unresolved feelings about him. That'd be too humiliating.

TJ's brow has begun to knit with suspicion. "Is this guy bothering you?" He shifts his body so he's partially shielding me from Noah, which is completely unnecessary. The only thing Noah has done is break my heart over and over again, and there's nothing TJ can do to protect that particular bit of my anatomy.

"Nope. And he's going to leave now, *before I call the police*. Noah?" I say, indicating the door. But the second the name slips from my mouth, I wince. Shit. Now TJ knows who it is.

TJ scowls at Noah like he's a rat he'd love to trample on. I shake my head at him—an incident at the bakery would *not* be good for business. Still, his nostrils flare and hot air puffs out, like an angry bull. His eyes rake Noah up and down, then he tilts his head like whatever he's seeing doesn't compute.

"Is this the loser you've been wasting your life over?" he demands.

"It's called having feelings for someone," Noah says. "And I care about her, too."

The added part cuts me, and I try to keep my expression calm. How easy it is for him to say what he doesn't mean, and how irritating is it that I'm so affected by it. "TJ..." I lace my voice with a warning. No way am I letting my cousin get into a discussion about how much Noah managed to hurt me. I have my pride. "You want those apple pies or not?"

"Fine." He whips around and sticks a finger in Noah's face. "You hurt her, I'll fucking kill you. Slowly." He stalks out without waiting for a response, the baked goods clutched in his hands.

"Did he pay for that?" Noah asks, like it's the most unfair thing in the world.

"Doesn't need to. Unlike you, he's special."

"I understand. Some of us have special needs. You going to marry him?"

I can't help smirking. Wait until I tell my cousins this weekend. We'll have a good laugh over our chicken wings and apple pies. "What's it to you?"

"He can't give you the kind of life you want."

"Oh, really? You just real sure about that? He's been here for me more than you. He was here when the bakery opened. And in case you're wondering, he also came to get me from the hospital when you couldn't bother to show up."

Guilt fleets over his gorgeous face, soon replaced by determination. "A man who can be controlled with an apple pie isn't somebody you want as a life partner."

"Don't worry. He only reacts like that to *my* apple pie, not just any pie." I give him a thin smile. "Unlike some people." *Unlike you.*

"I've been faithful to you."

I laugh. "Right. I'm supposed to believe you haven't had sex in a year."

"That's right." His response is immediate and firm.

"And Rim-Me is...what?"

"Nothing. I'm telling you, she really was a misunderstanding. Some hired hooker or whatever."

"Uh-huh. Look, stop with the lies." If he hadn't had any in a year, he wouldn't have let me go like that at the steakhouse. Rammi or no

Rammi, he would've screwed me until we both turned into puddles of goo. He was always insatiable in bed.

"It's not a lie, Bobbi."

"I'm supposed to believe you can't bother to keep your promises, but you've remained 'faithful' to me for over a year?"

"Yes."

I snort. "Well, I haven't." It's sort of untrue. I've gone on a few dates, but I haven't had sex with anyone else since I met Noah. There's no way I'm admitting that to him, though. It'd only encourage him.

He shakes his head with a small laugh. "Don't lie to me. I know you, Bobbi."

His confidence irritates me although I'll be damned if I let him know he hit the mark. "Think what you want. Like I said, you aren't part of my manifested future."

"That's too bad, because you are part of mine. So what happens when two people are manifesting two conflicting visions?"

"You quit." I point my finger at him. "Or you forget about me. You're good at that."

"Or whoever manifests harder wins."

"Listen, I've been working on my future a lot longer than you. You butting in uninvited because you suddenly can't stand the idea of not having ready access to me every time you're bored isn't going to make a particle of difference."

Noah looks at me like I stuck a knife in his gut. "I'm not doing this out of boredom. I told you I love you."

It requires a lot of control to hide the pain his empty confession of love brings. But it doesn't matter how outwardly sincere he seems. There's always something he loves more than me, and I want to be first on my future husband's priority list. "Well, here's the thing, Noah. I don't believe you."

"You say that now, but I'll convince you."

He looks at me with an unbelievable amount of earnest confidence, like he's certain he can make me see things his way.

"You know that guy who just walked out? He can shoot straighter than you. He's been here for me more than you. *Much* more. I don't want to hit a big milestone that I've worked hard to achieve, and then feel disappointed because you didn't show up to celebrate with me." Finally, the bravado leaches from his expression. But instead of bringing me vindication and satisfaction that I scored a point, it makes me a little sad and more determined than ever to insulate myself from the effect he has on me. "You not showing up for the opening here was the last straw. I have no reason to stay in a relationship where I'm just your..." I can't think of anything appropriate. "...emotional punching bag."

"Bobbi, I'm sorry." His voice is solemn.

The apology carries a gravitas that I didn't think he was capable of. The air in my lungs goes still even as something in my heart stirs. *He means it.* Part of me wants to give him a chance. But I just can't convince myself that he's capable of changing. "I'll accept your apology if you'll stay away."

"No deal."

"What?"

"I'm not staying away, Bobbi."

20

BOBBI

THE FRESH HEAVY CREAM CHURNS, mixing with the sugar and a dash of vanilla, getting the consistency I need before I can start decorating the cake. I introduced Josie to Japanese-style nama cream frosting, and she immediately became obsessed. Since I'm taking five apple pies for TJ, who will likely not share even one, I'm baking a cake for Josie and Cassie.

Nama cream is my favorite to work with because it's easy to decorate with and tastes fantastic. Luxuriously rich without being overly sugary. I'm also loving it that more and more people I introduce it to agree with my assessment. But there is a downside: using it tends to trigger memories of Mexico.

I run the electric whisk to beat the cream. I added a bit of yellow food coloring, and the shade is just right—bright and cheery without looking radioactive. The choice between nama cream frosting and fondant was hard, but in the end, the former won out. Noah will like it better anyway. He's apparently never had nama cream frosting before, and I want him to taste it on his birthday, even if it's going to be more difficult than fondant for the particular cake design I have in mind.

The already cooled cake is sitting on the rack. I take two round sheets, then cut them into the right shapes. I put plenty of cream on top of one, then lay the other on top. Now it looks right. I want to make a cake with the theme of a guy getting kissed by his girlfriend. There isn't enough time to get super fancy, so I'm keeping it simple, making both of them look like round yellow emojis.

Dark frosting out of a piping bag becomes the male emoji's hair, the shade an exact match for Noah's. And I do the same for the female emoji with golden frosting. Molded chocolate pieces for the eyes and mouths...voilà!

It was amazing luck that the Airbnb I rented has a fully stocked and generously sized kitchen. And even though it's on the Pacific coast of Mexico, all I had to do was hit the local grocery store for the ingredients. Excitement and anticipation swell like balloons in my heart. Noah doesn't know I'm planning to do anything special for his birthday. Hopefully, he'll like what I'm making. I've baked for him before, but never a cake.

He'll probably love it. He's one of the most rewarding people to cook for. His appreciation is instant and honest. A blinding smile splits his gorgeous face and his eyes sparkle. Then he looks at me like I've given him the greatest gift possible.

It's such a shocking yet lovely contrast—I used to bake for Dad, too, but his reaction was a grunty nod while his eyes stayed glued to whatever document he happened to be reviewing for work. He'd eat mechanically, but his expression always remained flat. I might as well have given him yellowed boiled brussels sprouts.

I put the finished cake into a box and drive to the beachfront cottage Noah got for his vacation here. It's only ten minutes from my rental, and he invited me to stay there, rather than splitting my time between mine and his. He doesn't know the reason I was at my place was the kitchen. His is cramped. Plus, I want this to be a complete surprise.

"Hey," I say as I walk inside with the box. The windows are open, gauzy curtains swirling in the briny breeze as the ceiling fans spin lazily. The sound of waves slapping the white sand fills the house. "Noah? Hello?"

I put the cake on the glass-top dining table and head to the deck to check if he's on the beach. He loves to swim and laze around on the sand to "work on his tan." Funny since he's already sun-bronzed. I'm the one who could use some extra pigmentation.

A soft groan comes from the deck. "Fuck..."

I head toward the sound. Noah is on one of the cushy deck loungers in nothing but swim trunks and sunglasses, showing off ridged abs and his surprisingly thick chest. His eyebrows are pinched together, forming a deep triple furrow. Sweat beads around his hairline, and his long fingers twitch. Despite the warm, slightly humid air, his complexion is slightly chalky. He murmurs something and jerks once, violently.

"Noah? Noah. Hey, it's okay." My voice is gentle, but loud enough that he can hear me over the surf. "It's just a dream." I put a hand on his shoulder, keeping the touch light and soft, so he doesn't feel threatened as he pulls himself out of the nightmare.

He jackknifes up and swivels to sit sideways on the lounger. A hand snakes around my wrist and squeezes hard for a second before he lets go. He yanks his sunglasses off his face and blinks up at me. Three heartbeats pass before he opens his mouth. "Bobbi..."

"Wakey, wakey, pretty boy." I smile, looking down at him and pretending the grip on my wrist didn't hurt. He didn't know what he was doing in his sleep, and there's no reason to make a big deal out of it.

He exhales softly, his shoulders sagging as he pulls me down to him. "Wow." His arms wrap around me, his heart thundering against my chest. "Thank God."

"Bad dream?" I run my fingers through his hair, trying to soothe him.

"Yeah. It was... I was stuck in a dark tunnel and couldn't find my way out. It was so weird because I knew it was a dream, but..."

Shock pokes a cold finger into my chest, and sympathy immediately fills my heart. I have a similar kind of nightmare, and it can leave me disoriented for a few moments after I wake up, especially if it's still dark. "I sometimes have the same dream. If it's a lucid one and I can tell I'm in a dream, I just breathe deeply a few times and remember to put my hand on the wall and follow it. I eventually hit the end, and the dream ends. Try it next time and see if it works."

"Or I can just hear your voice to end the nightmare." He seems almost fervent. Another effect of just waking up.

I laugh softly. "That, too." I stroke the back of his neck, which is very tight. "Happy birthday."

He pulls back. "Huh?"

"Happy birthday, Noah." I smile, then kiss his cheek.

"You remembered..."

He sounds really surprised, which is odd. He's wealthy and extroverted.

Doesn't he have a lot of people to celebrate his birthday? Make a big deal about it, even if he doesn't want to?

Or maybe he just has shitty friends and family. You never know the pain people carry inside. "Of course. It's an important date. And I got something for you. Come see!"

I tug at his hand, taking him inside where I pull the cover off the box. He looks down at my cute, delicious creation while I hover, waiting for his reaction.

Something jagged and complicated fleets through his eyes. Small goosebumps cover my arms...probably his mood after the nightmare is affecting me. Although we've only known each other for a couple of weeks, our moods are unbelievably in synch. It'd be scary if it weren't so exhilarating. I've never experienced anything like it—as though our hearts are tied to each other with a string that vibrates and communicates how we're feeling.

"This is the best gift I've ever received."

My belly flutters. "Seriously?"

He gazes at me. "Very seriously. Nobody has ever made me feel glad I was born."

The air in my lungs seems to vanish. I never thought I could mean this much to someone. But when Noah's looking at me like this, it's like I was born to be the center of his universe.

"I know our time is limited, and...we initially agreed to a vacation fling," *Noah says.* "But we don't have to limit ourselves, do we?" *His earnest eyes peer into mine.* "I want more time with you, Bobbi."

"Me too...but I don't know about a long-distance relationship." *I want somebody local, somebody I can see regularly and potentially build a life with. I can't just move from SoCal—I have friends and family there. And I don't feel right asking Noah to make the sacrifice, especially when our relationship's so new that he might be too wrapped up in emotion to think straight. When he's back into real life and going through the everyday grind, things might change.*

"Not an issue. I'll move to wherever you are." *His hand wraps around mine, squeezes with determination and need—and maybe even a bit of desperation and longing.*

It was the last two things and the fact that I was falling for him that had me nodding before I realized what I was doing. If I'd known our problem wouldn't be physical distance but him not giving a damn, I would've never agreed to see him after our time in Mexico ended. Nor would I have been so happy that he turned out to live here in L.A.

I shake off the bittersweet memories as I place white and dark chocolate shavings on top of the white frosting the way Josie likes. I'm done being nice to people who don't appreciate me.

Okay, no more thinking about Noah. I need to start picturing the perfect man, the one I want by my side. I pull the ring from around my neck and look at the sparkling blue stone as I conjure up the kind of man I'd love to have. Somebody reliable. Kind. Honorable.

Someone I can invite to hang out with my cousins. Hell, someone I can show to all my friends and know he can be part of my life for good.

Señor Mittens sniffs past the food I laid out for him. I study his fur, which is even glossier than before. He's definitely gained a bit of weight, too. Maybe he's just gotten bored with the food I bought because it's the same thing I've been feeding him forever. Is he hunting for little critters like he used to when he was a stray? He hasn't done that since I took him in, but maybe that's his way of varying his food options. I make a mental note to try a different brand of cat food on my way back from TJ's.

"Be good." I shake a finger at Señor Mittens, who spreads out like a fat, cat-shaped rug on the floor. "No more hunting for food. You aren't a stray anymore."

A huge feline yawn.

"I'm responsible for you," I remind him.

His tail twitches.

"I don't want you to get into trouble and lose another toe."

He gives me a reproachful look. You think I'm still the same silly cat who lost his toe?

"Yes."

He stretches and closes his eyes for a nap. Or maybe he's just decided to ignore me. I carry the boxes of baked goods out to my truck.

"Hey there," comes a friendly voice as I shut the truck door.

I turn around and see a tall man in a tank-top and cargo pants standing a few steps away. Despite his lanky frame, his muscles are wiry, veins standing out on his forearms. He has friendly green eyes, and he'd be handsome if it weren't for the terrible burn scars on his face. I maintain steady eye contact to avoid staring at the marred skin.

"Trey Underhill. I just moved in." He indicates the house next to mine that used to belong to Mr. and Mrs. Park, who lived there since forever. I was wondering who they sold it to when they packed all their belongings into a large U-Haul last month. He extends a hand. The back of it is scarred, like his face, but he has a good grip. Strong and dry.

"Bobbi Bright."

"I was hoping to say hello a little earlier, but you seem really busy."

"I own a bakery, so I'm always up and out early."

He nods. "Got a cat, too, right? He sometimes comes by." Trey's voice grows affectionate.

Very odd. Señor Mittens doesn't like to leave the house unless he has to, and he doesn't like to hang out with neighbors. But maybe this man is the source of treats for Señor Mittens, which might explain why he hasn't been eating as much as he should at home.

"He gets along pretty well with Nero. My cat," Trey adds. "Got him after my last tour in Afghanistan. My therapist said it would be good for me."

"Thank you for your service." Thank God I didn't do anything to make him self-conscious about his scars. The people who fight for our nation deserve respect and gratitude.

"So anyway, I started cooking before I realized I'm out of salt. Mind if I borrow some?"

"Yeah sure." I smile, then lead him to my place. He limps a little, dragging his right leg—probably another sign of the sacrifices he's made for the country.

Señor Mittens blinks with utter boredom when we walk in, then goes back to his nap. "Not the friendliest cat," I say, half-apologetic my pet isn't being sweeter to the man who's fed him.

"Probably just sleepy." Trey looks at him fondly, then glances down. "Interesting floor there."

I chuckle. "Yeah. I don't know what my parents were thinking. I'm going to replace the tiles soon."

"Need help?"

"No. I got it. My cousin also volunteered, so..."

Trey nods, running his fingertips along the edge of the kitchen counter. "Well, you look like you can take care of the job. But if you need an extra hand…"

"Appreciate the offer." I don't plan to impose on him, especially when he's limping.

"That couch looks nice and new." His tone is slightly abashed, like he's just realized he was critical of my kitchen floor.

I laugh to let him know it's all good. "I bought it like two years ago after I got this place from my father."

"What was wrong with the old one? Don't tell me it matched those tiles."

"Ha! No. It was just worn out. Plus, I didn't want to dwell on the past. Felt it was time to move on." Thinking about my dad is still uncomfortable, especially because we were sort of distant, and I sometimes struggle with the fact that I didn't grieve for him the way I should, like dutiful daughters do in movies and books. I put a cup of salt in a Ziploc and turn to Trey. "This enough?"

"More than." The corners of Trey's eyes crease, although his smile is constricted due to the scars. He holds the bag up as he limps out the front door. "'Preciate it."

I lock up, get in the truck and head to TJ's, which is a two-bedroom house almost halfway between my place and Josie's. The livable space isn't that big—maybe two thousand square feet and smaller than the place Dad left me. TJ bought it for the big yard for Buster, although since Cassie wants children, he'll have to get more living space at some point if he proposes. I'm pretty sure he will since she's the sweetest, and he's crazy about her. His mom adores her too, which means she's a great catch. Auntie Bella is an excellent judge of character.

I climb out of the truck with the boxes of dessert and into the mouth-watering aroma of chicken wings. TJ must've decided to spoil me and taken out his charcoal grill, rather than half-assing it by baking them in the oven.

I walk inside the house and call out, "The pies are here!"

Buster greets me, tail wagging and barking with excitement. I kick the door shut before he can escape—he can get overly enthused when a car drives by and will chase it like a T-bone steak dragged on a string.

But I shouldn't worry too much. After giving me a doggy smile of welcome, he rushes to the backyard where the grill is, hoping TJ will give him a piece of chicken.

"Hey, long time no see." Cassie comes out of the kitchen. A pretty brunette with friendly wide-set blue eyes, she has the nicest smile. She's tiny—around five-four, but compensates for her height with a buxom figure I envy. She's in a ribbed red tank top and faded denim shorts, long hair twisted into a knot at her neck. She takes the boxes from me.

"Oh my gosh, did TJ stop by your bakery?" Josie gives me a hug. She's the exact opposite of TJ—pale and petite with long straight black hair and smiling gray eyes. Her demeanor is open and inviting. I don't know how she doesn't get a billion stalkers. The men who have seen TJ generally stay away, but he can't be around her 24/7.

"A lot of people have stopped by."

"Oooh, including Reggie? She came by Mom's house to drop us invitations to her engagement party and wedding! Like we'd go." Josie snorts.

"I thought you might."

"I value my mental health too much. Mom isn't going either."

"Reggie wants me to make her an engagement party cake."

"I hope you shoved a rolling pin up her ass."

I chuckle softly. "That'd be cruel and unusual punishment...for my pin."

Josie and Cassie chortle.

"Hopefully, she'll be a decent mom," I say.

Cassie looks confused. "Mom...?"

"Oh my God, did she tell you she's pregnant?" Josie asks.

"Oh yeah. A couple of times. Made a point of rubbing it in," I say.

"She's sooooo not pregnant. She just gained weight."

"How do you know?" Cassie says.

"Because her mom told me. I don't know what the deal is, but every time she sees me, her verbal filter disappears. She thinks everything she tells me is confidential because I'm a therapist. She doesn't understand the rule only applies to my patients." Josie rolls her eyes.

And Reggie acted like she had something I never could. Shaking my

Still Mine

head, I gesture at the boxes Cassie has put down on the counter. "Think I brought enough?"

TJ's girlfriend shrugs. "Probably not. He can never get enough of your apple pies. If yours weren't so great, I think I'd be insulted."

"Why? Did you try to bake for him?" I ask with a laugh.

"Yes, and he was like, 'It's good, babe,' and had exactly one slice and put the rest away."

"Really?" TJ? Putting away uneaten pie? I can't put the two ideas together.

"Uh-huh. And when I said he could have more, he said he was 'saving it for later.' But then when you brought an apple pie over, he ate the whole thing in one sitting. When I asked him about it, he tried to claim it was because you always bring pies that are about to go bad."

Josie rolls her eyes. "He can't lie for shit."

"Yeah, but you want to be with a guy like that. Transparent is good." If Noah had been more honest, I would've been spared a lot of heartache.

"True, true."

"Who's lying?" TJ says, coming into the kitchen. His black T-shirt strains as he leans over and kisses Cassie.

"We were just saying you suck at lying," Josie says.

"I'm an honest man." He takes out an ice-cold bottle of raspberry beer from the fridge and hands it to me. "Plus, I make up for it by being good at sex."

I pop the beer open and take a good swallow right about the time Josie makes a barfing sound. Cassie just looks amused.

Buster joins us in the kitchen, nails clicking on the tiles and looking up at us like he hasn't been fed in a month. I scratch behind his ears, making him smile and wag his tail. Meanwhile, TJ reaches for the baked apples I brought. They're Buster's favorite, and I always make sure to bring some when I come visit.

"Here you go." TJ tosses one to the golden retriever. His eyes on the flying fruit, he jumps up to catch it, bumping the bottle on my hand. The beer spills all over my shirt, leaving a large reddish-brown stain in the center of the cream-colored fabric. Thankfully none of it gets on my shorts.

155

"Oh crap." Cassie grabs a fistful of paper towels and hands them to me. I try to wipe off the beer, but it's too late.

Buster is too busy with his apple to realize what he's done. TJ cringes.

"Eww. I'm going to smell like I'm drunk." I wrinkle my nose.

"Ah, geez. Okay, I got something you can borrow." TJ gestures at me to follow him. We go to his bedroom, and he rummages in the closet. "None of my shit's going to fit, but..."

"That's fine. Who am I impressing here?"

"Buster?"

I laugh.

He emerges with a black T-shirt. "Smallest one I have. I only wore it last night to work out."

"Uh-huh. That explains why it smells like Satan's ass-crack."

TJ snorts. I make a show of spraying the clothes with the eau de toilette Josie gave him last Christmas, then sniff. "Much better."

"Har har. I'll let you change."

"Thanks." He leaves, closing the door behind him, and I switch tops. TJ's XXL shirt fits like a tent, of course. It says:

Hatorade

Why You Drinkin' It?

This is his favorite. I grin as I come out.

"He loves you," Josie says, noticing the shirt.

"I love everyone," TJ says.

"Except the people who cross you."

"Obviously. They're assholes."

Cassie laughs. "I love how consistently bad-ass you are."

"It's called being protective. Now you can add that to the list of my amazing qualities."

"Protective and honest are important qualities," I agree. Protectiveness is what made me like Noah more than I should have. He jumped into the fray when three lowlifes tried to mug me in Mexico. Most guys would've just pulled out their phones to record the fight.

"Unlike that Noah guy," TJ says.

I give him a baleful look. "Really? You have to bring him up?"

"Noah?" Cassie's eyes grow wide as she leans toward me eagerly. "Is this someone significant?"

"Tell me this is some other Noah," Josie says. She knows all about my history with Noah. I had drinks with her a few weeks after the bakery opened and shared more than I should have. But when she hangs on your every word and nods and makes sympathetic noises, you can't stop talking. The woman is a genius shrink.

"It's the same Noah," TJ clarifies.

"Wait, everyone knows about him but me?" Cassie says with a mock pout. "I feel left out."

I put a hand over my face. "Oh my God, this is embarrassing."

"What are *you* embarrassed about? He's the fucking disgrace!" TJ's always on my side, which makes me feel better. He thinks anybody who wrongs me is a disgrace. He can't stand Reggie for the same reason. Of course, she's just a bitch to begin with.

Josie starts in with an overview of my rather messed up relationship with Noah. Cassie gasps and nods in all the right places. She's almost as good as Josie. Must be from dealing with little kids all the time.

Meanwhile, TJ brings in the chicken wings and takes my pies and cake to the table. I bring out plates and utensils, blushing as Josie recounts my romantic missteps. Josie and Cassie bring drinks to the table, and we all finally sit down.

"And now he's back in her life," TJ says when Josie's finished telling the story.

Cassie's eyes widen. "What? No!"

Josie turns to me. "Are you dating him again?"

"No. You know me better than that." I grab a chicken wing and bite into it. The spicy sauce is perfect. I've begged TJ for the recipe, but he refuses. Says we can swap wings for pies.

"But he wants to?" Josie asks, reaching for the chicken.

"Well...yes. But that doesn't mean I will."

"Did he say why he didn't come to the bakery opening?" Cassie takes a sip of her lemonade.

"No. And I'm sure he won't. He didn't really explain himself when he didn't come to the hospital to pick me up after I got shot, either."

"That motherfucker." TJ bites into the biggest slice of an apple pie. He is a firm believer in "eat pie first."

"Did he at least apologize?" Josie asks.

"Not really. I mean, he said he was sorry, but then ruined it by saying he didn't want me to accept the apology if it meant never seeing me again. What the hell kind of contrition is that?"

"Shoulda shot him when you had the chance," TJ says.

Cassie blinks. "*Shot* him?"

"I thought he was an intruder when I saw him a few weeks ago."

"Perfect opportunity," TJ says, shrugging.

"I'm not shooting someone just because I don't like him! Besides, if I'd shot him, I'd have to see him even more because we'd be involved with the police and lawyers. Ugh. No, thank you."

TJ gazes off into the distance. "Depends on *where* you shot him..."

"You deserve better." Josie's voice is firm. "You deserve somebody who's going to be around, give you stability." She knows about my complicated feelings about my father and his absences. She's also aware that Mom was a bit hot and cold with me. She wasn't abusive or anything, but there were times she looked at me like she didn't recognize me. It never failed to make me uncomfortable, and recalling that now gives me that unsettled feeling again.

"I'll be fine," I say. "I mean, even Reggie seems to have found the love of her life. I can, too."

21

BOBBI

I have the empty cake and pie containers under one arm as I unlock the house after returning from TJ's place. All of a sudden, the hair on the back of my neck stands up, sending a chill down my spine. I stop and look around. It's late in the evening, and the streetlights are on, creating little halos of orange. Nobody's around. People are either in for the night or out partying and clubbing if that's the plan. Nothing seems amiss on the street; nobody's having people over.

Still, something feels off.

Weird. Am I just getting rusty after leaving the personal protection biz? My senses were always on alert during my years as a bodyguard. But I quit being so jumpy after I became a baker.

If this were a rougher neighborhood, I might assume I was about to get mugged. But it isn't.

Maybe it's talking about Noah and Reggie that's left me feeling unsettled. I turn the doorknob and step inside. The chilly sensation intensifies.

Somebody's in the house.

I put the boxes on the tall stand by the door where I drop my keys and mail. Whistling softly, I flip the light switch by the foyer, flooding the entryway with light.

"Señor Mittens, where are you?" My voice is casual as I start toward the kitchen to grab the Glock.

A brush of something warm against my bare arm. I react without thinking, twist and grab the intruder's shirt and use the momentum of my motion to throw him. A strong grip around my shirt—shit—and as his big body goes down, he pulls me down too, his leg swiping at my ankle.

I aim an elbow at his chest, ready to crack his sternum, but he blocks it as we land in a heap with me on top. I'm not a waif, so the impact should knock the air out of him, but it doesn't. We roll a bit and I end up on the living room floor on my back.

"What a welcome."

"Noah?" I scowl up at him. "You couldn't have just said 'Hi Bobbi?'"

"Yeah, but then we wouldn't be lying here together in your dimly lit living room."

"Ack." I struggle to get up but he won't let me. "What the hell are you doing here?"

"What the hell are *you* doing *in a man's shirt?*" He sniffs. "You smell like him too." His voice is low and seething with something dangerous.

Instead of backing off or explaining that the T-shirt belongs to my cousin, I laugh. "So? Nobody's stopping you from putting on a woman's blouse and smelling like her."

"Oh baby, the only woman I want to smell like is you." He rubs himself against me like a cat—that's the only way to describe how he's moving over me. "The only woman I want to taste is you."

"Shut up."

Desire flares in his eyes. Too late I remember what happened the last time I told him to shut up. His mouth swoops down and claims mine ruthlessly. There's no finesse or tenderness, just raw need and possessiveness as his tongue thrusts into my mouth like he's starving for me.

I shouldn't take anything he does at face value, but part of me starts to melt a little. His mouth feels so good. It's unfair how well he remembers what I like. The exact pressure I love, the teasing strokes I crave, and the dominating caresses I can't get enough of.

And the fact that I still crave him—and remembering that I've never felt the urge to sleep with another man after Noah—results in a surge of annoyance and embarrassment. I should never let him control me with sex. I deserve more.

I open my eyes, just a little, and see his face in the shadows. The long lashes over his high cheekbones, the heat of his body and the hardness of him nestled between my legs. If I had amnesia, I'd probably think he was my devoted husband and crazy about me. Maybe that's why I keep falling for his charms.

Well, no more.

I arch abruptly, shoving him off and bringing my knee up sharply so he can't continue to use his body to hold me down. It connects, but not the way I want; he grunts and rolls away.

He stares, eyes glazed with unfulfilled lust—which is rapidly dissipating. "Hey, watch the knee. I thought you wanted babies."

"Not yours." I sit up.

"You aren't having *his*." He points at my shirt.

"Really? Why not? You planning to get me pregnant and then not show up when my water breaks?" I loop my index finger around the chain and pull it from under the shirt, so Noah can see the blue diamond ring. "I deserve what this represents—a good, *reliable* man who doesn't lie to me. I deserve to be my husband's number one priority, to feel loved and respected. *Cherished*."

"Bobbi, I—"

"Do you remember the time I baked you a birthday cake and you said it made you feel glad you were born? In Mexico?"

"*You* made me feel glad I was born." His voice is rough with emotion. It begs me to lower the shield around my heart, but I won't.

"I want to be with a man who makes me feel glad *I* was born, Noah. I can't settle for anything less than that. My future shouldn't be less than that. I don't know why you're back in my life and what you're hoping to accomplish, but let's not..." I shrug, struggling to put my messy thoughts into words. "We can be friends."

"I don't want to be your friend, Bobbi. I want to be more."

"That's the divide between us. And I'm not negotiating."

A beat of silence. "You said you'd give me a chance if your cat liked me."

161

"So? It won't do you any good."

"We'll see about that. Yes or no?"

I stare at him and then sigh. "Yes. But it won't change anything." Señor Mittens is antihuman. And Noah doesn't have the patience to woo my cat.

"Here, kitty, kitty, kitty," he says, putting a hand out.

I laugh despite myself. "It isn't going to work."

"Just give him a minute."

I cross my arms. "Yeah sure. Take your time, but you need to go after an hour."

"Have a little faith," he says mildly. "Here, kitty! Oh, Señor Mittens~!"

I prop an elbow against the couch and rest my temple against my knuckles. Noah seems ridiculously confident as he holds his hand out. But then his self-assurance is one of the sexiest things about him. He must've never failed at anything, which is why he's so sure he can win my cat over—and me.

Personally, I need a vision board, meditation and a lot of friend-support to help shake off doubts and negative beliefs about myself, what I want and my success. The objects help remind me of what I deserve—what I should strive for.

Señor Mittens slowly emerges from the kitchen, looking bored. If he could speak, he'd say, *What lowly animal is calling my name?*

Still, the fact that he's come out at all is a miracle. I stare at Noah in shock. He might as well have parted the Red Sea.

He grins.

Okay, time to end this. "Señor Mittens," I say in my sweetest voice. "Come here, baby."

"Come here, kitty," says Noah. He makes a little kissy sound with his lips.

My cat gives me a glance, then trots over to Noah and rubs his head against his hand. Not only that, he *purrs*.

I gasp, sitting up straight. "Traitor!"

"Not a traitor. He just loves me."

"How?"

I stare at my cat, wondering if Noah somehow swapped him with a different animal. I reach over and pull him into my arms and check his paw. He's missing the toe. But even if he weren't, I'd know that disdainful expression and those slitted eyes when he's pleased. I hold him for a moment longer, then put him down and gaze at Noah, who's looking on with a lopsided grin.

"What have you done to my cat?"

22

NOAH

BOBBI LOOKS AT ME, half-horrified, half-mesmerized. If this were back in the late sixteen-hundreds, she would probably try to burn me at the stake.

"What have I done? Nothing." I grin. "I just happen to be a pussy whisperer."

A war erupts within her—the struggle not to giggle. She bites her lip but the corners twitch up. Then she has to break eye contact and look anywhere but me. Finally, she just gives in and lets it go, and her laughter rings through the house

No matter what happens, she doesn't lose her sense of humor. It's making me fall in love with her all over again.

I let her ride her hilarity out before saying, "So...my chance?"

"Fine," she says primly, although her lips are still twitching. "Unlike you, I'm a person of my word. But the second you bail on me—or lie to me, we're done."

I nod. "Understood. Now, take off that T-shirt."

"Why?" She sounds genuinely confused. Suddenly she narrows her eyes. "Are you trying to get me topless?"

"No, I'm trying to get you out of another man's shirt. You're mine, Bobbi. You don't wear another man's shirt or put on his scent."

Something that's half amusement and half dare fleets over her gorgeous face. "Well, as it happens I'm wearing both. Whatcha gonna do about—"

I close the distance and plunge my fingers into her hair, holding her tight, as I plunder her mouth. A low laugh rumbles in her chest, but it soon turns into a soft sigh when my tongue brushes hers and our breaths mingle. She tastes like sugar, spice and herself—something heady and beautiful I can't stay away from no matter what.

Her breathing roughens, and she clutches my shoulders. She's always been so responsive to my kiss, and I love the way she ravages my mouth, like she wants me as desperately as I do her and can't get enough.

I tug at her shirt, pull it upward. She lets me get rid of it. Then impatiently we seek each other's mouths again, fusing our lips. Her simple nude-colored bra encases her beautiful little breasts. I run my knuckles over the swell, feel goosebumps breaking out over her creamy skin.

As her skin heats, the scent of that male cologne hits me again. Fiery jealousy and possessiveness swell hard and fast, urging me to find the man who put his scent on her and blow his brains out. But murder isn't a good way to prove one's romantic commitment.

Instead, I unhook the bra and let it fall to the floor, then pick her up, determined to get her away from anything that smells like the other man. With a small yelp, she wraps her arms around my neck. I relish her solid weight as I carry her to the bedroom. The fact that she isn't a tiny waif is another reason I love her so much. She doesn't feel like she's going to break if I hold her too tight. And I plan to hold her very, very tightly.

I lay her on the bed. Only the street lights come in through the gap in the curtains.

She looks up at me, her eyes glittering in the duskiness. "Take off your shirt. I want to see you."

I pull it off in one swift motion. My persona may be lackadaisical, but I make sure to stay in shape. Sometimes it's the difference between surviving and dying, but the side-benefit is that my body looks damn good. I spread my arms so she can see better. The tight abs, the flaring lats and the thick pecs. "All yours, my light. Every square inch. I've been yours since the moment I laid eyes on you."

Her breathing hitches a little. "Then kiss me."

And I kiss her like the light of my life that she is—the only woman I ever valued more than my own existence. I coax her, tease her, stroking her tongue and brushing against the roof of her mouth, lick and suck on her pillowy lips. I run my fingers through the warm silk of her long hair, relish her soft sighs, the gentle way she kisses me back. It's like we're in Mexico again, lost in each other.

I cup her tits, run my thumbs over the tips. She twists, moaning as her nipples grow harder. Stroking them gently, I run my mouth all over her torso, determined to erase all trace of the other man with my kisses.

I don't know why she was in that shirt or why she smells like another guy, but I don't give a fuck. *She's here. In my arms. Mine.* Writhing under my body, panting for the pleasure I'm giving her.

"Noah... Please," she begs.

I thread my fingers through hers, then pull a nipple into my mouth. Her back arches, a choked cry caught in her throat. I start to suck, trapping the tip between my tongue and the roof of my mouth, and position myself between her legs. She tilts her head back, exposing her stunning neck. Feet flat on the mattress, she rocks against me, her hips lifting. Her stomach muscles tense, and she tightens her fingers linked with mine.

I hollow my cheeks and suck hard, rubbing my tongue against her impossibly pointed nipple. She twists, her head tossing left and right as she fights for air and rides the wave pushing her higher and higher.

Yes, baby, oh yes...

She screams, her whole body shaking and her legs wrapped around my waist. "Oh my God," she pants mindlessly. "My God."

I kiss her fluttery eyelids and cheek. "I'm here, Bobbi. Right here."

I hold her as she shudders her way down from the orgasmic peak. My dick is aching like crazy, desperate to be inside her, but I wouldn't miss this moment for the world, when she's soft and warm and slick with post-orgasmic sweat. Her defenses are gone, and she clings to me like I'm her sanctuary.

She seeks my mouth, the touch tender and sweet. I let her take the lead, working on her pants. As much as I love to have her come from getting her breasts sucked, I want to see her orgasm in other ways, too.

Her mouth still on mine, she lifts her hips to help, pulling off her shorts and panties at the same time. I cup her ass, feel the taut curve against my palm. She whimpers softly. I swear, every part of her body is an erogenous zone.

My hand drifts until my fingers touch her slick core. She's scorching hot, and I let out a low, satisfied laugh against her lips. I rub my finger against her clit, and her kiss grows more needy and demanding. Her pussy is flooded, and my blood is hot and thick, my cock desperate to get inside her.

I place pillows under her head and torso so she can see me better, then spread her thighs and keep them there by lodging my shoulders between them.

"My light, tell me who's making you feel so good." My eyes on her face, I run the flat of my tongue down her pink flesh, tasting salt and Bobbi.

She bites her lower lip, her fingers digging into my hair.

I tease her with my tongue, brushing the tip against her clit. Shudders run through her.

"You, Noah," she whispers breathlessly. "You."

"Do you want to come?"

"Yes."

"How?" I kiss her inner thighs. She's so wet, her slickness has dripped down there too. Her desire stokes my own need, but I rein it back hard, refusing to give up what little slippery control I have over myself.

"Lick me. Suck me. Fuck me. Do what you do best."

I laugh softly. She doesn't beg even when she's completely exposed and vulnerable. She commands, as though in her deepest conscience she knows I won't fail her.

My tongue runs over her hot, dripping core. I pull her clit into my mouth and suck hard. Her pelvis lifts from the bed as though touched by a live wire, and a choked cry shudders out of her. Her chest rises and falls and her breasts jiggle, the tips pointed skyward. Her mouth is parted as she sucks in air, and her hair is a beautiful mess around her shoulders and neck.

I bury my face in her, licking and sucking her sweetness. The tensing of her muscles and the sexy sounds she makes are the best reward. I could eat her pussy forever.

Her heels dig into my back as she flexes her legs. I move up slightly and devour her as I push two fingers into her slick pussy. She tightens around them instantly, tight and greedy. I move them hard, ruthlessly pushing her to her climax. She grips my hair, holds me tight, rocking against my face.

Oh yes.

I give her all that she wants. Her breathing grows impossibly shallow and fast. Her entire body starts to tremble as another orgasm rushes toward her, ready to break.

Her back arches. "Noah. Oh my God," she sobs out her bliss, her fingers clenching against my scalp. I give her another push, so she can fall into another climax.

She convulses again against my face and around my fingers, tasting even sweeter in her orgasm. I suck her even harder, thrusting three fingers inside her, filling her and stretching her, rubbing against the little bump in her pussy.

She doesn't get to come down from the high before she screams again. Her voice breaks as she whispers my name over and over again, while saying, "Please."

I kick off my shoes and shed my pants and underwear in a nanosecond. I'm so hard, I feel like my dick's going to break if I don't get inside her. I grab a condom from the box I brought and have in my pocket—boy scouts aren't the only ones who're prepared—and I sheathe myself fast.

Then, kissing her, I push inside, filling her still convulsing pussy.

She's so wet, so soft and so welcoming. A missing piece of my life and a homecoming rolled into one. I go slowly, fisting the sheets and trying not to embarrass myself by coming after only one thrust, but it's been so damn long.

She gasps, then brings her hands to my cheeks, cradling my face. When she does this, I could give her my soul and never miss it.

I shift my pelvis to the angle that gives her the most pleasure, then drive into her. We kiss, our tongues tangling in a carnal dance. She moves with me, deepening each thrust and driving me crazy. When she's greedy for me like this...

My control slips away.

An animalistic groan tears from my throat, and I push into her hard and fast, air sawing in and out of my lungs. The blood in my veins is so heated, I feel seared from the inside out.

"Yes, yes, yes," she urges.

Fuck. Her voice is an aphrodisiac I can't resist. I'm too close. Reaching between our bodies to rub the pad of my thumb against her clit, I plunder her. She spasms, her pussy gripping my dick hard. It pushes me over. My fingers dig into her ass as I shudder and empty myself.

Then I hold her like she's the greatest treasure in my life. Because she is.

23

BOBBI

I GROAN as muscles not generally used ache in protest of last night's vigorous sex. The gap between the curtains lets in the light, which looks like late morning. But then I needed the sleep.

Thank God it's Sunday.

Despite the soreness, I feel fantastic. I haven't had so many orgasms in one night in a long time—not since Noah ghosted me. And as much as I like my toys, they can't deliver the intensity and intimacy Noah can. It's ironic that the man who's disappeared on me more than anybody else also gives me the most intense emotional connection I've ever felt.

Feeling silly-happy, I roll face-down and slide my cheek along the sheet. It's a bit warm—so he hasn't been up for long—and it smells like him. A small voice warns me to be wary. After all, where's the proof he's changed? But at the same time, I promised to give him a chance. Doubting him wouldn't be fair. And constantly worrying about bad outcomes won't help the situation.

Still, that doesn't mean I'm going to ignore what he's done wrong. He needs to explain his behavior. Why didn't he show up? Why didn't he call? Why did he ghost me over and over again? He needs to offer some real answers if he's serious about wanting to be part of my life. We can't keep doing the same thing and expect a different result.

Noises come from the kitchen. Noah must be looking for food—maybe even nonexistent croissants—there. He might be entertaining Señor Mittens, too. I'm stunned my cat isn't here in bed with me, demanding to be petted and fussed over.

I stretch, then roll over and out of bed. Time to grab a quick shower and start the day. I walk into the master bathroom naked, then stare at myself in the mirror. What the...?

Hickeys cover my torso, like somebody carpet-bombed me with kisses. Noah was acting jealous, but I thought he got over it once we started to make out.

"Marking his territory. Mature. Very mature," I mutter, then laugh, a flush spreading over my face. Is it weird of me to be pleased that he was so possessive last night? It makes me feel like I matter—and that he cares. Even my own parents didn't care what happened to me as long as they never got a call from school.

I shower quickly and put on a red tank top with cotton boxer shorts, then follow the heavenly aroma of fresh coffee to the kitchen. Noah's in there, dressed only in shorts. The sunlight pouring in through the windows hits his body just right, showing off the incredible lines of his abs and shoulders that make my breath hitch. But the best part is his forearms. He practices martial arts—he didn't take me down with a quick judo move by just being pretty—and he has forearms that a top-level practitioner would envy. They're thick but so lean that every muscle and vein is visible. Most importantly, they're strong. When he grips you, it's nearly impossible to get away.

And right now, he's hanging on to me with everything he's got, in every way he can.

His back and shoulders are scored with scratch marks going every which way, which is a little embarrassing—I marked him up pretty well, too. Guess I lost control, but he drove me absolutely crazy. It was probably the best sex we've ever had.

Noah hands me a mugful of coffee. "Here. With a dash of sugar."

I raise my eyebrows and take a sip. "You remembered."

"Of course."

I sigh with appreciation as caffeine starts to seep into my veins. "You make the best coffee. I don't get it. It's the same machine, same beans and same water, but it tastes better when you do it."

"Because I make it with *lurve*."

I laugh.

But he continues, "It's the same way you bake better than me even though we use the same recipe, oven and ingredients."

"Because I bake it with love?"

"I believe you do." He flashes me a wide grin, the corners of his eyes crinkling.

This scene feels so blissfully ordinary, a normal vignette out of a regular couple's life. I've dreamed of having that with Noah, but it's a little weird to experience after having decided it would never happen. When I wanted it I couldn't have it, but after I gave up, thinking it wasn't in the cards for me... Now I get to live it. Why?

To hide my unsettled emotional state, I drop my gaze. Señor Mittens seems to have no such existential uncertainty as he tucks into his breakfast. "What's he eating?" I squint. "Are those *bugs* in his cream?"

Noah chokes back a laugh. "No, I wouldn't feed Señor Mittens bugs! Ew." He pulls out a bag of egg bagels from my pantry, the movement easy and familiar. He must've been busy reacquainting himself with my home while I was sleeping. "Want one?"

"Yes. But what *are* those black things?" They might not be bugs, but they definitely look iffy. I've never seen cat food that looks like that.

Noah cuts the bagels and dumps them into the toaster. "Fish eggs. Caviar, to be specific."

"You're feeding my cat *caviar*?"

"He already ate the filet mignon."

I gape. "You gave him filet mignon, too?"

He nods. "Caviar doesn't provide all the proper nutrients. You didn't know that?"

His tone says he's shocked I didn't know, but I'm too stunned to comment on that. "But *caviar*? *And* filet mignon?" Then it hits me, and my eyes narrow. "Just how long have you been feeding him?"

"As soon as it became clear how important he was going to be in my quest to get another chance, and I ramped my efforts up after you bought that ring. But don't worry. I've varied his diet—beef, tuna, wild salmon..." he says when he notices my expression. "I've been *very* conscientious about Señor Mittens's health and nutritional needs."

Oh my God. "So what have you been doing? Lurking around, luring him outside so you could feed him?"

"Uh, *no.* That would be weird and stalkerish. I just fed him here when you weren't home. Or, you know...were sleeping."

"I changed the locks!"

He gives me a look. "And? Come on. You know that no lock can keep me away when you're the only one I want."

There it is again. He constantly tells me I'm the only one, so I should be used to it. But every time he says it, my heart still leaps like it's the first time. "That explains why Señor Mittens refuses to touch my food." I try for a normal tone of voice, not wanting him to know just how deeply he's affecting me. We haven't established all the ground rules and expectations, and while the sex is fabulous, sex was never the reason our relationship faltered.

"Nothing beats a sashimi-grade ahi tuna steak topped with caviar." His light tone is a little forced. He's aware of my unease and is trying to keep the mood from growing too heavy.

"Seems like a lot of effort to go to."

"I also petted him, brushed his fur and bought him some toys. Well, the toys were secret, but I'm not sure how well he hid them from you."

"I never noticed because I was too worried about him not eating. I wondered why he wasn't as grumpy as he used to be."

Noah takes my hand in his and gently squeezes, linking our fingers. "You said you'd give me an opportunity if I could win your cat over. I would've done anything for a chance with you."

"You keep telling me that, and I'm not going to deny our chemistry is still amazing. But Noah, I need more than that to be sure it's going to work out between us."

"I know." He puts the toasted bagels on two plates and pulls out a tub of whipped cream cheese—my favorite. It's a new tub; he must've bought it earlier. "Let's eat and talk. More coffee?"

I nod and grab another cup of coffee. Noah heads to the storage closet in the living room. He must've hidden something there while I was out. So much for the *secure* lock.

I take a stool by the counter, spread cream cheese on a bagel and start eating. A few moments later Noah brings out a canvas and carries it sideways into the kitchen.

My eyebrows arch. "Are we having an art show?"

"I was going to show it to you yesterday, but then you decided to attack me."

"I thought you were a burglar!"

"I was going to say something, but then I realized you were with another man."

"I wasn't." I prop my elbow on the counter, then drop my chin in my hand. "And as much fun as it is to watch you get all jealous, it's pretty gross to hear you talk about my cousin like we have something going on."

He goes still for a moment before a gorgeous smile splits his face. "Thank you. I was going crazy inside."

"Just inside?" I look down at myself. "My torso looks like somebody decided to open up a hickey farm."

His index finger tips my chin up as he looks into my eyes. "When the only woman I've ever loved comes home like that... You should worry if I *don't* react."

My pulse picks up at the stark intensity of his tone. A deeply buried sense of self-preservation says I should put up my shields—and *fast*—because too much honesty will leave me exposed. At the same time, if I can't be honest with him, I can't expect him to reciprocate. It's scary as hell, but...

"I know," I say softly. "And...I liked it. It made me feel like I mattered to you."

"You matter. I was thinking about you when I made this." He starts to fuss with the canvas. It's a bit awkward to arrange it in my rather small kitchen. "Remember how I said I was manifesting my future with you? I don't know if that stuff really works, but I wanted to be specific in case it does. And I wanted to put some effort into it rather than cutting up magazine photos or something. That's boring."

"What I remember is you putting your face on my vision board," I say. "Don't tell me you printed out our faces and put them over pictures."

He shakes his head. "Oh, no. Better than that." He finally gets the angle of the canvas right and whips the cover off. "Behold! The vision *painting!*"

I steel myself not to say the first thing that pops into my head. It's not an abstract or post-modernistic piece like I was forced to endure when my former clients went to galleries full of super-weird art you must love if you want to be considered cool. But I'm not a hundred percent sure what it *is* either. It's an oil painting, that much is clear...but there are so many random objects on the canvas, and none of them are particularly well-drawn or to scale. A couple stands in the center with four strollers. The man has dark hair and is wearing a tux. The woman must be the bride with yellow-brown hair with specks of ivory mixed in. Her dress is long and white, the skirt huge and puffed out. But the man manages to stand next to her anyway—ditto for the overly large strollers that surround the two. White globs circle the couple. They are too big to be rocks. I squint at them. Maybe ghosts?

On their left is something that reminds me of *The Last Supper*, except there are seven men and seven women at the feast with little puppies— or kittens?—in colorful clothes crawling underneath the table. To the right of the couple is a house on a yellow cliff over pounding waves the color of fresh bruises.

And are those flying croissants, cupcakes and...a donut in the sky? They might be interesting interpretations of UFOs, except thematically they feel off because I just realized the thing that I thought was a glazed donut is actually a sapphire ring. It's just that the stone is so big, I thought it was a glob of unblended paint.

Not an unfair assessment, based on the artistic talent displayed.

"Did you commission it?" I ask, debating what it's supposed to represent. Or, if it's a present, where I'm supposed to hang the thing.

"Commission it? Baby, I *did* it." Noah beams. "So every aspect is *exactly* the way I envision things. This is actually my third try. The first two weren't that great."

"Oh. Well, third time's the charm, and all that." Now I'm morbidly curious what the first two were like. He looks at me expectantly, reminding me of Buster when he's done something he believes is particularly clever. I smile, doing my best to appear excited. "Wow. It's, um, amazing."

"Thank you." He laughs a little, the tips of his ears turning slightly red. A sheepish vulnerability tinges his smile, and I realize with unexpected tenderness that he knows his masterpiece is no da Vinci, but it was the best he could do.

I study the painting again. After the initial shock, it doesn't seem *that* bad. And most importantly, I appreciate the effort he put in.

"This way," he says, "everything that I'd like in our lives is properly represented. I was going to use color pencils, but that would have taken too long. Plus I didn't want to mix them with crayons. It's not a kindergarten art project."

"Definitely not. It's far too serious." I try not to giggle as I imagine the little toddler Noah working with crayons to draw something pretty for his mother. Or the teacher he had a baby crush on. "Why don't you explain what this picture is supposed to represent?"

He puts a hand on my shoulder and points. "Okay, so the couple in the center? That's us—married. Your wedding gown. All white and pretty."

"Where's the ring?" I tease a little since he was so adamant about buying me a suitable ring at Peery Diamonds.

"Over there." He points to the flying sapphire ring. "A blue diamond stone because you seem very partial to that."

I blink slowly. "That rock is totally not drawn to scale. It looks as big as my fist."

"Nah, just your thumbnail, maybe. You can find one that large, no problem. And I plan to get one so everyone knows you're mine, and how much I value you." He lifts my hand and kisses the back, his lips warm and firm. His eyes are on mine, shining with earnestness. Hope stirs, dancing in my heart like a little fairy under the moon. "Bobbi, I'll lay the world at your feet if you'll just give me a chance."

He is charming his way back into my heart, so effortlessly. But I'm not ready to fully accept him yet, not after what he's put me through.

I sniff. "Why are we surrounded by ghosts?"

"Ghosts? Where?"

"There." I point to the white blobs circling us and the strollers.

His jaw drops. "Those are calla lilies!"

"Calla lilies don't get as big as strollers."

"They're for our wedding." His cheeks are slightly flushed. "As for the size, put enough of them together and they'll make a sort of, you know...corsage that's that large."

Laughing, I lay my forehead on his shoulder. He's surprisingly cute and vulnerable. "What about the cupcakes and croissants?"

"Your career as a baker."

"I don't bake flying cupcakes."

"It's, like, allegorical. They represent soaring success." There's such a deep level of faith and humor in his tone.

I laugh again.

"I thought it looked better than having Bobbi's Sweet Things buried under a giant pile of money," he says. "I tried that, but it ended up looking like somebody moved your bakery to a pot farm."

I'm to the point of wiping tears from my eyes. "And that brooding gothic mansion?"

He frowns. "Gothic? Does it look gothic to you? That's the Malibu house."

I lean closer. "Your place is not on a cliff."

"That's *sand*."

I shake my head, then giggle. "It's a good thing you're independently wealthy."

"Agreed," he says sincerely, good humor sparkling in his gorgeous eyes. "I thought you might like living there better. It's on the beach, which, see, is represented by *that sand there*, and bigger. The kitchen's pretty impressive too."

"With a much prettier floor."

"That too." His expression softens. "But if your commute is too sucky, we can live here."

The offer is surprising. I know how amazing his house is. "You want to downgrade to here?"

"It's an upgrade if I get to be with you. Plus we could buy a house we like better. Or I can just buy you a helicopter and you can use that for the commute."

"And how am I supposed to pilot it and where am I supposed to land it?"

He waves a hand. "I can get you a pilot. The Malibu place doesn't have a helipad, but I can put one in, no problem. And the building your bakery is in has a big enough roof—enough to support a small helipad."

"Floyd—my landlord—is a dickhead."

"I'll make it worth his while."

I suddenly realize Noah is totally serious, even though I was half-teasing when he got too extravagant for my middle-class mindset. He's thought a lot of this through, put a lot of effort into visualizing what he'd like us to have together.

"But really, that's just details," he says. "What's important is that you and I will be together. That's why we're in the center, holding hands."

"With four kids...?" I glance at the strollers around the couple in the picture.

"Well, I thought you'd want more than one."

"But four?" I ask, surprised he painted the ideal number of children I had in mind.

"Thought it'd be a good upper limit, although we can have more if you want. I'm flexible."

The way he says "I'm flexible" makes me want to double-check. He shouldn't think only about what I want, not if he hopes to build a future together. It should be what *we* want. "Don't you have an idea of how many *you*'d like?"

"Nope. I'm not the one carrying them for nine months. I have more than enough money to support them financially, and it's about you being happy with the family we end up creating."

"What about your happiness?"

"Making you happy makes me happy." He tucks a wayward tendril behind my ear, his fingertips brushing my sensitive skin and sending warm shivers down my back.

"What if you do something that makes me unhappy?"

"I'll kick my own ass." The response is prompt and serious.

"I don't think you're that flexible."

"I'll work on it. Or you can ask Griffin. One of my brothers, who does kickboxing. His kicks hurt like hell. I'll be limping for days."

I snort, then laugh at his exaggerated expression of pain. "Did you guys fight a lot?" I ask, curious about his childhood. I realize that we've never really talked about our families. I wasn't in the mood to talk about mine since it hasn't been that long since Dad died, and I didn't want to dampen the mood, especially when I wasn't even that close to him. And since I wasn't going to talk about my family, I didn't feel comfortable probing about Noah's. I didn't even realize his father was Ted Lasker until Noah crashed that godawful "date" with Joey.

"Nah. I mean, we argue and give each other shit as much as any siblings. But we've been always tight since it's just us against the world." A fond smile crosses his face, then he must see something in my expression because he adds, "Our parents just aren't always around. And it turned out better that they mostly stayed out of our lives. We're happier on our own."

I nod. "I'm glad you have your brothers." I wonder if I would've been less distraught over the loss of my mother and father if I'd had siblings. Although I'm close to TJ and Josie, I felt so bereft when my parents died overseas.

Okay, time to reset my mood. Don't want to dwell on the past right now. I gesture at the final section of the canvas. "And *The Last Supper*?"

"*The Last Supper*?" Noah chortles, then tilts his head. "I guess it bears a passing resemblance... Does this mean my painting's almost as good as a da Vinci?"

"Well... If you cut this section out from the rest of the canvas..."

"Can't do that. It's part of the whole manifestation."

"With flying cupcakes and croissants. And a ring."

"Yes. But you'll notice there are no crème de la hairballs. Anyway, it's the brothers and the wives getting together," he explains.

"Do they have a lot of dogs?"

"Dogs?"

I point at the animals around their feet.

Mock horror crosses his face. He probably thinks I'm messing with him. "No! They're the *kids*. Can't you tell from the onesies?"

"I thought they were dressed up puppies."

Noah looks mildly insulted. "They don't look anything like dogs. See? No fur."

"You might've tried to *draw* fur and failed."

"No." His shoulders shake with mirth. "Oh man, just wait until I tell my brothers. They'll give me shit about it."

"So just don't tell them...?"

"Nah, it's fine. We always do it." He grows sober. "I haven't introduced you to them, but they're important to me, and I want you to like them. All of us can be together and make a bigger family unit that has each other's backs."

"That sounds amazing."

"Yeah. They're fantastic. And your family can be part of the picture, too. I just didn't know how to fit them in since I wasn't sure who you like and who you want to delete from your life. I can add people, though."

"I'm sure my cousins and aunt will appreciate that," I say with a small smile.

He points at a white dot near us and the stroller. "The cat is Señor Mittens."

I keep a straight face and nod. "How about a dog?" I ask, in case one of the wraithlike globs is a puppy Noah always wanted.

"Can't. That'd be cruel to Nicholas."

"Nicholas?"

"Another brother. He's allergic to cats and dogs. About once a month or so, the brothers go around and host boys-only brunches, while the women get together for their girls-only fun time. None of us have pets, so Nicholas can join us without any problem."

"Oh..." How will that work with Señor Mittens? He's part of my life and I can't imagine giving him up. But Noah's brother matters, too.

Noah says: "But Señor Mittens is an important part of the family, so I can host the brunch elsewhere when it's my turn. You shouldn't have to give anything up, Bobbi. I don't want you to, and none of my brothers would expect you to, either."

It's such a lovely vision that my wariness is starting to dissolve. But my logical side says he still hasn't explained why he hasn't been keeping his word to me. Unless I can be sure he won't do that again, I can't be certain that everything he's told me just now isn't just an empty promise, like before.

I consider what I'm about to say with care, so I don't come across as unappreciative or dismissive of his effort. Turning to him, I meet his eyes with a little smile and place my hand on his. "That's really nice and specific. Thank you for sharing. But I'm kind of having a problem trusting that it's really going to happen the way you've laid it out."

24

NOAH

Bobbi needs reassurance. But more than that, she needs me to explain why I let her down and how I plan to ensure it won't happen again. Although my past actions were motivated by a desire to keep her safe, they ended up hurting her deeply. I have to do better if I want more than just a chance, but for her to really accept me.

"I need your honesty, Noah," she says, "or I can't do this. I don't want to live feeling like I'm on a train that can derail at any moment."

No way to avoid fessing up. It was the one thing I wanted to get around, so I wouldn't have to lie by omission. A lot of what I've done is classified. But keeping it to myself will cost me Bobbi. And beyond that, it would hurt her, make her feel like she's being deliberately kept in the dark.

Share enough so she can understand, but not so much that it will get you in trouble for spreading state secrets.

I take a moment to gather my thoughts—and courage. Failure here will mean the end. There won't be any further chances given. But if I can convince her, she'll give me a fair shot. She's too honest not to.

"I think I was a little afraid. I didn't have the best family life or role models. My parents aren't married, and they're basically only interested in their careers. Although I shouldn't complain too much. Dad paid for me and my brothers, so we grew up with all the material comforts you could imagine. Private schools, expensive vacations, cars, clothes... You name it."

She runs a hand over my forearm. "That stuff isn't everything."

"I know. I've always been confident about providing for you, but I wasn't always confident I could give you the personal and emotional support that creates a real relationship." *I wasn't sure if you would be okay knowing that side of my life.* But most importantly, my long-ingrained belief to keep my professional life secret from everyone kept me from opening up. My work is very fucking dangerous, but also necessary to make the world a safer place. And the fewer people who know about it, the better it is for everyone. "So even when I made promises, I stayed away because I chickened out."

"But why? What could've been so bad? The worst thing that could've happened is that we'd break up. But then you leaving me behind and breaking promises led to the wrecking of our relationship anyway. We never had a chance." Her tone isn't accusatory, just clouded with confusion.

I inhale. Bobbi's skepticism is understandable. I'd feel the same if the situation were reversed. It's killing me that full honesty isn't an option, and I have to choose my words carefully. "I had this idea that when we were together, we'd have a lot of adventures together."

"Like going to Africa on photoshoots?"

"Yeah, like that. But then I saw some pictures of a guy I knew getting mauled by hyenas..." I blink, trying to keep the image of what happened to Mike Swain and his fiancée out of my head.

"I'm sorry." Her voice is soft, full of sympathy. She squeezes my hand, so I turn mine and thread our fingers together, the warmth from her palm driving out the chill settling along my spine.

"His fiancée was there, too. She didn't make it, either." That's the kindest way to put it. "And I kept seeing *us* in those photos, and it messed me up."

"Oh, Noah. It was just an accident. We wouldn't have been attacked like that. Besides, you know I can handle myself. You saw me in Mexico."

"I know, but these are animals." Fucking terrorists who consider raping women an enjoyable way to pass the time. They mutilated Swain's fiancée. My belly knots again. "I just couldn't stand the idea of anything happening to you."

Bobbi wraps her arm over my shoulder and neck, her hand resting on the back of my head. Her lips press against my forehead, offering comfort. I close my eyes and let it soak into me, soothe the frayed edges of my nerves. The men responsible are gone now, their heads blown apart thanks to my cheetahs. But their deaths couldn't undo what the couple had to suffer.

After a long moment, Bobbi asks softly, "So what changed?"

"I was on a plane after I shot some cheetahs on an assignment." True enough—my cheetahs fired off a lot of bullets. "The pilot had a fatal heart attack, and there was a problem with the engines." More like sabotage, but that's an irrelevant detail. "The plane crashed—"

Bobbi gasps. "Oh my God."

"—but I survived."

"Well, yeah, obviously. But were you okay?" she asks, looking me over and running her hands down my shoulders and arms.

"Pfft, sure, it was nothing." I love her concern for me, but there's no reason for her to be worried at this point. "Found a working parachute under the pilot's seat of all places."

"Thank God." Suddenly she drops her hands from my body and flushes a little, like she's just realized what she was doing. So I take her hands in each of mine and kiss their backs, one after another.

"But what fueled me on that plane was the thought of you. I had no regrets about my family, but you... I kept wishing we hadn't ended the way we did. That I'd been more courageous. I would've sold my soul to the devil if he'd guaranteed I'd get to see you again."

"Noah..."

"It's weird when you're about to die. What's really important and what's just bullshit—it all starts to crystalize." I give her a self-deprecating smile. "Took me a while, didn't it?"

"Yeah, it did," she says softly, but her beautiful caramel eyes brim with concern and care. "And now I understand where you're coming from a lot better." She looks away and takes a moment to think.

Time ticks by, anxiety pooling in my belly. Is she going to ask for proof of the crash? It wasn't reported anywhere—obviously—and I can't really share more than this.

She expels a breath, then lifts her chin and faces me squarely with the resolute expression she wears when she's come to a decision. It's sexy as hell, but at the same time, I know that whatever conclusion she's come to will be final. The muscles around my neck and shoulders grow taut.

"I will give you another chance, Noah."

"Thank you." *Thank God.*

"But I'm setting a limit. Three months. If I'm not convinced within that time that we can have a future that's right for us, I want you to accept it and leave me alone. As in *alone* alone. Permanently. Can you do that?"

"Yes." Based on the way she goes whole hog after what she wants, she sometimes appears reckless. But she's too smart to not leave herself an exit. And it's irrelevant what she wants if I'm unsuccessful. I don't plan to fail.

25

NOAH

—EMMETT: Hey, can we make our lunch a potluck?

I scratch the spot between Señor Mittens's ears, which earns me a soft purr, and mull over the group text that arrived early Wednesday morning. Just what is Emmett aiming for here?

The lunch he's referring to is this Saturday, with not only the brothers but their wives and children, so Bobbi can meet and—hopefully—approve of them. It's a major milestone in our relationship, especially since family is so important to her. I need to prove to her that mine isn't a total loss, which is why I'm not inviting Mom or Dad. But if Bobbi tastes something Emmett brings, that'll be the end of us. Not even a terrorist under interrogation deserves to be subjected to my brother's food.

—Sebastian: Depends. Are YOU going to cook?

—Emmett: I was thinking about it.

—Griffin: He's probably taken out life insurance on all of us.

Spoken like a true economist. But it's one of the more plausible explanations for Emmett's sudden desire to kill us.

—Emmett: Veerrry funny. No, Monique wants to try it.

Ah crap. He pulled the Monique card. Time to shut this down before my brothers start to picture our beautiful niece and cave.

—Me: I've already arranged for catering. Let's do potluck next time.

—Emmett: Shit.

—Grant: Why do you hate your daughter? She'll never forgive you if you make her eat your "cooking."

—Emmett: She had a playdate, and some girl bragged about having a potluck lunch. Now she really wants to try it.

May the lightning strike the kids who brag about potluck lunches. Why can't they brag about something more ordinary? Like how their daddy bought them a special edition Barbie or something?

—Me: It was probably a catered potluck anyway. Who cooks these days?

—Nicholas: Well, it might not be too terrible if we stick to things that require minimal cooking—or none at all. Like ham, cheese and crackers? Maybe caviar if we want to get fancy?

—Me: That's cat food.

—Sebastian: Cat food? Wait a minute! You feed Bobbi's cat caviar?

—Me: Well, not every day.

—Huxley: WHIPPED!

At least I don't have my family conspiring against me! I don't type it since that would invite some awkward questioning. I already made an effort to alert Huxley. If he failed to notice, it isn't my fault.

—Me: Don't be jealous her cat deserves better than you. I expect you to be on your best behavior this Saturday.

—Nicholas: Unlike you, we know how to woo a lady. We're married. You're barely a steady BF.

I make a face. I can't even give him shit because he never treated Molly wrong or screwed up.

—Me: Yeah, well, if you all manage to act civilized on Saturday, maybe on Sunday I'll BE engaged.

—Sebastian: So that's why you ordered a ring from Luce?

I raise my eyebrows. Can't decide if he's upset or just surprised. Probably a little bit of both. Every brother so far has used Sebastian Jewelry for their rings.

But that was before Lucie became family. Why shouldn't she get some love too?

—Me: Yeah. She has great sensibility. Love the Peery Diamonds designs.

—Sebastian: I can't decide if I should feel insulted.

He's too pussy whipped to be annoyed by my subtle dig. Heh. It's sort of cute, an adjective I never thought I'd associate with my asshole brother. He's so freaking competitive, he believes in torching the other team until there's nothing left. That attitude almost cost him his wife, but he hasn't changed. He just changed the direction of his focus—now whatever Lucie does is right.

—Me: Not meeting your quarterly financial goal?

—Sebastian: Ha! We're on target.

—Me: Good. Keep making me rich.

I own a lot of shares in Sebastian Jewelry. I'm also a major shareholder at Peery Diamonds.

—Me: Besides, buying from Peery Diamonds is like paying myself money. The more I buy, the more I get!

I don't need to be in the same room as Seb to know he's rolling his eyes.

—Nicholas: Does Bobbi really need a ring? I thought bakers don't wear jewelry on their hands.

—Emmett: Engagement necklace!

—Me: I'm doing it the usual way.

Bobbi is surprisingly traditional despite her independent attitude. Wants a loving, supportive husband, kids, the whole deal. And I want to indulge all her desires. If she decides she wants an engagement necklace too, I'll get her one.

—Me: Plus I want everyone to know she's mine. Men don't check out women's necks. They check the ring finger.

—Griffin: Perhaps. But the second step is checking YOU out, to evaluate the competition, before deciding whether or not they should poach.

I snort. *Competition?* Whatever. I'm confident I can make Bobbi happy. All I have to do is convince her over the next three months.

Speaking of which...

I should make dinner. Women love that sort of stuff. I pretend I can't boil water without burning down the city—after all my cover is a spoiled billionaire, not someone capable of surviving anything. But I know my way around a kitchen. When I'm on assignment out in some shit jungle, it's up to me to shift for myself or subsist on bugs. That spurred me to learn real fast.

A simple, semi-homemade pasta with roast beef should do the trick. Since Bobbi likes tomatoes, I'll make a tomato, basil and fresh mozzarella salad with vinaigrette dressing. Unfortunately, I can't do dessert, but I don't want her to have to bake when she's home. I make a mental note to grab a tub of premium hand-churned gelato.

A call from my mom pops up. *Crap.*

–Me: Call from Mom. Gotta go.

My brothers joke that at least it isn't Dad or Joey. They don't know how much worse a call from Mom can be, especially now. But then to them, Nora Blane is an eccentric travel writer, not a deadly government assassin who recruited her son to join the team.

She never calls to say hello or see how I'm doing. Even after the plane crash, she didn't check up on me. When Mom pops on my phone, it's about one thing: somebody needs killing.

"Yeah?" I say.

"Time to go shoot your precious cheetahs."

"Not available."

"What?"

"I said, I'm not available." Maybe the connection's bad. It's possible.

There's a pause. "You can't 'not be available.'"

"Well, I'm not. Pretend I didn't survive the crash. Problem solved."

"Noah, you're a government asset."

"Who is currently on a three-month mission of a personal nature. I'm not vanishing for a week or longer. Use someone else."

"Noah—"

"Sorry, about to drive through a tunnel. Do you hear that sta—?" I hang up. Wish I could take out the phone's battery and disappear, but she already knows where I am. Probably having me watched too.

Regardless, there's no time to waste debating Mom. It's going to be mid-morning soon, and I need to hit the florist and drop by Bobbi's bakery so I can give her flowers in person. I've been doing that religiously even before she decided to give me another chance. Anything to make her happy.

As I step out of the house, spinning the key ring around my finger, my senses prickle. I look toward the porch next door. A scarred man with aviator sunglasses sits in an old rocking chair, looking slightly bored as he slips his hand underneath a mildly dingy T-shirt and scratches his belly. His shorts are denim so faded they're almost white.

He's the guy I saw walking around the block before, the one with the limp. Seems completely uninterested, but something about him leaves me unsettled. He's projecting harmlessness, but there's something lurking underneath. Something dangerous, like a sea snake hiding under the calm ocean surface. It reminds me of all the human trash I've had to take out.

Bobbi never had a neighbor that raised my hackles before. I checked all of them out when she inherited this place. Besides, the house whose porch he's occupying used to belong to Mr. and Mrs. Park. The Korean immigrant couple sold their home to another Korean immigrant family, and I'd bet my left nut that man isn't a Korean national. A black Subaru Forester sits there, the bottom half of the SUV mottled with dried specks of mud and dirt.

He looks over, noticing me. "Hey."

I paste on my usual vapid rich-boy face. "Hi. You new?"

He smiles, flashing perfect white teeth. "Yeah. Just moved in not too long ago. You Bobbi's boyfriend or something? I thought I heard her go to work this morning." His eyes slide to Bobbi's driveway, my gleaming Bugatti the sole occupant of the pale concrete.

"Fiancé," I say with an innocent grin.

The man's smile widens, but lacks genuine affability. Bet if I yank those sunglasses off, his eyes will be cold and flat. Does he have the hots for my woman?

"Oh. Well, congratulations. Didn't realize she was engaged." Conversational, inviting me to share details.

My mask doesn't falter. The grin I give him is full of amiableness, which he matches. We might as well be in a competition to see who has the cheesiest smile.

"Yup. Now you know." Even my voice is congenial. I should get a medal.

"Where are my manners?" he says. "I'm Trey."

"Noah."

"Nice to meet you." He shrugs like he's slightly self-conscious. "Probably noticed the scars. Got 'em in Afghanistan."

Slid that little nugget in, did you? "Oh, wow." I feign being impressed. "Thank you for your service." *Assuming you served.* Guys sometimes lie about things like that. You immediately get some respect and cred, and how many people will actually check your service record?

"Second tour. Didn't go as well as I hoped."

"Sorry to hear that. Why can't the bad guys just surrender when we show up, huh? It's so stupid we have to actually fight."

"Seems like some folks are just plain stubborn."

I nod. "There's gotta be an easier way. I say press the button and turn the whole region into a sea of glass. Then punch a hole in it and drain off the oil." I flash him my best simple-minded-rich-moron grin. "I mean, why have all those nukes if we aren't going to use 'em, right? It's like living on a ranch and refusing to eat beef."

"You might have a point there."

"Sure. It's a waste, is what it is. We need to use what we've got. I'm not paying taxes so they can sit on stuff while good men like you get hurt."

"Well, I appreciate that." But he can't quite hide a slight sneer.

I shake my head. "Yeah. Welp, time to go see my fiancée." I give him an oblivious wave and head to my car.

Then, pretending to fiddle with the sound system, I pull out my phone and hit one of the "social media" apps. I enter a few strings to verify that it's me and look up the property details of the house next door. Still owned by that immigrant family. This guy must be renting. Trey is too common a name to get a decent hit. I raise my phone as though checking my texts, then take a shot of his face and upload it to the app.

I drive to the florist, which should have a magnificent bouquet of pink peonies ready, while face recognition AI does its magic. The technology is scarily accurate now. People think a pair of shades or a mask can hide your identity, but that's not the case. There are billions of people running around with their phones, snapping shots of you without you realizing. You could be in the background of some stranger's picture, and it's fed into the system that scours the Internet.

The AI returns six possible matches in SoCal. The scars on his face are problematic. Isn't that convenient?

Two served in the military. Both did a tour in Afghanistan and got injured there. So he checks out...sort of. But why does he give me the vibe I get whenever I first see a target in person?

As I pay for the flowers and return to my car, a text from Mom pops up.

—Mom: Are you stalking Bobbi's new neighbor? If you have time for that, shouldn't you take the job?

—Me: Are YOU stalking ME?

—Mom: I'm keeping an eye on you. For obvious reasons!

Yeah right. She's just upset I declined to go blow the brains out of somebody of her—well, the government's—choosing.

—Me: He's new and I wanted to make sure he was okay. I just got a weird feeling from him.

—Mom: He's probably wary and not doing a good job of hiding his nerves around you. He's trained to kill. Or maybe he's wondering what the hell he was doing overseas, sacrificing himself to protect somebody like you. You can lay it on too thick at times, so much so that even I feel embarrassed to say you're my son.

She's probably rolling her eyes, while spinning a knife between her fingers to relieve tension.

—Me: Still not going. I've rearranged my priorities.

A moment of silence.

—Mom: You can't quit.

—Me: Nobody does this forever.

—Mom: You're too young.

—Me: Bobbi wants to have babies. You could be a grandmother.

—Mom: That's disgusting.

—Me: You'd be able to make Nikki insanely jealous...

Mom despises Nicholas's mom. Calls her too fickle. Unreliable. Annoying. Poor Nikki has no clue, though. She's under the impression that Mom adores her, the belief encouraged by my mother who has a policy of being friendly to everyone because you never know when you might need to use them.

—Me: I can't talk to you now anyway. I have to cook.

—Mom: Cook? As in, prepare food? There are no sanctioned targets in the city.

—Me: Very funny. Now go away before I do something to the pasta and kill someone. Think of the paperwork!!!

26

NOAH

MY SATURDAY COULDN'T START BETTER than waking up to the muted pounding of the Pacific waves and the soft sound of Bobbi's breathing. The room's dark from the blackout curtains, and she's taking advantage and continuing to sleep. Bobbi in my arms, in my bed, is a dream come true. I can't believe I didn't know this was exactly what I wanted until now.

It's been a week since I made my case to Bobbi. We've been staying at her place since it's easier for her to make the commute from Sherman Oaks than Malibu. Our routine is simple. She wakes up at the crack of dawn, tells me to keep sleeping, and heads to the shower. I get up anyway and prep a tumbler full of fresh coffee, then hand it to her with a kiss and a cheery "Have a great day!" and wave goodbye as her Tacoma peels out from the driveway.

After coffee and a simple breakfast, I take flowers to her bakery around ten after the crazy rush of carb-desperate commuters is over. I started with white calla lilies—which she kept this time, much to my satisfaction—and to vary things a little, I bring pink roses, purple Thai orchids, white and pink peonies and lavender hyacinths depending on the day. The smile she gives me is the greatest reward, along with cupcakes that are like the cherry topping on a sundae...even though they aren't croissants. She'll offer those when she's ready—and she's truly forgiven me.

I regard her lying next to me on the bed. Although I acted shamelessly to get her to agree to give me a chance, there's no question that I treated her badly before. If the situation were reversed, I might've shot me dead on the spot. The plain fact is that Bobbi's heart is softer than I deserve. I have a lot to make up for. Which includes taking care of Señor Mittens, who was there for her when I wasn't.

After visiting the bakery, I return to her place to play with the cat and feed His Feline Majesty a feast fit for the Prince of Wales. Although he regards me with the usual cat-like disdain, the little kitty loves me, I can tell. And he came through when I needed him the most.

Thinking of this reminds me of Bobbi throwing me down...which honestly was hot as hell.

My cock stirs. I shift closer and bury my nose in the warm silken tangle of her hair. Her feminine scent never fails to excite me. I could live to be a hundred, and she'd still be the only woman to inflame me like this.

I run my hand gently over her sweet curves, my blood starting to simmer. She thinks her body isn't particularly sexy because she doesn't have giant tits or massively flaring hips, but the strength in her lean muscles is more erotic than any breast could ever be.

My phone buzzes behind me, rattling against the night stand. *Shit.* I quickly reach over and grab it, praying the sound didn't wake Bobbi up. *Mom again.* I slide my finger over the red, cutting it off. A text pops up.

–Mom: This isn't funny.

Neither is your calling me early Saturday morning. She's been hassling me since Wednesday to go kill some terrorist. You'd think I was the only sniper left in the country.

She even offered some protection for Bobbi as a sweetener. Ha! The day I can't protect her is the day I quit living. Mom thinks she got me because of my unease with Trey, but he hasn't been around since our encounter a few days back. Hopefully, he's busy with his job. Or he's found the love of his life—who happens to live in Riyadh or Lahore or some other place far, far away from Los Angeles.

Bobbi turns toward me, rubbing her eyes. "Who's that?" Her voice is husky with sleep.

"Nobody important."

A beat passes. A flick of a switch, and the lamp by her side of the bed casts a warm glow over us. "And this unimportant person has your number?"

"Sorry. I shouldn't have been so dismissive." That isn't the kind of future relationship she wants. "It was my mother."

"Shouldn't you have answered it?"

"*No. She just wants me to do some chores.*" But of course Bobbi will wonder why I'm unwilling to be nice to my mom. "*At her house in Dubai.*"

Bobbi blinks. "In Dubai? As in *the Middle East*?"

"Yeah. It'll take at least a week." Probably longer, although that isn't something I'm willing to discuss in detail. "And I'm not spending a week overseas when I promised to be with you."

"But if she's calling, you might be the only person who can help."

I shake my head. "There are plenty of people who can do it. I already gave her several referrals. She just wants to be difficult about it."

"Maybe she misses you, and this is her way of getting you to visit."

It's hard to keep a straight face. "Uh, yeah, Mom's not the most gregarious person." If Bobbi knew what Mom is really like, she'd never think that. On the other hand, if she knew what my mother is really like, she wouldn't be in bed with me. Who wants a sociopath for a mother-in-law?

On my birthdays, she sends me bullets. On Mother's Day, she wants nothing but knives. Christmas? The only thing stopping her from giving me the names of all the people she wants dead is the fact that I only do sanctioned kills.

"Besides, I visited her a few weeks ago," I say. "And this isn't about her needing me to pay for something. She is as loaded as I am." She has plenty of assets to choose from. It doesn't have to be me, even if I'm one of the better and more convenient tools. "She just likes to see me jump when she snaps her fingers, regardless of my availability."

Bobbi grows quiet, then finally nods and cuddles with me. The little knot in my gut eases, and I enjoy the simple pleasure of her warmth. I hold her close, then slowly rub my cock against the taut skin of her belly, my palm skimming over her back, then cupping her ass. Her breathing quickens.

Lust starts to build. But I want her for intimacy and closeness, not just orgasms. And now that it's the weekend, we have plenty of time to indulge ourselves.

"What time is it?" she asks sleepily.

I'm more interested in feeling her up than checking the time. "I don't know. Eight-forty?" It was eight-thirty-ish when Mom called, so close enough.

"Shit!" Bobbi jumps up, pushing my hands off.

"What?" I ask, but immediately focus at the sight of her nude body rushing toward the bathroom. That ass, those legs... I sit back and enjoy the view.

"I'm late!"

"Late? It's Saturday." Maybe she has the days confused.

"For lunch with your family!"

"I told you, they're coming here. Come back to bed." I pat the spot next to me invitingly. A sadly wasted gesture since she doesn't bother to look in my direction.

"Even so, I'm still late. And no, I'm not going back to bed."

"I'll be quick." I sound like the devil tempting Eve. *Just one bite, pretty lady.*

Bobbi knows me too well. "Ha! I don't believe you."

She slips into the ensuite bathroom. I jump off the mattress and hurry toward her. "Okay, well... Let's shower together."

Her gaze drops to my erection. A hint of wistfulness passes over her, and I smile. She lifts her eyes to my face, and something firms in her expression. With an I-don't-think-so smile, she shuts the door in my face. A metallic click says I'm locked out.

"Come on. You're wasting water." *Appeal to her civic-mindedness.*

"Ha! Us in the shower together will waste more."

"I need to shower, too."

"There are seven bathrooms in this house."

I let out a theatrical sigh. "Cruelty, thy name is Bobbi."

The sound of the water cuts me off. I can just picture her determined face, her lips pursed and eyes slanted watchfully at the door between us.

I shake my head with a small laugh. Well...nothing to do but go to another bathroom and grab a quick shower myself. I'm not going to miss watching her get ready.

I throw on a gray T-shirt and shorts and get comfortable on the rumpled bed. Bobbi comes out a few minutes later, face freshly scrubbed and rosy. A fluffy white towel is around her, stopping at upper thighs and revealing those endless legs. Maybe I should get her an anklet. She's fond of blue, so maybe something with sapphires... *Hmm.*

She pushes the pump on a bottle, and the tiny opening squirts a generous dollop of white goo onto her palm. It looks like cum, and she slathers it all over her face and body. We could've done something similar —her full lips wrapped around my shaft and her fingers in her pussy as she made herself happy while sucking me off. And the finale would have her climax with me coming on her face. Or on her chest. I'm accommodating.

Oblivious to the dirty fantasies in my head, she goes through her skin-care routine, then drops the towel and dons a pale mint green bra with matching lace thong that hug her body perfectly. My mouth dries, my cock hardening painfully. Mint's supposed to be cool, but on her it's scorching hot.

Great. Now I'm going to think about her in that lingerie all day. She pulls on a pale azure fitted sleeveless top and a flaring short skirt in the same shade as the Thai orchids I gave her on Thursday.

She gathers her hair into a top knot and skewers it with a stick lacquered in pink. The updo reveals the graceful lines of her neck and shoulders. And a hickey on the back of her neck.

My woman, I think with satisfaction.

She runs her hands down the shirt and skirt and turns left and right, checking. Then she reaches into her bag and applies mascara on her already long and thick lashes. Her eyes drop to her phone, then she frowns a little before running some red lipstick over her mouth.

"What's the matter? It's not even nine thirty," I say.

"Right. Not enough time." She slips her feet into nude slingbacks.

"You need a necklace."

"What?" She stops and looks at her reflection. "You think so?"

"Yeah." I get up and grab a long box from the drawer in my closet.

Peery Diamonds sent it a while back, but there hasn't been a good opportunity to give it to her.

I open the lid and show her the glittering rubies and the huge diamond in the center that shines like the sun. Her lips part as she stares at the stones, her fingers over her mouth. "Oh my *God*."

"You like it?" I grin.

"Noah." She lifts her gaze to meet mine. "It's so extravagant."

"You aren't answering the question."

"Well, yes, of course. It's gorgeous, but—"

I kiss her. "No buts."

"But—"

I kiss her again. "Just say thank you."

She sighs. "Thank you."

"Good girl." I pick up the string of gems and put it around her neck. My eyes catch hers in the mirror, and I smile. "Beautiful." It's even more amazing on her than I imagined when I first saw the necklace in the Peery catalog. Without breaking eye contact, I kiss her neck, taking in the warmth of her skin, the soft sweet fragrance that somehow always surrounds her.

We have plenty of time before the guests arrive. I slip my hand under her shirt, stroking her taut belly. Her breathing hitches, and I bring her close, so she can feel how much I want her right now.

"Noah..." She sighs my name like it's both a torment and pleasure, then she pulls away. "I *can't*. I'm rushed for time as it is."

What?

She dashes out of my arms, then out of the bedroom entirely.

I follow her to the kitchen. "My brothers and their wives aren't arriving until eleven thirty or later, in case you forgot."

"I'm baking." She reaches into one of the brown bags she brought with her last night, then pulls another from the fridge.

Perhaps I didn't make the purpose of the lunch clear. I want my family to impress *her*. I'm the bird doing his best to woo a mate by displaying everything he's got. I put my hands on her shoulders and spin her around. "Relax. I didn't bring you here to cook."

She breathes out. "I know that, but I want to. Having people enjoy my food makes me happy. I want to bake for your family. Nothing special. Just three pies and two cobblers."

Of all the times to suddenly get domestic. I sigh, but respect her decision. "Let me help you then."

"Okay."

I set the ovens to the temperature she asks for. For once I'm glad my place has four ovens, even though until now I've never had an occasion to use any. She peels, cores, pits and cuts up apples, nuts, and cherries and peaches with an ease that would impress even my mother. Her comfortable expertise is a massive turn-on. I'm acutely aware that she doesn't really need anybody—and she certainly has no need for my money or influence. She's too capable, too smart. The people in her tightly knit social circle are ones she has a deep affection for, and relief and pride twine through me in the knowledge that she considers me worthy.

I measure sugar and butter and hand her spices as she calls for them, my forearms and fingers brushing against hers. Her breathing stills when we touch, and a pretty flush colors her sculptured cheeks. Electricity hums under my skin.

Finally, she puts the pies and cobblers into the ovens, sets the timers on each unit, then lets out a breath.

"You shouldn't worry so much," I say. "You're going to be the most popular person."

"How can you be so sure?"

"Because nobody can eat diamonds or dildos. Or the money GrantEm makes. Or Griffin's academic papers..."

She chokes, then lets out a lilting laugh.

"I'm serious." I kiss her smiling mouth. She kisses me back softly, her tongue flicks against mine in a silent gesture of apology for ignoring me earlier. I take advantage and fuse our mouths, plunder her, taste the mint from the toothpaste and the sweet honey of her.

The need for her thrums in my veins. The heat of the kiss burns through me, slowly pushing away a small bit of anxiety that's a by-product of my overwhelming desire to have this lunch be perfect.

Her soft whimper stokes my lust, and I slip my hand underneath her top and bra and knead her soft breast. She threads her fingers into my hair and clenches, until my scalp prickles from the tight pull.

The tightness of her shoulders betrays her nerves. The fact that she wants to make a good impression on my family soothes some of my own nerves. I run my lips and tongue along the sensitive curves of her neck, then push the top out of the way and pull her nipple into my mouth.

She sobs out softly. Her breasts are so beautifully responsive, and the pleasure pinkening her skin is my greatest reward.

I maneuver her backward until her ass is at the edge of the counter. I prop her up, and she tugs at my hair. "The caterer," she gasps.

"We've still got time."

"But—"

My hand slides under her skirt, my fingers dragging over the quivering muscles of her inner thighs. I push aside the small band of fabric between her legs and run the pad of my thumb over her folds. She bites her lip as her hot juices coat my hand. "We can't have you greeting my family like this."

"Noah…"

"And you're way, *way* too wound up."

"Anybody would be when they're meeting the family of their boyfriend for the first time."

"I know. So let's take the edge off."

She looks at me, needs for physical release and reassurance mingling in her half-glazed caramel eyes.

"You're perfect the way you are." My thumb brushes over her clit, causing a small tremor to ripple through her. I drop to my knees, spread her legs and lay kisses on her inner thighs. "They're going to love you, even if you don't make a single damn thing." I look up at her, not hiding all the love and adoration in my heart. "You're like the sun. Nobody can resist you."

She goes absolutely still, gazing at me. Smiling, I press my mouth on her, through the thin strip of her thong. The delicious scent brings me an addictive high, and I tongue her wetness, groaning at the heady flavor I can't get enough of.

I spread her legs wider and push two fingers inside, knowing it drives her wild when I rub her G-spot while sucking on her clit. Her back arches, and her knuckles whiten, gripping the counter. Another tremor snakes through her, harder and faster. I pull her sweet flesh into my mouth, adding another finger and fucking her, making sure to bump the little button inside that drives her crazy.

She screams as she comes, her thighs tensing and tightening around my head. I don't give her time to come down from the high. I'm just getting started.

I devour her, lapping her up like a man who hasn't had a drop of water in days. She's a dripping mess, but I love how turned on she is—that I'm doing this to her. Her fingers digging into my hair, she rocks against my face, moving her pelvis to the rhythm set by my furiously thrusting fingers.

The next two climaxes hit her back-to-back like wrecking balls. She convulses over my face, and I grip her ass hard. "Oh God," she moans, her entire body quivering.

"Yes, my light." I get back to my feet, wipe my jaw with a careless swipe of my palm, and pull her into my arms and kiss her. She's unsteady on her feet, orgasm-drunk, and drives her tongue into my mouth.

My steel-hard dick presses against her; she undoes my belt and pushes the shorts down. Her eyes shift to the wall behind me. "Ten minutes left."

"Then we better make it fast. And hot." She starts to lead my cock toward her pussy, but I pull back. "No condom."

She bites her lip, then a devilish gleam sparks in her eyes. Her hand wraps around my shaft, forming a tight sheath. My erection pulses against her bare skin. *God, she feels so damn good* is the only thought I can muster over the roaring of overheated blood in my ears.

She pumps me, her mouth on mine. I drive into it, feel the precum dripping over her strong fingers enveloping me. Soon a climax begins to swirl beneath my skin, my balls growing tight.

She nips my earlobe. "Will you come for me, Noah?" And then her other hand is on me, the tip of one finger touching the tip of my shaft, and I can barely say "yes" before my vision goes white, and I spurt in her hand, my lungs struggling to drag in air. I come so hard, the cum hits her chin, splatters over our clothes.

The sight is so fucking hot, my cock spews again, although not so much that anything hits her face again.

A moment or two pass before I can speak. "Fuck," I groan. "Jesus, I love you."

"Not Jesus. Bobbi," she corrects me, then laughs just as the oven timers start dinging.

27

BOBBI

THE LAST SUPPER-ESQUE portion of Noah's vision painting didn't come close to capturing the raucousness of his brothers and their wives and children. Although his place in Malibu is huge, with so many large men around it starts to feel kind of cozy.

A cute curvy brunette introduces herself as Molly and beams at me. "I knew it!" She turns to Noah, looking at him like he's her star pupil. "Told you being yourself works!"

I look at her, wondering how much advice she gave Noah.

"So you're the master baker," Amy says. She's a friendly blonde and a regular. And Emmett's wife.

"And now," Grant says, "Noah doesn't have to be the mastur*bator*." Two of the other brothers are walking by; the high-fives occur almost eight feet in the air.

"I feel like I should buy even more Danishes from you now," Aspen says. I recognize the redhead—she used to come to the bakery all the time to grab goodies for her office.

"Thanks," I say with a smile.

"So, has Noah finally earned a croissant?" This one looks suave, all polished charm and pleasantry, but I can picture him breaking someone's legs without breaking that smile. *What was his name...?* *Huxley.* Mr. Harvard Law who doesn't want to be a lawyer.

"I haven't given him a croissant since we got together." He hasn't asked, and I haven't offered. Giving him a croissant might come across as meaning everything's all good. Maybe it's because he loves my croissants—or maybe it's because that's what he filched that night he promised to come to my bakery opening. But I'm not sure if it's wise to declare everything's perfect when it's been only one week into our three-month trial.

"Sounds like you're giving him enough." Again the smile, but this time it comes with a wink that makes it okay.

Sierra slaps him on the arm. "Don't be crude. By the way, I love your desserts." She's the CEO of Silicone Dreams, which makes some of my favorite vibrators.

A Nordic blonde even taller than I am is here, making me feel less conscious about my height, although among these men I feel almost slight and girlish. She's Lucienne Peery, the heiress to Peery Diamonds. She seems a bit tired and doesn't have much of an appetite. She's barely touched the massive spread that Noah had catered. It could come across as just a tad stuck up, but she genuinely seems apologetic she isn't more fun to be around.

Her husband Sebastian sits next to her and takes care of her, pouring her water, having her try different fruits and bread. She has a couple of bites of crusty whole-grain bread, then shakes her head.

My phone buzzes. I glance at the screen.

—Floyd: Why aren't you responding to Reggie?

Ugh. A text from the last person I want to hear from on a day like this. I blocked Reggie years ago, but I can't block my landlord.

—Floyd: Remember—a month to design and make the cake. Reggie and I want to see the design before you bake it, to make sure you do a good job. You don't want to humiliate yourself.

I hope your butt explodes with gluten. I'm so tempted to call him out on his fake gluten intolerance, but I don't want to waste energy on this man-roach, who'll insist until his dying breath he has it even though he doesn't. Probably to feel special or get attention because he's just that pathetic. I dump the phone in a drawer and turn my attention back to lunch. Pigs will sing Taylor Swift's entire catalog before I bake anything for Floyd and Reggie.

Amy, Aspen, Molly and I go to the kitchen to get the pies and cobblers. The caterer reheated them just in time for dessert, and they're bubbling perfectly.

"These smell *so* good." Molly looks like she wants to bury herself in the cobbler she's holding.

"There's also a key lime pie." I reach into the fridge to pull it out. I whipped it up yesterday at the bakery and brought it over last night. It's simple to make, and perfect for the unusually warm weather.

"It's good to see Noah with someone he loves. I never thought he'd settle down," Amy says.

I raise an eyebrow.

"He's always been so wild and carefree. Prototypical bachelor for life."

"He's had other girlfriends," I say, feeling slightly awkward. His sisters-in-law are acting like I'm definitely going to be part of the family, and I don't have the heart to tell them Noah and I are on a three-month trial run.

"Maybe... But if he did, we never met any of them. His brothers, either. Grant told me he was shocked when Noah asked for this lunch, and then ordered everyone to behave or else," Aspen says with a laugh.

"He hasn't proposed or anything," I say.

"He will," Amy says. "But don't say yes until you're sure."

I blink. "I thought you liked him."

"I do, but I like you too. And in a relationship affection has to go both ways. If you aren't ready, or you don't want it, it doesn't make sense to commit."

"Definitely. Sometimes the timing isn't right," Aspen says somewhat wistfully. "Grant and I almost lost each other forever."

Molly pats her hand. "It worked out in the end."

My anxiety over meeting his family wasn't just about making a good impression, I abruptly realize, but over how they might side with him and subtly pressure me to just say yes now. Although Noah hasn't said anything more about proposing, I know he'd like to get married, just like in his vision painting.

But his family just wants to meet me and honestly seems to hope for the best for me and Noah. Something loosens in my chest. "Thanks. Really." An easy smile splits my face. "Now, are you guys ready to help me take these treats to the table?"

When we return, everyone's eager to grab a piece of pie or cobbler. One of Griffin and Sierra's triplets, Ellen, is fussing—Noah takes the little girl from them and bounces her on his knee while making funny faces. Emmett samples my key lime pie and groans. "Oh man, this is like crack. You're going to make me fat before my time."

Amy filches a forkful from his plate and her eyes grow round. "Wow! Better than the one we had in Florida."

"Thanks." I smile, my cheeks warming.

"I can't believe I haven't seen this at your bakery."

"It's not a regular item."

Noah reaches over and takes the biggest slice. Ellen looks up at him, drool gathering around her mouth, but he shakes his head. "Too tart for you, Princess." He turns to me. "But Emmett's right. This is crack." Then he turns to the little girl and tries to get her to eat some toast—without much success.

Lucie looks torn for a moment, then whispers something to her husband, and he grabs a slice of key lime pie for her. She takes a bite, then sighs with bliss, mingled with relief.

"What's that about?" Nicholas says. He's a quiet guy, his expression somber, his demeanor steady. He seems like one of those people with an extra-long fuse that blows up spectacularly when pushed to the limit.

Sebastian looks at his wife briefly, and she nods at him with a smile. He turns to us. "We thought about having a party to announce the news, but why not do it here? Luce is pregnant."

Gasps go up along with shouts and laughter. "Congratulations!"

The women get up to hug her, and after a brief hesitation I squeeze her too. Grant, who is sitting to the right of Sebastian, slaps him on the back. A huge smile stretches Sebastian's mouth.

Lucie beams quietly next to him, her head on his shoulder, then takes another bite of the pie. She closes her eyes and sighs. "Oh thank God. I almost feel human again."

"I know you said you don't make it often, but I'll give you anything if you can make it for Luce." Sebastian's all sincerity. "She hasn't thrown up, but she can't stomach eating anything. She says everything tastes like sh—uh, dirt."

"Oh, no need to pay," I say, pleased and flattered that my pie is helping. I saw how it was with Ivy and Yuna. Both had weird food cravings and couldn't tolerate a lot of food that they normally enjoyed. "I'll be happy to make some for your wife. Just let me know when and I'll have it at the bakery for you to pick up."

Lucie looks at me like I just single-handedly protected the world from a zombie apocalypse. "You're a life saver."

Sebastian and I exchange numbers so he can figure out when he should come and pick up the pies. Meanwhile, Noah feeds Ellen some peach cobbler filling after blowing on it to cool it off. She takes it from the small plastic spoon, smacking her lips as she eats it, then sticks her tiny tongue out. "Too delicious, huh?" He laughs.

The girl opens and closes her adorable rosebud mouth, slapping at his wrist with her little hand.

"Yes, Your Highness."

Molly leans closer. "Ellen's a picky eater," she whispers. "Although I think she's more particular about who feeds her rather than what she gets fed. Noah managed to charm her into eating mashed broccoli last time we had a family meal. She never lets her dad come anywhere near her with anything green."

Noah feeds Ellen another spoonful with a grin, then busses her rosy cheeks. Drool drips from her mouth, and he wipes her tenderly with a napkin, then praises her. "Look at you, eating like a champ."

The sight is so ordinary and beautiful. My womb just shivers in a spontaneous ovulation.

Emmett and Amy's little daughter Monique trots over and taps Noah on his leg. "Unca Noah."

"Yes, Monique?"

"I'm gonna marry you."

He laughs. "Are you now? Why me?"

"Mommy says I should marry a man who's nice to me," she says primly, her chin tilted up.

I press my lips together hard to contain a laughter bubbling in my throat.

"Hey, I got you a princess tiara!" Sebastian says in a feigned outrage.

"Yeah, but you're married, Unca Seb. Also Daddy said only the SOBs take their presents back."

A stunned silence falls over the table. Amy recovers first. "Emmett!"

He raises both hands, palms out. "I never said that in front of her!"

"He said it on Zoom," the little girl clarifies, "I heard him." She turns to Noah again. "You have to buy me a ring."

"Sorry, Princess, but I'm taken."

Monique's eyes widen. "Who?" she whispers, like her world just ended.

"It's a secret right now." He flashes me a smile. "But she took my heart, so I can't marry you."

"Oh." Her shoulders sag so forlornly it's all I can do to bite my lip and not laugh.

"But guess what? You bring home a boy and I'll look him up and make sure he's worthy of you. How about that? I know exactly how to be nice to you, so I'll know when I see the right boy."

Monique thinks about it for a moment. "Okay. I'll tell you first, then Daddy."

Emmett stares at his daughter like she just stabbed him in the gut, which elicits a laugh from everyone.

I drape my arm over Noah's shoulder, feel his lips on my palm, and decide this is better than his vision painting.

When everyone's gone, I stretch, then prop my chin on his shoulder. "That was fun. Your family's amazing."

He grins. "Glad you liked them."

"So. What kind of adventures do you have when you aren't home? I'm curious about what you do when you go off on your own to take photos of wildlife." I want to know more about Noah, understand his dreams, separate from mine.

"Then why don't we do something together next weekend?" he says, his eyes alive with excitement.

"Deal."

28

BOBBI

"Wow..." I look up at the orange-brown layers of rock that form Antelope Canyon. I didn't know what to expect when Noah said he'd take care of everything we'd need for the weekend. But his excitement was enough to get me to go along with the plan sight unseen.

Noah chartered a turboprop plane for a hop to northern Arizona. Apparently, the airport in Page isn't big enough to accommodate a jet, and there are no convenient commercial flights to the area.

"Time is of the essence." He winked, saying he didn't want to waste hours driving from Phoenix.

I've heard of canyons in the area, but I've never been to any. When I was younger, I was overseas with my parents and adventures of any kind were strictly forbidden. My mom absolutely refused to go anywhere that could be deemed dangerous, even though the State Department provided security when we moved to regions considered less than safe by the government. Dad was too preoccupied with work to bother. I doubt he would've taken me anywhere even if he hadn't been busy because he hated arguing with Mom. She was impossible when she felt threatened, and logic wasn't her strongest point. And by the time I finished college, I was working.

I'm glad Noah chose this canyon for our first adventure together as a couple. The photos I've seen didn't do it justice. The cool air inside provides a respite from the baking sun, and the early afternoon light beams straight into the canyon, creating beautiful highlights. Noah threads his fingers through mine as we follow our very competent looking Navajo guide in on a group tour. Apparently, the canyon doesn't allow individual tourists to wander around unescorted.

"The weather forecast called for rain later this afternoon, but hopefully it won't lead to a flash flood." Our guide looks up at the sky that's bright blue at the moment. It was cloudy a few minutes ago. "We had one two days ago—lasted about half an hour and washed away a lot of the soil." The green beam from his laser pointer hits a line a little over a foot above the ground. "That's where the floor used to be two days ago."

A few of the people in our group make shocked noises. I frown at the old soil level still marked on the stone. Water powerful enough to swipe away a foot of sediment in a few minutes isn't something I ever want to take on, no matter how "adventurous" it might be.

"Just how dangerous is it?" a woman to my left says with a slight French accent.

"People have died here," the man responds. "If it happens, there'll be no hesitating. We turn back and head for the bus."

I glance at the opening behind us. Noah leans closer until his breath tickles my ear. "Don't worry. I'll protect you."

"Really? How's that going to work?"

"I'm an excellent swimmer."

"You can outswim the crocs in the Nile?"

"Oh, easily." The corners of his eyes crease into fans. "And worse. A flash flood is no match."

I laugh quietly at his bravado. "My hero."

"At your service, milady." He winks.

The guide points out at the section ahead of us. "That's the bear."

I squint, unsure what I'm supposed to see. Noah puts a hand on my shoulder and pulls me more toward his angle of view. "See it now?"

I narrow my eyes. And then finally see it—a bear on its hind legs, right ahead of me. "That's *so* cool."

Noah and I snap a shot, then take a selfie together with a wide grin. The guide notices and gestures for the phone. "Let me."

I hand him my phone, and he has us stand in front of a cool sandstone formation with layers and layers of different shades of orange. He takes a picture of Noah and me, arms around each other's waists, and hands me the phone. It's a good shot, almost professional, and I smile at our relaxed expressions. Noah in particular looks very comfortable, like he's done this hundreds of times.

I send him the photo, and he grins. "Damn, you look amazing. I'm going to set this as my new background." He fiddles around, then flips the phone. "One of the best things that's ever happened to me."

His tone is so earnest and open, his eyes bright with hope and love. And the wall I had erected around my heart starts to crumble like wet sand. He's like an emotion ninja. No matter how strong my castle's defenses are, he always finds a way in.

Just as I start automatically refortify the walls, I pull myself back. It isn't fair to continually put obstacles in his way just because I'm feeling unsure. He's trying to reassure me, and I should try to accept his gesture in the same spirit, until he does something to betray me. Still, it's scary as hell—a little exhilarating, too, honestly—but very, very scary.

"That's the dragon's eye." The guide's words pulls my focus back to the tour. He points to the light coming through a particular gap above us.

I look up. Little bits of wet dirt crumbles from the stones soaring over us. I put up a hand to keep the dust and soil from getting into my eyes, then snap a shot of the dragon's eye. Unlike the bear, this one is obvious, the pupil glowing in a glorious orange fireball. It looks amazing.

"An adorable little dragon." Noah grins at me.

"Adorable? How? Where?" *Am I missing something?*

He puts an arm around me. "Right here."

I laugh. "Oh, okay. Adorable, huh?"

"Mmm-hmm. Fierce, too. And sexy."

"If I'm a dragon, what are you? A bear?"

"Of course not, silly. I'm the treasure."

"You want me to sprawl on you?" I say, as images of old drawings of dragons coiled around a pile of gold and gemstones fleet over my mind.

"Totally." He lowers his voice. "Thighs on either side of my head... your pussy on my face."

I look around to make sure nobody in our tour group is paying attention. "Noah," I chide, although the laughter in my tone undermines my intent.

His clever fingers stroke my side. "Come on. I'll make it worth your while."

My cheeks heat. From the way he can bring me to one mind-destroying climax after another, I'm sure sitting on his face would be more than worth my while. Wetness pools between my legs, which is a little shocking. I've always enjoyed sex, but with Noah, my body craves it. There's something about him that puts me in a constant hum of excitement.

From the wicked gleam in his eye, he knows it, too. His fingers slip lower. More bits of wet dirt fall from the opening of the canyon. Some non-dirt moisture comes through, feeling like a sprinkle. A moment or two later, there is a trickle of water flowing toward us along the canyon floor.

Our guide looks up, squinting, then at the ground. He turns to the group. "Flash flood! All right, people, back to the bus!"

The people in our group start to mill around. A few of them glance upward, searching for some sign of torrential rain or water pouring in. Several more drops fall—more liquid than dirt this time, but they don't seem threatening.

"Look," Noah says, nodding at the ground.

Small currents of water are now slithering along the brown soil like snakes. I look up at him. "Uh-oh."

"Like the man said. Time to go."

People turn and start to run. A few scream, and a woman in strappy heels complains in Italian. I shake my head. Who wears high heels to walk in a desert? The tour site and pamphlet specifically asked everyone to wear sturdy and comfortable shoes.

Noah takes my hand and escorts me at a steady pace. Around us, the crowd is hopping and running over the puddles and streams of water that are becoming increasingly wide. He shields me from a trio of guys in their early twenties who rush out cursing, bumping into others on the way. Other tour groups are also darting toward the field where the buses are.

Maybe they're panicked or scared. But I'm surprisingly calm. The warmth of Noah's hand on mine is reassuring—somehow, I feel like we're going to be fine no matter what. The little currents are now much wider and deeper, water flowing faster and creating small ponds and eddies in places. The rapid pace of water pouring down from the rocks above us should inspire fear, especially after the guide said that people have died. But knowing that Noah is with me leaves no room for alarm, just the exhilaration of experiencing something unexpected.

I know he's going to keep me safe.

By the time we're halfway back to the entrance of the canyon, brown-orange waterfalls that didn't exist when we entered are pouring over us. Piercing screams and shouts are everywhere. I pull my shoulders together as cool water and dirt run down my back; Noah wraps an arm around me, not caring that he's getting caught in the deluge as well. I press closer, seeking his warmth through our clammy and gritty clothes as we walk rapidly toward the mini-bus with its sturdy tires.

The guide boards last, does a quick headcount and gets behind the wheel. The rain beats on the roof of the bus in a deafening staccato. I look up, then at Noah. He grins. "Ever been in a situation like this?"

I shake my head, then smile as he puts an arm around me.

Somebody sitting in front says something, but the words are lost in the general chaos. Everyone gets tossed around as the guide throws the bus into gear and then does an amazing job of maneuvering the sliding, skidding, jouncing bus over what was dry desert ground less than an hour ago but is now an expanse of mud and gravel that can barely be seen through the rain-spattered windshield. I sigh and move closer to Noah. Despite the crowd and the racket, somehow it feels like we're alone sharing a secret adventure together.

The bus tosses us up and down, left and right as though we're on a roller coaster without a safety bar. Laughing, I tighten my hand on Noah, who squeezes it back. He's so warm, and I can smell the musky scent of him over the dirt and rain. The driver leans left and right as he wrestles the heaving bus over the terrain like a ship in a stormy sea. But instead of being terrifying, it's fun—probably from being such a change from my regular life. Or maybe it's being with Noah.

"I didn't know weather could turn so fast," I say as the rain, impossibly, grows even more furious.

"It happens out here." Noah grins. "You should see it in Africa."

"I bet." I gently push wet hair off his forehead. "So is this the kind of adventure you have?"

"Sometimes."

"Probably cooler in Africa." My tone is more wistful than I intend.

"But not as much fun." He gives me a soft peck. "You weren't with me there."

I laugh, then kiss him back. His eyes twinkle, and I'm falling in love with this side of him. At the same time, a sober voice slides into my mind with a warning.

We could only manage a canyon tour for a weekend, but if it weren't for my schedule, Noah probably could've gone on a bigger adventure. One with more excitement, discoveries and new experiences. How long will he be satisfied with just coming over to the bakery to give me flowers, taking care of my cat and placing his own exciting life on hold?

29

BOBBI

"I'm working on my magnum opus."

I roll Noah's response around in my head as I knead the dough early in the morning with Victor. It was more or less immediate when I asked him what he did with his free time while I was at the bakery.

"I always wanted to write a novel, and now I have the time," he said. "You can be the first to read it, before it's published."

"Sure, love to." Will he miss photography? Maybe not, since he hasn't hung any cheetah shots in his house. But then I don't have trays of bread and pastries in *my* house, so—

"Hey, Bobbi? You okay?"

I jerk my head up and see confused concern on Victor's face. "Yeah. Why?"

"You seem really distracted. Keep muttering under your breath." He clears his throat. "I asked if you're gonna need me this weekend —twice."

My cheeks heat with embarrassment. "Sorry. I was just thinking about some stuff. Um... Yes. I'm going to need some help with that cake Saturday morning." Victor told me he finally managed to get a date with the UCLA blonde. He hasn't said when, and I don't want to take up his weekend unless it's absolutely necessary, but I can't handle transporting a ten-tier cake by myself.

Besides, thinking about this Saturday only stirs up the unsettled feeling in my gut. Noah asked me to be his plus-one to a luncheon party, and I told him I couldn't since I had to work. The cake is going to be unbelievable, with cascading roses, lilies and orchids, along with forget-me-nots molded with modeling chocolate and gum paste. It's for an I've-Been-with-the-Love-of-My-Life-for-Two-Months celebration and is *completely* over the top, but Rachel Griffin, the former model turned influencer who hired me, thinks it's critical to celebrate every milestone of her new relationship. I don't have the heart to tell her the jailbait she's with is probably more in love with her money than her. She's old enough to be his mom, but she's also a client who doesn't want to listen to anything that doesn't confirm her own notions about life. And if you're in business in SoCal, you need to play ball when dealing with the rich and fatuous.

But that also means I might miss out on some of the things going on in Noah's life. "No worries. I can go alone," he said with an easy smile.

"Seriously? You okay without a date?"

"I'm not taking some random piece of arm candy just so I can have a 'date.'" The light way he said it made me feel worse, like I'm not doing my part somehow.

"I'm sorry."

"Why? Your career is important."

"But so are your trips to take photos and social obligations. Maybe we should talk about those things and work them out."

He shrugged. "Pfft. Nothing comes close to you. Now listen. No more frowning." He stroked the lines between my eyebrows, moving his index finger back and forth like an eraser.

I smiled, then laughed. But we do need to sit down and have a serious conversation about how we're going to weave our lives together, even though he's dismissing the idea. He shouldn't have to wake up one morning five years from now and ask himself, "What the hell have I been doing all this time?"

RACHEL'S PARTY is at Ted Lasker's multi-million-dollar mansion. He's letting her host it at his place because she gave him a son—Griffin, whose keen intelligence and academic accomplishments make his father proud—and he's fond of her.

But beyond that, he obviously just likes to party. The man is legendary for having fathered Noah and his six brothers in four months, and he's never married any of the mothers. Yuna's husband Declan was cast in a Ted Lasker film last year, and she said the director has probably produced more children. "There was this Chinese emperor who had thirty-eight sons and forty-two daughters. *Eighty* kids! I mean, this was before effective birth control, but he died when he was like fifty-two with something like twenty wives. Ted is already older than that and now we have Viagra. And I bet you he's screwed more than twenty women. Men should totally do a paternity test with the woman they want to marry, just to make sure they aren't fathered by the same guy."

Ivy choked and I made a face, but ten mudslides between us made us all laugh away an image that had nothing to do with us.

Except... It definitely does have something to do with me! If I marry Noah, Ted will be my father-in-law. Although I never got the feeling that Noah and his brothers were close to their parents, the possibility of being related to somebody that famous is a bit...weird.

With Victor tagging along behind me, I'm rolling up the winding driveway, through lush green scenery, when another thought hits: the disastrous date with Joey. *Eww.* Is he also going to be part of my life if I marry Noah?

Okay, don't think about that. Noah's painting didn't include Joey, and we don't need to have anything to do with him. Ever. Better just to focus on the future Noah and I would like to create for ourselves.

God, I hope I don't run into him and another ridiculous attempt to get me to have a grandbaby for Ted. If two of his sons don't want Ted near their children, it's probably him, not them. Or maybe it's Joey doing a terrible job of representing Ted's desire to be closer to his grandchildren. The guy couldn't even represent himself without using a million filters first.

Victor and I pull the cake out from the truck with extra care. It took forever to make, even with Victor's assistance, but looks amazing.

Three of the tiers are invisible, with crystal support columns, flowers and figurines that represent the most memorable dates Rachel and her boyfriend had. My chest puffs with pride. It's some of the best work I've ever done. I already took a shot of it for Bobbi's Sweet Things's social media profiles. I plan to take more once it's in place at the actual party.

The main caterers come out in starched black and white uniforms and stop dead when they see the cake. "Wow…"

"Amazing, isn't it?" Victor says with a grin.

"Totally." One of the women nods and takes charge. "Okay, let's move this and set it up by the main tables next to the pool."

They carefully push the cake cart through the mansion, and I follow, praying that nothing happens before it's put into place. Soaring Topiaries of topless women line the giant pool on three sides, giving it a semblance of privacy. Heart-shaped balloons in bright pink and red sway in the air, and a DJ is playing upbeat love songs. Guests, many recognizable from commercials and movies, dance and laugh in bathing suits. The catering team sets up the cake by a fountain where rosé champagne fizzes.

"This is perfect," the woman says.

"Agreed. Mind if I take a quick photo?" I say, pulling out my phone.

They move aside, and I snap a few shots, making sure to capture the cascading flowers and sparkling columns. I also get a few close-ups of the flowers and faux pearls so people can see the details of the decoration.

I shove the phone into my back pocket with thanks to the crew who set up the cake. I tell Victor he can go, and he immediately heads out. *Good luck, buddy.*

The catering manager signs off on the delivery sheet, and I sigh with satisfaction over a job well done. The stunning cake, towering over the buffet table, was worth the hours of delicate work that left my hands aching.

"Nice cake. So. You're the reason Noah won't leave L.A."

I look to the left. A tall woman with short dark hair and a pasty-pale face is studying me. Her skin looks fantastically white against the black bikini that's on her lean body. She wears a friendly and curious face, but her tone doesn't hide a mild rebuke, although I'm not sure if her displeasure is directed at me or Noah. Or both of us.

"I'm sorry, do I know you?" I ask in a neutral tone.

"Nora Blane. I'm Noah's mother." She extends a hand, and I shake it on autopilot. *This is Noah's mother?* Despite her wiry frame, she's shockingly strong. It feels almost as if she's trying to break my hand. I match the tight grip, and a flash of respect glints in her eyes.

"I'm Bobbi. But I guess you know that. I thought you were in Dubai."

"Yes, but since my son refuses to talk to me over the phone, I had no choice but to come talk to him in person."

Whatever she wanted Noah to take care of must be *really* important to make that trip. He said he wouldn't spend an entire week away from me, and again I feel uneasy because Noah is neglecting his life to prove himself to me.

He's definitely going to wake up at some point and realize he doesn't have a life. Midlife crises happen when people don't feel comfortable with the life they're leading anymore, and that's often because they went along with whatever everyone else around them wanted.

"On the other hand, perhaps speaking with *you* would expedite things." Nora wears an expectant smile and seems certain I'll side with her.

This isn't what I bargained for when I agreed to deliver the cake. As much as I want to be friendly and get along with Noah's mom, it wouldn't be right to commit Noah to a task when I know nothing about it. I'm just about to tell her as much when her eyes shift to focus behind me and her expression sours.

"Mother? What are you doing here?"

Noah?

Once I told him I had to work, we didn't discuss further details. It never occurred to me that he'd be at this party. If I'd known, I would've brought a change of clothes, so I could join him after the cake was delivered.

Noah breathes hard as he rakes his fingers through his hair. He glares at his mother like she's his number one enemy, a rather odd reaction since I thought he'd be okay with seeing his parents at parties, even if they weren't particularly close. He pulls me close and kisses me but keeps his eyes on her.

"Since calls and texts weren't accomplishing anything, I decided to show up in person," she says smoothly. "I miss you, too."

Noah shifts, positioning himself like a shield against his mother. "Surely you didn't leave your toilet clogged all this time."

I cover my mouth with a hand to contain a sound somewhere between laugh and incredulity. She flew all the way out here over a clogged toilet? Or does "clogged toilet" mean something else?

"Sadly toilets get clogged all the time if they aren't taken care of by experts. Which is where you come in." Nora's tone is flat and serious.

"No, I don't. Not at the moment, anyway."

"You know your duties."

Filial duties shouldn't include having him fly from Los Angeles to Dubai just to thrust a plunger into her toilet, no matter how good he is at the task. Does she often make unreasonable demands? Is that why she isn't part of the vision painting he created?

"I'm not leaving Bobbi's side to unclog your toilet, no matter how inconvenient it is for you. Get someone else. There are plenty of plumbers."

"Oh for God's sake, don't fight over something as inconsequential as plumbing," Ted Lasker booms as he comes closer.

Finally, a voice of sanity.

He's in surprisingly good shape for a man his age with lean muscle and a visible six pack. The black trunks hang loosely around him, and he's holding a glass of champagne.

Nora's face scrunches with disappointment and annoyance. Noah merely sighs.

"I know the best plumbers in the city. I'll have Joey get on it." Ted snaps his fingers.

And my last disastrous date pops up from behind Ted with a tablet. I try not to make a face.

"Which mansion requires attention?" he asks Nora.

"Noah is the only one who can unclog it," she says in a friendly tone.

Joey's eyes shift in Noah's direction with something akin to wariness. Then they widen when he notices me. "You!"

I do my best to not cringe. Talking about that date would be humiliating.

"I thought you didn't want him! That's why I had to get Rammi!" Joey looks at Noah like a scared bunny, then returns to me. "You got me into so much trouble!"

Noah starts to take a step forward, but I put a hand on his forearm. I got this. "Don't blame me for your issues. I would've never agreed to meet you if you hadn't lied."

Joey turns red. "If you'd just communicated better, I could've avoided the trauma of...that visit."

"What's traumatic is your existence," Noah says.

"What's going on here?" Ted asks, while Noah glares at Joey.

"She's the one I told you about a few months ago as a perfect fit for either Noah or Huxley. You know, the chick who wanted to have children. Guess she settled on Noah." Joey looks absurdly satisfied with himself. "I, you know, said some nice things about him to help speed up her decision."

Like you have any influence on me. I step forward. "Look, I knew Noah long before I met you. You had nothing to do with us being together."

Joey huffs. "Denying me the credit I'm due won't change the facts of the matter."

"It's all good, Joey." Ted talks to his assistant like he's a chihuahua that needs a bit of coddling, then suddenly turns and hugs me. "Welcome to the family, Barbie! So how many babies are we talking here? And how soon?"

I squeak. He's squeezing too hard, and it's awkward as hell since his hand is way *way* too low, not even an inch above my ass.

"No!" Noah's panicked shout cuts through the small crowd. He rushes up and rips his father's arms off me. "Bobbi, remember the vision painting?"

"Yes." *Is that the right thing to say here?* This whole situation is *so* bizarre.

He points at his parents and Joey. "They aren't part of it. Because they're weird."

"Ow. That hurts," Nora says in a monotone.

"Your babies will get ponies," Ted goes on, like no one else has said anything. The man has tunnel vision and apparently tunnel hearing. "Not even my own kids got 'em." He gives me a you-know-what-I-mean wink.

I just stare at him. If Noah and I had babies, our kids would enjoy more material comfort than others. He is a billionaire after all. But there would still be very definite limits on what they could have—getting everything you want all the time can't be healthy.

Nora puts on a smile, but it doesn't reach her eyes. "Lovely idea, Ted. But where are they going to *keep* the ponies?"

"Here." He rolls his arms vaguely in an I-don't-know-what-the-problem-is gesture. "I can build a stable. Joey, look into it."

Joey taps his tablet. "Right away, sir."

"Of course. And riding through a colonnade of penis cannons would be *fabulous* for a child's psychological well-being and emotional development. I can't wait to see how Noah and Bobbi's offspring turn out," Nora says sweetly.

What cannons?

Ted lets out a booming laugh. "Hey, having fun is important! Look how well Noah turned out."

A muscle in Noah's jaw ticks. Regardless of the amount of *fun* he may have had frolicking among...penis cannons, it looks like he wants to murder his father.

"Let's take this somewhere else." Noah hooks one arm under his father's shoulder and the other around his mother's waist and drags them away. Joey follows, tapping his tablet.

Noah looks back and mouths, *Wait for me, we have to talk.*

No kidding. Except my brain doesn't know exactly what we should be talking *about.* I'm barely wrapping my mind around the fact that Ted Lasker is even weirder than I expected and Nora isn't capable of hiring a plumber in Dubai.

Despite Noah saying that his folks aren't part of the painting, will they be willing to stay out of our lives? And how about our kids? Should they be deprived of their grandparents?

Too much to think about right now. I head toward the buffet for something to drink, and just as I get there Reggie, the person I'd least like to see, stops right in front of me.

Her judgmental gaze sweeps me up and down, and a sneer twists her bright red lips. "Jesus, Bobbi, you look like the hired help."

Although many of the guests are in bikinis, she's in a flowing sundress and high heels. Not because she wants to look fashionable. My money's on her not having a toned enough belly that she deems worthy of displaying in front of the movers and shakers of Hollywood. She's exhaustingly critical of both her own appearance and that of others, and can't stand it when she doesn't measure up in some area. I don't know how she—or anyone—can live her entire life comparing herself to others, from her body to clothes to what she puts in her mouth.

Floyd stops right behind her. He's in red, white and blue trunks with the U.S. Air Force emblem on them. Aviator shades cover his eyes, and he's nodding in time with the music. He probably thinks his outfit and those sunglasses make him look like Tom Cruise in *Top Gun*.

I'm way too dazed and emotionally drained from meeting Noah's parents and Joey to deal with Reggie or Floyd, so I start to go around the cockroach couple. Better to find some quiet place to settle my thoughts until Noah returns.

"Hey, I'm talking to you," she says.

"And I'm avoiding you. How did you get in anyway?" She isn't important or famous enough to rub shoulders with Ted Lasker.

"I know people, unlike you. Rachel's boyfriend is a good friend of mine."

Translation: She slept with him in the last two years. If it had been longer than that, she would've labeled him "an old friend."

She plants her palm on my chest as her gaze zeroes in on the cake. "Did you make that?"

"Yup." I say, while debating whether to just push her hand off my chest or break it. The former would be the professional way to go, although the latter would be *much* more satisfying. "Gorgeous, isn't it?"

Her face turns red, probably since she's dying to tell me it's fugly as hell but can't. Calculations race behind her feverish eyes. "Not bad," she finally says. "So when are you sending the designs for my engagement cake?"

"Never. I already told you I'm not baking anything for you."

"You can't talk to my fiancée like that!" Floyd says, trying to look aggressive.

"Don't you have a gluten allergy? Aren't you feeling faint? Maybe experiencing a little shortness of breath?" My eyes slide to the cake and the huge pile of pastries. I'm not sure how many of these super skinny Hollywood people are planning to indulge, but Rachel spared no expense to make sure her party had everything, including a giant flakey pastry baked in the shape of swans with their beaks touching.

"Look, I'm giving you a chance to redeem yourself and get some good publicity," Reggie says.

"More like a chance to be a sucker. I know you, Reggie. You're going to say shit about my cake anyway because this isn't about my redemption but about you being too cheap. You never liked me because you could never get TJ to like you and you blamed me. But you know what? The real reason he never liked you is your awful personality and selfishness. You don't have the guts to go up to him and ask him why he doesn't like you. The only thing you can do is come after me because you're a coward and you think you're better than me because your tits are bigger. But guess what? I'm not jealous of your tits or your Instagram followers or that car lube commercial you did ten years ago. I don't even think about you—ever—until you show up to bother me. Like roaches aren't on people's minds until they crawl out from under a Dumpster. And in case you still can't figure out my answer to your demand: I'm not baking you a fucking engagement cake, and there's nothing you can do about it."

Reggie and Floyd turn bright red. A matching couple.

Over their heads, I spot Noah striding toward us. I start walking to him.

Floyd is the first to recover. "Who the hell do you think you are?"

His anger seems to embolden Reggie. She grabs my arm. "Where do you think you're going after talking to me like that?"

She shoves me with surprising force. My heel catches on something on the ground, and I trip.

Damn it, *the cake!*

I twist, trying to avoid knocking over the buffet. Everything happens in slow motion. Noah rushes forward. I try not to flail my arms. My hip bumps against the table where the cake is set, and it trembles like a building in an earthquake. The crystal columns in the naked tiers shake dangerously. My skin prickles as horror shivers up my spine.

Reggie's eyes glint with viciousness, and she kicks one of the table legs. Some of the gum-paste rose petals fall from the upper tiers, landing on the smooth surface of the buttercream tiers below. One of the crystal columns tilts to the side and all five of the layers above sway. I raise a hand, like a super hero with telekinetic powers, to stop my gorgeous creation from tipping over.

But it happens anyway. The cake slumps, then topples, crumbling and falling over me. Cool buttercream smears my face, neck, chest and shoulders. Fire burns across my forearm, but I ignore the pain as I stare at the ruins of my masterpiece in absolute shock.

"What the *fuck*!" Noah's sharp cry pulls my attention back to the present. "Are you okay?" He holds my arm, raising it.

"My cake…"

"Who cares about the cake?"

I look down and see blood trickling from a long, jagged cut on my forearm. On the ground is a cake cutting knife. The catering people must've put it by the cake after we set it up.

"We need to get you to the hospital," Noah says.

"But the cake—"

"Fuck the cake." His eyes burn with barely banked rage. I swallow. I've never seen him this furious. Actually, I didn't realize he was capable. "Forget the cake, Bobbi. Let me handle this for you. Please."

30

NOAH

If Bobbi weren't staring at me in shock over what just happened, I'd probably take the opportunity to kill Reggie Hopkins and Floyd Baggett on the spot, witnesses or no. It would only take a moment, and I don't need a gun.

Instead, I put my arm around her, hustle her into my car and take her to the hospital. *Four fucking stitches.* Every time the doc's needle pierces Bobbi's skin, I feel like a bullet is tearing through my guts.

Bobbi pats my arm like I'm the one who needs to be soothed. It just makes me want to murder Reggie and Floyd more.

The doctor says Bobbi is fine, but what the hell does he know? Doctors always say everything's fine. Fuckers.

You're being unfair, a cold rational voice points out, but I ignore it. What's unfair is what happened to Bobbi.

The doc sends her home with a lot of pain meds. If she were really fine, he wouldn't have to give her anything.

Bobbi studies my expression. "It doesn't hurt that much. I'm all right," she says, but the tight hollowness in her eyes tells me not to trust her words.

There is physical pain, but the meds are containing it. Worse is the emotional damage. She's upset because she didn't just make the cake to be a pretty decoration at the party. She imagined people enjoying the beauty of what she'd created and marveling over its delicious flavor. To her, baking is about nourishing people's souls and bodies.

Reggie and Floyd ruined it. And they will pay. I'll make sure of it.

My phone buzzes.

–Griffin: Is Bobbi okay? How badly is she hurt?

–Me: Four stitches. Pain meds.

–Sebastian: What the hell.

–Grant: Shoulda been there to lend support. I didn't realize you and Bobbi would be attending Rachel's party.

–Me: Rachel loves me, and I was trying to be nice.

–Nicholas: I should've gone. I honestly didn't think anybody was going except Griffin.

–Emmett: When I heard about what happened to the cake and Bobbi, I couldn't believe it.

What he can't believe is that anybody would be stupid enough to ruin a party at Dad's place. He hates people who interrupt him, but what he absolutely loathes is a good party gone wrong. In his mind, the purpose of life is to party.

On top of that, the disgusting duo made a big mistake in injuring Bobbi. Dad might never remember her name—memorizing such details is an effort and that's what Joey's for—but her being my girl and wanting to have babies is etched in his mind forever.

–Griffin: You should've seen Mom's face. I've never seen her that angry.

–Emmett: Bet Dad was pissed too.

–Nicholas: What a way to ruin your career. They were hoping to break into acting, right?

–Me: At least the girl was.

–Griffin: Mom's going to blame them when her relationship implodes.

And her little romance with her boytoy of the moment will expire within the next four weeks—at the outside. Her relationships don't last more than ten or eleven weeks, tops. But it'll be blamed on Reggie and Floyd now. In Rachel's world, nothing is ever her fault.

I put the phone away and look at Bobbi.

"I gotta go pick up some stuff from my place," I say. "It won't take long."

She nods, her eyelids drooping. "Don' worry 'bout me." Her words are slurred from the meds. "I'll be fine."

Remains to be seen is on the tip of my tongue, but she doesn't need an argument right now. She needs some tender attention.

I wander around the house, grabbing stuff she might need. Her phone, Kindle, TV remote, a bottle of water. *Anything else?* I look around, but the items in my hands seem adequate. If she weren't injured, I might bring her wine, but no alcohol until she's fully healed.

I leave them on her nightstand. She watches me with amused affection. "Y'know my legs are fine, right? Hands're fine, too."

"Believe me, I know your legs are fine." I kiss her. "Now, shush. Bedrest. I'll be back soon."

Heading out, I open the app on my phone. Mom's going to blow a fuse when she discovers what I'm about to do, but my girl deserves justice.

Let's see... What the hell is Floyd up to right now? Reggie's post pops up first—tagging Floyd. It's a photo of them in a hot tub, enjoying some champagne and laughing. Candles surround them, and she captioned it:

The best way to end the evening. Nothing cleanses away the ugliness of the day like being with the one you love.

The ugliness of the day? They aren't the ones with stitches. If I had the power to reach into photos, she and Floyd would have broken necks.

I tap the photo and run it through the AI. Geo-recognition AI isn't as sophisticated as the facial programs, but it should be accurate enough.

Within seconds, it spits out a location. I smile grimly. *Bingo.*

The assholes are at a house in one of those secluded canyon communities with lots of trees and bushes. It's one of the two Floyd inherited from his mother, and he uses it when he wants to impress a woman and get laid. The place isn't swanky, but it has its charm with lots of privacy—there aren't any houses in the area except for one a mile away—and a hot tub, adequate for two adults.

During my drive, the app spits out a detailed dossier on Reggie, who is clinging to Floyd, both literally and figuratively. She has nothing but debt to her name. Spending every penny that comes into your account tends to do that to you. For a has-been with no prospects, character or brains, Floyd is the best option. The second she can upgrade, she will, although it won't be easy in a city where youth is the most prized currency.

I park my car far away enough that nobody will hear the engine noise, then pull out my tools from the hidden compartment in the trunk and head toward my targets. I position myself in the trees around the house, and take a look.

Reggie and Floyd are in the hot tub, oblivious, and my scope is good enough to see that they're sipping Jaume Serra Cristalino Brut Cava. She whines and pouts. I read her lips. She's pissed off that Rachel got upset and my dad kicked her out. "How am I going to be a star at this rate?"

There's always porn.

Floyd puts his arm around her and kisses her temple. "I know, baby, but I'll take care of you no matter what."

For sex. I don't need to be able to read minds to know that's what he's thinking.

"Thanks, love. In spite of all the crap, it was so satisfying to see that bitch's cake land on her." She tilts her head back in a raucous laugh.

My earlier rage returns, tightening my skin. *What's gonna be satisfying is seeing you shit your pants.* I drag a black balaclava over my head, bend back down to the sight and pull the trigger on my cheetah.

Bullets puncture the hot tub without hitting the trashy couple. Water begins to spew out through the holes. Reggie and Floyd look around, their wide eyes wild. The silencer muted the sound, but they know what just happened.

There is the usual moment of paralysis. Then Floyd flings a hairy arm like a panicked one-winged chicken, his elbow knocking the bottle of the bubbly over. The laser sight on my rifle puts a red dot on Floyd's chest, causing Reggie to scream, and he slides under the water, like the rapidly plummeting water surface will stop the next bullet. Reggie continues to screech, but nobody's going to hear her. The only occupied house in the area is full of drunken teenagers, partying to music loud enough to permanently damage your hearing.

I fire more shots. She scrambles out of the tub. Floyd finally seems to realize that water isn't Kevlar and heaves himself over the edge to land in a heap on his wooden deck. I rise from my position and walk toward them, rifle by my side.

"Oh my God, don't kill me!" Reggie says. She's scrambled off the deck and into the yard; now she puts her hands high above her head. "I'll do anything!" She rips her bikini top down, displaying her tits.

Agh, my eyes! Why do women like her think guys want to see them topless? Or that showing their tits will make a difference?

I pull out a pistol from the back of my waistband with my left hand. My ambidexterity is something not even my brothers know about, but I can shoot more accurately with my left hand.

Floyd tries to get up but stumbles. Tears drip from his eyes. "Please. Don't kill me. I'm too young."

"My name is Reggie Hopkins. Short for Regina. I'm only twenty-nine."

"Why the fuck do you think I care?" My voice is distorted from the little chip on my neck. The government spends a lot of money on things like that, calling them "toilet seats for the Pentagon."

"Doesn't knowing my name humanize me?"

She's watched too many movies. "Naming a rat doesn't make it a human."

"What?" The blood drains from her face, making her appear ghostly.

"You're lucky I'm not that good with knives. Otherwise, I'd skin you both." Mom did that once. The other guy deserved it.

Reggie and Floyd scream, their eyes so wide with terror the white shows around their irises. Then they sob. From the smell, one of them definitely peed. Or maybe they both did.

Still not enough.

I raise the pistol and fire twice.

31

BOBBI

SOMETIME IN THE NIGHT, the mattress dips. I stir as Noah slips in and puts his arm around me.

"Hey, you're back. What time is it?"

"Like midnight?" He kisses me. "Sorry I woke you up."

"I wasn't really sleeping. Sort of dozing. It took you a while," I say, turning and burying my nose in his chest and inhaling the fresh shampoo and body wash. His skin is a little damp from a recent shower.

"A fender bender. And it rained a little, too."

I sigh. I can only imagine what the traffic must've been like with rain. One drop of water from the sky and all of L.A. turns into a parking lot.

Noah's phone buzzes on the night stand, but he doesn't check it.

"You should get that, in case it's your mom."

"She doesn't need a plumber that bad." But he picks up the phone anyway, then shakes his head. The dim light shows a reluctant smile on his face.

"What?"

"Here. You can read it." He hands me the phone. "Group text. Hux just added to it."

–Griffin: How's Bobbi doing?

–Nicholas: I finally saw the videos Molly found. That's assault, isn't it?

–Huxley: No point pressing charges. She'd get a slap on the wrist, if that.

–Griffin: Dad should've waited before dragging them out. I never got a chance to kick 'em.

"When Griff kicks you, something breaks," Noah says.

I let out a short laugh. "Good to know. Next time you see him, tell him thanks."

"Tell him yourself when we have another get together."

I realize he's right. And his talking about our future like he's going to be around—of course!—sends flutter of hope and optimism. "Yeah, I will." Smiling and placing a hand on his arm, I return to the text.

–Emmett: You kick women now too?

–Grant: She's a bitch, but she's still a woman...

–Griffin: No, I don't kick women. But I would've kicked him twice. One for him, one for her. She's his fiancée. He should take full responsibility.

–Me: Very medieval of you.

–Griffin: Not my fault he's engaged to an animal.

–Huxley: There are ways to sue them into oblivion. No need to get violent like savages.

–Griffin: Say that to my face.

–Nicholas: I don't think Bobbi would appreciate you fighting.

–Me: I wish I could dump them in the middle of a jungle with a single canteen of water.

–Huxley: I know a guy who might know a guy.

I lift my eyes. "Is he serious?"

"Could be. You never know with Huxley."

Another text pops up. I let Noah tap it. He looks at it for a moment and then tilts the screen back my way.

–Amy: Is Bobbi okay? Does she need anything?

–Lucie: I can't believe it! That cake was so beautiful. And her cut looked terrible.

–Sierra: I can drop by with some dinner if that helps.

—Molly: There's this poultice I found on the Internet that's really good for cuts.

—Me: Thanks. I'll ask Bobbi what she needs. She got four stitches, so she might need some help.

—Aspen: If she needs help with the bakery, I can totally do it. Not with the baking, but with the coffee pots, displays and cash registers. I worked at a café in college, and I was good at it.

"Wow..." I swallow a small lump. I can always count on my cousins —and Yuna and Ivy—but I never imagined I'd get the same kind of absolute support from Noah's family as well. I thought it might take a while to win them over.

"They care about you," Noah says, kissing my temples like he knows exactly what I'm feeling right now. "You're part of the family, Bobbi."

"Isn't this a little...premature?" My voice trembles slightly. "We aren't even engaged or anything."

He takes the phone from my hand and puts it on the night stand, then shifts carefully to avoid touching the injured arm and holds me tight, so I can feel his heart beat against my skin. "None of that matters," he says in the dark. "I've never brought a woman home to introduce or hosted a lunch like what we had. They know you're the only woman to hold my heart."

I lay my arm over him, the unease I've had since the trip to the Antelope Canyon dissipating like a handful of sand in the ocean.

We should be fine as long as we love each other and have each other's backs.

32

NOAH

"It's really nothing."

Bobbi's reassurance makes no difference. Every time my eyes settle on the bandages on her arm, I wish I'd peeled Hopkins and Baggett like a couple of potatoes. Just because I don't have the talent with knives that Mom does, doesn't mean it can't be done. I just wouldn't be able to peel off each layer of skin.

"You still have stitches," I say.

"Stop acting like I can't even go to the bathroom on my own. My legs work fine."

My brain understands that. But my heart says it's my fault she's hurt, and I gotta protect my woman. "But the stitches..."

She lets out an exasperated sigh, but a hint of amusement glitters in her burnt caramel eyes. "I know you're anxious because you care, but you shouldn't be wound so tight."

She starts toward the kitchen and reaches for a mug. "Hey, hold on. Let me." I run over and grab it for her.

"Noah, it's just a cut. I've had worse, believe me." She points to her belly.

"You're not making me feel better here." Regret and fury pool in my gut. Siccing the IRS on that psycho bitch was too lenient. I should've just gut-shot her. An eye for an eye. Hammurabi had the right idea. There would be a lot fewer assholes around if we did unto them what they do unto others.

"I should've been there," I say. "I'm never going to forgive myself for not being there for you."

She shakes her head. "We aren't going to rehash the past. And you know why? Two reasons. One, because that isn't how you get to the future you want." A soft brush of her lips over my chin. "And two, because otherwise I will *never* forgive you."

"I know. I've been a complete bastard."

I pour freshly brewed coffee into two mugs and have Bobbi sit at the kitchen counter, then toast a couple of bagels and fry up some bacon. "I talked with Rachel. She said she'd pay the bill for the cake. And she also wanted to know if you're okay. So did my dad."

Bobbi sighs. "It's too bad Rachel didn't get to cut the cake. She was looking forward to doing it with her boyfriend." A sudden smile pops on her face. "I was surprised your dad had Reggie and Floyd thrown out. It was pretty awesome." She's been around fame-chasers long enough to know that stuff like this can be fatal to their quest for stardom.

"That's Dad. You fuck around, he'll make sure you find out. And ruining a party hosted at his mansion definitely counts as fucking around." I spread a generous dollop of cream cheese on a slice of warm bagel and hand it to her.

She takes it with a murmured thanks, looking vaguely relieved that I don't try to feed her myself.

"So what's up with your father?" she asks when I sit down with the rest of the bagels and bacon.

"He won't be around that much, if that's what you're wondering. Not that relevant to our lives." I've always known she has a particular distaste for the Hollywood celeb types, most of it formed due to her idiotic clients. I didn't want anything to count against me, especially when I was trying to get close to her for the job. And then later... Well, our father is a cross my brothers and I bear.

She shakes her head. "So he's really that serious about having new grandkids? Even though he already has four? I thought Joey was exaggerating."

"Oh, not at all. Dad's absolutely that obsessed, but only because Emmett and Griffin won't let him near their children. For good reason."

"Was he a terrible father to you, growing up?" Sympathy softens her voice.

"He wasn't that bad, considering. He provided for us financially, even though he never had any time for us."

"No holidays together?" She sounds a little wistful. If even half the stuff from the dossier on her father, Otto Bright, was true, he was a shitty human being and a shitty father. He was always working—mainly to dig up state secrets and find the highest bidder for them. And her mother wasn't much of a parent, either. She whined about having to move all the time, but never provided any kind of emotional stability for Bobbi.

I wish Bobbi and I had met when we were younger. Then we could've hung out and she would have felt less lonely while we were together. Otto took assignments in some of the worst parts of the world and often took his family with him, uprooting Bobbi constantly. The only time he didn't was when the State Department instructed him to leave his family behind because his new assigned post was too dangerous.

"Not unless your idea of a holiday involves orgies."

She looks at me, then lets out a skeptical laugh. "Seriously?"

"Yeah. That's just how he is. Like him nagging me and my brothers to give him grandchildren. He isn't doing it out of a desire for more family members to love. He wants them because he needs a musically talented grandchild—ideally one who can sing well—to rub into his rival's face. He was asking Emmett, but these days he's been harassing Griffin."

"Because of Ellen? She's really cute."

I snort. "He doesn't even know her name. He thinks she might be better than Monique because Griff can carry a tune. He's one of the few who can sing a Freddie Mercury song without embarrassing himself. That's how he wooed Sierra."

"Awww, that's so sweet." Bobbi leans closer. "Can you do it?"

"Not without causing you severe trauma. So I'll stick to what I do best." I kiss her, and she giggles against my lips.

Suddenly, the door to the house opens. An alarm blares in my head, and I jerk back, automatically assessing the situation and cursing because I have no gun. The next best option: the knife I used to smear cream cheese on our bagels.

Three people walk in—her cousin TJ, the huge guy I saw at Bobbi's bakery and who I researched thoroughly. And a couple of women: Bobbi's other cousin Josie and the Kodiak bear's girlfriend, Cassie.

"Oh my God, are you okay?" Josie says, rushing toward Bobbi. She opens her arms to hug, then stops, hands hovering, unsure if she can touch Bobbi without hurting her. That's an automatic ten bonus points.

Bobbi hugs her instead. "I'm fine."

The women take seats at the counter. TJ remains standing and glares at me like I just stepped on an apple pie. "What's he doing here?"

"Nursing her," I say. "How about you?"

"Checking up. She's family. Gotta take care of her."

"Who's this?" Cassie asks.

"Noah."

Josie narrows her eyes at me as she speaks to Bobbi. "*The* Noah? The one who ditched you over and over again?"

"Who are these people?" I ask Bobbi. I'm not supposed to already know.

She makes quick introductions. "My cousins TJ and Josie. That's Cassie, his girlfriend."

"I see. And you haven't told them about our relationship?" I'm a little hurt. After all the effort I've made, does she still have enough doubts that she doesn't think she can tell her family about me? I address the other three. "I'm a reformed asshole."

"I didn't really call you an asshole," Bobbi mumbles.

"Oh yeah, you totally did," TJ counters loudly, which earns a glare from Bobbi. His lips flatten, but he drags a chair from the dining table and sits down.

"Need some couple therapy? I can give you a referral," Josie says, shooting me a bland smile.

Bobbi sighs. "That won't be necessary, thank you. But seriously. What are you guys doing here? And what's with all this 'you're going to take care of me' stuff?"

"We saw the videos." Cassie bristles. "What that bitch Reggie did! It's all over the Internet."

"Uh..." Bobbi blinks slowly. It's like somebody just told her that her car just went over a cliff—but it's okay because the car got smashed to pieces without killing anybody. Guess she didn't expect she'd be the star of a viral video or two. But people don't go to parties at my father's mansion for discreet fun. They go to flaunt, to be seen—and thereby let the world know they're important enough to warrant an invite. And they post whatever they think is interesting and dramatic. There's no way people at the party *wouldn't* have posted clips of the cake falling, much less security hauling off Hopkins and Baggett.

"I'm just pissed somebody got to them before I could," TJ says.

Bobbi frowns. "What do you mean?"

Biting back a smug smile, I look at TJ. *Yes, tell her what I did.* It sucks I can't take credit for it, but then I can't take credit for most of the good I've done for the world.

"Home invasion," TJ says. "Got roughed up some."

"Seriously?" There's no shock like feigned shock.

"Uh-huh. Reggie called me, begging me to hook her up with some exclusive security that's not going to break the bank."

Josie makes a face. "Because nothing says exclusive—or secure—like cheap."

I nod inwardly. I like this woman. "So what happened?"

"Somebody shot up the hot tub at their house—actually, her fiancé's house. Which I sort of feel not that bad about since she was always so obnoxious about it, like nobody but the two of them have ever had a hot tub." Cassie rolls her eyes.

Bobbi looks at me, eyes wide, and mouths, *Huxley?*

Why would she think my almost-lawyer brother would do something like this? Oh, wait—the text! I firm my chin to hide my amusement as I shake my head, then turn to Cassie.

"But *they* weren't shot, right? So what if somebody messed up their hot tub?" I shrug. "Just get the insurance to pay for it."

TJ gives me a look. "They *were* shot. With tranq darts. And then tied up."

"*What?* Are they okay...?" Bobbi says.

TJ grunts. "Some money and some valuable sports memorabilia were taken. Floyd's computer. Also, Reggie supposedly had her hair sheared off almost to the scalp."

"That hair is her pride and joy," Josie says, wincing.

That's right. The sports stuff and money were to throw the police off the track. I threw all of it into the Pacific. But the bitch said shit about Bobbi's pride and joy when the bakery first opened, so the hair was more eye-for-an-eye justice. *These are the worst croissants I've ever had, my ass.*

TJ continues: "And your landlord? He got shot in a ball."

"Jesus!" Bobbi gasps, her jaw dropping before she cringes.

"Again, just a tranq dart." TJ raises his eyebrows. "Coulda been a *lot* worse."

"Coulda been blown off with a bullet," Cassie says viciously.

TJ shudders.

I do my best to not smile with pride. Damn, I'm good. Floyd let out a cry somewhere between a dying cow and a rutting hyena. He passed out even faster than Reggie. Then again, the pain probably knocked him out before the tranq drug hit.

"Then he got four cuts on his arms."

One cut per stitch, which will take at least sixteen stitches total to fix. Or so I think. I'm not as precise with knives as Mom, and might've gone a little overboard because I'll be damned if he'll only need fifteen.

"You look awfully pleased," Bobbi observes.

I shrug, but the twitching of my lips betrays me. "I think whatever karmic force is responsible for what happened to Reggie and Floyd did a helluva good job." I make sure to hold Bobbi's eye for the next line: "It should get the Nobel *Fleece* Prize."

She laughs, shaking her head. Josie and Cassie join in.

TJ gives me a hard look for two heartbeats. "You're not wrong." A corner of his mouth pulls upward. Then he adds in a voice just loud enough for me to hear: "Maybe you aren't a completely useless bastard after all."

I feign confused innocence.

He shoots me a don't-play-dumb smile. "Every rich guy knows a guy who knows a guy."

He doesn't realize—I *am* the guy. But revealing that wouldn't do any good for my future with Bobbi, so I just give him more confusion and turn to talk to the ladies. A lie of omission is better than a lie of commission.

Isn't it?

33

BOBBI

"You. Out. Now."

Noah gives me a sad puppy face, but I refuse to be swayed, no matter how progressively more forlorn his expression grows. It's been a week since the injury, and he's still hovering like I'm some brittle sugar candy about to break.

He's reacting out of love, but it's just too weird. I'm taller than many men, with a sturdy frame and strong muscles. I throw guys around in judo and am trained in three or four other martial arts on top of that. I'm just not used to having somebody follow me around and act like I'm about to collapse every time I move my arm.

Plus, I'm a fast healer—and the cut is now fine. The doc was actually a little shocked.

"Don't you need some help with the housework?" Noah asks, looking around my living room.

"Are you calling my house dirty?"

"Just offering my assistance. I'm good at chores."

"Which is why your mom's been calling you. But my toilets are fine. You need to go visit your brothers."

"Why?"

"Because you like them? For male bonding? Family time?"

"They don't need help." His eyes fall on my arm again.

I'm going to scream. Then murder Reggie with my "bad" arm. Griffin had qualms about kicking her, but not me. "Noah, sometimes you need to stay away to get closer."

He considers for a moment. "But—"

"Just one day."

He bites his lip, a sign that there are more arguments he wants to make, but knows better.

"Come on. You're driving me nuts here."

He sighs. "Fine. But don't do anything taxing. Especially the floor. I'm going to help you with it." He glares at the boxes of tiles that arrived last Wednesday.

"Go. The tiles aren't your enemy."

He looks at Señor Mittens for backup, but the cat merely gives him an aloof look and grooms himself.

"Traitor," Noah mutters, then leaves.

When the door finally closes behind him, I half-sigh and half-laugh. Maybe it was a blessing in disguise when he ghosted me after the gunshot. If he'd been around, he would've driven me insane with overprotectiveness. And all this time I thought *TJ* was overzealous and overbearing.

I'm going to show Noah I'm perfectly fine, I think, looking at the ugly kitchen floor. Ripping up these disgusting tiles up should do the trick.

I rummage through the toolbox TJ brought a few weeks ago and find what I need. Señor Mittens gives me a reproachful look. "Keep your opinions to yourself," I say.

I don't want to work in silence and under my cat's disapproval, so I put on a Korean spy drama Yuna recommended. It apparently involves a lot of backstabbing. It's dubbed, so I can work and listen to the dialogue.

The trim work around the kitchen floor is solid oak and very nice, so I take care removing it and stack it to the side to be reused. Then I grab a chisel and hammer to pry away the first tile. After a couple moments of gradually increasing pressure, the grout cracks and the tile comes off.

What the heck? I stare at the oak underneath. It's in surprisingly good condition, despite dust from the grout and other gunk. A bit of buffing, staining and applying topcoat, and the kitchen will have gorgeous hardwood flooring. What was Dad thinking? He wasn't the type to care about real estate appreciation, but it seems wild that he would've actively *de*valued his home.

The existing tiles are much sturdier than I expected. I pull out one of the newly delivered ones and compare. The old ones are at least three or four millimeters thicker. Wonder if that makes a difference. *Should I have bought tiles that were equally thick?* On the other hand, all the options basically had the same dimensions. Where did Dad get these ugly, thick things, anyway?

My phone rings. *Is Noah checking up on me already?* It hasn't even been an hour.

I glance at the screen. Yuna and Ivy, requesting a video conference call. I hit the green button.

"Hello, ladies. Don't worry, I'm fine," I say, going back to chipping away at the grout. They texted me on Sunday after TJ, Josie and Cassie left, and I reassured them I was all right, although Yuna acted like the world was ending because I might get scarred. She told me to sue Reggie, then brought over some Korean ointment that's supposed to prevent skin discoloration and pitting.

"Good to hear," Yuna says. "But I just had a conversation with Eugene, that brother of mine." Uh-ho. Whatever he said must've upset her to call him "Eugene, that brother of mine." "How could you not have told us about your steakhouse lover boy?"

"Eugene told you?" I say, feeling slightly betrayed. He seemed like a stoic, silent fellow who wouldn't gossip.

"It came up. I understand him not telling me when it happened because he's a guy and guys tend to not recognize what's important. But *you?*"

"We feel hurt and unwanted," Ivy adds, laying it on thick. She's been with Yuna for too long.

"Sorry," I say. "I was kind of upset and distracted at the time."

"Buildup but no payoff?" Ivy asks.

"So is that why you didn't end up with your porterhouse passion? Eugene hinted you had a quickie with him at the restaurant."

My face heats. *Of course he knew.* He isn't blind, just too gentlemanly to show he noticed. I hammer the chisel with more force than necessary. "Um... I actually *did* end up with him."

"*What?*" my friends say in unison.

"It was Noah."

Ivy gasps. Yuna mutters something in Korean.

"Well, that explains why you didn't tell us," Ivy says.

"Yeah, it seemed like a one-off thing. I assumed he was just jealous of Eugene and acting like a savage."

"Well, he shouldn't have been. Jin isn't getting married any time soon, although our parents keep sending him dossiers of info on possible merger wives." Yuna went through the same thing. She actually fled Korea when her parents tried to pressure her into marrying some rich guy for some business merger, and Eugene tried to cut her off financially until she complied. "I'd laugh at the irony if it weren't for the fact that this is Round Two for him."

"Tell him I wish him luck. Look, this floor needs my undivided attention. Once I'm done, we'll get some margaritas and you two can *pry*"—I wave the chisel in front of my phone's screen—"to your hearts' content."

"Fine. I can take a hint," Yuna says.

I place the chisel and give it a quick whack with the hammer. "Good."

"Should you be doing that, though? Doesn't your arm hurt?" Ivy asks.

"It's *fine*. It was just some cuts, not a broken bone. Stop sounding like Noah."

"He's probably just worried. If I got cut like that, Tony wouldn't have let the host drag the duo away."

"Yes, but Tony is famously paranoid about your safety. And I understand why." He almost lost her—twice. "But I can't live like that."

We say goodbye, and I go back to the floor. Four more tiles come off relatively easily. Then I get to the base of the counter and the first one there won't budge. It also looks slightly newer, although the top is scratched and worn like the others.

I spend about five minutes of fruitless effort hunting for a good spot to pry it up. *What is this stuff made of, adamantium?*

No dice. I sit back and think. Maybe it would be better to break the tile in half and pry it up from the middle.

I place the chisel in the center of the tile and hit with a bit more power. Sure enough, it breaks cleanly in half. Success!

I pull off the bottom part and dump it into the box with the others. Then notice a black spot on the floor. *Oh, no. Is that mold?*

Shit, shit, shit. Holding my breath, I bend down and squint, but up close it doesn't look like mold. In fact, it looks like...*a microSD card?*

Huh. No brand name or anything. It's pristine, so it couldn't have been that Dad dropped it while installing the floor. So where did it come from? I pick it up, then the discarded half-section of tile. On the bottom of the tile is a shallow gouge about an inch long. So... Did somebody hide the memory card under the tile? The slot looks deliberately created.

And just what's on the card that this much effort went into hiding it?

Curiosity spurs me to get off the floor. I find the memory card adapter that came with the microSD card I bought for my phone a while back. Then I dust the card off, stick it into the adapter and plug it into the slot on my laptop.

A folder pops up. I click on it, see a pdf file named OttosFavoriteThings. Did this belong to Dad? Otto isn't exactly a rare name, but it isn't that common either.

When Dad died, there was no will, no last words. But then his death was abrupt and violent. I'm curious what he'd consider his favorite things and why he'd hide a file about it in the kitchen floor. He sometimes acted like he was starring in a Bond flick. Was this another example of that? Did he ever mean for me to find it?

I open the pdf. The first page shows a black-and-white photo of a woman and CLASSIFIED stamped in red.

I look away for a moment. *This better not be porn...*

The top line reads ASSET: LAURA BENNETT. Lots of blacked out lines in a document that looks like the CIA dossiers from *The Bourne Identity*, except the agency is nothing I've ever heard of, and I don't recognize the olive-wreathe-over-a-shield-and-spear emblem.

What *is* this? Some kind of weird role-playing game he did with others? Except wasn't he always too busy to fool with stuff like that?

Or maybe he never had any time because he spent so much of his energy on the game. There are people who get so into games they basically live online.

The rest of the pages about her are mostly blacked out, but dates and locations and targets can still be read. Wonder what the difference is between the blacked-out ones and not blacked-out ones.

I scroll down some more...and my heart jumps to my throat.

ASSET: NOAH LASKER. Lots of lines are redacted, but I see a hand-written note in the margin: *Nora Blane's son and favorite asset*. The writing is blocky, with familiar overly looped *a*'s and *e*'s—Dad's.

Noah's mom introduced herself as Nora. And she wanted him to "unclog her toilet" in Dubai. Even flew all the way to SoCal to get him to do it. I thought she was just an eccentric wealthy woman—one thing money can't buy is common sense. But what if she's something else...?

Besides, if this was just a harmless game my dad played with her and Noah, wouldn't they have said something? Noah knew who my father was. When he first visited me at this house, he saw a family photo pinned to the fridge and I told him they were my parents.

I scan the pages for clues that this is just a big prank. Words jump out. Outwardly unserious. Possible sociopath. Unpredictable. Difficult to control. Unmanageable. Highly trained and skilled. Prolific. Refers to his rifles as "cheetahs."

I shoot cheetahs. Noah's statement about what he does for a living fleets through my mind, icy apprehension slithering down my spine.

I close the pdf, unable to process what I've just seen. Of course this is a joke. Dad had basically zero sense of humor, so maybe he thought this would be funny... Noah? A possible sociopath? Come on! The man is tight with his brothers. Ellen adores him. Who puts stuff like this on a microSD card and hides it in a kitchen tile? There's another explanation for all this. Has to be.

But...

Every innocent scenario I come up with to explain the document is ridiculously unbelievable.

Señor Mittens meows, obviously bored with my stunned stillness. He hops down from the window sill, purposely knocking over the tablet on which the Korean drama is playing, chin held high in a disdain that demands I entertain him.

Not too interested in humoring you at the moment. I go over to pick up the tablet and check to make sure it didn't get damaged.

The male lead on the screen stares at his girlfriend. "You saw?"

"I saw *everything*," she spits out, the wind blowing her hair into her face. Her eyes are red with gathering tears. "You never loved me. You only cared about the secret you thought you could extract from me." She throws papers at him. The red CLASSIFIED stamps flash as the documents swirl in the air.

The man's jaw tightens, and he pulls a gun on her. She lets out a hollow chuckle. "I'm right, aren't I?"

The man glares at her. She suddenly puts a hand behind her, as though reaching for a gun, and he fires. Red bursts on her chest, terrible against the white of her shirt. She falls on her side, and there's nothing in her waistband.

The tablet suddenly goes black—out of battery.

I stare at the dead device, feeling like I've just seen a bad omen. *You only cared about the secret you thought you could extract from me.*

My eyes slide to my laptop. A chill slowly settles over me, swirling through my veins as the gears in my head start to turn. Noah and I met in Mexico right after my father died. Then he spent more time with me, came over to spend the night at this house—which I inherited from my father. He was here when I replaced some of the old furniture and mattresses. He helped me go through some of my father's things and held my hand when I needed to get over the grief of losing him. And he helped with the weird guilt I had over the fact that I didn't grieve as much as I should have because Dad and I just weren't that close.

Then he disappeared for a while, and when he came back he said his near-death experience in the plane made him realize what was important. But what if there's more to it than that?

What if he approached me because he was looking for the file Dad left behind? If I were a spy or mercenary, I wouldn't want it lying around. After all, keeping your identity secret is part of the game. He didn't think I had it, but maybe something happened to make him think it was hidden in the house. That would explain all the breaking in. And spending so much time here.

He's trying to prove he's the one for you, my heart argues. My brain feels like melting ice cream as I shove away the rebuttal.

As I try to sort my thoughts and emotions, I recall something TJ said when he came by with Josie and Cassie.

Maybe you aren't a completely useless bastard after all.

He said it quietly, but I heard it and know he directed it at Noah. He said something else too that I didn't catch, but didn't think anything of it at the time. What does he know?

Instead of texting, I call. TJ picks up after two rings.

"Bobbi, you okay?" I don't call unless it's an emergency.

"I'm fine." The response slips out automatically. I shake my head, grateful he can't see my physical reaction. He can be shockingly perceptive. "Listen, I just have a quick question."

"Okay." His tone is uncertain. He's probably wondering what's wrong because I didn't ask him if he was free to talk, either.

"Remember how you said that Noah might not be a completely useless bastard after all? You know, when you came to tell us about what happened to Reggie and Floyd?"

"Uh-huh."

"What did you mean?" My heart races as I wait.

"Well, the timing and all seemed pretty convenient."

"So you think he went after them?"

"Himself? No. Guys like that don't dirty their hands. They have too much to lose. But he probably knows a guy who, you know..."

"You think he's capable of something like that?" Clammy sweat slickens my palms. My cousin's more objective than I am. His heart isn't involved.

"In a heartbeat. You saw the look in his eyes, didn't you? If he thought he could get away with it, he would've killed them, no hesitation." TJ's tone is full of approval. He is, as they say, heavily into revenge.

I'd like to think Noah is just a carefree billionaire adventurer who likes to take photos of wildlife, but my cousin's radar for potential threats is much more fine-tuned than mine...which is why he enjoys his job, whereas I never really cared for my bodyguarding career. "I see. Okay." There doesn't seem to be anything more to say. "Thanks."

"That it?"

"Yeah."

"Okay. It might not be him, you know," TJ says. "Reggie likes to run her mouth, and she's pissed off a lot of people. One of them might've decided to seize the moment. Or it could've been Floyd. He could've banged somebody he shouldn't have."

"Ew."

"Yeah, you're right. Doubt he has talent in that direction. But he could've owed money to a bookie or something."

"It's possible. Okay, thanks. I'll talk to you later."

"Of course. Call if you need anything. And don't go doing that floor on your own. You'll open those cuts up again and have to go back to the hospital."

I roll my eyes. "Buh-bye," I say, and hang up.

As soon as I drop the phone on the sofa, my forced cheeriness evaporates. The call with TJ only stokes my uncertainty, fear and anxiety until I can't sit still. I jump to my feet and start pacing.

If he thought he could get away with it, he would've killed them, no hesitation.

But Reggie and Floyd aren't dead.

On the other hand, Noah was out late...way, way too late.

And the dossiers...

I look at the laptop. I wish I could say the dossiers were just pranks. But my father had a top-level security clearance. He coordinated a lot of projects with other departments and agencies, and he worked on things I'll never find out about.

I shove my fingers into my hair, then bend down and grab the hammer. My knuckles turn white around the handle.

You only cared about the secret you thought you could extract from me.

Bang.

34

NOAH

INSTEAD OF THE usual homey scent of bread and flowers, a stench of acrid dust hits me when I open the door to Bobbi's house around six p.m. The kitchen tiles are ripped out, and I run a hand over my face. The notification on the app had a post complaining about construction noise next door, and I knew exactly what she was doing after I left. It took all my self-control to not barge in and take over the task.

"Bobbi, I thought you were going to wait," I say.

Intellectually, I understand she needs to use her body. She isn't one of those people who likes to sit at a desk and sign papers. She was chafing at what she called my overbearingness. But seeing her bleed was like being hit in the solar plexus with a baseball bat, and it's my prerogative to take care of her to my heart's content when she's injured, even though she believes she's immortal. People are incredibly fragile. If she'd had her arm angled differently, the knife could've sliced the radial artery in her wrist, which could leave her blacked out in half a minute and dead in as little as two.

Just thinking about it makes me want to encase her in metal armor... except she'd run the other way, calling me crazy. So I've been hovering between the desire to hide her away in a padded room with nothing that could hurt her and the desire to accept what my brain has been telling me—that she's fine and I need to back the hell off unless I want her to lose her temper and throw my ass on the ground just to make a point.

"I was, but then I wanted to prove to you that my arm's fine." She sounds stiff, probably defensive, since she must be expecting me to be upset. Not moving from the couch in the living room, she gestures at the box with the old tiles. "All yours."

"Well, glad you waited for me to take them out, at least." I grin to let her know I'm not upset with her.

"No, I mean you can have them."

"What?" Finally I register the tight set of her jaw and mouth, the ticking of the muscle under her right eye. "What's wrong?"

I start toward her, but she doesn't meet my eyes. Instead, her heel bounces in that way she has when she's preoccupied with something that she doesn't want to think about.

My gut shivers with warning. I'm in the presence of a ticking time bomb. Just what the hell happened after I left?

"Do you really call your guns cheetahs?"

It takes a moment for my mind to process the abrupt question. My blood turns to ice. My brain says I should act dumb and give her my most charming and lighthearted smile. As I start to grin, her eyes meet mine, and I freeze, unable to continue with the ruse.

She knows.

"Here," she says, giving me a microSD card. "What you've been looking for."

I stare at it like it's a leech.

"My father's papers," she adds when I don't move to take it from her. "You weren't being fully honest before."

"Bobbi—"

"You aren't a wildlife photographer or an adventurer. Who do you work for?" She looks at me like she doesn't recognize me, and that shrivels my heart. "Who *are* you?"

I should deny everything, except she's seen the dossiers. Fuck. She must've found them in the floor, but how? My team and I went through everything, including the floor, which was the first place we looked. But we found nothing. "Where did you get the memory card?"

She grabs my hand and slaps the card onto my palm. "It was hidden in a groove inside one of the tiles."

Shit. No wonder we didn't find it. We were very careful to rip out each tile without breaking it. Otto picked out the ugliest tiles, ones that couldn't be replaced, and we didn't have the time to replicate them.

"So who are you?"

Desperation mounts. I'll lose her if I say a single wrong word. "Bobbi. I'm still the Noah you know."

"No, you aren't. You're an asset. For who?"

"For the United States government. I belong to an agency nobody knows about because we do things that other known entities like the CIA can't get involved in."

Two beats that feel like an eternity. "Did you approach me for the papers?" she asks, her voice hoarse.

I wish I could say anything but the truth. "That was part of it."

She pales. "Why didn't you tell me, then? I would've cooperated."

"We weren't sure if you were colluding with an enemy state."

Her eyes narrow. She's working fast to put things together. "Did my father..." Her voice hitches. "Did he take the dossiers to sell?"

I exhale harshly. I never wanted her to find out. "Yes."

"To a foreign state?"

"Yes."

"So he was a traitor. Were you ever going to tell me?" Her voice cracks.

"No. It's irrelevant. Why torture yourself with the knowledge?"

"It isn't *irrelevant*," she hisses. "You approached me for the dossiers. You thought *I* might be a traitor. Is that why you kept ghosting me? Because you couldn't be sure?"

"No!" My denial rings like a wild gun shot.

"When you came back..." Her breath shudders, and she stops for a moment to gather herself. "Was it because you wanted another shot at the dossiers? You know yours is included, don't you?"

"Yes, but I didn't come back for the dossiers. We thought they were gone."

She regards me. "But our meeting in Mexico. That wasn't a coincidence."

Fuck. I wish I could make up some story, but I respect her too much. Furthermore, she's too smart to buy my lies. There are enough pieces for her to get the full picture. "Our first meeting"—I run fingers through my hair—"was a setup. The thugs who attacked you weren't really thugs. They knew what they were doing, and they just wanted to scare you, so I could come to your rescue and get close to you. Instead, you kicked their asses, and that was that." My palms go clammy with cold sweat. Desperation fuels me as I look into her eyes. "Please, Bobbi. I fell in love with you."

Her composure crumbles a little, and underneath the crack, I glimpse immeasurable pain. Remorse pounds at me. I should've done better. Found some way to keep her heart protected.

"But you couldn't tell me the truth. Even after you came back and said you wanted another chance..." Her jaw trembles, and she clenches her teeth.

"I couldn't. I'm sorry. Everything I've done... What I am..." I sigh heavily. "It's all classified at the highest level. Not even my brothers know."

"Your mother knows."

"Because I report to her. She's an asset as well." Regret and self-recrimination congeal in an ugly, bitter mixture. I wish Bobbi hadn't found out. I wish the dossiers had remained hidden. The hurt and confusion warring on her face isn't worth it.

"My father's death... Was it an accident or..." She struggles for the right word to describe what she instinctively knows happened.

Oh sweet Jesus. Terror runs through my veins. If I tell her, she might never regard me the same way again. Maybe even despise me. Otto Bright was a damn traitor, but he was still her father. She and he weren't very close, but still...

She seems to have guessed the answer from my hesitation. "Did you have something to do with it?"

Don't tell her. Lie. She'll never find out.

Even if she never does, I can't play her for a fool. She deserves better. "Yes." My voice is hoarse as I struggle to speak through the tight ball of fear, panic and regret lodged in my throat. "He was my mission. I had to stop him from selling the dossiers and retrieve them."

"So you shot him."

A beat as bitter despair that I'm going to lose her spirals upward from my gut, all the way to my racing heart. I resist an urge to wipe my clammy hands. "Yes."

A tear falls from her eye. Panic that she's slipping away blazes through me. I reach for her, wishing I could soothe her and cling to her at the same time, but she pulls away. The rejection twists a knife in my heart. I tighten my jaw to contain a groan.

"Stop. I just...can't." She raises her hands, palms out. "I need some time to myself. I don't know what to make of us—of this—anymore."

"How long, Bobbi?" I say, my whole body numb with a certain defeat.

She looks at me, her eyes glazed with tears. "I don't know. But right now, I can't do this."

35

BOBBI

THE DOOR CLOSES QUIETLY BEHIND Noah, who takes the box of tiles like I asked. If I hadn't discovered the memory card, I'd think he was taking them out for me and smile. But now I know it's so he and his agency buddies can pull each tile apart and look for more memory cards—if there are any.

A suffocating silence descends on the house. Although it was quiet after the tablet ran out of juice, it feels like a mausoleum now, the ceiling and walls closing in.

I can't process all this, especially with the new information from Noah. I don't even know what to believe anymore. I never suspected Noah was anything but a photographer and adventurer. Guess he's good at his job.

Just like Dad was good at his.

Thinking of him sends icy slivers into my heart. He deserved to be punished for what he'd done. He was lucky the truth didn't come out after his death, sparing his name and reputation. Hell, *I'm* lucky the truth remained buried. If it hadn't, my life would've become a nightmare with reporters coming after me. The government would have wanted to know if I knew or suspected anything. If I'd participated or benefited somehow. Although we weren't close, the government might think we were faking estrangement. After all, Dad's distance from me wasn't out of a desire to protect me. He was just too damn busy selling his motherland out.

Noah didn't elaborate, but grabbing those dossiers to sell to the highest bidder couldn't be the first time my father betrayed the country. People simply do not, out of the blue, decide to commit such a serious crime without any deliberation or practice, especially for someone like my father who was nothing if not methodical. He didn't have money problems, and he despised gambling. Didn't drink or do drugs as far as I know. He left me a very modest sum, and I wonder if there's an ill-gotten fortune hidden somewhere. Or maybe the agency knew about it and confiscated it. Either way, I don't want it.

What about this house?

Did he pay for this with the money he got from selling state secrets? I look around the home I inherited, and the place that has felt like a sanctuary suddenly seems like a filthy hovel. I cover my mouth as nausea roils in my belly. How many lives were lost because of my father's sins?

And wouldn't Noah think about that when he sees me? I don't look much like my father, thank God, but I'm still his daughter. Noah's face twisted with pain when we talked.

He might've lost someone dear to him because of Dad. Or maybe he was thinking of how he got so close to having his identity revealed. That would've gotten him killed—and his brothers and their wives and children he adores so much might not have been safe, either.

Is that why he ghosted me? Or was it because he couldn't see a way for us to be together? He knew his lifestyle and all the dangers it entailed.

My thoughts spin in frustrating circles. I pick up my phone, needing to call Yuna and Ivy to talk, then slowly drop it back on the sofa cushion. I can't tell anyone. Even if this weren't a top state secret, I couldn't. A sudden chill shivers my skin. I'm truly alone, with nobody I can lean on, in this matter.

I change and slip under the sheets in the quiet bedroom, but sleep eludes me. My brain won't shut down. Everything I've learned in the last twenty-four hours churns dangerously.

The next morning, I get up with a head dull and heavy from the lack of sleep. Thank God it's Sunday so I don't have to go open the bakery. I dig the heels of my hands into my eyes, but the headache lingers. A hot shower doesn't help. I slip on a wrinkled tank top and jeans, then shove my feet into flipflops until I remember the state of my kitchen floor. I put on the first pair of shoes I find in my closet—ankle boots—and walk out of the bedroom.

The house feels empty and wrong without Noah. I open the pantry, then shut it at the sight of bagels. They remind me of him.

I give canned tuna to Señor Mittens, who looks at the offering with utter contempt. "Sorry, buddy. Caviar Man is gone."

Señor Mittens turns his nose up and pads away with a feline sneer. I should care that he doesn't want to eat, but right now, my mind is too preoccupied with tangled thoughts about Noah and Dad to make room for a cat.

I make myself coffee and sit in the living room. It's awful to be alone without anybody I can seek advice from. Josie is a therapist, so everything I tell her is confidential if I go to her as a patient, but I just can't. My dad betrayed the country and Noah. I can't betray the latter's secret.

Damn it, Bobbi. What are you going to do?

I remain with my head in my hands for a long while. Then there are knocks at the door.

My joints creak as I get up and wince at the stiffness in my neck and shoulders. The clock on the wall says it's a little after six. *Who could it be?* Noah's people, wanting to question me and see how much I know?

But wouldn't it be easier for them just to kill me? The dead can't speak.

As I hesitate, three more knocks punch through my anxiety. I start to reach for my Glock, then stop. What am I going to do? Have a gun fight with government assets trained to kill as efficiently as possible?

But at the same time, I can't bring myself to open the door without anything to protect myself. My sense of self-preservation rebels against it. I hide a small paring knife in my right boot as a compromise.

When I open the door, Trey is standing there. He grins. "Hi."

"Hi," I respond automatically, my voice slightly high-pitched in surprise. We don't have the kind of neighborly relationship where we visit each other in the evening or on weekends, especially in a crisply ironed button-down shirt and nice slacks. His carefully styled hair is that of a man on a mission to entice a woman for more than just dinner.

"Señor Mittens came over." He hefts my cat, who is hissing with disgust. "Guess he wanted to play with Nero. Anyway, just wanted to drop him off because I'm heading out for a date, and I didn't want you to worry."

"Ah," I say stupidly. He's going on a date. I accept Señor Mittens from Trey. "Thanks. I had no idea he'd snuck out."

"Maybe he got lonely while you were working."

"Could be. I've been doing some renovation."

"If you need help, just let me know." His smile grows a bit awkward. "I know your fiancé is around, but in case you need another pair of hands."

"Thank you." He starts to turn, and I blurt out, "Were you ever lonely?"

He stops and gives me a curious look.

"When you were in Afghanistan, away from your friends and family," I say, even though I already regret asking him. I just wanted to emotionally sort out the fact that I have nobody to talk about the cause of the suffocating knot in my chest.

"Lonely? Nah. Hard to feel lonely when I had my fellow soldiers and my family back home, who were rooting for me. It was a privilege to serve and help keep the people I love safe."

"I see." I manage a smile. "Thanks for your service. Again."

He nods. "Have a good evening."

"Good luck with your date."

He chuckles softly as he limps toward his SUV, waving at Darcy on the other side of the street. She waves back. I hold Señor Mittens, who swishes his tail and makes a vaguely displeased sound, then slip back into my house before Darcy notices me and comes over. I'm not in the mood for mindless gossip. I sit back down on the sofa with the cat on my lap, scratching his head absentmindedly. It was probably foolish to ask Trey if he was lonely—his identity as an American soldier wasn't secret. He had people to share his thoughts and concerns and fears and triumphs with.

Then it hits me that Noah doesn't have anybody. His mother doesn't seem warm and nurturing. At the party, she was more interested in getting him to take another mission than seeing if he was doing well. His brothers have no idea what he does. He can never tell anybody about what he does. The dossier calls him "prolific." So he's good at his job and likely has enemies who would kill him if they knew his identity. Does he ever feel afraid? He talked about the plane crash calmly, like it was nothing, but it must have something to do with his job. The exciting "adventures" I've worried he might miss are actually dangerous missions. If I stay in his life, I could be a target for the bad guys.

Do I want that?

No one excites me like Noah. Nobody can make me laugh and feel so beautiful and important. My eyes roam around the living room, then stop at his vision painting. It has none of the dangers or threats a clandestine life would bring. Just all the lovely things I've always wanted.

Are they empty promises or a vow to keep me safe?

My initial sense of betrayal at Noah setting up our chance meeting in Mexico fades as what was at stake sinks in. If I'd been in his place, I would've done the same. As a matter of fact, I might've done more— might've let it slip that Otto Bright was a traitor. Put pressure on me until I cracked.

Noah didn't do any of that. Actually, I was treated with kid gloves. The coolness in his mother's eyes said she would've done whatever was necessary to finish the job, and to hell with any collateral damage.

I stand up and pace. I've been thinking in circles since I found the dossiers yesterday morning. I can't continue to stew without driving myself insane. Besides, it isn't like me to fret endlessly. I figure out what I want, then make a plan to get it. I refuse to let my father's past strip me of control of my future.

I am in charge of my destiny.

My mind made up, I start to stand. My phone pings, and I reach for it with a racing heart. *Noah...?*

–Victor: I hate to bother you, but my car won't start, and I don't know who else to call for help.

He drives an old beat-up white Hyundai Elantra he got for almost nothing from some international student who had to move back home. When I asked him if it was reliable, he said rather proudly that he maintains it himself and that he's a pretty decent mechanic. It must be serious for him to reach out.

–Me: Sure. Where are you?

He sends me an address, and I look it up. A strip mall in a not so great area of the city. I switch to street view and see a greasy Chinese take-out place, a seedy bar and pawn shop. *What's he doing there?* Is he in some kind of trouble?

Confusion and concern rising, I grab my car fob. Something creaks behind me and the fine hair on the back of my neck bristles as chilly disquiet crawls along my spine.

Something cuts through the air as I turn. Pain explodes. Then everything goes black.

36

NOAH

I RAISE another glass of whiskey and toast the photo.

Bobbi glares at me from the wall, flipping me the bird. It's the enlarged shot from the security feed, which I printed and framed and hung in the room where I store my rifles. Wonder what the shrinks at the agency would say if they knew. Would they call me crazy? Obsessed? Hopeless?

I haven't been able to move from this lounger since I returned from Bobbi's house and let Mom know about the dossiers and the box full of tiles.

"I knew it!" she crowed. Nothing pleases her like being proven correct. "Did she see the files?"

"No," I lied. If she decides Bobbi saw more than she should, I might have to go rogue. And it would be the end of whatever bright future I could have with Bobbi. Besides, I'd really rather not have to kill my mother. She's a cold-blooded sociopath, but at least she's *our* cold-blooded sociopath. "I found the memory card in the floor before she could, and looked it over to make sure. Then I took the tiles, ostensibly to throw them away. It made a mess in my Bugatti," I added. The lie would be more convincing if it included whining about dust in the car.

Sure enough, Mom snorted. "Use your billions to clean it."

Zero sympathy. Like I said, a cold-blooded sociopath. But at least she's satisfied for the moment because she has the dossiers she wants and the tiles to break.

My eyes return to the picture of Bobbi, and a desire to drink until I can't think or feel anything surges up. Although she was angry and defiant when I shouldered my way back into her life, she gave me hope because she cared. And she didn't know what I did or the danger I posed or the fact that I killed her father.

I down another whiskey, wishing my problems were something I could just assassinate with my cheetahs. Alcohol probably won't help, but I reach for the bottle again anyway because what else is there to do? How the hell do we come back from this? I can manifest until my hair turns gray, but nothing will change.

Bobbi's a smart woman. Probably too smart for my own good. If she were a little slower, the type who'd just nod at everything I said, it'd be easier to manage the situation.

Dumb ass. If she were like that, you wouldn't have fallen for her.

Fuck. I've been thinking about how to fix this since I left her house, but haven't come up with a single solution. I can't talk with my brothers about it, because what the hell will I say? Hey guys, Bobbi's mad at me because she found out I'm a government spec-ops asset. Plus, I lied to her when we first met in order to get close to her and retrieve some dossiers on operatives we have stationed in foreign countries. Oh, and I assassinated her father a while back, too. Got any ideas how I can pull myself out of this hole?

Yeah sure. My brothers are going to want to know what the hell I've been snorting. And that's the *best* reaction I could hope for because disbelief is better than the alternative. Just how messed up is my life?

I roll the square box in my free hand. The ring from Peery Diamonds arrived yesterday, after Bobbi asked for some time off. I pop the lip open, stare at the ten-carat, circular blue diamond surrounded by twelve square white diamonds that together look like a clock. Two pairs of smaller, moval-cut diamonds on either side complete the piece.

When I received the preliminary sketch of the ring, I knew this was it. The clock motif seems to symbolize the lifetime Bobbi and I will spend together, and I also like the four smaller diamonds because they could represent the four points of the compass, signifying our freedom to build a life in any direction we choose.

But the longer I study the sparkling stones, the more despair and misery weigh me down. What good is a ring without the woman I love? I cling to the fact that Bobbi hasn't dumped me outright. Time and space do *not* equate to "Sorry, it's me, not you."

But that doesn't mean the outlook is good. Bobbi wanted time to think. And when a woman says she needs alone time, it rarely ends well.

I struggle to maintain self-control. Rushing back to Bobbi to try to talk—forcing a conversation when she isn't ready—would be a recipe for disaster.

Huxley would say that remaining silent is the best course of action. I haven't felt this nervous since my first mission to snipe some shitty dictator's right-hand man. He was in the market for chemical weapons *and* raped little girls on the side. A mission I later came to think of as a twofer.

I snap the ring box shut with a flick of my wrist. Even if Bobbi says yes to the engagement, what about the wedding? She won't have a father to walk her down the aisle. Otto Bright might have been a traitor, but he was also her parent. She wasn't close to him, but still. My brothers and I grouse about our dad's ridiculous antics, but if he were to die, we'd stop. Death tends to elevate a person a few notches, so ordinary guys become saints and assholes somehow become just... misunderstood. You have to be an absolute shitshow to continue to be vilified.

And what Otto did might not reach that level with Bobbi. It's impossible to tell.

A panicked voice inside my head screams at me to talk to her now. Fuck giving her time. Confront her. Make her choose you. All your brothers who got the women of their dreams went after them with all they had.

Yeah, except none of them offed their future father-in-law.

Besides, I'm not sorry I killed him. I'd do it again if I could go back in time because it was that or sacrifice too many of our people. What I regret is the impact on Bobbi and how she feels about me.

I open one of the social media apps on my phone to see if there's any update on Bobbi. Need clues on how she's feeling now. Nothing pops up. But there's a post about a job opening—an NGO position to build a wildlife sanctuary in Colombia.

It's a coded message from my mother: *Noah, take this damned job.*

Never satisfied, not even after I just delivered her the dossiers and the tiles to check. Scowling, I scroll down. Huxley's grandmother had another meeting with Andreas Webber. Either Hux hasn't put a stop to her machinations or she doesn't care about the consequences because she's going to do it no matter what. Should *I* do something about it? I'd hate to see Huxley forced to work at Huxley & Webber. It's a great law firm, but it isn't his dream.

The job opening post shows up again. *Very funny, Mother.*

Want a working vacation?

Take the chance of a lifetime in the beautiful countryside of Colombia. Great coffee, clean mountain air, and easy transport into the city.

Now it's an ad. A fake one, of course.

Not interested. I start to click away, then pause. As long as it doesn't take more than a week—and Mom said it would be quick—I could do the job and give Bobbi some time to think. It would have the bonus of getting Mom off my back.

Bobbi didn't say how much time she needed, but a week seems like it would be good. And the distance would force me to give her the space she wants. Plus, maybe a job would help clear my head. The cheetahs and I, working together toward a common goal... It has a meditative quality.

I type my response: Sounds great. Where do I send the résumé?

That done, I knock back the rest of my drink and reach into the safe for my cheetahs. My phone pings. I try not to sigh. Mom never wastes time.

–TLOML: Can we talk?

Bobbi. My heart pounds as expectations and hope stir. My hands shaking slightly, I type my answer.

–Me: Of course. Where?

–TLOML: My place.

37

BOBBI

I sputter at the splash of icy water on my face. I try to wipe it, but there's an unnatural stiffness in my shoulders and arms, preventing me from moving. The ringing in my ears adds to my disorientation.

Water drips from my face and soaks into my hair. A groan tears from my throat. Although I'm forced awake, I want to close my eyes and try to block out the splitting headache. It feels like an ax is wedged into my skull.

But that would be unwise. The last thing I remember is getting texts from Victor and blacking out. I blink, trying to clear my bleary vision and the fogginess clouding my mind. Something scratchy rubs against my cheek. A rug. Familiar couch and table.

My living room?

I realize I'm on my side. Duct tape is around my wrists, biding them together. My ankles are also taped and bound.

The home invasion incident with Reggie and Floyd slides into my head. Is this the same culprit?

No... Probably not. No bullets. And no tranq, based on how much the base of my skull throbs. Somebody swung something at me—maybe a sap... Or a baseball bat.

My thoughts start to unfurl in a torrid mess. *Victor.* Is he okay? He's waiting for me. I don't know how long I've been out, but he might try to reach me again. If I don't respond, he might text TJ because I told him to get in touch with my cousin if he needed something and couldn't get ahold of me.

And Noah... I asked him for some space, so he won't be dropping by to come to my rescue. The notion leaves me oddly bereft. Do I want him to save me like some action-movie hero? If I didn't know he was an agent, I'd be terrified of him getting caught in a situation like this. But—

"Wakey, wakey, Bobbi girl. Come on, now. No time for beauty sleep."

That voice... *Trey?* What's he doing here?

He looks down at me, holding an empty glass in his left hand and a gun with a silencer in his right. He's wearing a black Angels cap, a stretchy black top with long sleeves and jeans that are—naturally—black. His black sneakers have some dirt on the sides. "I didn't think I hit you that hard, but you were out for a while so I helped you along. Hope you don't mind." He gives me an I'm-such-a-nice-guy smile, which I'm dying to wipe off his face. Only if I weren't tied up. I'd love to face off with him right about now.

"If you hadn't hit me, this could've all been avoided." My voice is heavy with sarcasm. "Why don't you untie me and face me like a man?"

He smiles as he puts the glass on the coffee table. "It's an idea. But your dad said you were good at judo."

He knew my father? Some of Dad's colleagues and friends visited while he was alive—and at his funeral, but I don't remember ever seeing Trey.

He continues, "You act like you can take on anything. You are a pretty big girl after all. But Bobbi, I don't want anything to happen to you. You see, I've been waiting for this moment. Just two of us. Alone. Private." He smiles like I'm some kind of treasure.

What the hell? I've seen that look on a lot of the creeps my former clients hired me to keep away. "You're a stalker?" I can usually recognize them when I see them. They've got that unsettling vibe you can't ignore. It's different from the feeling you get when you are around other types of lowlifes. I can't believe my stalker radar failed with him.

"What?" He laughs. "Don't flatter yourself. You aren't my type." His eyes roam over my body. There's no particular heat or interest.

"Then why are you doing this?"

He leans forward. "Information."

"Care to be a little more specific?"

"The dossiers."

Time stops for a moment. Air sticks in my throat.

"Where are they?" he asks gently.

"What dossiers?" My response is calm with just enough faux irritation despite my racing heart. He might be one of the assets on the documents and wants to make sure his secrets are safe. But my gut says I need to play dumb. Besides, Noah said he was tasked to retrieve the dossiers. The government wouldn't assign another agent the same mission...would it?

"Otto's dossiers. Drop the innocent act. I know you have them."

"I still have no idea what you're talking about."

"That so? Well, let me jog your memory."

He takes a step and punts me halfway off the ground. Pain detonates in my gut. Air whooshes out, and I roll away as best I can, feeling like my intestines are turning black and blue underneath my skin. I haven't been kicked this hard in a while.

"I hate hurting women." Trey's voice is full of regret. "It's not very gentlemanly."

You motherfucker. "Then don't," I wheeze.

"But you're being a bitch, Bobbi. And bitches get beat."

Shit. I roll some more, bringing my knees up, then twist my arms a little until I can reach my boot. The small paring knife I hid is still there. Guess Trey didn't search me for weapons. Or maybe he doesn't think it will matter because he has a gun.

I grab the blade and shift my body so I can hide cutting the tape around my wrists. It is difficult to maneuver because I'm trying to make sure he doesn't realize what I'm up to. Once I cut my wrists free, I'll need to do the same for my ankles before I can make a move. Let's see if he's still as smug after he gets his ass kicked by a woman.

"You ripped the floor out, and I bet you found something. Your idiot boyfriend didn't look too happy when he left yesterday and he didn't come back today. You were probably trying to protect him from the fallout. How much did you read? Find anything interesting?"

I glare at him, sawing away at the tape. He's twisted the duct tape multiple times, until it's like a rope and difficult to cut through. The skin around my wrists stings from the nicks I leave every time the blade slips in my sweat-slickened hand.

"Otto was *so* good at digging up secrets. Preternatural, almost. I greatly admired his talent. A shame he died the way he did."

"Obviously, since he worked for the State Department. How do you know my father?" I ask, pretending that I know nothing about what my dad really did.

"I worked with him. Helped him broker some lucrative deals." Trey is smiling, but his eyes are soulless.

He was Dad's partner in treason. Did Noah know Dad didn't work alone? Did his agency look for Trey and somehow miss him? "So you never served in Afghanistan?"

"What, and waste my life away in that hellhole? Not bloody likely."

Damn it. I've been too gullible, believing the lies about his military service.

Regardless, there's no point in playing dumb now. If he worked closely with my dad to sell our country's secrets, he knows about the dossiers. "I'm not a traitor like my father," I say. The tightness around my wrists loosens. I just need to cut my ankles free without him firing at me.

Trey laughs. "Wait, you're doing this out of some misguided sense of patriotism?" His eyes sparkle with evil amusement. "No, it's simply too rich." He laughs harder, throwing his head back. "My dear, you aren't even American."

"Of course I am." He's insane if he thinks I'll believe such a ridiculous lie.

"No. You're actually British although it's true you don't sound like it."

"Because I'm not British." I say it dryly, without too much sarcasm, because provoking him too much wouldn't work out. My belly doesn't need another kick. Regardless, I don't understand what he hopes to gain by calling me British. He might just be crazy, which would be very bad. You can work with the rational. Not so with the insane.

He chuckles. "My dear, your father was a British diplomat, and your mother was from London. That does, I believe, make you British."

"My mom was born in Los Angeles." Not gonna let him mess with my head with his bullshit.

"Unfortunately, no. Your father was not, as you've been led to believe, Otto himself, but Otto's best friend. They golfed together, spent time together, conversed over aged Scotches and French cheese. You see, your father was from a well-to-do family, although obviously not an aristocrat or anything of that sort. He left a nice flat in London worth quite a bit of money, but sadly, that won't be yours. His younger brother took it and sold it off. He's a little shit with money problems. Never seen a horse he didn't want to bet on. But at least he's popular with the ladies. He would've liked you. You're his type." He rakes his eyes over me again, making my skin crawl.

Although my main focus is on freeing myself and finding an opportunity to overpower him, part of my head is struggling to process what he's saying. Is any of it true? The story he's spinning is outrageous. Besides, I just can't picture Mom having an affair.

He adds, "But to continue about your father and Otto—their wives were tight, too. Always having their tea parties. Earl Grey and scones. Very British and civilized. But then Otto liked to wear a veneer of respectability, and your daddy was one of many props."

I move the knife up and down faster. My impatience earns me two more nicks.

Suddenly, Trey wags his finger and my heart almost stops. "But then your dad had to ruin it all. He found out about Otto's extracurricular activities, and instead of letting it go like a smart man would, he confronted him. Apparently, nobody taught your father that the way to go when you discover a scheme like that is to join in the profitable venture. There's a demand for state secrets from Great Britain as well. Some of my buyers would've paid good money for them. We could've all been rich together." He shakes his head. To this asshole, destruction and deaths of the innocent mean nothing. Everything's about what's in it for him.

"He did the right thing," I say to keep him talking.

"No, he did the stupid thing. You see, Otto didn't take it well. He thought their friendship should mean more. After all, nations..." He shrugs. "They're so faceless." He waves his gun and leans forward again. "They lack *intimacy*, if you get my meaning."

If he expects me to nod and agree, he's going to be disappointed. I continue to stare at him levelly.

He pulls back at my lack of reaction. "So..." He points the gun at me, and my pulse jumps. A fresh coat of sweat pools in my palms; the knife almost slips from my grip. "*Bang!*"

My heart in my throat, I flinch.

He smiles. "Goes the diplomat. And *bang!*"

This time I manage to keep still, but my skin is clammy all over.

"Goes the wife." He sighs with a theatrical mournfulness. "Then you... You were just a little baby."

"So where's 'bang, goes the baby'?" My voice is shaky despite my resolve to stay strong. This story has to be fake, but it's still terrible.

He has the audacity to place a hand over his heart, but the unholy amusement in his eyes says he's enjoying this entirely too much. "We aren't monsters."

"Right. How do I know you aren't making this story up to get me to hand over the dossiers?"

He blinks. "But why would I lie? There are so many ways for me to get what I want without"—he waves the gun vaguely—"fabrication. If you play nice, I'll even make your death quick and painless."

We'll see about that last part. Not letting him kill me without a fight. "Then how did I survive? Why didn't my mom think it was weird that Dad brought me home from his dead friend's house? Didn't she know I was somebody else's baby?"

"Oh, my innocent little child." Trey tsks and shakes his head. "By coincidence, Sarah's own daughter had just been killed. Blown to bits by a suicide bomber while the family was in Jenin. So when Otto brought you home, she was ecstatic. And if she thought something was weird...? Well..." A Gallic shrug. "Better to think her baby was alive than dead. For her own mental health anyway. She was never quite right in the head to begin with."

271

I want to deny it, but Mom *was* always a bit weird. Sometimes smothering, but oftentimes distant and withdrawn. I thought she was just moody, but what if...?

"Not that that was a problem for Otto. He liked it that his wife didn't have her shit together. Easier to lie and gloss over things. The kind of things he did aren't so easy to hide if your spouse is observant and clever. Like you."

No way. No freakin' way. Trey is playing with my head. "You're lying."

He shrugs again. "Get somebody from your mother's side of the family and do some DNA testing. Otto was an only child, but Sarah wasn't."

"Nope. You're lying." But doubt spreads like poison in my head.

"Believe what you will. No skin off my nose. But no matter what you tell yourself, you aren't Otto's, and you aren't American." All humor drains from his face. "Now. Where are the dossiers, Bobbi?"

"Like I said, I don't know. And unlike you, I don't lie."

He regards me, still as a reptile. "Don't make things difficult. If you keep on this way, I'll really have no choice."

"No choice but what? To kick me again? Take some neighbors hostage?" *Just a little more time with my knife...*

"How about your cat?"

I go still, trying to hear Señor Mittens.

"Cutting off his toes would be motivating, don't you think? Or perhaps his tail, say...an inch at a time?"

Outrage and dread flood through me. That poor cat already lost a toe. He shouldn't have to lose more because this subhuman trash is a psychopath. "Stay away from my cat, asshole!"

"Or how about your boyfriend? He's coming, you know. I texted him from your phone. Most men dread hearing their women say, 'We need to talk,' but he seemed eager. I imagine he thinks he's getting you back."

Oh *shit*. Noah is undoubtedly capable. An experienced, in-demand operative. But he doesn't know he's walking into a trap. Even if I scream, it'll be too late.

I can't let him be ambushed. My knife cuts through the last of the twisted tape. *Finally!*

"I didn't come this far to fail, Bobbi. My buyer is an impatient man. One way or another, you're going to give me those dossiers."

Trey is watching me too closely. I'll never get a chance to free my legs before he shoots me.

Time for Plan B.

I smirk. "Trey, that bit about being a war vet was pretty good. Gotta admit, I didn't see you coming. But now you're starting to disappoint me."

His eyes narrow. "What do you mean?"

"Oh my God, they *all* say, 'I didn't come this far to fail.' It's like in the B-movie evildoer training manual or something."

"I warn you, Bobbi—"

"But people fail all the time. What's the big deal? And why are you still chasing after some dossiers that don't even exist? You must've made a fortune selling your country out. What have you done with all that money? Lose it betting on horses?" He frowns, and hopeful anticipation swells—along with a dread that this is *really* going to hurt. I brace myself. I'm not going to go quietly. "No, wait. I know—you squandered it all because you want to live larger than you're capable of! Expensive cars and wine. Maybe expensive women, too... I mean, nobody would want you unless you paid. And now this is your one big shot. You think you can get back to where you want to be with one last big score. Right?"

"You have no idea what you're—"

"You know what? Even if you're right and I'm British and know where the dossiers are, I'm not giving them to a loser like—"

"Shut up!"

He kicks me in the gut again, *hard*. Holy *fuck*, it hurts! Raw adrenaline pumps in my veins. I curl up, and he keeps kicking everywhere he can reach—my hips, back, and head. I roll around to lessen the impact and to make it harder for him to see what I'm doing and cut at the tape around my ankles. Don't have to be as careful with the blade since my leather boots provide protection.

As soon as my legs are free, I swivel on the floor like a break dancer and kick him as hard as I can, catching him behind the knee. Shock flares in his eyes, and he crashes down. A shot fires from his gun, and a hole appears in the ceiling above us.

I slash at his right wrist hard, making him drop the gun. I kick it away, then thrust the knife at his eye. He twists, and the tip of the blade cuts a jagged gash on his temple.

"Cunt!" he screams. "I'll kill your boyfriend in front of you, make you tell me where the fucking docs are, then kill you and your goddamn cat, too!"

He grabs my wrist, his thumb digging into the cuts. Pain burns, and my grip on the knife loosens. It falls with a clatter, but before he can jump on it, I kick it away.

We both regain our feet. Blood dripping from his face, he swings. I duck, then kick, aiming for the same knee but getting the shin. He curses, then lunges at me, the limp completely gone. His fist connects with my face hard enough to jar my brain. Something hot drips from my nose, leaving a coppery tang on my lips. Great, a fucking nosebleed.

We close, and I get in a good hard shot with my elbow to his sternum. Grunting, he twists to take himself off center-line and tangles his legs with mine to limit my leverage. We struggle, lose balance and collapse on the floor in a bloody heap.

The second we hit, I use our momentum to roll him onto his back and unload another elbow into his face, all my bodyweight behind it. In my peripheral vision is the gun he dropped. It's not close, but probably within reach if I lunge for it. If I grab it, it's game over. But he notices where my eyes have gone, and sees the gun too. And his arms are longer.

We both pounce. His hand closes over it before mine as he kicks me away.

He rolls, the gun pointed at me. Deadly exhilaration lights his eyes, while my head screams, *Fuck fuck fuck!*

"Who's the loser now, bitch?" he rasps.

38

NOAH

I PULL into Bobbi's driveway. The lights are on in her living room behind closed curtains. The engagement ring feels like a box of lead in my pocket, rather than a beautiful dream and hope. Bobbi said she wanted to talk, not take me back.

Besides, I want to propose to Bobbi in an unforgettable way. A gorgeous villa on a stunning beach with a thousand white calla lilies, a thousand candles and the beautiful strains of a violin. Plus a bucket of champagne and her favorite nama-cream cake.

That's the least she deserves.

But I exit the car with the box in my pocket anyway, like it's *my* manifestation ring. My hand closes over it like a talisman. Bobbi has a ring to help manifest her future, so why not me?

The late evening air feels cooler than usual. I stretch my neck left and right, trying to ease the tension.

When a woman says she wants to talk, it usually doesn't have a happy ending. But Bobbi is different. *We're* different. We have to be.

I start toward the house. Something white streaks across my path, and I jump back, adrenaline pumping.

"Jesus..." I squint. "Señor Mittens?"

The cat hisses.

"Whoa, what's the matter? You forgetting I'm the one who brings you caviar and cream?"

Señor Mittens's eyes narrow. If he could speak, he'd call me a dumbass.

"What's the deal?"

The hair on his back rises, and he lets out another sharp hiss. The sound skitters like a viper, and all my senses bristle with warning.

My eyes dart toward the house. At the lights in the living room. Señor Mittens shouldn't be out and about, reacting to me like this.

Bobbi's cat doesn't normally go out of the house, not like this. Every time I snuck in to lavish luxurious meals on him, he'd stay put. And in the evenings he prefers to sit by the window and groom himself or curl up next to Bobbi, even while acting like it's a torture to be close to a human.

Something is definitely off.

I glance at the house next to hers—Trey Underhill's home. Empty driveway, and the lights are out, except for one in the back. I return to my car and grab some of my go-to tools. I've never been in the Boy Scouts, but I live by their motto: *Be prepared.*

This might be nothing. I could be making things worse. Señor Mittens might've decided he hates me because Bobbi's done with me. But every instinct screams danger.

I screw the suppressor on to my gun, then check to make sure it's fully loaded and ready. Satisfied, I put on four-tube night vision goggles and slip into Bobbi's laundry room through the secondary entrance in the back. Thankfully, the hinges remain quiet. My steps are silent and sure. Grunts and the sounds of fleshy impacts come from the living room. A chill ripples over me.

"Who's the loser now, bitch?"

No, Bobbi!

I flip the main breaker and darkness swallows the house. A swift curse follows. I step out of the laundry room into the hallway.

Time slows as my heart thunders in my ears. A few more paces and I'm at the door to the living room. Trey and Bobbi are on the floor, blood on both their faces and clothes. He has a pistol with a silencer in his hand, wavering between Bobbi and the doorway I'm standing in.

"Give it up, Trey," I say.

"Too late, hero!"

He swings the gun in her direction as a half-smile, half-grimace stretches his mouth. It's the face of a man who knows he's fucked and refuses to go down alone.

Boom, boom, boom, my heart beats like a war drum. "No!" *Bobbi!*

Suddenly Trey swivels back toward me. *Bobbi was a feint!* Twisting against the hallway wall to present a smaller target, I shoot.

There are twin *poots* from the pistols, and fire explodes in my ribs as I'm slammed against the wall. Trey drops with a muted thud, a hole smack between his eyebrows. The left side of my torso hurts like hell, but the pain is worth it.

Damn, I'm good, I think with a weird mixture of pride and dazedness.

Bobbi scrambles to her knees, then gets up.

"Noah?" Her voice is shaky.

"Right here, baby." My response is light. She needs reassurance and confidence. The wound is tiny. Besides, it's starting to hurt less. God bless the high pain threshold I got from Mom. "The fucker's dead, so don't worry," I add since she can't see what just happened.

"Are you okay?" Her question is more of a sob than spoken language. She's blinking in the dark, trying to adjust her vision.

"Uh, yeah. Don't move. Lemme get the light." Pulling off the NVG, I drag myself to the laundry room and flip the main breaker back on. I blink at the blinding brightness, then look down and see the blood seeping out of the little wound in my chest, around my ribcage. It's surprisingly warm and wet and smells like copper and rust.

I head back out to check on Bobbi. The NVG showed she was injured, but I didn't really get a chance to see exactly how much she's hurt and where.

She's taken some damage. Her face is a mess. The blood under her nose and over her mouth is crusted, but nothing fresh is coming out. Her nose isn't broken, thank God. At least four bruises to come, no black eye. Little cuts to her wrists and bruises there. There might be more under her clothes.

But what I can see so far stokes my rage. I shouldn't have shot the motherfucker. That was too damn easy. I should've kept him alive so I could skin him. I might not be able to peel him like Mom could, but I could pour salt water over him during the process. That's the least he deserved for what he did to Bobbi.

"Oh my God, you're shot." Tears fall from her eyes. She tries to reach for me, but pulls back, as though she's scared to hurt me with her touch. Her entire body shakes as she places her hands over her mouth.

She's worried. That's a good sign, isn't it? Even if she was thinking about breaking up with me for good, this means she's changing her mind...right?

"Let me find my phone," she says, sniffling.

"Wait, don't call 911." I take out my phone and text "911 gf house" to Contact2608.

–Contact2608: Acknowledged. Wait 10.

I relax slightly. He'll make sure everything's taken care of and a proper story is crafted to explain the death of Trey Underhill to the authorities.

My knees feel a bit rubbery. I don't think Trey's bullet hit anything important even though it hurts to breathe, but the blood keeps flowing out. I lean against the wall and slide down, smearing it with my blood. Shit.

"Sorry about the mess." I gesture at the red.

"Who cares about that?" Bobbi says furiously, then wipes away her tears. She puts pressure on the wound. "You're bleeding so much."

"It's not that bad." I grin at her, feeling slightly loopy now. When my body hits a certain level of pain, it generally makes me lightheaded... almost like I'm high.

"I can't believe you showed up the way you did. I didn't think I'd survive tonight without a miracle."

I grip her hand. "I will *always* come for you. I'm your miracle, my light."

She wipes her tears with the other hand. "How did you know I was in trouble? Trey said he texted you pretending to be me."

"It was Señor Mittens. He was hissing and acting weird. I figured something was up. Speaking of which, I need to figure out what to give him that's better than caviar and cream. Maybe top them with gold flakes?"

She laughs a little, just like I want.

"You've given me a lot of firsts," I say. Bobbi's in a receptive mood, and I want to get it out.

"Are you trying to tell me you were a virgin when we first met?" she says, half-exasperated and half-unbelieving.

"Oh hell no. You wouldn't have wanted to sleep with me a second time if I'd been a virgin."

She chokes on a small laugh.

"Anyway, lemme talk... You're my first love. The first person who made me glad to be born. The first to make me dream of a normal life. And this?" I point at my side. "First time getting shot." I grin. That sounds impressive. She should be flattered.

She glares at me. If she were a meme, the caption would read: *And should I be happy?*

"I never caught a bullet for anyone. Never wanted to," I add.

Her face scrunches. She presses her lips together hard, like she's trying to contain a sob. Air shudders in and out, and she clenches and unclenches her hands. "You should've *ducked*," she says finally.

"Then I would've missed, and he would've shot you next. We can't have that."

Silent tears pour down her cheeks. I swipe my thumbs over them.

"When I manifested the perfect man for me, taking a bullet for me was on the list..." Her breath hitches.

I grin. "So does that mean I'm your perfect man?"

"I didn't want it to happen for real!"

"Come on. It isn't that bad," I say. "I have a very high pain tolerance. If I were a woman, I could pop a baby out without an epidural, no problem."

She shakes her head, then lets out a teary laugh. "You're impossible."

"And crazy about you." I hold her hand, threading our fingers. My head feels like a balloon full of helium, ready to fly high in the sky. "I love you, Bobbi Bright. You're the light of my life. And that will never change, till death do us part and beyond."

She runs a hand over her wet cheeks. "My God."

"Not your God. Just me. Noah Lasker." I kiss the crown of her head. "Now, tell me you love me, too."

She barks out a laugh. "You can't just *demand*—"

"You're going to be sad if you let me die without telling me how you feel."

"I thought you were going to survive this." The fire in her eyes says if I don't, she'll never forgive me.

"Well...yeah. Of course. But just in case."

"I'm not telling you anything until you're fully recovered."

"Is this your way of making sure I get better?"

"It is." She presses her lips together, but they tremble anyway.

She couldn't look more beautiful. And she's mine. My woman. My life. My everything. I can take another bullet for her, although if I tell her that, she'll probably kill me. "Fine, then. I'll get better."

It's been almost ten minutes. Contact2608 is going to arrive any second. His team is always punctual. I exhale, then strip my face of all humor. "Hey. You gotta promise me something."

"What?" she whispers.

"You can't tell my brothers about this. Seriously. Like, never."

"Of course not. I'll never tell your secrets to anyone."

"Thank you." I give her an easy smile. "I don't want to survive getting shot only to die of second-hand embarrassment as they fuss over me like a bunch of pussies." My fingers brush over the bruises starting to form on her face. "And you promise to get better too, okay? See all the docs you need to see, patch up everything that needs patching up."

She takes my hovering hand in hers. "Okay. I promise."

39

NOAH

WHEN YOU WAKE up after surgery that follows saving your girlfriend from a sociopath, the last thing you want to see is your mother. Especially if said mother is assessing you like you're a used car some smarmy dealer is trying to unload on her.

"Where's Bobbi?" My voice is hoarse. I gingerly reach for the bottle of water next to my bed. Mom isn't the type to hand it to me. Nurturing isn't her forte.

Sure enough, she doesn't offer to help or ask if I need anything else. "Not here."

"Did she go home?" I hope she got treated for her injuries and went home to rest.

"Yes, I made sure of it. She doesn't know you're awake yet."

"Has she seen someone?" Nothing looked broken when I checked her out, but I don't have X-ray vision. She could've been hurt quite seriously fighting Trey, and given the circumstances, she wouldn't have said anything because she was too upset about the damn gunshot wound.

Mom cocks an eyebrow. "She's doing better than you, so worry about yourself."

"Wait, what? Was that actually some maternal concern? It's terrifying. You should see an oncologist. In case you have cancer."

She blows air out between slack lips. "Always the comedian."

"Everyone loves me for my sense of humor. Anyway, you can go. You're my last choice for a nurse."

"Ha. Ha. Ha. Very amusing. You aren't hurt enough to rate a nurse. The wound just looks impressive from the outside." Her eyes drift toward the ceiling. "Rather like your father, come to think of it."

"Oooo, nice one."

"Your surgeon was shocked the bullet went through without tearing up anything important. He said it was a miracle."

More like Bobbi's miracle. I smile to myself.

Mom's eyes come back to me, and a chill enters them. "I saw Bobbi. How much does she know?"

Shit. Bobbi can't lie like Mom and I can. "Didn't you ask?"

"Couldn't very well do that and tip her off, now could I?"

"She knows her father was a no-good traitor."

"You sure she doesn't know what you really are? You shot a man in front of her, and it was an impressive shot."

"Don't have to remind me. I know I'm good." I blow on my fingertips.

"Spare me the self-aggrandizement."

"But self-aggrandizement is one of my most endearing traits." I give her a thin smile. Time to switch her focus. "But even if she noticed my amazing shot, so what? I'm retiring."

Exasperation simmers in Mom's eyes. "You keep saying that. Why?"

"I want a normal life."

"Know thyself, Noah Lasker. You'll get bored. Grow restless."

"Funny, I've never once thought that while I was with Bobbi." My words come out measured and steady.

Sighing, Mom scrutinizes me. Her eyes never warm up, and she doesn't smile. She isn't showing it, but she's beyond frustrated and irate. "I can't let you retire permanently," she says finally. "The world needs people like us, even if we do our work in the dark. Think of all the bad actors you've taken out. They would've bombed our country—and worse—simply because they could. Your acts might've saved thousands of innocent lives. More, perhaps. You might've even saved Bobbi, for all we know."

That's about as much of a concession I'm going to get out of her. But then I wasn't one hundred percent sure they'd let me go without forcing some sort of compromise. "There are others who can do that work."

"*Noah.*" Her eyes flash.

Time to give in a little. "Fine. But no more than once a year."

"Three months."

"Two years."

"Don't be ridiculous. Six months."

"Nine. But not while Bobbi's pregnant or our babies are young."

"You're going to make babies for Ted?" Mom's lips curl in distaste.

"Nope." I smile, thinking of the vision painting I created. "We're going to make them for Bobbi and me."

40

BOBBI

ALTHOUGH I HAVEN'T BEEN to the bakery since the weekend, and devoted the time to rest and recovery, my body still feels like it's been beaten from scalp to toes with a meat tenderizer. I got in touch with Victor on Sunday evening and told him to close the bakery.

"You sure you're okay?" he asked. I've never closed the bakery like this before. I gave him a story about getting into an accident to explain why I couldn't pick him up. A good lie, since it also explained the bruises and cuts, which are going to linger for a while.

I smiled at his concern. "Yeah, I'm fine. It'll be paid time off, so it'll be good for you, too." No need for him to worry about paying his bills. Although I ensure he makes enough to be okay, SoCal is expensive.

"Nah, I don't need that. Listen, Bobbi... I don't think you have to close for a week. You've been teaching me how to bake. I think I can man the fort while you get better."

"You don't have to. I don't want you to take on too much." Although I've been teaching him my recipes, he might get overwhelmed if he has to do everything on his own.

"You have no idea what your kindness meant when I had nowhere to go. I never told anybody, but I felt like I didn't have anyone. Family was useless, and my friends mostly vanished once I became homeless. It felt like I was just...done."

Sympathy for the lonely Victor wells up. Nobody should ever feel that way about themselves.

He continued, "You took a big risk when you decided to feed me, and a bigger one when you hired me. I'm going to show you that you made the right decision."

"You don't have to prove anything." My voice was soft with affection and pride. "I already know I made the right decision."

"Well. I'm going to do it anyway," he said gruffly, then hung up.

Now it's Wednesday afternoon, and Noah probably isn't available yet. If he were, he would've noticed all my texts and calls and reached out.

When a bunch of people in paramedic uniforms arrived to take Noah and me to the hospital, I wanted to stay with him the entire time, even if he was asleep. But his mother said she needed to make sure I was okay in that scary inflectionless voice of hers, then dragged me off to see a bunch of doctors who pumped me full of painkillers and other drugs that I know weren't just for easing the pain. Afterward some police officers—assuming they were real cops—questioned me for over an hour, ostensibly to understand what happened, then one of them drove me home.

When I recovered from the loopiness from the meds and went back to the hospital the next morning, Noah had been moved, and people were less than helpful.

"I'm sorry, but what's your relationship to him? Family or...?" The receptionist at the information desk gave me a look that said unless I provided a satisfactory answer, I wasn't getting anything out of her.

Here went my fifty-fifty shot. "Girlfriend."

She shook her head, said, "Family members only," and gave me a sorry-not-sorry smile.

Her smile was more annoying than the hospital's privacy policy. Mainly because I resented her condescension even as I understood why the hospital was reluctant to give out patient information. One of my former clients had a stalker who pretended to be her fiancé in order to gain access at a gynecology clinic.

All my calls to his phone are going to voice mail. Doubt he's reading my texts either. And I have no idea how to reach Nora, who may have confiscated his phone and undoubtedly knows where he is. She spoke with me a few times on Sunday, mainly asking what happened that evening...maybe she wanted to trip me up because she wasn't satisfied with my answers to the "cops." Then she asked how I felt about Noah, and I told her I wasn't telling her when I haven't told Noah yet. She gave me the flat, assessing look of a snake debating whether or not to strike, and it bugged me that she didn't seem to care at all about Noah's well-being. My dad—I mean, Otto—never cared about me that much, but now that I know he wasn't my real father his attitude makes more sense. Noah is Nora's son! What kind of mom remains so blasé about her own child getting shot by a freakin' traitor?

I was so disgusted, I left without asking for her number. Unfortunately, manifesting won't give me her number, so I finally gather my courage and text Noah's brothers.

–Grant: I don't think anybody knows.

–Griffin: Why don't you ask Noah?

Because he got shot saving me and is lying unconscious in some unknown hospital.

–Me: I'm planning a surprise.

–Emmett: Joey might know. But then you'd have to talk to Joey.

Ugh, not Joey of a Thousand Filters. On the other hand, I'll put up with him if it means seeing Noah and making sure he's okay.

–Nicholas: Don't bother. When my mom asked because she wanted to invite Nora to a trip to Berlin last year, he said he didn't know.

–Grant: Then how does he send her invites to Dad's parties?

–Nicholas: He emails Noah. Bobbi, do you have to involve Nora? She's rarely available.

–Me: Probably not. Thanks.

I put my phone down and let out a frustrated breath. I should've asked for Nora's number even though she annoyed me with her cold attitude! I kick the bare floor of the kitchen and curse. It doesn't make me feel better.

The door bursts open, making me jump. My heart settles when I realize it's TJ barging in, his shoulders bunched. From the wild look in his eyes, it's shocking he's not frothing at the mouth.

"I go out of town with Tony for a couple of days and come back to *this?* What the fuck happened?" he shouts, face twisting as he takes in my bruises. "Victor said you got hurt, but he didn't tell me you had a fight with a semi!"

"Yeah, but you should see the semi." I shoot him a cheeky grin. "How they hangin,' cuz?"

He lifts a thick finger and wags it in my face. "*Don't.*"

He's about to blow. Time to defuse the situation. "TJ, I'm fine. It was just an accident."

"And the car fucked up your face?" He is shouting again. "You can lie to your little assistant, but not to me."

I sigh. "Looks worse than it is. And seriously, you should've seen the other guy. Before, you know, I shot him." I look away briefly, hoping I sound convincing. It's difficult to take credit for killing Trey Underhill, but to protect Noah's secret...

I don't know what strings his mom pulled, but the detective—the real cop, not the fake ones who did the detailed questioning after I was doped up in the hospital—in charge of investigating this case agreed that I was right to defend myself and called Trey's death "justifiable." The entire interview lasted all of five minutes, and the case was wrapped up so fast, I wondered if Nora's people had pre-written police reports they hand out for occasions like this.

"Come on. Let's sit." I gesture at the sofa and take a seat.

TJ parks himself next to me, jaw flexing. Hopefully he doesn't grind his teeth too hard. Dentists are expensive.

"I told you we should've put landmines around your house!" His voice shakes with fury and regret. "Then none of this would've happened."

"I don't know," I say vaguely. "The other guy was really motivated." Trey was also devious, claiming to be a veteran with a cat to get my guard down. He would've found a way around the landmines. But I keep my mouth shut about it; TJ would only come up with some even more outlandish way to keep me safe.

"Who was it? A stalker?"

"No. Someone who had a beef with Dad's work. Apparently he blamed Dad for some treaty that didn't get ratified or something. I wasn't sure what he was talking about to be honest. Most of Dad's work was classified, so..." I shrug.

"So what happened? My buddies at the precinct can't find a report or anything."

That explains why he didn't buy my initial lie about an accident. Again, I wonder just how much influence Noah's mom has. "We got into a physical fight, obviously. He pulled out a gun, but I was faster with the Glock."

TJ stares at me but then nods slightly. His fury starts to cool. "So... You okay? Maybe you should see a shrink about the whole thing. Talk about the trauma."

"I'm fine." After all, I'm not the one who shot Trey. *Is Noah unavailable because he's seeing a therapist?* I assume people like him don't need to because they're used to death in their profession. James Bond never lay on a therapist's couch. But this isn't a movie.

"You sure?" TJ puts a gentle hand on my shoulder, as though he's afraid of breaking me. "Bobbi, I know you're strong, but you can lean on others for help, too. Cassie, Josie and I are here for you."

"I know. Thanks." I smile wanly as Trey's revelation floats on my mind. He said I wasn't my father's child. Not that I think he was being entirely truthful, but what if I'm not related to TJ? Would it matter to him? I could pretend like Trey never said anything, but I keep thinking about it. Besides, what he said explained my mother's behavior so well. "Hey, TJ."

"Yeah?"

"Would it change anything if you knew I'm not really your cousin?"

He gives me a look. "What are you talking about?"

"That guy...the one who came and did this"—I gesture at my face— "said I was a baby Dad found while stationed overseas." I don't mention the diplomat. In a way, my version isn't entirely untrue. Revealing the information about the diplomat and his wife would be impossible without coming clean that Otto Bright was a traitor.

"Oh, that? Yeah, I knew you were adopted," TJ says.

"What?" A vice suddenly clamps down on my chest.

"Uncle Otto and Aunt Sarah never brought it up, but I knew. When you got shot that time, you needed a blood transfusion. I offered, but we weren't compatible. You're Rh negative. Everyone in the family is Rh positive. Your father was too."

I stare at him. "But you never said anything!"

He shrugs, all awkward now. "I thought you knew. Besides, why would that make a difference? You're still my cousin. I don't know what that motherfucker said, but if you think being adopted makes a difference to me, I'm gonna get insulted."

The tightness around my chest eases. What was I thinking, letting Trey's toxic words get to me? TJ is right. He and I are family no matter what. If the situation were reversed, I'd still love him. Feeling a little choked up, I sniff. "Thanks. Want a freshly baked apple pie?"

A ghost of smile touches his lips. "Taking a rain check. You need to rest and recover. Don't even think about going to the bakery. You'll scare all your customers away, and poor Victor will lose his job."

"Is that so?" I raise an eyebrow.

"Yes. It'd be a tragedy since he finally started dating that little blonde chick. Be a shame if he couldn't afford to take her out to a nice restaurant and movie. You know, before he bones that poor girl half to death."

41

NOAH

I'm discharged on Friday. Mom wanted me in the hospital longer, probably to keep me away from Bobbi while she works on convincing Bobbi I should do my patriotic duty. Mom understands how much influence Bobbi has over me. The problem is, she and I don't share Mom's vision for my life and future.

She also reluctantly had to give my phone back. She had Contact2608 take my phone, ostensibly to grab evidence, a.k.a. texts between me and Trey disguised as Bobbi. I know better. She wanted me isolated from the world. Why? Who the hell knows. She works at her own pace, does her own thing and toes the line. But sometimes I have no idea what's going through that devious head of hers.

The first thing I do when I finally get my phone back is check for texts and calls. My brothers sent me tons, and I respond I've been out of town shooting some cheetahs. That satisfies their curiosity—I generally go AWOL when I'm "working."

Bobbi sent me lots, and even called. Damn it. Anxiety streaks my system. Has she been feeling abandoned and unwanted? Does she think I'm ghosting her again? She hasn't been by the hospital because Mom moved me after sedating me. Ostensibly for security reasons, but she didn't have to keep Bobbi in the dark. My girl will never forgive me if she thinks I'm pulling another disappearing act.

I debate between texting and calling, then settle on texting. She might be busy at the bakery.

–Me: Finally back home. Sorry I couldn't answer your texts and calls!

Her response is almost immediate.

–TLOML: Finally! But why are you already out? Actually, don't say anything. I'm coming right now!

Bobbi arrives within an hour, having driven like a maniac through L.A.'s horrendous traffic. She marches into the house, feet slapping the marble floor, and holding a bag from Bobbi's Sweet Things.

I take in her beautiful presence after having missed her so much over the last few days. The bruises on her face have faded to a sallow yellow, and she's moving well, so no lasting damage to her joints, thank God.

She opens her arms, then hesitates, her gaze dropping to my torso. I hug her tightly, bury my nose in the crook of her neck and breathe in her sweet scent. Every cell in my body relaxes in homecoming.

This is exactly where I belong.

"Shouldn't you still be in the hospital?" she murmurs, holding me tightly around the shoulders. "You were shot."

"Nah. I got lucky." I finally pull away and grin. "Clear exit. Nothing major was hit."

"A miracle," she whispers, her fingers stroking the spot.

"That's what the doc said, but I think it was you."

I lead her to the couch and sit down, pulling her onto my lap. She settles there, like that's where she belongs. She doesn't protest that she's too big—one of the many things I love about her. In her worldview, a man who whines about her being too big or heavy doesn't deserve her.

"I don't see how," she says. "You're the one who came to save me."

"True, but you and I *both* manifested a future where we were together. So of course the universe wasn't going to let some worm like Trey screw things up." I touch the tip of her nose.

"But you bled so much." The shadow of memory dims the light in her eyes.

"It just looked impressive. A trick they teach you in spy school." I keep my tone light and carefree, to bring the glitter back into her gaze. And it really wasn't that bad. I'd cut off a limb to protect her. "I can recover just as well at home as in some boring hospital. The surgery went well, and I'm healthy as a horse. On top of that, I can't stay away for too long. My brothers would suspect something was up. Now, enough about me. How are you feeling?" I really wish I could go back in time. Not to spare Trey's life and torture him, but to go back far enough that I could kill him the second I laid eyes on him.

"I'm fine. The bruises are still there, but the swelling's gone and nothing hurts. Victor's been managing the bakery during my absence since—according to TJ—my appearance would scare away all the customers. And he's been doing a great job, much better than I expected. I also had him hire someone to help out."

"That's good," I say, pleased to note the life she's worked so hard to build hasn't been messed up by Trey and Otto.

"By the way, there's something I want to tell you. Before Trey got violent, he said I wasn't Otto's daughter."

"What?" If she weren't Otto's real daughter, it would've been in the files I received before the mission. But I never saw anything about it in any of the documents, and nobody mentioned it in briefing. "If he's not your father, who is?"

"Some British diplomat. Trey said Otto killed him and his wife and took me from them."

I shrug. "Could've lied."

"I thought that too, but TJ also said Otto wasn't my biological father."

A beat. "Do you want me to find out who your real father is?" It would take some work, but I'm sure I'll be able to figure it out for her.

"No. Part of me is curious, but another part wonders what purpose it would serve. My life is here. My friends. My bakery. My family—blood relatives or not." She gives me a smile. "And you."

Hope and love bubble in my chest. Maybe this is going to work out after all.

"I was upset before, but when I thought about it, you did what you thought was right based on what you knew. You had to find the dossiers before somebody like Otto or Trey sold them and put you and others like you in danger. And I don't want to let what Otto did stop us from having a wonderful life together, especially when he wasn't even my real father."

I press my forehead against hers, closing my eyes in a brief prayer of thanks to whatever entity out there is watching over me—and her. The anxiety and despair I felt over the fact that she might never fully forgive me for killing her father ebb. The air suddenly seems lighter and sweeter.

She thrusts the Bobbi's Sweet Things bag at me. "Here. For you."

I take the bag and open it. Fresh croissants are nestled inside. I jerk my gaze up at her.

"I swore I'd never let you have my croissants again because they reminded me of the last time you made me a promise and broke it. You loved my croissants then, too, saying you'd sell your soul for them. But when you didn't come, I thought keeping your promise to me wasn't that important to you."

Regret and sorrow throb dully in my heart. I should've gone, no matter what. I should've put Bobbi above my own misgivings, uncertainties and fears.

"Even after I told you I'd give us three months, I didn't really give us a clean slate. Part of me was just waiting for you to disappear on me again. But now... Well, now I feel like I can trust a guy who caught a bullet for me to keep my heart safe too." The smile she gives me is bright and precious. My mouth dries as hope and love dance in my heart.

"You slay me," I rasp, then laugh as my vision blurs a little. "You have to marry me because you've ruined me for other women. I'll die alone, lost and miserable without you. You're the light that I didn't know I was willing to die to protect."

Bobbi stares at me, her mouth softly parted and her eyes wide and teary.

"Wait wait wait, don't answer," I say as I realize what I've done. "I'm going to propose properly."

She covers the bottom half of her face with her hands. "How are you going to propose better than this?"

"A white beach with an aquamarine lagoon attached. A thousand white calla lilies, and a thousand—actually, make it *two* thousand— candles, with chilled champagne and chocolate-dipped strawberries and the nama-cream cake you love so much. And I'll drop to one knee." I give her the vision I've held in my head since I saw the ring I ordered.

"That sounds really beautiful, but I love the proposal you just did, too."

"Come on. I didn't even give you a ring." *How could I have botched this?*

She smiles, looping her arms around me. "Fine. You can propose again and impress me. But no matter how or where you do it, my answer is always going to be yes."

42

NOAH

I can't do the beach, white calla lilies and candles. They seemed perfect in my imagination, but now that I've told Bobbi, the whole thing would be anticlimactic.

And my brothers agree.

—Emmett: This is why you keep things to yourself!

—Nicholas: I know you can't keep a secret, but this is...I don't even know what to say.

—Sebastian: Just buy her extra jewelry.

—Grant: The world doesn't revolve around diamonds.

—Sebastian: Or around the tango!

I smirk at Seb's irritation. He's unhappy because Lucie wants to learn the Argentinian tango with him since she was so impressed after watching Grant and Aspen dance. But Sebastian isn't the best dancer, certainly not compared to Grant, and his competitive streak can't stand it.

—Grant: Not my fault I can romance a woman without jewelry. Up your game, bro.

—Nicholas: Anyway, back to Noah's problem, give her something she'll love more than diamonds.

Easy for him to say. All he has to do is order a crateful of autographed romance novels to please Molly.

Bobbi is more complicated. And sensitive.

She deserves the world.

So a month after my rather pathetic and impulsive proposal, I head to Bobbi's Sweet Things one morning. The ambrosial scent of baked goods greets me as I step inside. Bobbi smiles from the counter. "Hey, babe. You're just in time. Give me a sec."

She slips into the back, then returns with a croissant. "Came out of the oven ten minutes ago."

It's still warm. I kiss her, then take a bite of the pastry and marvel at the incredible light flaky texture. "Perfect. I swear your croissants get better each day."

"Flattery will get you absolutely everywhere."

"I have something for you."

"What?"

"Here." I hand her the papers.

She looks at them curiously. "This can't be a prenup. Too thin."

"Hey, you know I'd never ask you to sign one."

She laughs. "I'm just kidding. So what is it?" She starts reading. The grin fades, then slips entirely from her face. She gasps, blinks, then squints at the words on the pages. Finally she looks at me. "Did I read it right? *I own this building?*"

"Yup." I smile.

"How did you get Floyd to sell?"

"Much as I'd like to take credit here, it wasn't me. It was Uncle Sam wanting his fair share. Floyd's been a very bad boy, not paying his taxes on time. He's going to have to sell the house his mom left him because he also owes the state." The house I shot up. I don't mention that detail though. Nor do I mention that Reggie dumped Floyd because she "deserves better," but her prospects aren't great. She can't even hawk diet teas online, not after what my dad did to her.

"Oh my God." Bobbi stares at the papers again, which tremble in her shaky hands. "I... I was so worried I might not be able to afford the higher rent Floyd was insisting on."

"Ah, fuck him. Why waste your energy on someone like that when you have me?" I loop my arm around her waist. "Don't forget. You've got a billionaire who's dying to give you the world. My money is your money."

"And my money is yours?" she teases through happy tears shining in her eyes.

"Nah. Your money is yours. The only thing I want is *you*."

She places a hand over her mouth and inhales hard. "I don't even know what to say."

"You don't have to say anything." I kiss her, hold her tight and quietly count my blessings. "People reap what they sow. You sow love and happiness, so..."

"And you?"

I grin. "Not sure, but I must've done *some*thing right to hold the light of my life in my arms." I drop to a knee, then pull out the ring box and pop the lid open in one smooth motion.

Her breath catches.

"Bobbi, I want to make you the happiest and most beloved woman in the world. Will you marry me?"

Tears fall from her shining eyes. "Like I said before... *Yes*."

43

NOAH

THIS IS SUPPOSED to be a fun, relaxing night with my brothers at our favorite steakhouse, while Bobbi and her friends hang out and have her last girls' night out as a bachelorette. But instead, the mood is positively funereal. Maybe a little alarming. Not because I have a problem with my nuptials—I can't wait to make Bobbi mine.

It's Huxley, who arrived in a state of shock and fury. He looked so awful, I had to ask if somebody wrecked his new Lamborghini.

"Worse. Much worse. I'm stuck. I have to marry Grace Lain." His eyes narrow.

"Well... At least she's not a Webber...?" For once, Emmett seems unsure of himself.

Catalina is desperate to use a marriage to cement the ties between the Huxleys and the Webbers. So far, Hux has done a marvelous job of evading her attempts.

"She's a fucking Webber in disguise! She misrepresented herself!"

Uh-oh. An undercover Webber. That sucks. I try not to clear my throat too loudly. Anything can set Huxley off when he's in this kind of mood.

"You sure? I've never heard of Grace Lain," Emmett says. He's pretty close to Andreas Webber because he's done work for the firm.

"She's the daughter Nelson Webber had with his side piece." Huxley looks mad enough to eat a tree stump.

"Do you have to marry her? There's gotta be a loophole," Grant says.

"She claims she's pregnant with my baby."

"Well... Is she *really?*" I ask. He's too meticulous to screw up birth control.

But if Grace is pregnant... Well. Catalina won't let the opportunity go. Not only will the baby—along with the marriage it will necessitate —bring the families together, but it might pull Huxley closer to the legal dynasty, like she's always wanted.

"She thinks she's won, but I'm going to ruin that conniving little bitch." Both of Huxley's hands are clenched into white-knuckled fists.

I munch on some bread, feeling a smidgeon of pity for Grace Lain. Huxley didn't choose to be an ad executive because he was a nice, sweet guy who couldn't swim with the sharks in the legal field. He can be the nastiest of us when he's crossed. He's too smart, too rich and too powerful to rein himself in when he feels he's been wronged. He is scorched-earth personified.

"You might not want to judge so hastily. Just in case," Sebastian says. He almost lost his wife over a decision made in anger, and he probably doesn't want to see Huxley suffer the same fate.

"She crawled into my bed! Did Lucie crawl into yours?"

"No. But her sister crawled into my brother's."

Something Sebastian's going to be grateful for for the rest of his life —otherwise he would've never had a chance to marry Lucie.

"She's going to wish she'd never met me."

"How about the kid?" Nicholas says.

Huxley looks like he can't decide between kicking something or ripping his hair out. "I don't know. It probably isn't mine anyway."

"You sure?" Emmett asks.

"Gonna have to check, but I am extremely careful with contraception."

"Still could've failed." Griffin gestures around the table—all of us are the result of our father's failed vasectomy.

"I didn't get a vasectomy from a second-rate doctor," Huxley says.

"Neither did I, but…" Griffin shrugs. He got his wife pregnant purely by accident during a one-night stand in New Orleans.

Huxley closes his eyes briefly. "Yeah. Sorry. I shouldn't have said that."

"It's cool. I know you're upset." Griffin claps him on the shoulder.

Hux shakes his head. "We should have some fun here." His voice is grim. But he said we should have fun, so he'll do his best to have it.

Grant pours Huxley his favorite scotch. I feel vaguely guilty about not keeping an eye on what's been going on between the Huxleys and the Webbers because I've been distracted with Bobbi. It's unfair for Hux to have to be stuck with a Webber—a member of a legal family he does not want to get involved with—when the rest of us are happily married to the women we love.

Huxley meant what he said about having fun. The man can throw himself into a party like it's a competitive sport. But the gleam in his eye says his mind is on revenge.

44

BOBBI

"You're so beautiful!"

"You look like a Sugar Plum Fairy!"

I smile at the chirpy voices of the little ones as they surround me in the enormous bedroom I'm using as my dressing room. They're pretty, too, in their pink and ivory dresses with little sparkly sequins and ruffles. Monique has a tiara from Sebastian resting on her head, and Lilian and Katherine are wearing stunning butterfly and flower pins made with amethysts and sapphires. Noah and I are getting married on the beach by his Malibu home. The cloudless SoCal sky is so blue it barely looks real, and waves lap the sand gently.

"You really are stunning." Ivy's admiring eyes roam over my white silk tulle dress with a sweetheart neckline and Watteau train. She hugs me. "I'm so *happy* for you!"

"I always knew it." Yuna embraces me—and Ivy as well, probably unable to wait until the latter moves away. Yuna isn't known for her patience. "The manifestation ring was so inspired."

"I can't believe it. It's just so incredible." Josie fans herself. Unshed tears shine in her eyes. She always gets emotional at big family events.

The door opens, and my soon-to-be sisters-in-law walk in, dressed as colorfully as their warm personalities. Lucie gasps. "Oh my God! Yuna?"

Yuna spins around and stares. "Lucie! I didn't know you knew Bobbi."

"She's going to be my sister-in-law. You?"

"Oh, we've been friends forever." Yuna grins.

While Yuna and Lucie gush about how small the world is, Aspen and Sierra hug me. "Welcome to the family!"

"How are you feeling? Hopefully not too nervous?" Amy asks.

"I'm fine. Ready to take my vows."

"Speaking of ready..." Josie hands me a pretty silver bracelet. "Something old." She smiles. "It's from Grandma."

"Thanks." I watch as she loops it around my wrist, my chest starting to swell with anticipation and hope. *This is it.* I'm going to become Mrs. Noah Lasker in a few minutes.

"Something new." Lucie pulls a diamond pin from the small box she's holding and pushes it into my updo. The stone sparkles like all the blessings in my life.

"Something borrowed." Molly puts a tiny heart-shaped silver charm on the bracelet from Josie, then gives me a shy hug.

"And something blue." Yuna wraps a vivid blue satin ribbon around my bouquet and ties it into a gorgeous bow.

"Sixpence in your shoe." Grinning, Sierra pulls out a bright penny. "They don't make sixpence coins anymore, so we're substituting. This was minted the year you were born." She puts it on my palm and folds my fingers over the warm coin. "I'm so happy we're getting another sister."

"Thank you so much, everyone." I smile.

The door bursts open, and the boys barge in, dressed in tuxedos. "Look! Señor Mittens is ready!"

I put a hand over my mouth. Noah told me the cat should be part of the ceremony. After all, he is our Cupid and guardian angel. But I never imagined this was what he had in mind.

A pair of wings made with actual feathers. A long white cloth wraps around him like a Roman toga, and a bow is attached to his back with an arrow tipped with a red heart. Señor Mittens glares at me like it's my fault he's been stripped of his feline dignity.

"Oh wow..." I breathe out.

"Isn't he *cool?*" Liam shouts.

Señor Mittens's narrowed eyes say I better answer wisely or else.

"Um... Yes?"

He lets out a growl. Guess that wasn't the correct response.

"Wow. So Joey actually did it," Aspen says in half in awe, half horrified.

"What?" *Joey?*

"Grant said that Noah ordered Joey to make them. I mean, he'd know who to ask to get the best costume, right?"

"Did he wrangle an invitation for Ted?" Amy asks, scandalized.

Aspen shakes her head. "Not a chance."

Amy lets out a relieved sigh. "Thank God. Grandfather or not, I'm not letting that man near Monique."

Yuna's phone buzzes. She glances at the screen, then chortles softly.

"What's so funny?" I ask as I check my reflection for the last time. The makeup artist did an amazing job. And she made sure that I still look like myself, not someone who has a thousand layers of plaster on her.

"Mom says congrats, and she wants to know if you can send her some of your marriage luck because she's having the hardest time getting Jin to marry a proper heiress. So I told her to cut off his allowance."

The suggestion has me gasping with shock. "He gets an allowance?"

"Of course not." Yuna laughs gleefully. "But they cut me off when I said no to an arranged marriage. I just felt like being bratty."

"Arranged marriages aren't that terrible." Josie's voice takes on a serious-therapist tone. "Provided the couple shares similar values. Love may not last, but values are forever."

"Oh, we don't pick our spouses for values," Yuna says lightly, like she's discussing the beautiful weather outside. "This is a merger marriage. Billions are riding on it."

I shake my head at the wild pressure that type of union would bring. On the other hand, who am I to think about pressure on others? I'm marrying a man who pre-emptively assassinates terrorists and other bad actors who threaten our national security.

Molly checks her watch. "It's time."

We step out together, and the ladies disperse toward the beach. TJ stands outside the door in a tux that fits his huge frame surprisingly well. A tear glints in his eye as he offers his arm. "Ah, Bobbi. I'm so happy for you."

"Thanks, TJ."

"If that fucker does you wrong, you lemme know. I've always got your back."

Instead of placing my hand on his arm, I hug him. "Thanks, TJ. I have yours, too. We're family."

He nods, offers his arm again and we stroll out to the beach in a stately manner.

The briny breeze ruffles my dress, and the train billows from my shoulders. The sun is a bright white coin in the sky, and I look at the love of my life standing at the other end of the silk-covered aisle.

Noah is absolutely stunning in his black and white tuxedo. The wind runs its fingers through his hair, tousling it. A brilliant grin splits his face, and his eyes shine with love. He looks at me like I'm all he could ever want in life. Emotions surge, my heart in my throat as thousands of butterflies flutter in my belly.

As Ivy plays "Here Comes the Bride," I take the first step toward my new future with the love of my life.

45

BOBBI

"WHAT IS life without proper parties to celebrate its milestones?" Yuna says raising a glass.

Music is floating in the air and people are dancing. The liquor flows freely as well. It's the seventh round of drinks she's serving to the guests at our intimate reception. She must've secretly worked as a bartender because she makes the soju and champagne bomb shots with such ease and flair, lining up the specialty flutes and dropping the soju shots in a sort of domino motion.

"It's like everyone's winning at life and love." Cassie grins. TJ proposed a couple of months ago, and she now sports a gorgeous solitaire ring on her finger.

"Winning is important," Josie says, slurring slightly. She's the cheap date of the family. "Nobody remembers the losers."

"Is that what you tell your patients?" I ask, laughing even though I'm not sure what she said is funny. But it feels funny to my brain.

"You should, cuz you're honest," Ivy says.

"I'm just glad I got married first. Mom would've been impossible," Yuna says, then giggles.

"Baby, I don't think you need another shot," Declan says, pulling her from the bar. "Let's dance."

Just as he says it, the music dies. Declan frowns, and Yuna sighs. "Guess it's time for another shot after all."

Suddenly a dramatic tune from "La cumparsita" hits the crowd. Grant and Aspen clasp hands and begin moving to the music with shocking expertise. I had no idea they could tango so well. Meanwhile, Sebastian looks pained, while Lucie tugs at his hand with a smile that's slightly loopy from too much sugar and happiness.

"Come on, Seb," she says, then laughs.

Sighing, he rests his hands on her waist and leads her. Instead of moving with him to the beat, she wraps her arms around his neck and clings. He laughs, looking at his wife fondly. A giggle bubbles from her, and she buries her face in his shoulder.

Noah places his hand on my bare shoulder.

"I can't tango," I say quickly.

"Don't worry. I'm not going to attempt a tango in front of those two and make an idiot out of myself." He angles his head to whisper into my ear. "Let's get out of here."

"Seriously?" He has to be joking.

But his expression is dead serious, except his eyes are bright with mischief.

"Noah! We can't leave our own wedding reception."

"Sure we can. Nobody's going to notice. We fed them and plied them with alcohol." His hand glides down my arm, sending delicious goosebumps over my sun-kissed skin. "Don't you want to experience the genius behind Silicone Dream's Lick-a-Lass?"

Silicone Dream is Sierra's sex toy company. And I've actually heard of that toy. I jerk my head up. "*You're* behind that one?"

"Hell, yeah. I was intimately—*intimately*, I tell you—involved in product development."

"Huh. So the Five Heavenly Motions come from you?"

"Ah, I see that you're a woman of experience. But why settle for a mass-produced imitation when you can have the one and only, the original, the nonpareil *human* Lick-a-Lass?" He cocks an eyebrow lasciviously.

I giggle, then shriek with laughter when he picks me up and carries me away.

His brothers call out something I can't quite catch. Someone starts a champagne shower, and the priceless Dom lands on us as Noah's long-legged strides eat up the distance, taking us to the house—our home.

"Don't worry about the champagne. I'll get you clean with my tongue," Noah murmurs.

I giggle at his faux gravitas, but soon it turns into a soft moan when his mouth fuses over mine.

Vaguely I register us moving up the stairs and then along the cool corridor that seems almost as long as our kiss. Finally, we enter the bedroom. Noah gently stands me up. The backs of my legs hit the mattress and he tugs at the small buttons and lace ties on my bodice. His lips and tongue plunder my mouth with such urgency I expect him to lose patience and rip the dress off. But he takes his time, like a man given a gift so precious he can't bring himself to be rough, even with the wrapping.

I cradle his cheek, then pull at his bowtie, letting the strip of silk slide down his tux. His kiss deepens as I undress him, revealing more of the gorgeous physique I adore for its beauty and strength. My bodice loosens and droops. He drags the dress down, the priceless silk pooling at my feet with a soft whisper. He runs his mouth over my exposed body, every touch of his lips searing. There is a reverence and possessiveness to the kisses he rains all over me. He doesn't have to speak, and I still hear it—*mine*.

I tremble with need and love. Sex with Noah is always amazing and hot, but the sweet tenderness of the moment undoes me.

He strips me out of my underwear, and I lie panting. My nipples bead in the cool air, and he runs his tongue over the pointed tips, one by one, making my toes curl.

He pulls one into his mouth and sucks. A low moan swells in my throat, and I clench his hair. He tugs at my other nipple. The callused tips of his clever fingers know exactly what to do to drown me in a pool of desire and pleasure.

"Please, please," I beg, desperate for deeper intimacy. My legs move restlessly against him.

He spreads my knees. His breathing has roughened, but his touch couldn't be more tender. He runs his mouth over my quivering inner thighs. "Mine." A kiss. "Mine." A kiss closer to my core. "Mine." A lick that results in an impossible ache and pooling of liquid heat in my flesh. *"My wife."*

Our eyes lock. Warmth suffuses my cheeks, and a breath shudders out of me. His eyes blaze.

He dips his head. His tongue moves up, licking me like he's devouring the fluffiest nama-cream. I arch my back at the pleasure twisting through me, my fingers scratching the sheet. He links our hands, our palms pressed tight, and then uses his lips and tongue on me, his breath fanning against my sensitive flesh.

Sweat mists over me as a blinding bliss overpowers my senses, leaving me sobbing my husband's name. But even as I begin to shake with orgasm, there's an aching emptiness. He senses my need, grips my hips and pushes inside, stretching me and filling me all the way. I gasp at the rightness of it, the sheer intimacy of the union.

His forehead rests on mine.

"Hello, Mrs. Lasker," he whispers.

"Hello, Mr. Lasker." I lay a loving hand on his cheek. "Welcome home."

A stunning smile breaks over his gorgeous face. And we rock each other into a blissful oblivion.

46

NOAH

—SIX YEARS later

I MAKE it home just in time for Mother's Day. I told Mom if I missed it because of a logistical fuckup, I'd never shoot the cheetahs again, and voilà! Magically I got a flight back home out of a shithole where I had to wait in position to kill some authoritarian thug who'd been wanting to blow up one of our embassies.

I slip silently inside the house. Bobbi's probably still sleeping. Victor's been invaluable, and he's now the manager at Bobbi's Sweet Things, giving my wife a more flexible schedule while she juggles four kids.

I grab a quick shower in the bathroom on the other side of the house so I don't disturb her, then quietly round up our three oldest. The youngest is only eighteen months old, so she won't be able to help.

"Okay, boys, we're going to treat your mom to a fabulous Mother's Day breakfast," I say as we arrive in the giant kitchen.

"Oooh, can I toast the bagel?" says Aiden. He has his mother's bright eyes and smile. Steve and Ryan—the oldest and second-youngest, respectively—have my eyes and jaw, but Bobbi's mouth. It's amazing how I can see her in them. And that makes me love them even more each day.

"Yeah." I help Aiden cut the bagel, while Steve gets water for the coffee, and Ryan gets the cream cheese. I scoop out the premium beans, grind them and start the coffeemaker. No breakfast is complete without fresh java.

Señor Mittens watches us, looking bored from his favorite spot right underneath the Marilyn Monroe picture. He's gotten quite plump from all the cream and caviar and tuna and steak, although we've cut back on treats due to the vet's concern that he might have a heart attack or develop gout. He resents his vet and probably wishes *he* would get gout, but the man is rail thin and fit from his daily runs.

The kitchen starts to smell like coffee and toasted carbs. I pull out a tray, and Ryan spreads cream cheese on the bagel before placing it on a plate. Aiden pours some fresh mixed berries into a small glass bowl. We assemble everything on a tray, and Steve picks it up since he's the oldest and most likely to carry out the task without an incident. I carry our little princess Evelyn so she can join in the celebration, even though she's busy sleeping at the moment.

By the time we reach the bedroom, Bobbi's lazing around in bed. She knows the Mother's Day breakfast comes at nine thirty every year. When Steve was too little I did it myself, and then after that I did it with our children to show her how much we all love her.

"Happy Mother's Day!" the boys say in unison.

"Oh my goodness, is this for me?" Bobbi says from bed, with a huge smile. "Wow, thank you." She kisses our boys.

Then it's my turn to kiss her.

"You're home," she says. "Everything go well?"

"Of course." I smile. "I missed you and our kids."

"Did you get some good shots, Dad?" asks Steve.

"I got one *very* good shot. But let's not talk about work right now."

"No, let's not," Bobbi says. Her hair's rumpled and she looks a little sleepy, but she couldn't be more lovely. I swear she's going to be the most beautiful woman to me even when she's a hundred years old.

And it's all come together—surrounded by our precious children, with the scent of fresh coffee wafting and laughter ringing in the air. Our love, family and home have been manifested in exactly the way we envisioned.

TITLES BY NADIA LEE

Standalone Titles

Beauty and the Assassin

Oops, I Married a Rock Star

The Billionaire and the Runaway Bride

Flirting with the Rock Star Next Door

Mister Fake Fiancé

Marrying My Billionaire Hookup

Faking It with the Frenemy

Marrying My Billionaire Boss

Stealing the Bride

The Lasker Brothers

Still Mine

Finally Forever

Contractually Yours

The Ex I'd Love to Hate

My Grumpy Billionaire

Baby for the Bosshole

The Sins Trilogy

Sins

Secrets

Mercy

~

The Billionaire's Claim Duet

Obsession

Redemption

~

Sweet Darlings Inc.

That Man Next Door

That Sexy Stranger

That Wild Player

~

Billionaires' Brides of Convenience

A Hollywood Deal

A Hollywood Bride

An Improper Deal

An Improper Bride

An Improper Ever After

An Unlikely Deal

An Unlikely Bride

A Final Deal

~

The Pryce Family

The Billionaire's Counterfeit Girlfriend

The Billionaire's Inconvenient Obsession

The Billionaire's Secret Wife

The Billionaire's Forgotten Fiancée

The Billionaire's Forbidden Desire

ABOUT NADIA LEE

New York Times and *USA Today* bestselling author Nadia Lee writes sexy contemporary romance. Born with a love for excellent food, travel and adventure, she has lived in four different countries, kissed stingrays, been bitten by a shark, fed an elephant and petted tigers.

Currently, she shares a condo overlooking a small river and sakura trees in Japan with her husband and son. When she's not writing, she can be found reading books by her favorite authors or planning another trip.

To learn more about Nadia and her projects, please visit http://www.nadialee.net. To receive updates about upcoming works, sneak peeks and bonus epilogues featuring some of your favorite couples from Nadia, please visit http://www.nadialee.net/vip to join her VIP List.

Made in the USA
Columbia, SC
08 June 2024

36866796R00193